THIS IS THE END OF THIS GRAPHIC NOVEL!

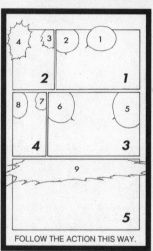

FOLLOW THE ACTION THIS WAY.

To properly enjoy this graphic novel, please turn it around and begin reading from right to left.

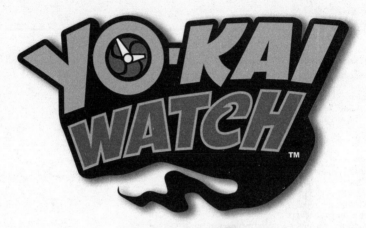

STORY AND ART BY
NORIYUKI KONISHI

ORIGINAL CONCEPT AND SUPERVISED BY LEVEL-5 INC.

YO-KAI WATCH™
Volume 10
DON'T BE A BRAT
VIZ Media Edition

Story and Art by Noriyuki Konishi
Original Concept and Supervised by LEVEL-5 Inc.

Translation/Tetsuichiro Miyaki
English Adaptation/Aubrey Sitterson
Lettering/John Hunt
Design/Shawn Carrico
Editor/Joel Enos

YO-KAI WATCH Vol. 10
by Noriyuki KONISHI
© 2013 Noriyuki KONISHI
©LEVEL-5 Inc.
Original Concept and Supervised by LEVEL-5 Inc.
All rights reserved.
Original Japanese edition published by SHOGAKUKAN.
English translation rights in the United States of America,
Canada, the United Kingdom, Ireland, Australia and New Zealand
arranged with SHOGAKUKAN.

Printed in the U.S.A.

Published by VIZ Media, LLC
P.O. Box 77010
San Francisco, CA 94107

10 9 8 7 6 5 4 3 2 1
First printing, January 2019

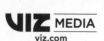
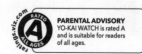

LEVEL5

VIZ MEDIA
viz.com

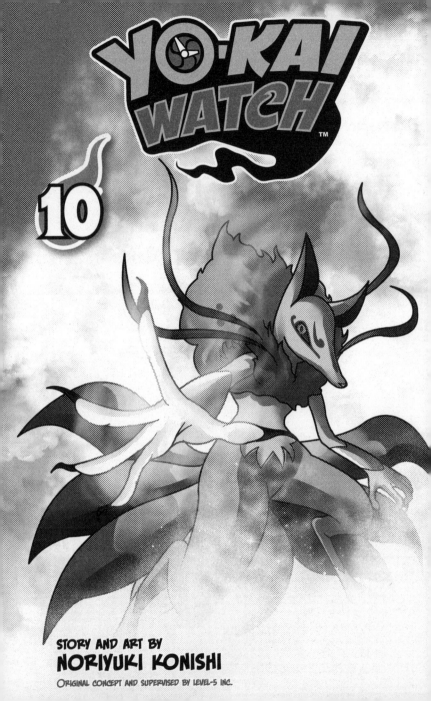

YO-KAI WATCH

10

STORY AND ART BY
NORIYUKI KONISHI

ORIGINAL CONCEPT AND SUPERVISED BY LEVEL-5 INC.

CHARACTER INTRODUCTION

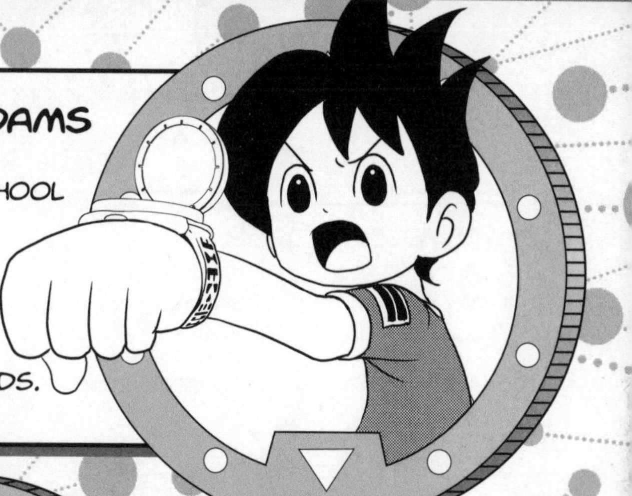

NATHAN ADAMS

AN ORDINARY ELEMENTARY SCHOOL STUDENT. WHISPER GAVE HIM THE YO-KAI WATCH, AND THEY HAVE SINCE BECOME FRIENDS.

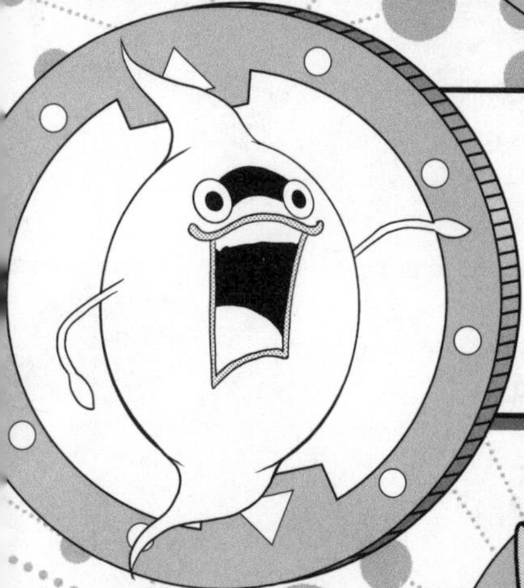

WHISPER

A YO-KAI BUTLER FREED BY NATE, WHISPER HELPS HIM BY USING HIS EXTENSIVE KNOWLEDGE OF OTHER YO-KAI.

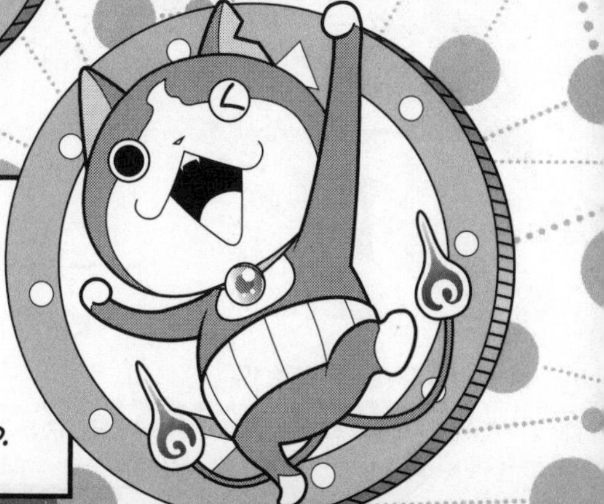

JIBANYAN

A CAT WHO BECAME A YO-KAI WHEN HE PASSED AWAY. HE IS FRIENDLY, CAREFREE AND THE FIRST YO-KAI THAT NATE BEFRIENDED.

BARNABY BERNSTEIN

NATE'S CLASSMATE.
NICKNAME: BEAR.
CAN BE MISCHIEVOUS.

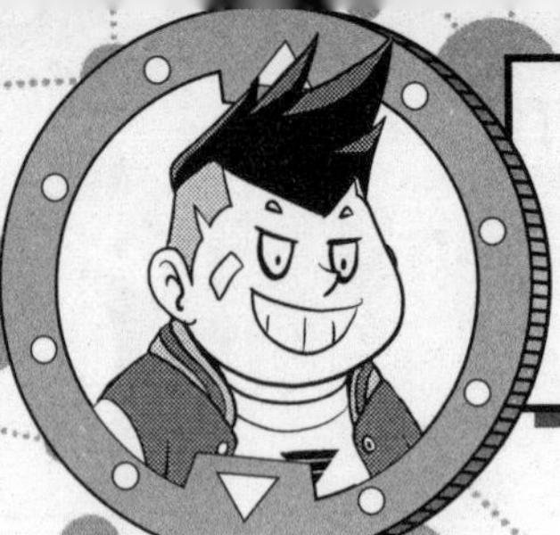

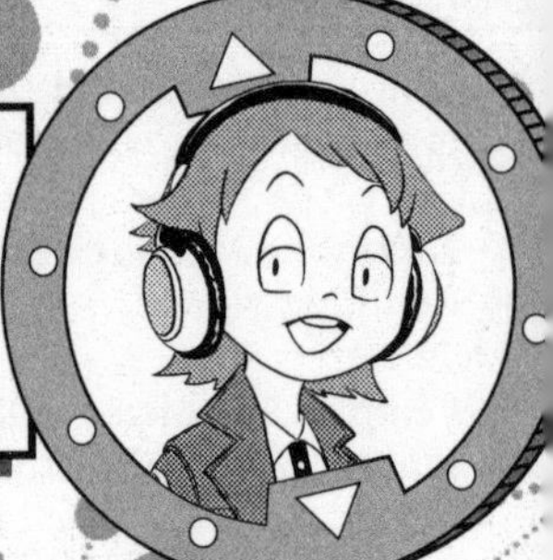

EDWARD ARCHER

NATE'S CLASSMATE.
NICKNAME: EDDIE. HE ALWAYS WEARS HEAD-PHONES.

KATIE FORESTER

THE MOST POPULAR GIRL IN NATE'S CLASS.

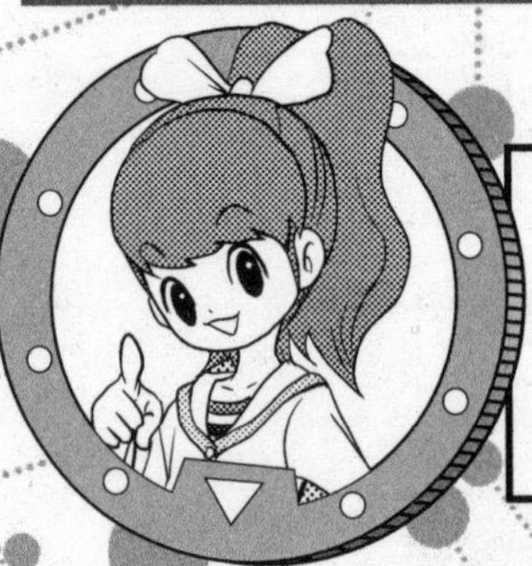

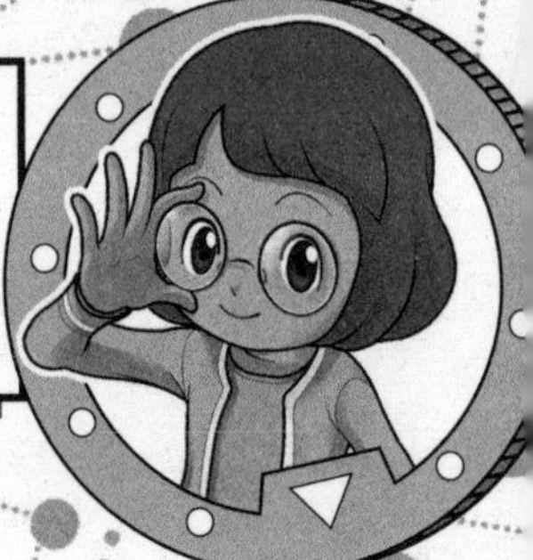

HAILEY ANNE THOMAS

A FIFTH GRADER WHO IS A SELF-PROCLAIMED SUPERFAN OF ALIENS AND SAILOR CUTIES.

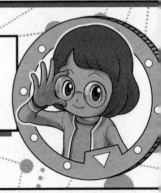

USAPYON

A RABBIT-ESQUE YO-KAI IN A SPACESUIT. HE'S SEARCHING FOR SOMEONE.

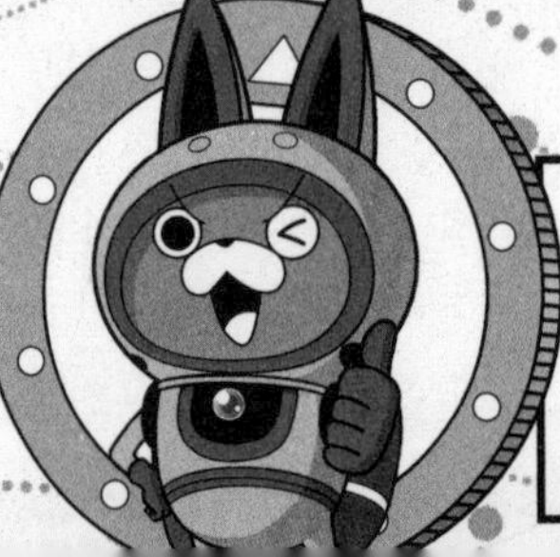

TABLE OF CONTENTS

CHAPTER 88
THE ATTACK OF THE NEW AND IMPROVED ROBONYAN!
FEATURING FUTURE ROBOT YO-KAI ROBONYAN F

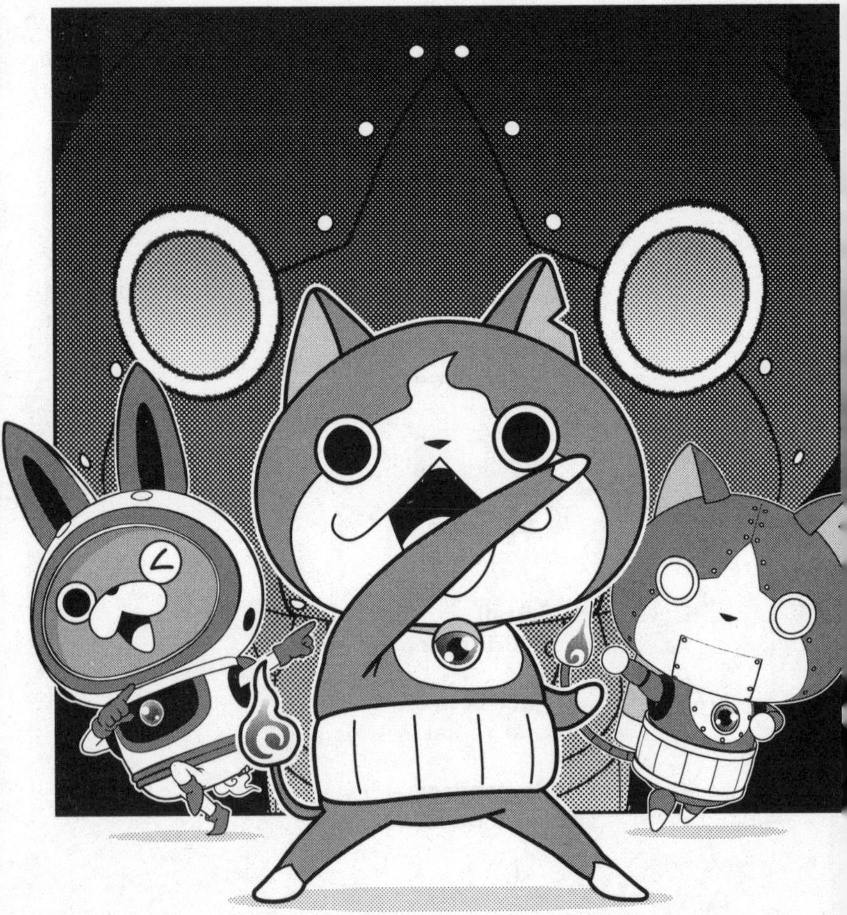

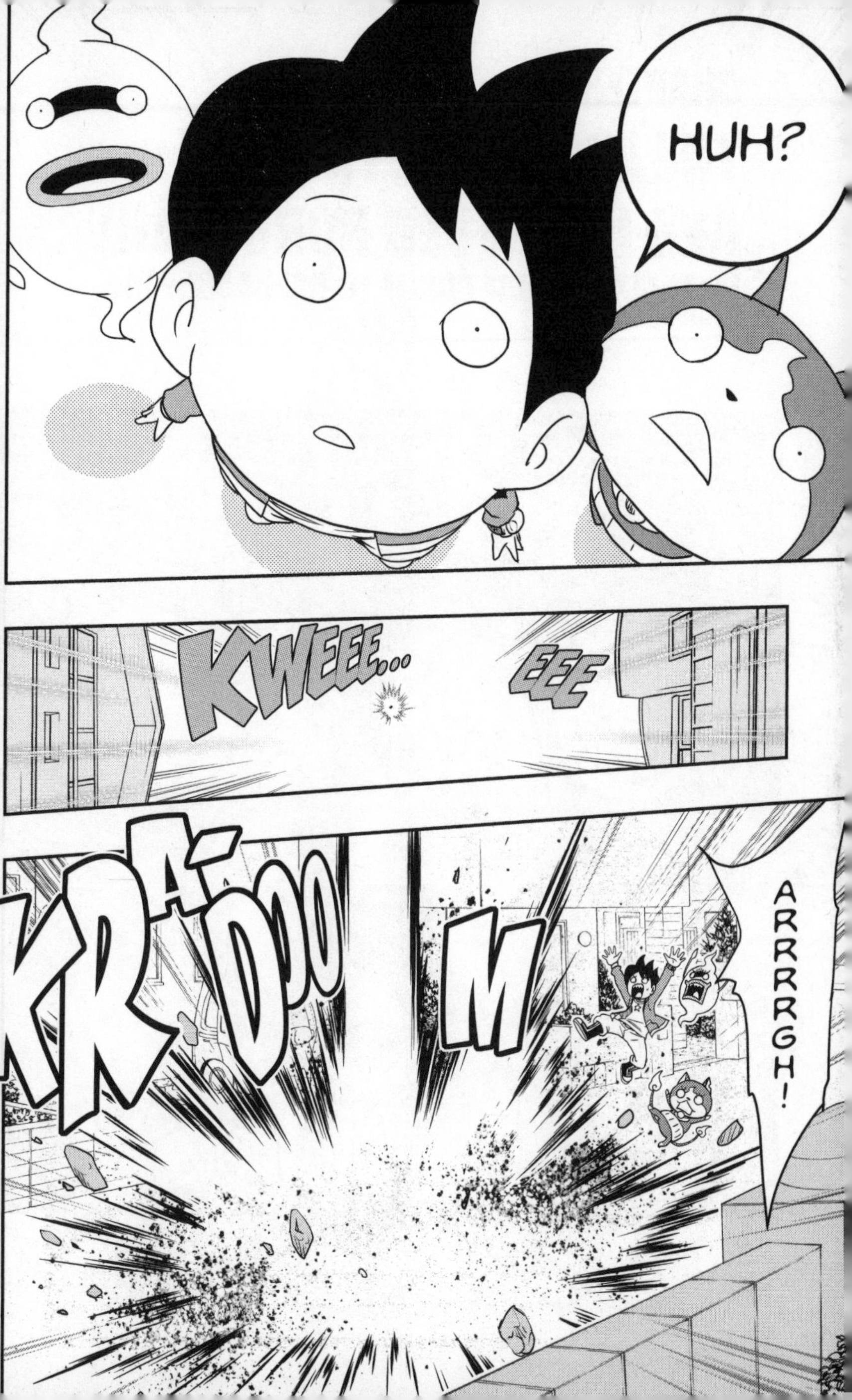
HUH?
KWEEE... EEE
ARRRRGH!
KRA-DOOOM

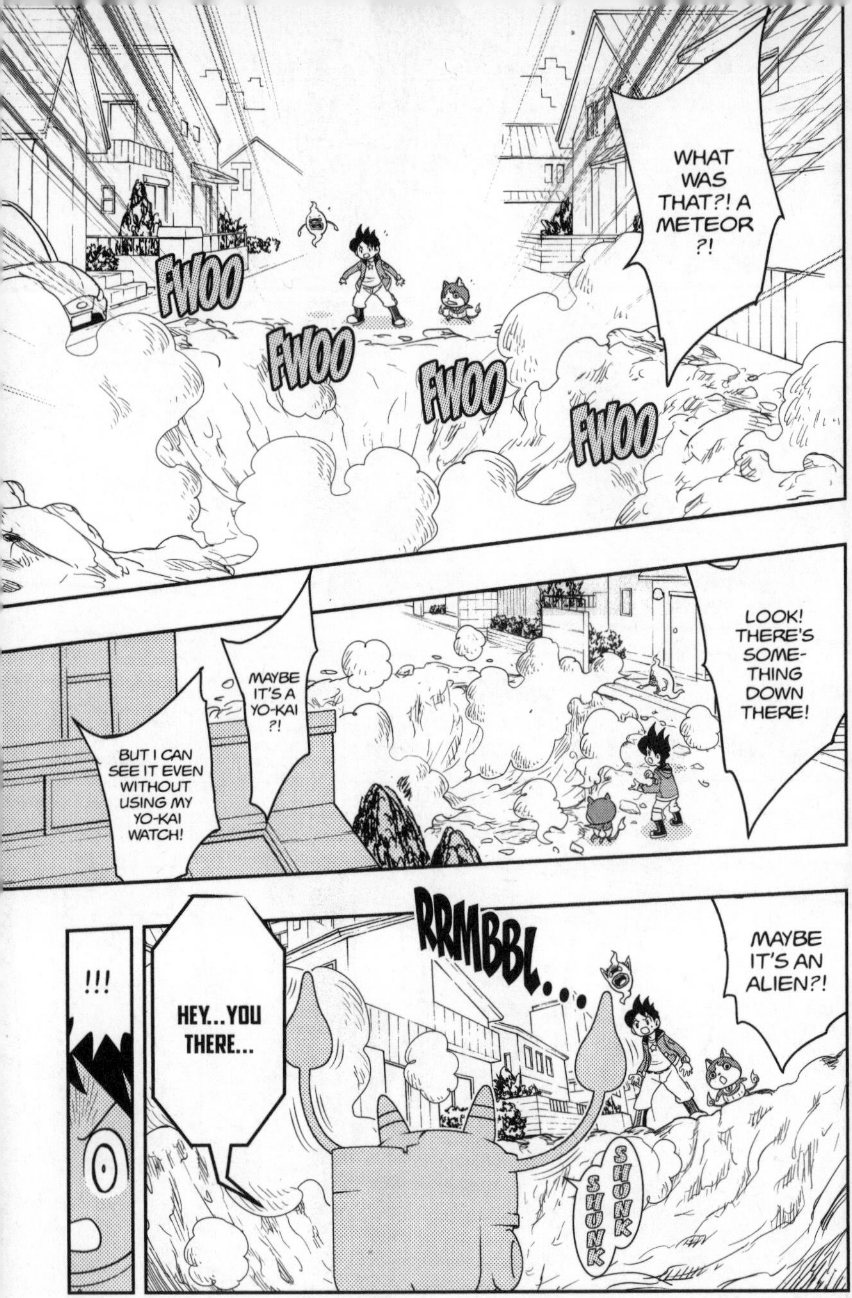
WHAT WAS THAT?! A METEOR ?!
FWOO
FWOO
FWOO
FWOO
LOOK! THERE'S SOME-THING DOWN THERE!
MAYBE IT'S A YO-KAI ?!
BUT I CAN SEE IT EVEN WITHOUT USING MY YO-KAI WATCH!
MAYBE IT'S AN ALIEN?!
RRMBBL...
SHUNK
SHUNK
HEY...YOU THERE...
!!!

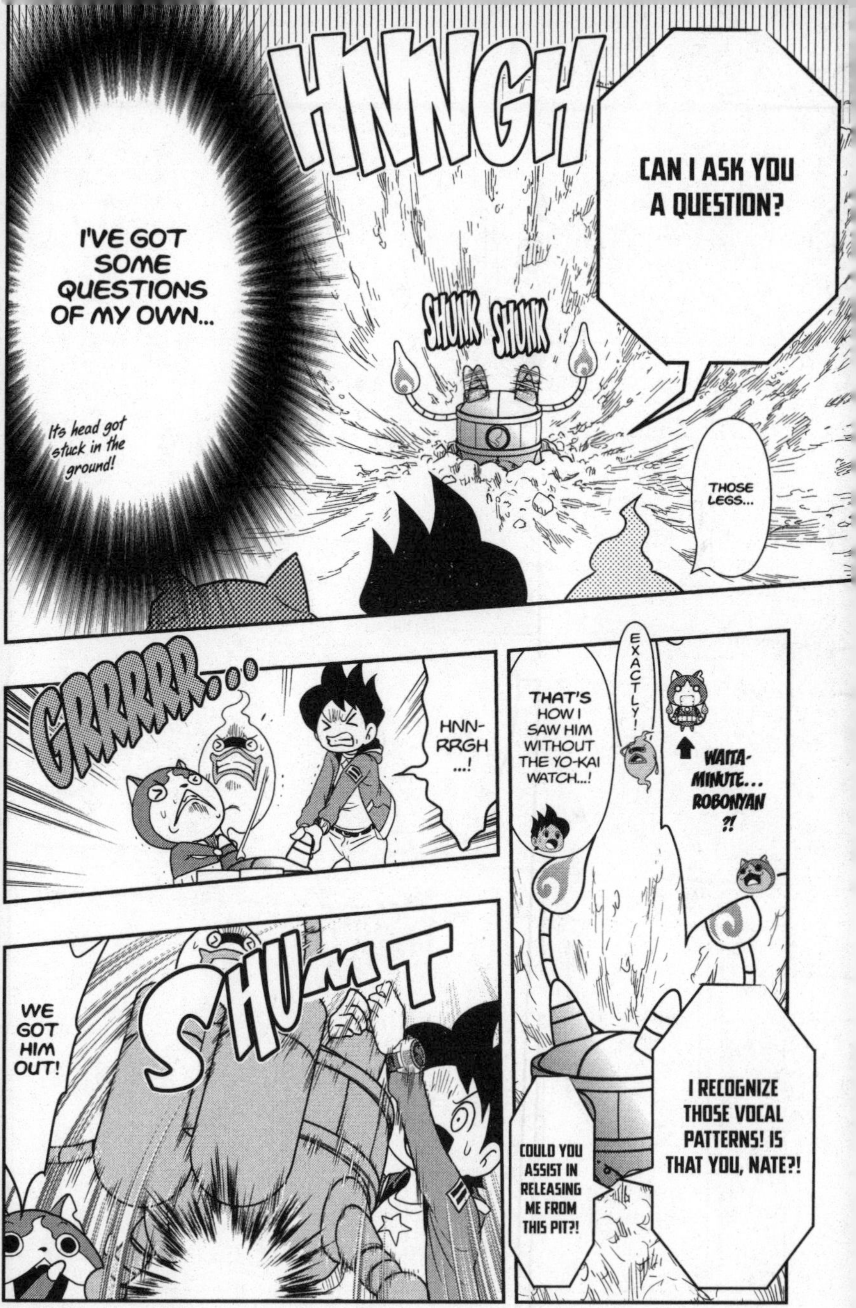

CAN I ASK YOU A QUESTION?
HNNNGH
SHUNK SHUNK
THOSE LEGS...
I'VE GOT SOME QUESTIONS OF MY OWN...
Its head got stuck in the ground!
WAITA-MINUTE... ROBONYAN?!
EXACTLY!
THAT'S HOW I SAW HIM WITHOUT THE YO-KAI WATCH...!
I RECOGNIZE THOSE VOCAL PATTERNS! IS THAT YOU, NATE?!
COULD YOU ASSIST IN RELEASING ME FROM THIS PIT?!
HNN-RRGH...!
GRRRRR...
SHUMT
WE GOT HIM OUT!

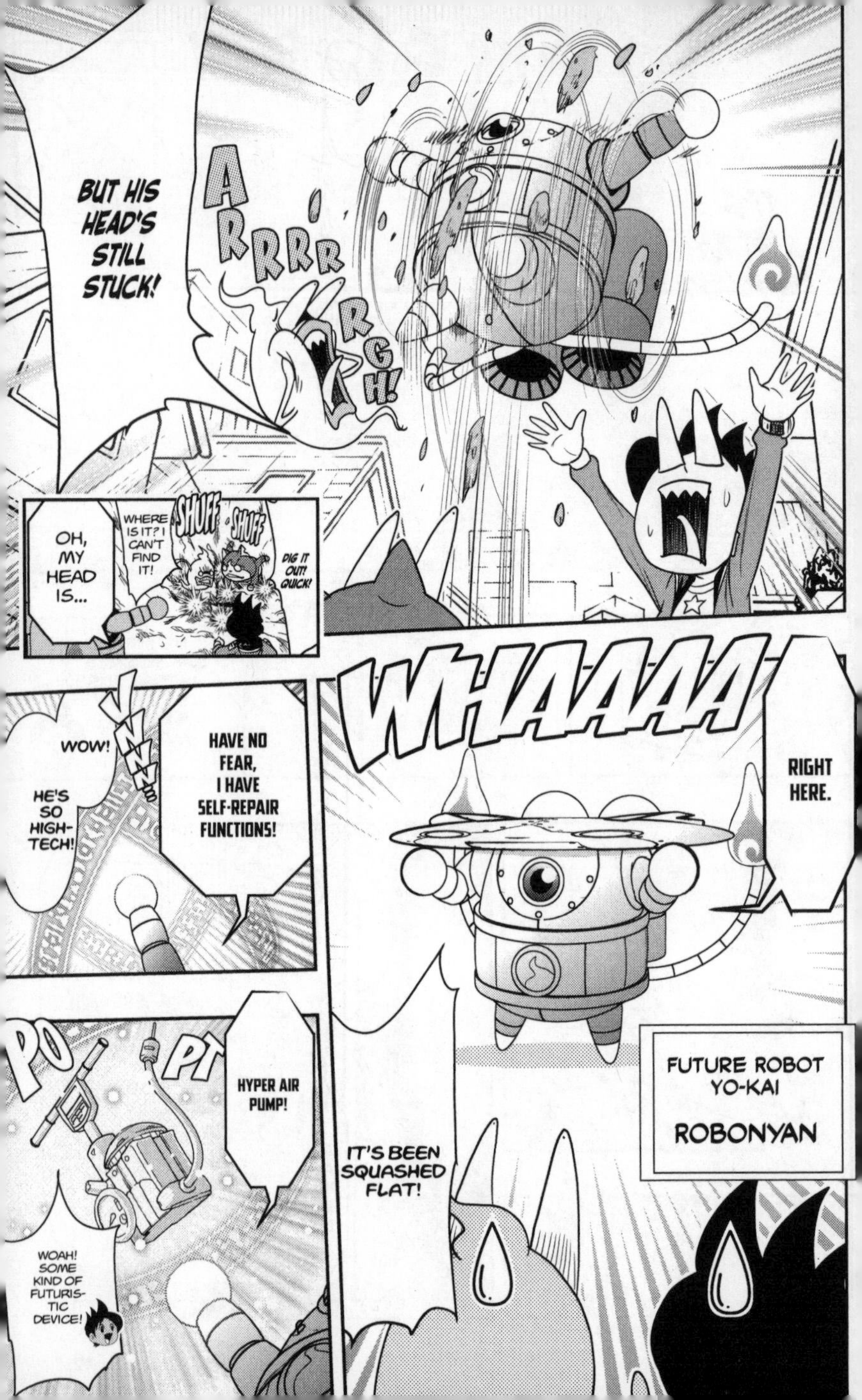

ARRRRRRGH!
BUT HIS HEAD'S STILL STUCK!
DIG IT OUT! QUICK!
SHUFF
SHUFF
WHERE IS IT? I CAN'T FIND IT!
OH, MY HEAD IS...
WHAAAAA
RIGHT HERE.
FUTURE ROBOT YO-KAI
ROBONYAN
IT'S BEEN SQUASHED FLAT!
HAVE NO FEAR, I HAVE SELF-REPAIR FUNCTIONS!
WOW!
HE'S SO HIGH-TECH!
HYPER AIR PUMP!
POPT
WOAH! SOME KIND OF FUTURISTIC DEVICE!

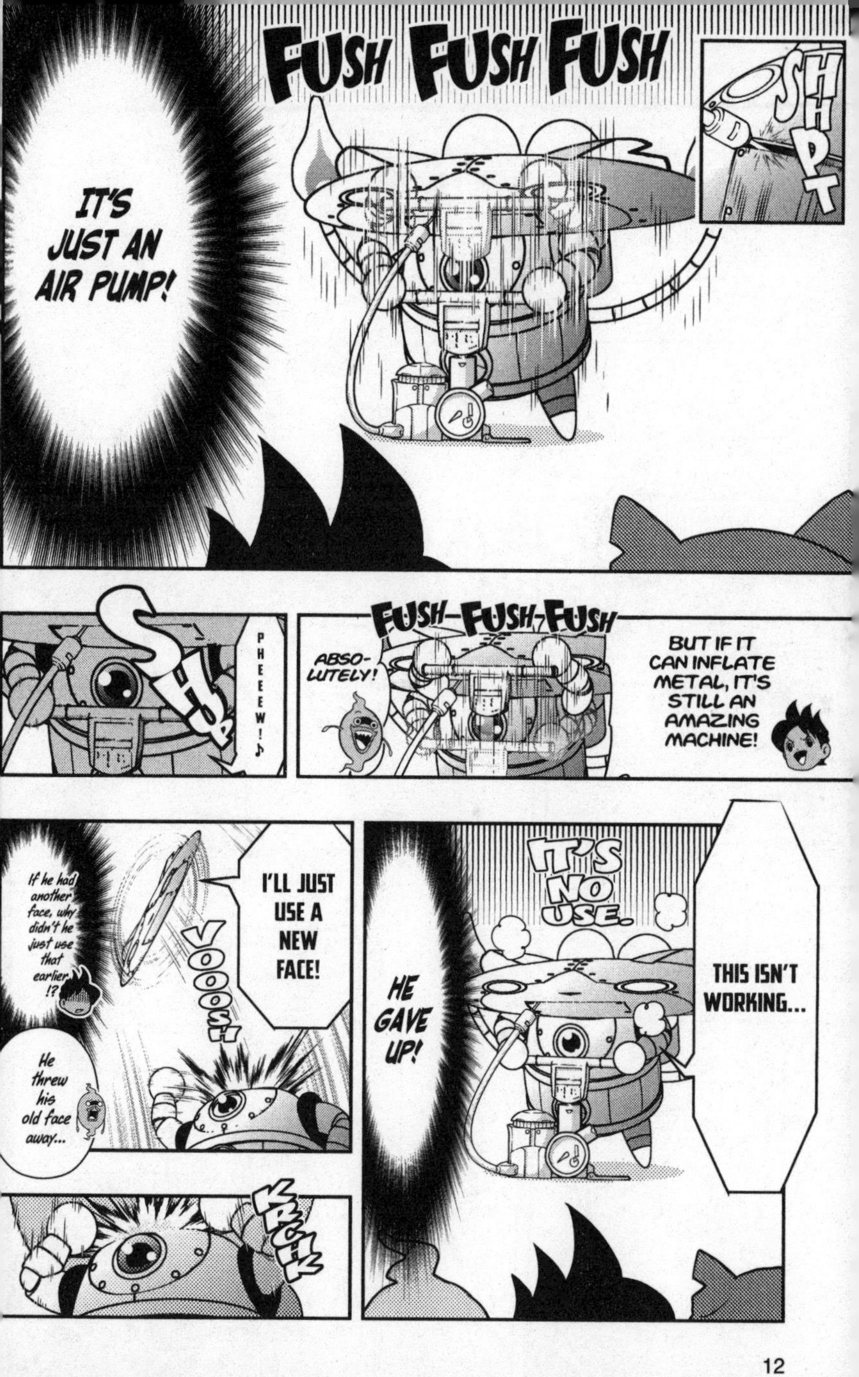
SHHPT
FUSH FUSH FUSH
IT'S JUST AN AIR PUMP!
FUSH-FUSH-FUSH
BUT IF IT CAN INFLATE METAL, IT'S STILL AN AMAZING MACHINE!
ABSO-LUTELY!
PHEEEEW!♪
IT'S NO USE.
THIS ISN'T WORKING...
HE GAVE UP!
I'LL JUST USE A NEW FACE!
VOOOOSH
If he had another face, why didn't he just use that earlier!?
He threw his old face away...
KRCHK

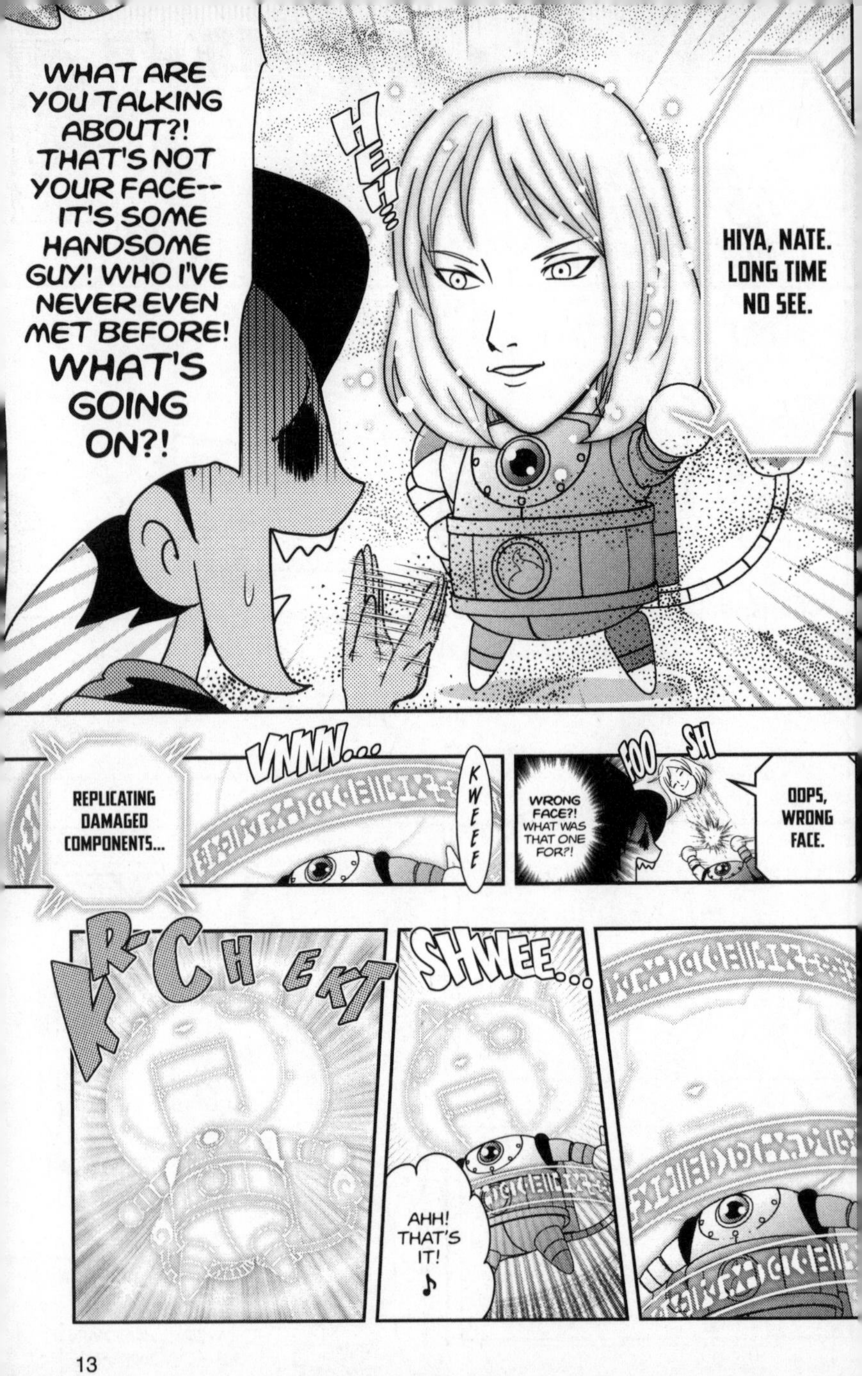
HIYA, NATE. LONG TIME NO SEE.
HEH...
WHAT ARE YOU TALKING ABOUT?! THAT'S NOT YOUR FACE-- IT'S SOME HANDSOME GUY! WHO I'VE NEVER EVEN MET BEFORE! WHAT'S GOING ON?!
FOO SH
OOPS, WRONG FACE.
WRONG FACE?! WHAT WAS THAT ONE FOR?!
VNNN...
KWEEEE
REPLICATING DAMAGED COMPONENTS...
SHWEE...
AHH! THAT'S IT! ♪
KR-CHEKT

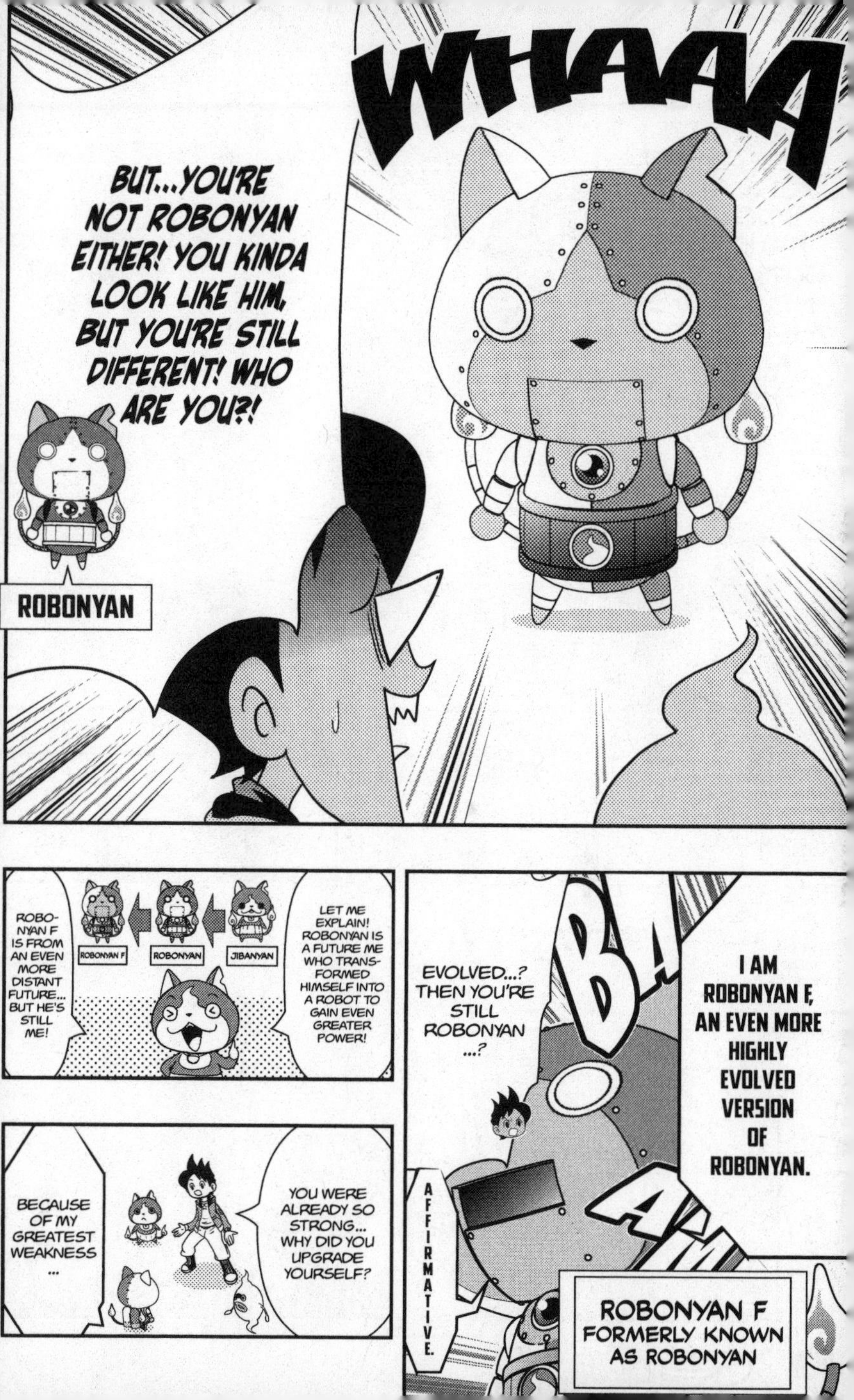
WHAAAA
BUT...YOU'RE NOT ROBONYAN EITHER! YOU KINDA LOOK LIKE HIM, BUT YOU'RE STILL DIFFERENT! WHO ARE YOU?!
ROBONYAN
I AM ROBONYAN F, AN EVEN MORE HIGHLY EVOLVED VERSION OF ROBONYAN.
BA
AM
EVOLVED...? THEN YOU'RE STILL ROBONYAN...?
AFFIRMATIVE.
ROBONYAN F FORMERLY KNOWN AS ROBONYAN
LET ME EXPLAIN! ROBONYAN IS A FUTURE ME WHO TRANS-FORMED HIMSELF INTO A ROBOT TO GAIN EVEN GREATER POWER!
JIBANYAN
ROBONYAN
ROBONYAN F
ROBO-NYAN F IS FROM AN EVEN MORE DISTANT FUTURE... BUT HE'S STILL ME!
YOU WERE ALREADY SO STRONG... WHY DID YOU UPGRADE YOURSELF?
BECAUSE OF MY GREATEST WEAKNESS...

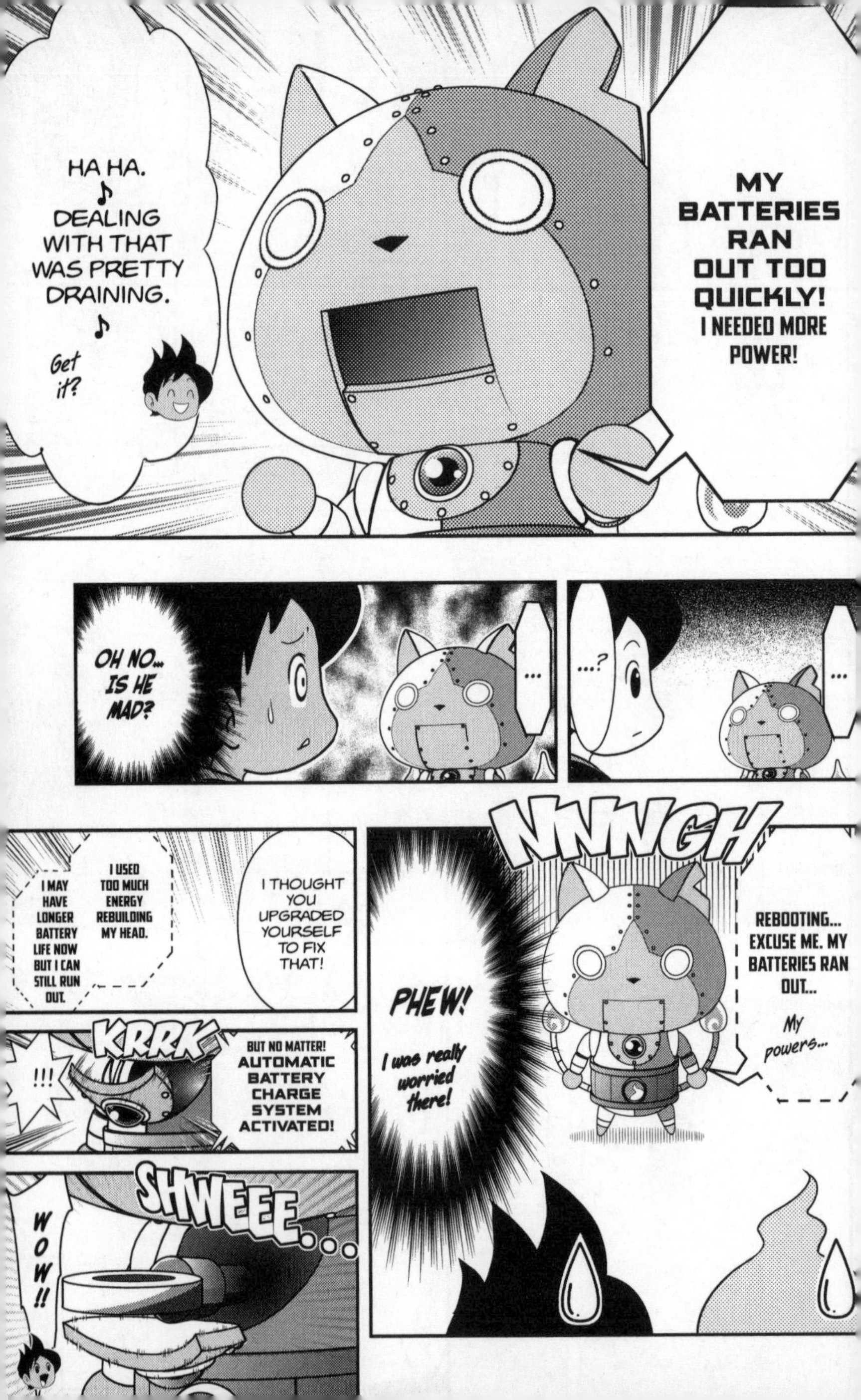
MY BATTERIES RAN OUT TOO QUICKLY! I NEEDED MORE POWER!
HA HA. ♪ DEALING WITH THAT WAS PRETTY DRAINING. ♪
Get it?
...
...?
...
OH NO... IS HE MAD?
NNNGH
REBOOTING... EXCUSE ME. MY BATTERIES RAN OUT...
My powers...
PHEW!
I was really worried there!
I THOUGHT YOU UPGRADED YOURSELF TO FIX THAT!
I USED TOO MUCH ENERGY REBUILDING MY HEAD.
I MAY HAVE LONGER BATTERY LIFE NOW BUT I CAN STILL RUN OUT.
BUT NO MATTER! AUTOMATIC BATTERY CHARGE SYSTEM ACTIVATED!
KRRK
!!!
SHWEEE...
WOW!!

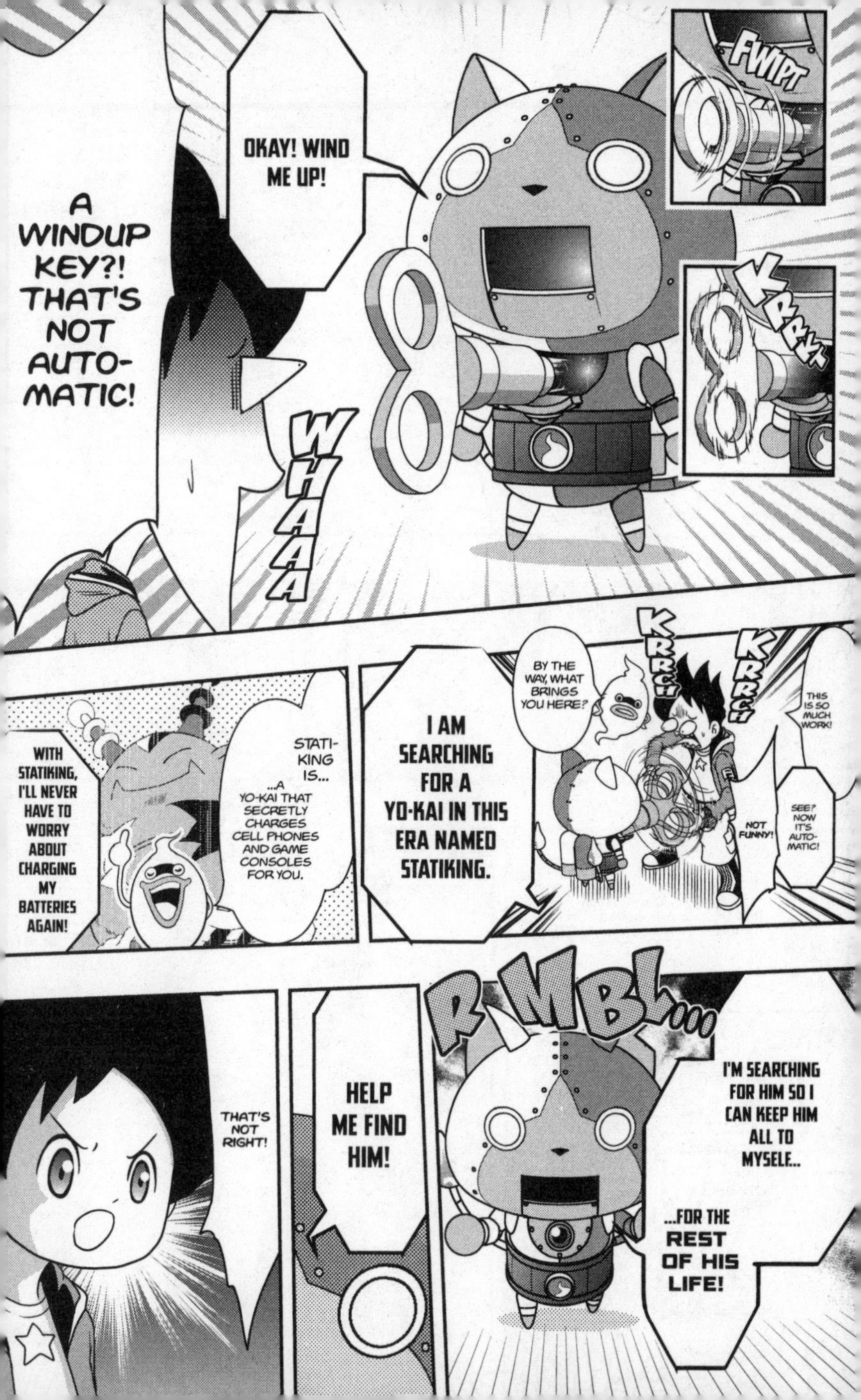
FWIPT
KRRKT
OKAY! WIND ME UP!
A WINDUP KEY?! THAT'S NOT AUTO-MATIC!
WHAAAA
THIS IS SO MUCH WORK!
KRRCH
KRRCH
BY THE WAY, WHAT BRINGS YOU HERE?
SEE? NOW IT'S AUTO-MATIC!
NOT FUNNY!
I AM SEARCHING FOR A YO-KAI IN THIS ERA NAMED STATIKING.
STATI-KING IS...
...A YO-KAI THAT SECRETLY CHARGES CELL PHONES AND GAME CONSOLES FOR YOU.
WITH STATIKING, I'LL NEVER HAVE TO WORRY ABOUT CHARGING MY BATTERIES AGAIN!
RMBL...
I'M SEARCHING FOR HIM SO I CAN KEEP HIM ALL TO MYSELF...
...FOR THE REST OF HIS LIFE!
HELP ME FIND HIM!
THAT'S NOT RIGHT!

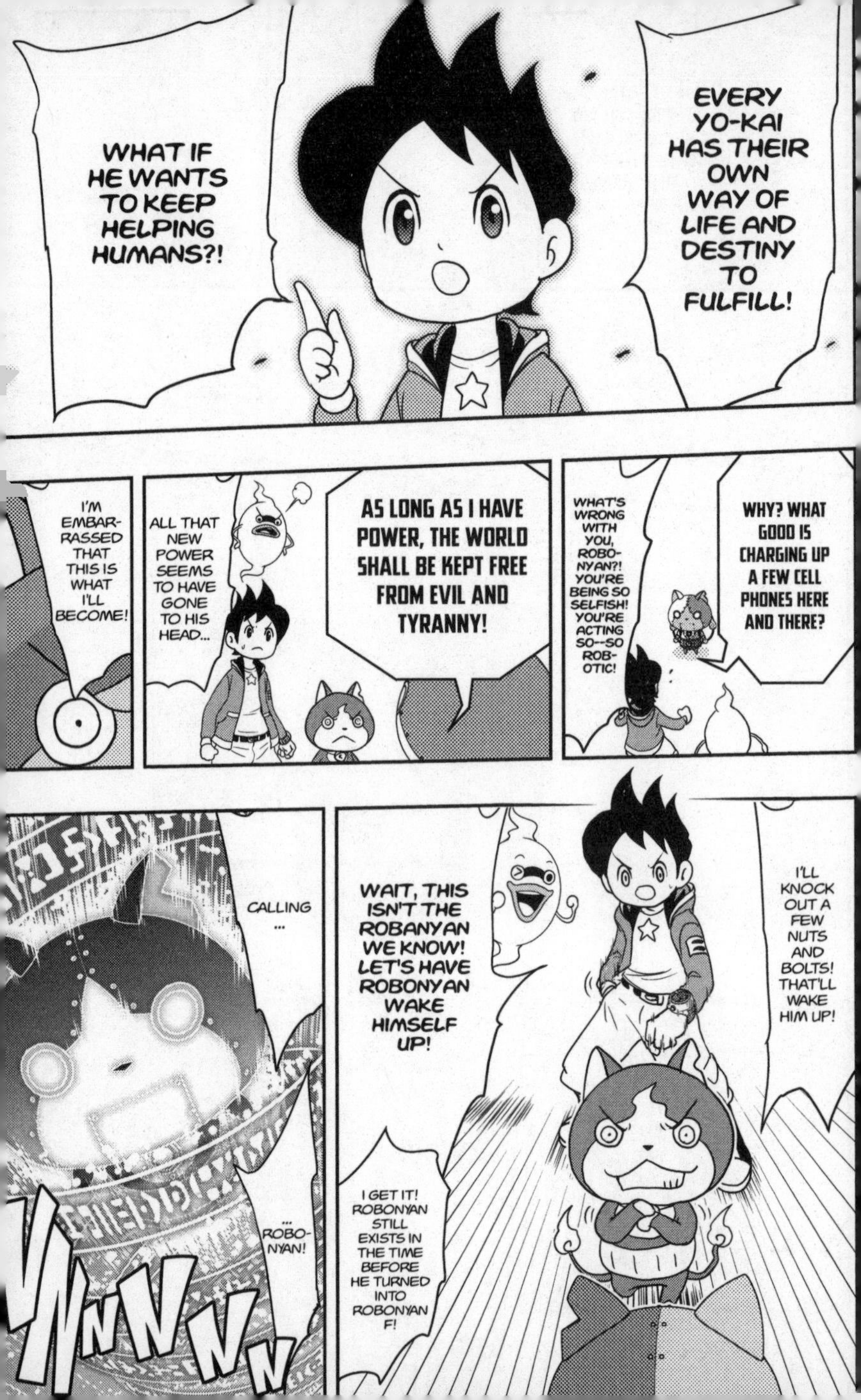
EVERY YO-KAI HAS THEIR OWN WAY OF LIFE AND DESTINY TO FULFILL!
WHAT IF HE WANTS TO KEEP HELPING HUMANS?!
WHY? WHAT GOOD IS CHARGING UP A FEW CELL PHONES HERE AND THERE?
WHAT'S WRONG WITH YOU, ROBO-NYAN?! YOU'RE BEING SO SELFISH! YOU'RE ACTING SO--SO ROB-OTIC!
AS LONG AS I HAVE POWER, THE WORLD SHALL BE KEPT FREE FROM EVIL AND TYRANNY!
ALL THAT NEW POWER SEEMS TO HAVE GONE TO HIS HEAD...
I'M EMBAR-RASSED THAT THIS IS WHAT I'LL BECOME!
I'LL KNOCK OUT A FEW NUTS AND BOLTS! THAT'LL WAKE HIM UP!
WAIT, THIS ISN'T THE ROBANYAN WE KNOW! LET'S HAVE ROBONYAN WAKE HIMSELF UP!
I GET IT! ROBONYAN STILL EXISTS IN THE TIME BEFORE HE TURNED INTO ROBONYAN F!
CALLING ...
... ROBO-NYAN!
VNNNNN

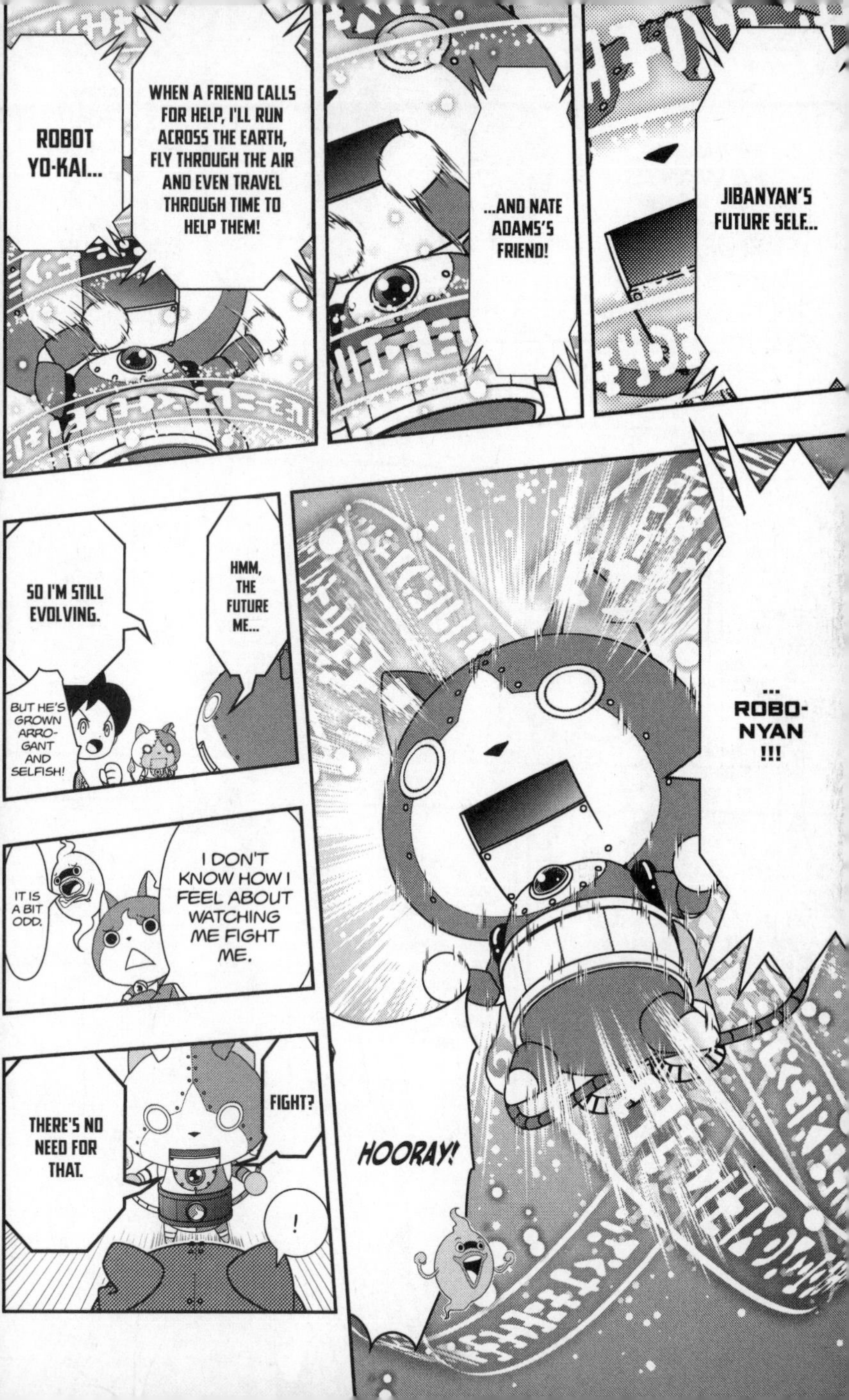
JIBANYAN'S FUTURE SELF...
...AND NATE ADAMS'S FRIEND!
WHEN A FRIEND CALLS FOR HELP, I'LL RUN ACROSS THE EARTH, FLY THROUGH THE AIR AND EVEN TRAVEL THROUGH TIME TO HELP THEM!
ROBOT YO-KAI...
... ROBO-NYAN !!!
HOORAY!
HMM, THE FUTURE ME...
SO I'M STILL EVOLVING.
BUT HE'S GROWN ARRO-GANT AND SELFISH!
I DON'T KNOW HOW I FEEL ABOUT WATCHING ME FIGHT ME.
IT IS A BIT ODD.
FIGHT?
THERE'S NO NEED FOR THAT.
!

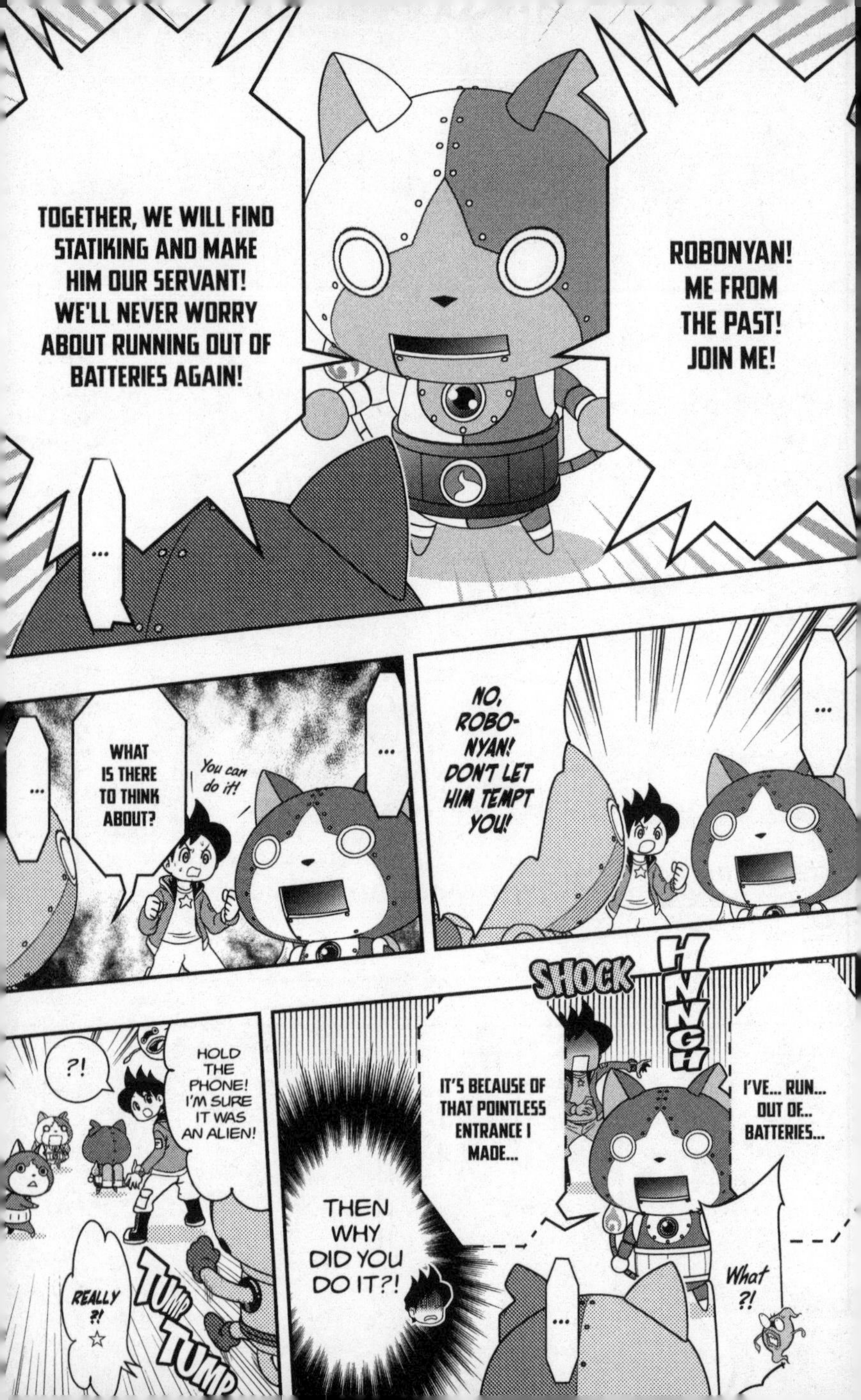

ROBONYAN! ME FROM THE PAST! JOIN ME!
TOGETHER, WE WILL FIND STATIKING AND MAKE HIM OUR SERVANT! WE'LL NEVER WORRY ABOUT RUNNING OUT OF BATTERIES AGAIN!
...
...
NO, ROBO-NYAN! DON'T LET HIM TEMPT YOU!
...
You can do it!
WHAT IS THERE TO THINK ABOUT?
...
HNNGH
SHOCK
I'VE... RUN... OUT OF... BATTERIES...
IT'S BECAUSE OF THAT POINTLESS ENTRANCE I MADE...
What?!
...
THEN WHY DID YOU DO IT?!
HOLD THE PHONE! I'M SURE IT WAS AN ALIEN!
?!
TUMP
TUMP
REALLY?! ☆

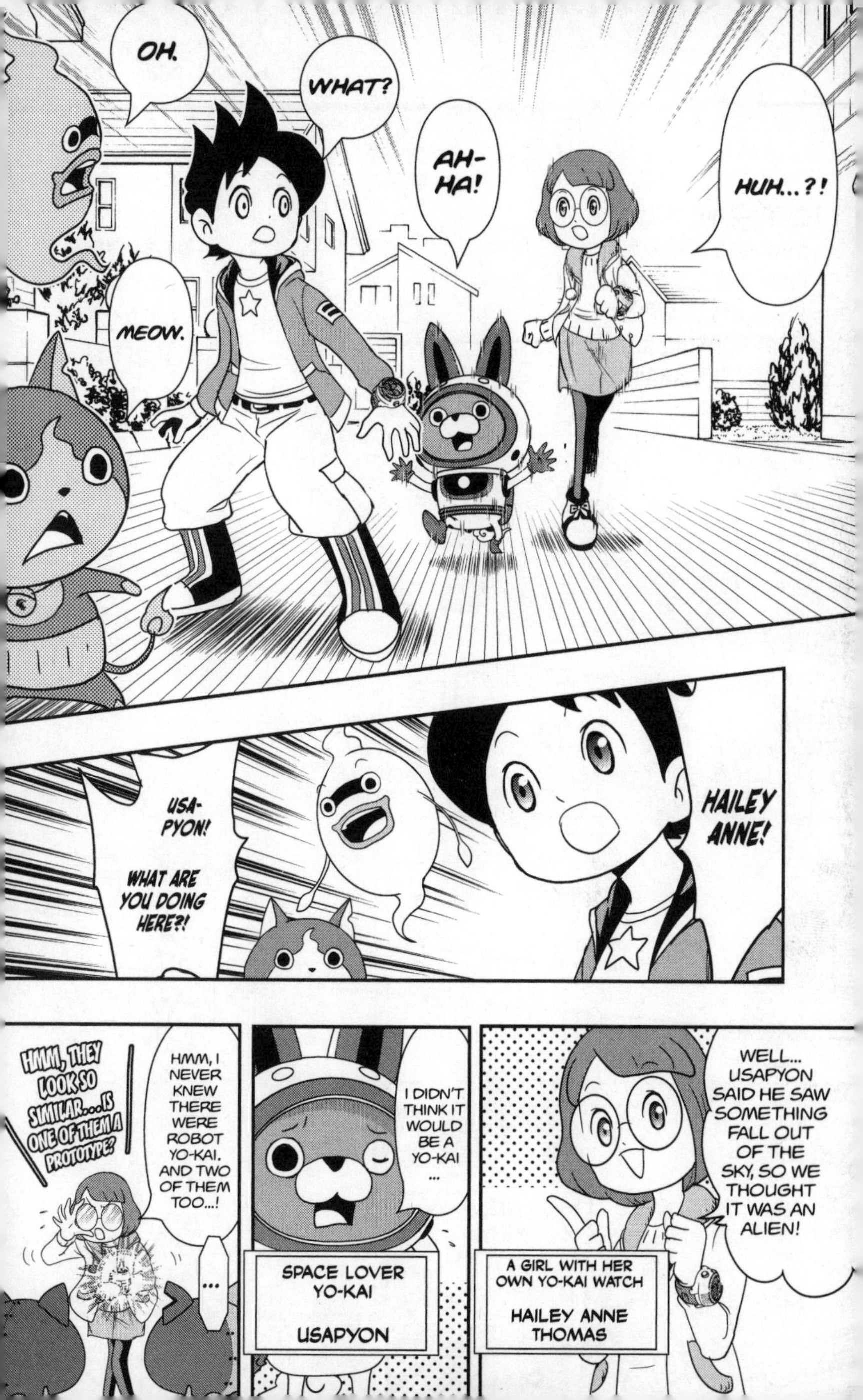
HUH...?!
AH-HA!
WHAT?
OH.
MEOW.
HAILEY ANNE!
USA-PYON!
WHAT ARE YOU DOING HERE?!
WELL... USAPYON SAID HE SAW SOMETHING FALL OUT OF THE SKY, SO WE THOUGHT IT WAS AN ALIEN!
A GIRL WITH HER OWN YO-KAI WATCH
HAILEY ANNE THOMAS
I DIDN'T THINK IT WOULD BE A YO-KAI...
SPACE LOVER YO-KAI
USAPYON
HMM, I NEVER KNEW THERE WERE ROBOT YO-KAI. AND TWO OF THEM TOO...!
HMM, THEY LOOK SO SIMILAR...IS ONE OF THEM A PROTOTYPE?
...

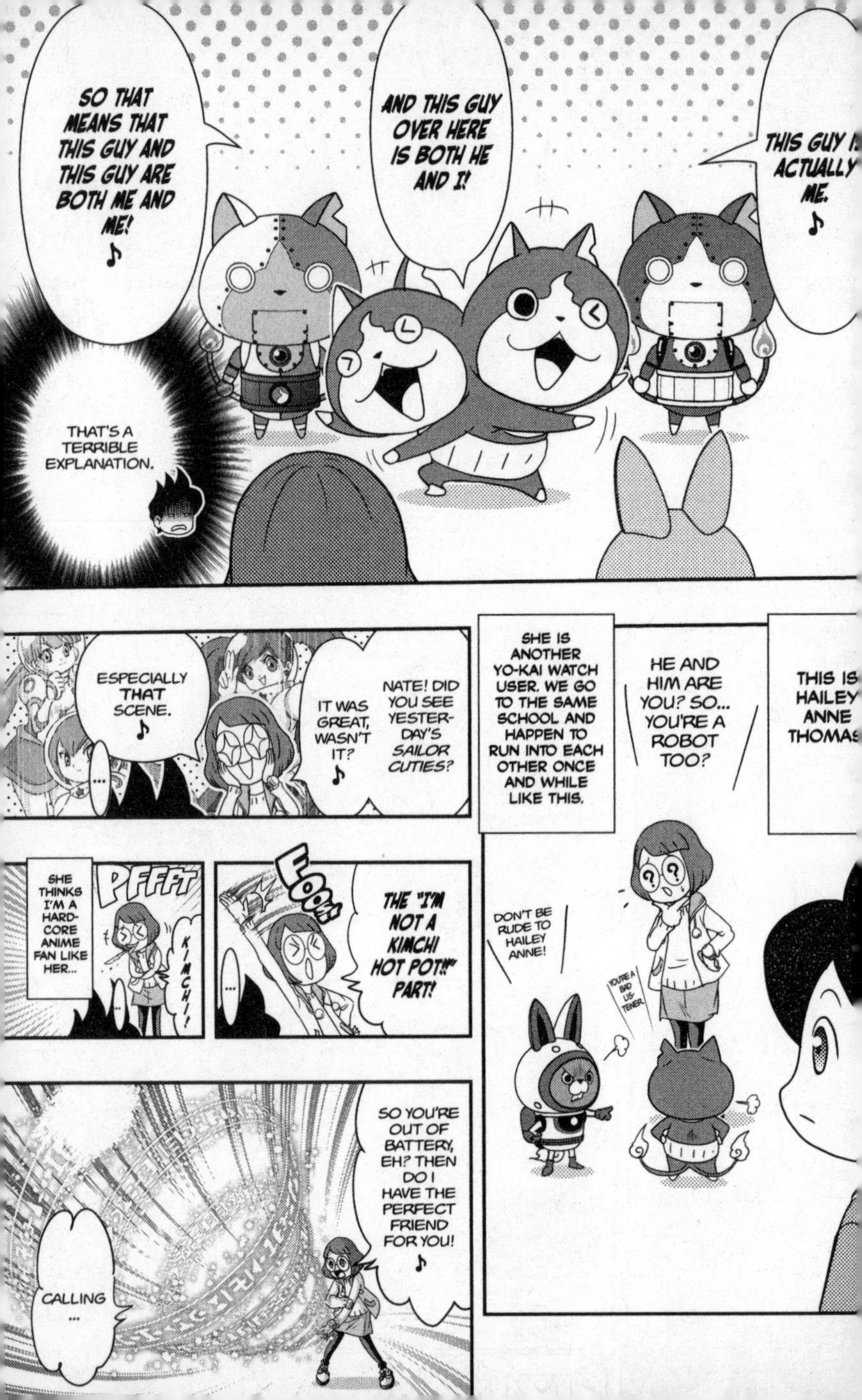
THIS GUY I ACTUALLY ME. ♪
AND THIS GUY OVER HERE IS BOTH HE AND I!
SO THAT MEANS THAT THIS GUY AND THIS GUY ARE BOTH ME AND ME! ♪
THAT'S A TERRIBLE EXPLANATION.
THIS IS HAILEY ANNE THOMAS
HE AND HIM ARE YOU? SO... YOU'RE A ROBOT TOO?
SHE IS ANOTHER YO-KAI WATCH USER. WE GO TO THE SAME SCHOOL AND HAPPEN TO RUN INTO EACH OTHER ONCE AND WHILE LIKE THIS.
DON'T BE RUDE TO HAILEY ANNE!
YOU'RE A BAD LIS-TENER.
NATE! DID YOU SEE YESTER-DAY'S SAILOR CUTIES?
IT WAS GREAT, WASN'T IT? ♪
ESPECIALLY THAT SCENE. ♪
...
FOOM
THE "I'M NOT A KIMCHI HOT POT!!" PART!
...
SHE THINKS I'M A HARD-CORE ANIME FAN LIKE HER...
PFFFT
KIMCHI!
...
SO YOU'RE OUT OF BATTERY, EH? THEN DO I HAVE THE PERFECT FRIEND FOR YOU! ♪
CALLING ...

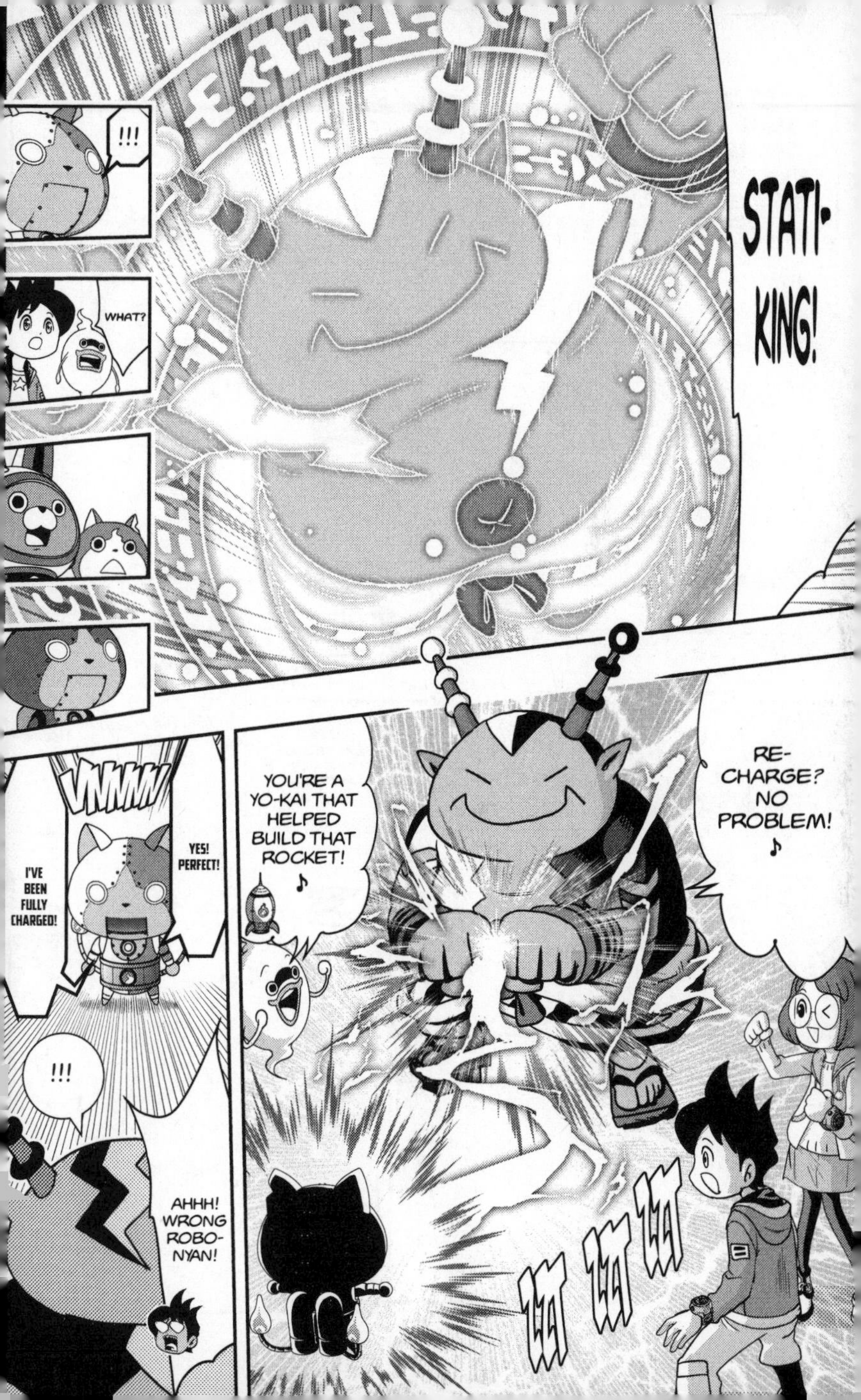
STATI-KING!
!!!
WHAT?
RE-CHARGE? NO PROBLEM! ♪
YOU'RE A YO-KAI THAT HELPED BUILD THAT ROCKET! ♪
VNNNN
YES! PERFECT!
I'VE BEEN FULLY CHARGED!
!!!
AHHH! WRONG ROBO-NYAN!

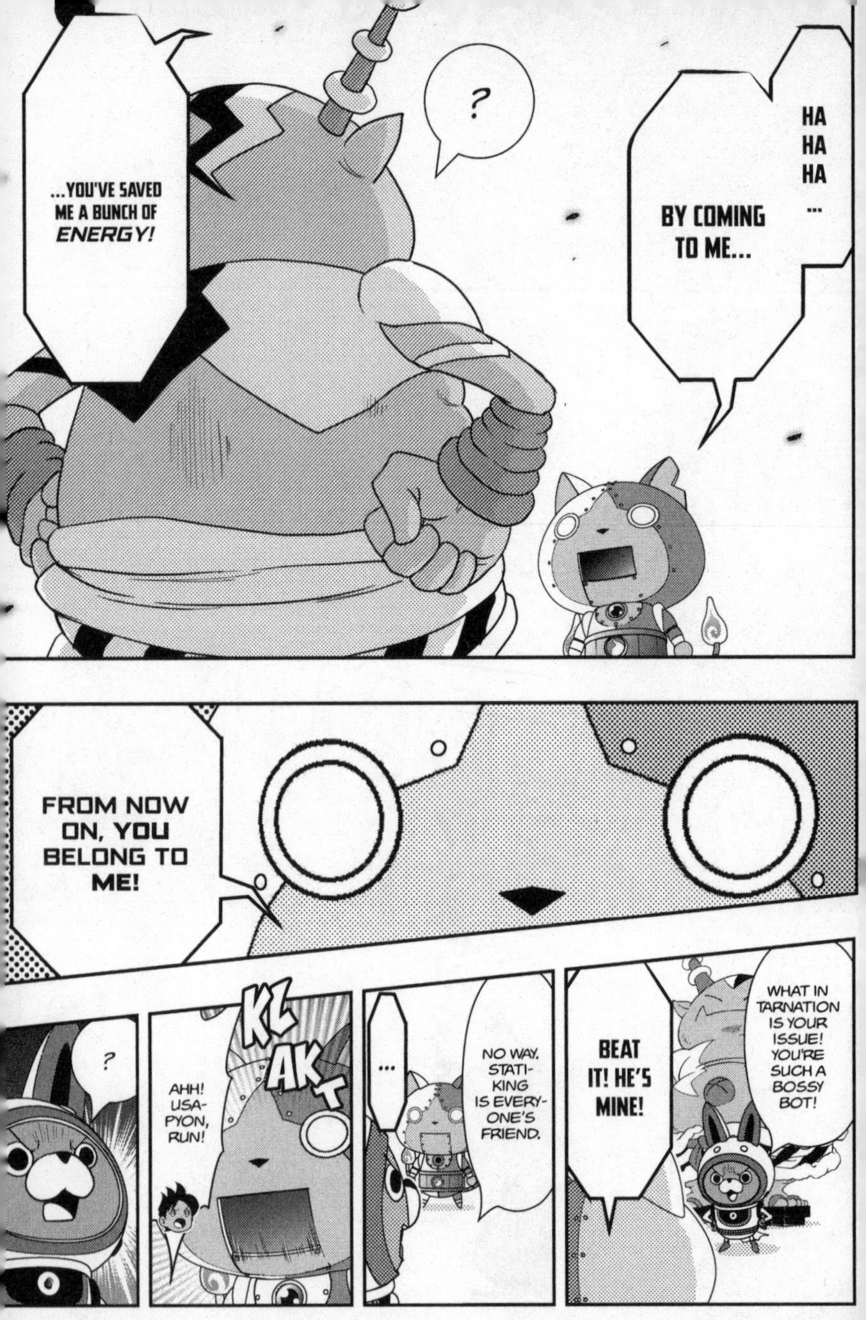
HA HA HA ...
BY COMING TO ME...
?
...YOU'VE SAVED ME A BUNCH OF ENERGY!
FROM NOW ON, YOU BELONG TO ME!
WHAT IN TARNATION IS YOUR ISSUE! YOU'RE SUCH A BOSSY BOT!
BEAT IT! HE'S MINE!
NO WAY. STATI-KING IS EVERY-ONE'S FRIEND.
...
KLAKT
AHH! USA-PYON, RUN!
?

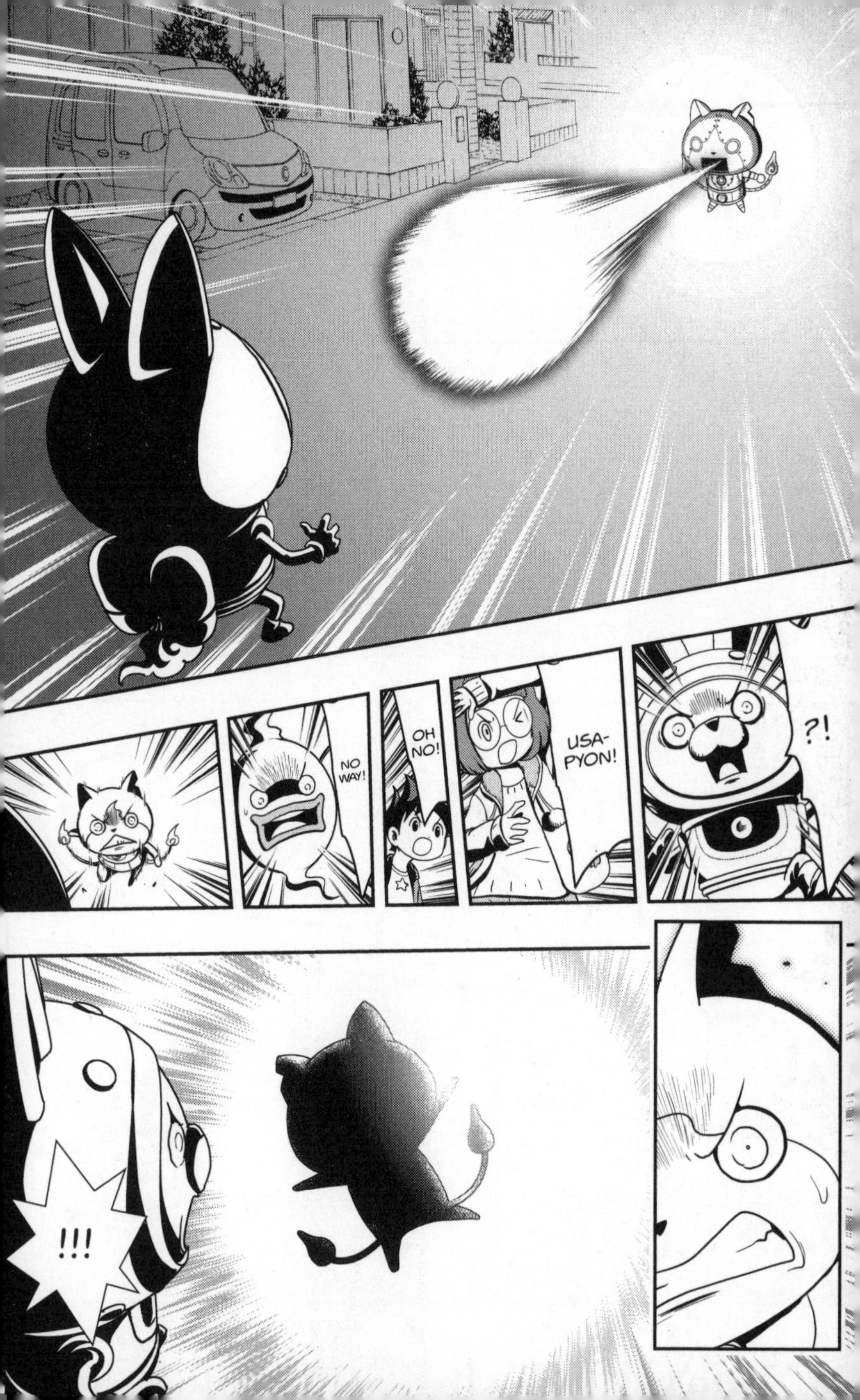
?!
USA-PYON!
OH NO!
NO WAY!
!!!

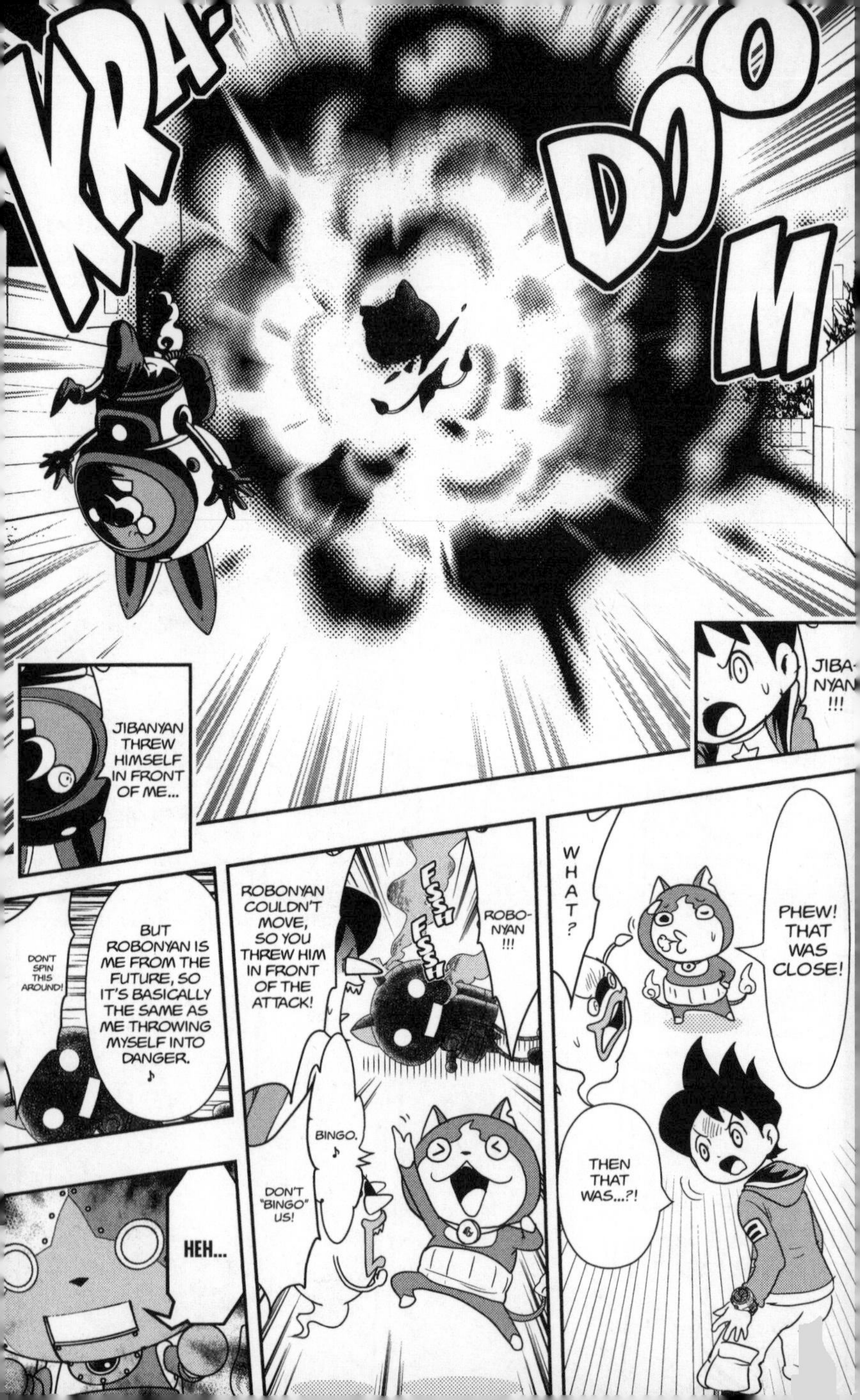
KRA-
DOOOM
JIBA-NYAN!!!
JIBANYAN THREW HIMSELF IN FRONT OF ME...
PHEW! THAT WAS CLOSE!
WHAT?
THEN THAT WAS...?!
ROBO-NYAN!!!
FSSH FSSH
ROBONYAN COULDN'T MOVE, SO YOU THREW HIM IN FRONT OF THE ATTACK!
BINGO. ♪
DON'T "BINGO" US!
BUT ROBONYAN IS ME FROM THE FUTURE, SO IT'S BASICALLY THE SAME AS ME THROWING MYSELF INTO DANGER. ♪
DON'T SPIN THIS AROUND!
HEH...

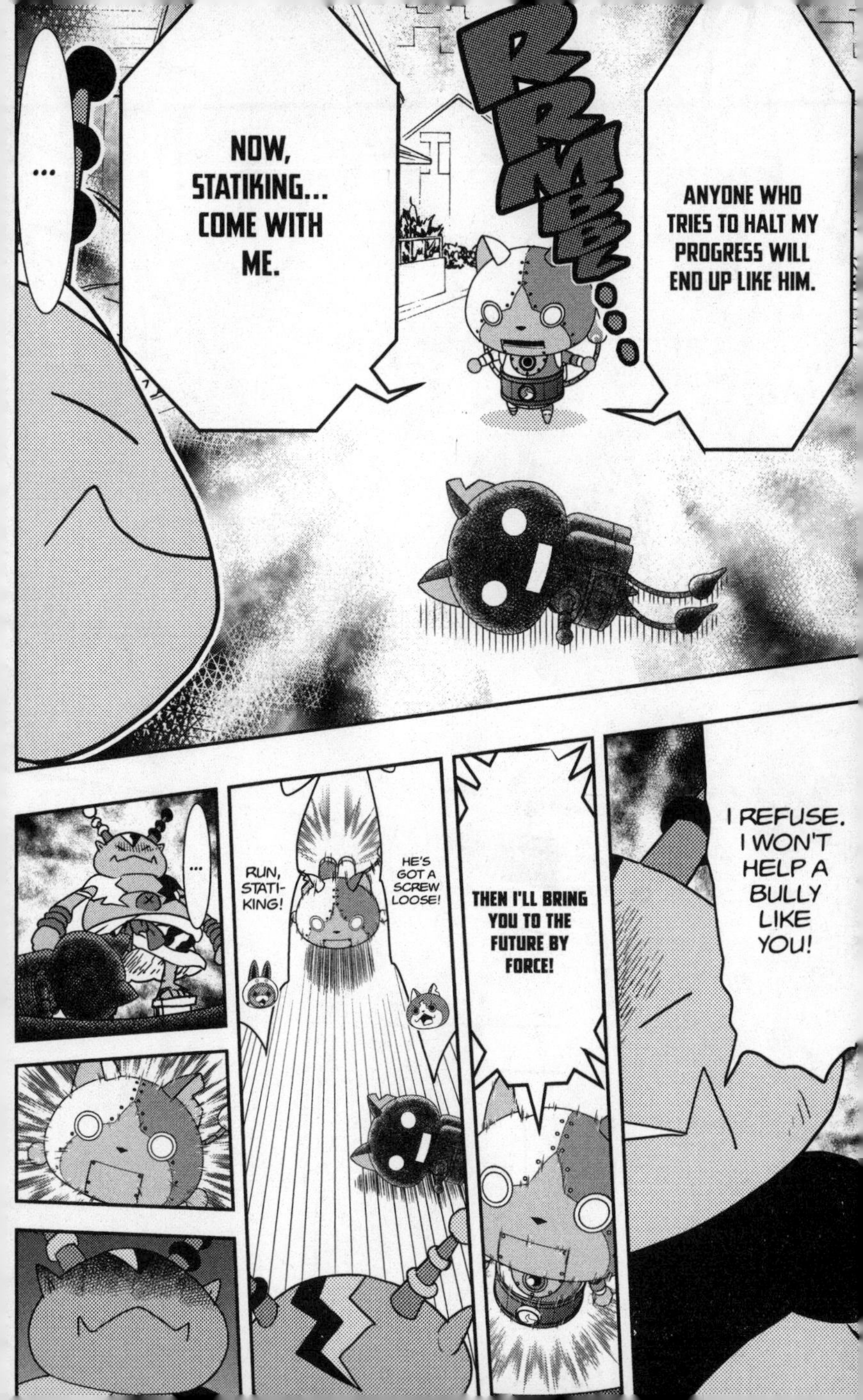
ANYONE WHO TRIES TO HALT MY PROGRESS WILL END UP LIKE HIM.
NOW, STATIKING... COME WITH ME.
...
I REFUSE. I WON'T HELP A BULLY LIKE YOU!
THEN I'LL BRING YOU TO THE FUTURE BY FORCE!
HE'S GOT A SCREW LOOSE!
RUN, STATI-KING!
...

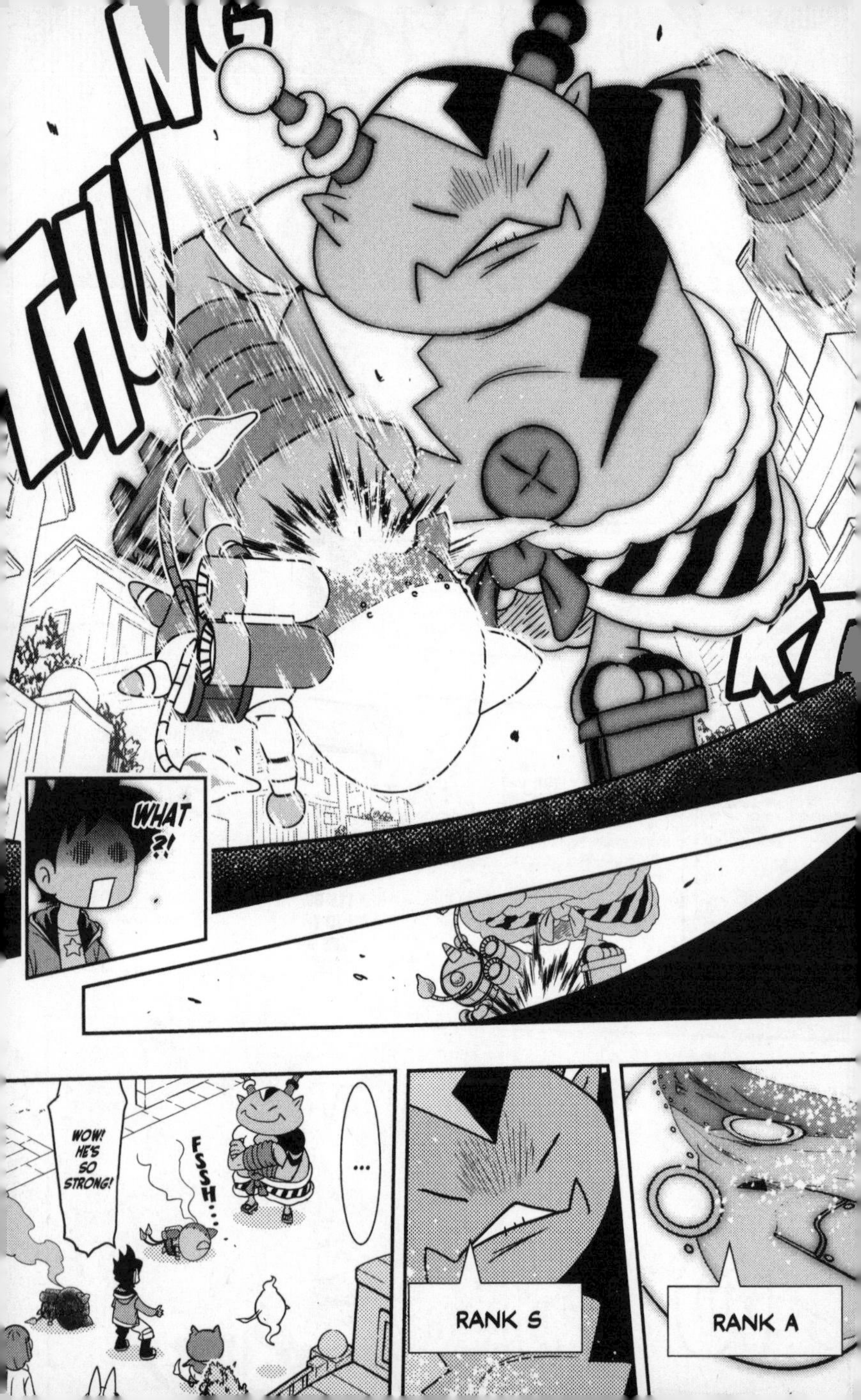
WHAT?!
RANK A
RANK S
...
FSSH...
WOW! HE'S SO STRONG!

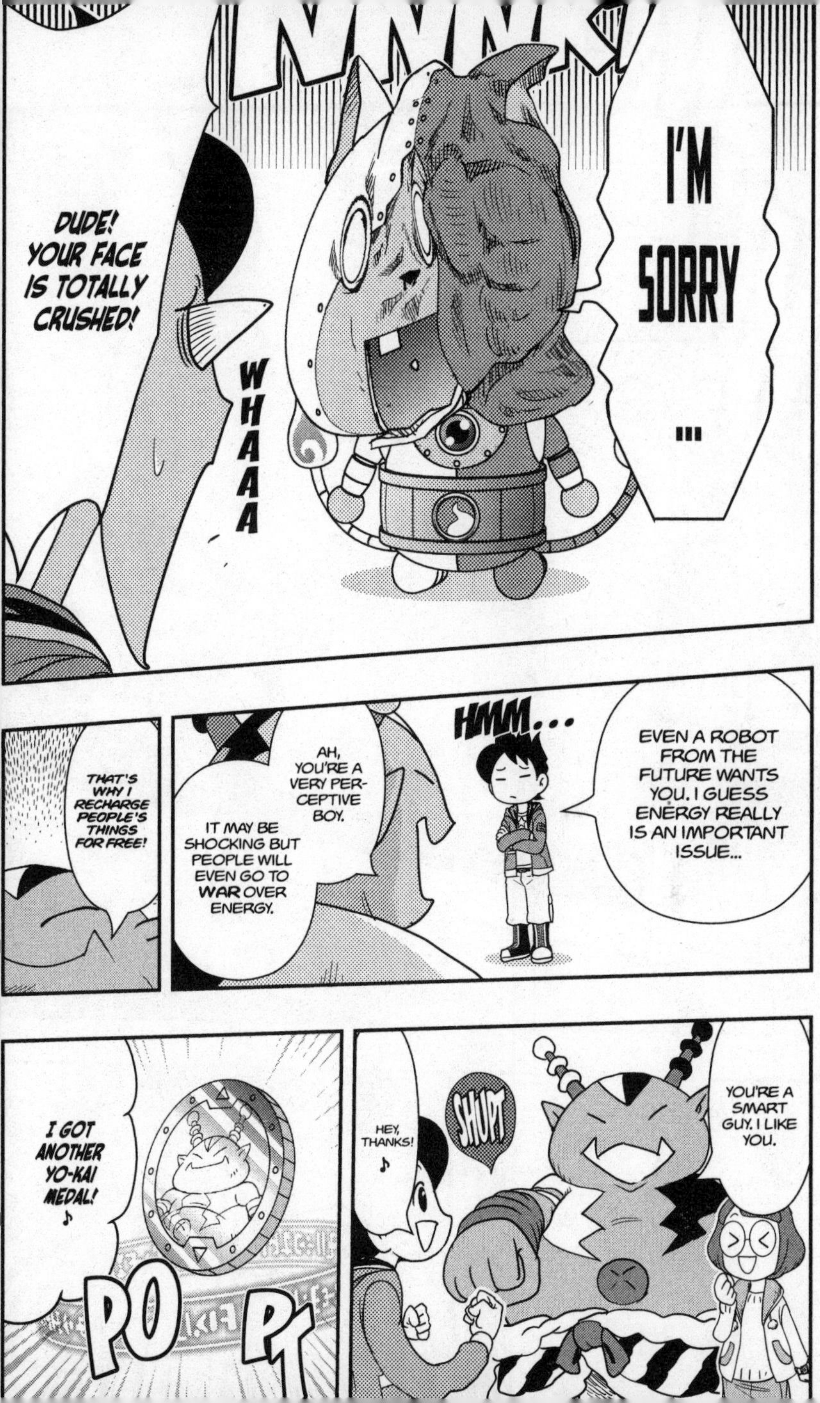
I'M SORRY ...
WHAAAA
DUDE! YOUR FACE IS TOTALLY CRUSHED!
HMM...
EVEN A ROBOT FROM THE FUTURE WANTS YOU. I GUESS ENERGY REALLY IS AN IMPORTANT ISSUE...
AH, YOU'RE A VERY PERCEPTIVE BOY.
IT MAY BE SHOCKING BUT PEOPLE WILL EVEN GO TO WAR OVER ENERGY.
THAT'S WHY I RECHARGE PEOPLE'S THINGS FOR FREE!
YOU'RE A SMART GUY. I LIKE YOU.
SHUPT
HEY, THANKS! ♪
I GOT ANOTHER YO-KAI MEDAL! ♪
POPT

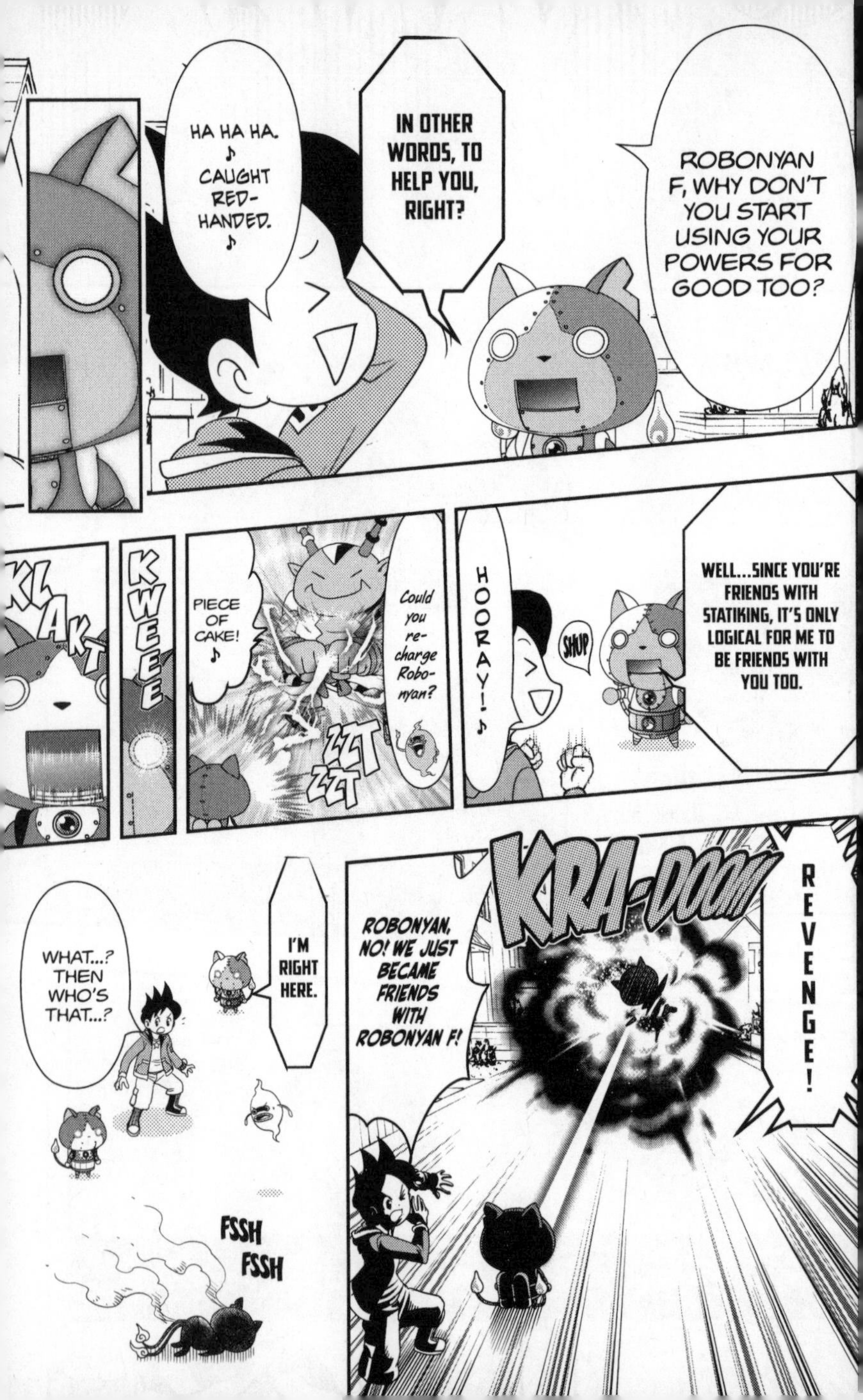
ROBONYAN F, WHY DON'T YOU START USING YOUR POWERS FOR GOOD TOO?
IN OTHER WORDS, TO HELP YOU, RIGHT?
HA HA HA. ♪ CAUGHT RED-HANDED. ♪
WELL...SINCE YOU'RE FRIENDS WITH STATIKING, IT'S ONLY LOGICAL FOR ME TO BE FRIENDS WITH YOU TOO.
SHUP
HOORAY! ♪
Could you re-charge Robonyan?
PIECE OF CAKE! ♪
ZZT ZZT
KWEEE
KLAKT
KRA-DOOM
REVENGE!
ROBONYAN, NO! WE JUST BECAME FRIENDS WITH ROBONYAN F!
I'M RIGHT HERE.
WHAT...? THEN WHO'S THAT...?
FSSH FSSH

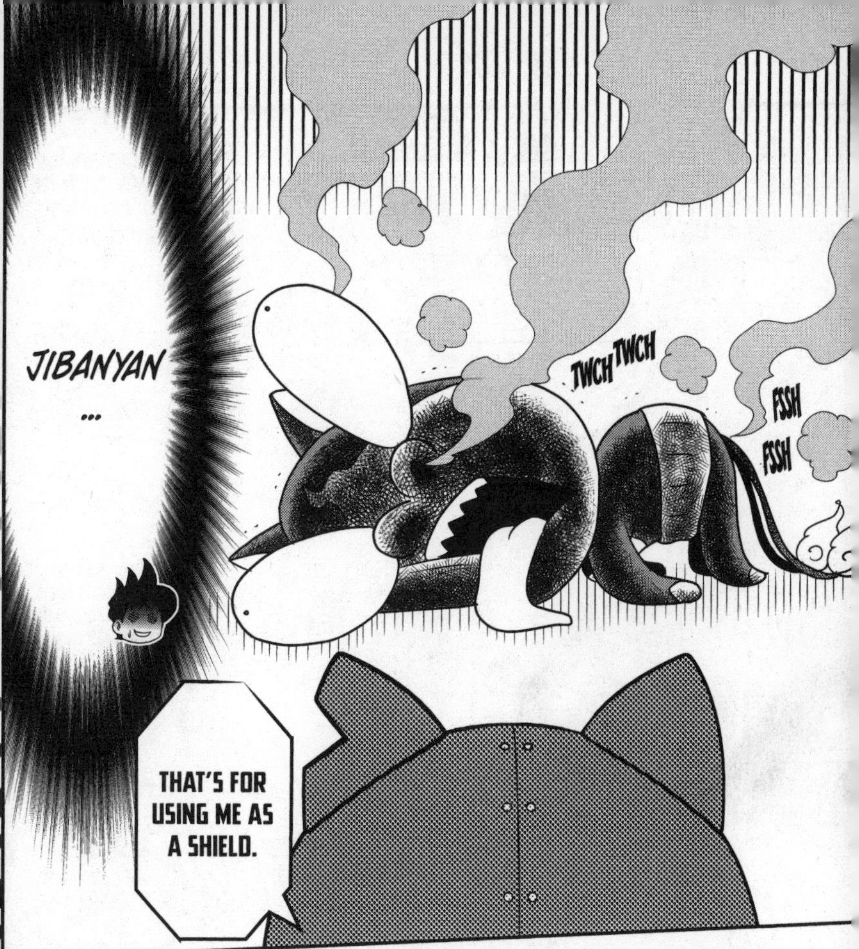

FSSH
FSSH
TWCH TWCH
JIBANYAN ...
THAT'S FOR USING ME AS A SHIELD.

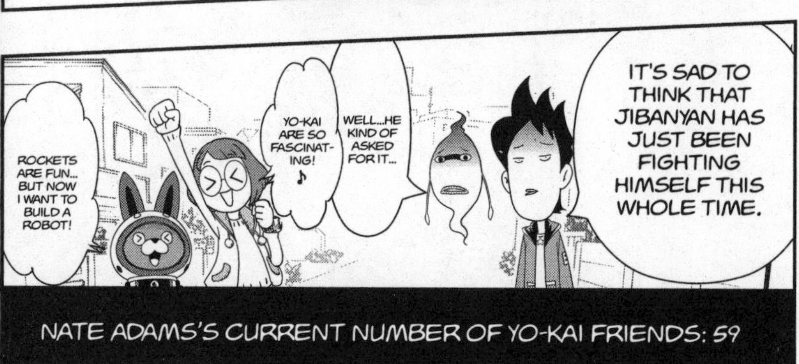

IT'S SAD TO THINK THAT JIBANYAN HAS JUST BEEN FIGHTING HIMSELF THIS WHOLE TIME.
WELL...HE KIND OF ASKED FOR IT...
YO-KAI ARE SO FASCINAT-ING! ♪
ROCKETS ARE FUN... BUT NOW I WANT TO BUILD A ROBOT!
NATE ADAMS'S CURRENT NUMBER OF YO-KAI FRIENDS: 59

CHAPTER 89
WHAT HAPPENED TO MY NECK?!
FEATURING NECK CRAMP YO-KAI CRICKY

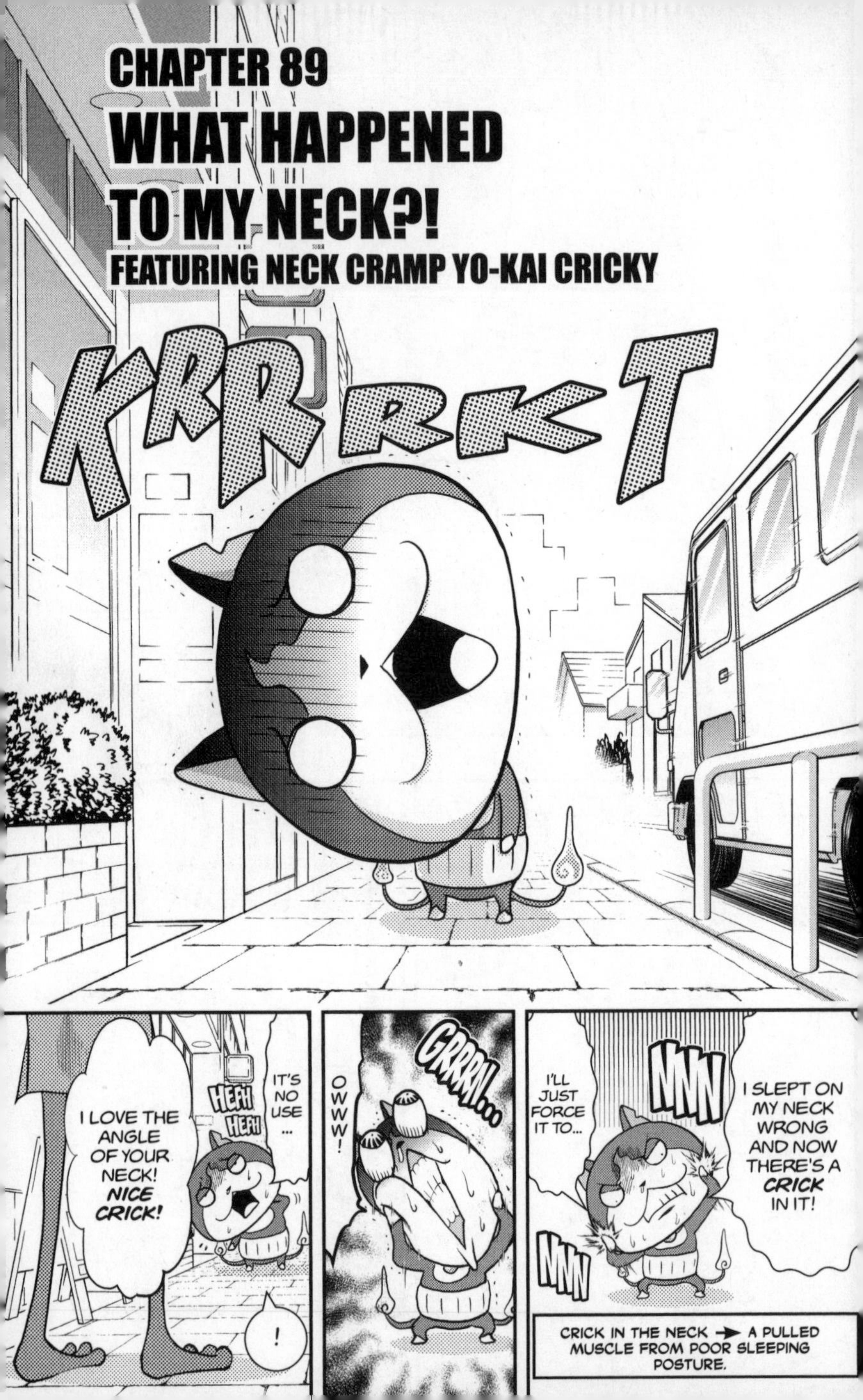
KRRRKT
I SLEPT ON MY NECK WRONG AND NOW THERE'S A *CRICK* IN IT!
NNN
I'LL JUST FORCE IT TO...
NNN
CRICK IN THE NECK → A PULLED MUSCLE FROM POOR SLEEPING POSTURE.
GRRRN...
OWWW!
IT'S NO USE...
HEFH HEFH
I LOVE THE ANGLE OF YOUR NECK! *NICE CRICK!*
!

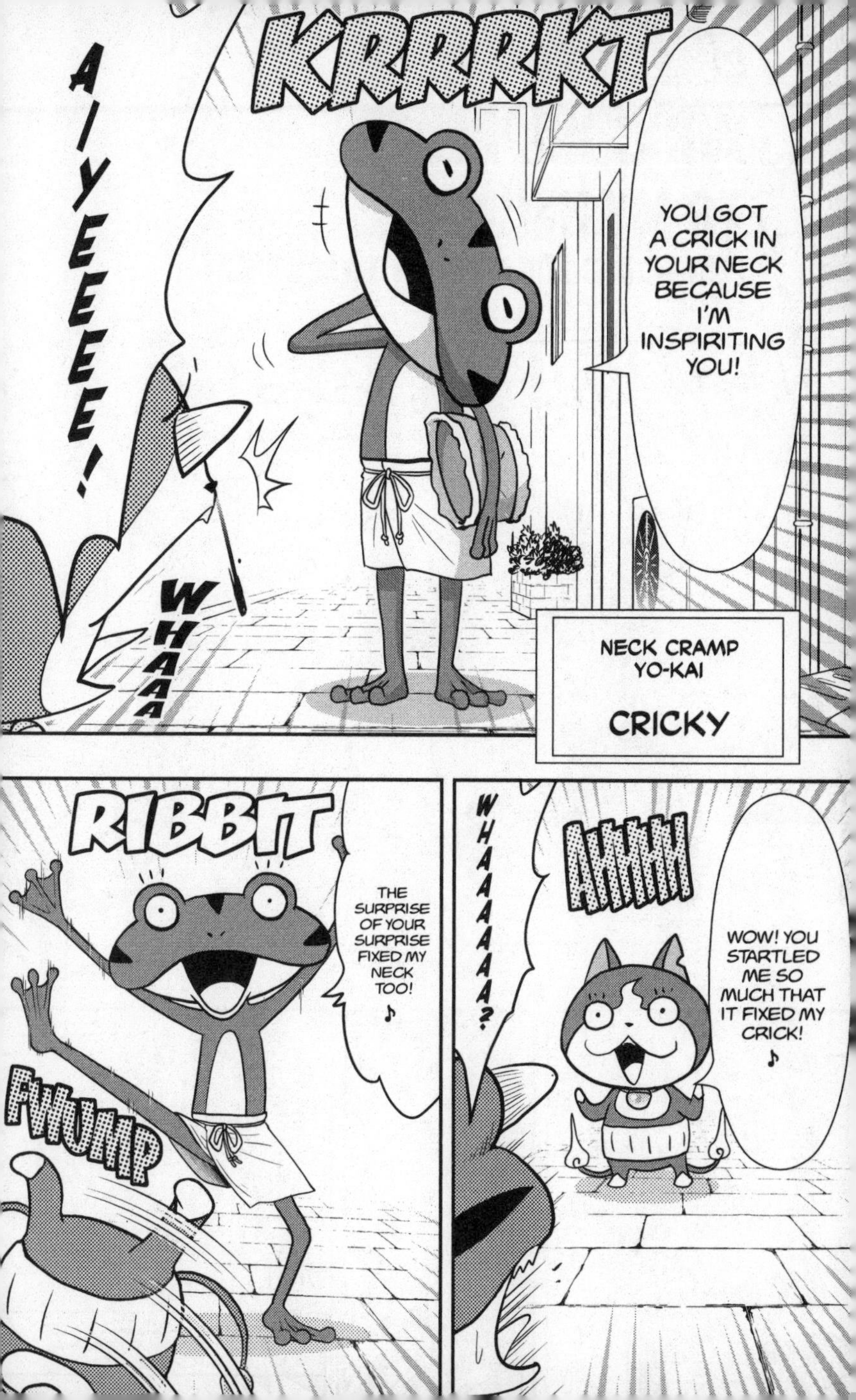

KRRRKT
YOU GOT A CRICK IN YOUR NECK BECAUSE I'M INSPIRITING YOU!
AIYEEEEE!
NECK CRAMP YO-KAI
CRICKY
WHAAAA
WOW! YOU STARTLED ME SO MUCH THAT IT FIXED MY CRICK! ♪
AHHHH
WHAAAAAAA?
THE SURPRISE OF YOUR SURPRISE FIXED MY NECK TOO! ♪
RIBBIT
FWUMP

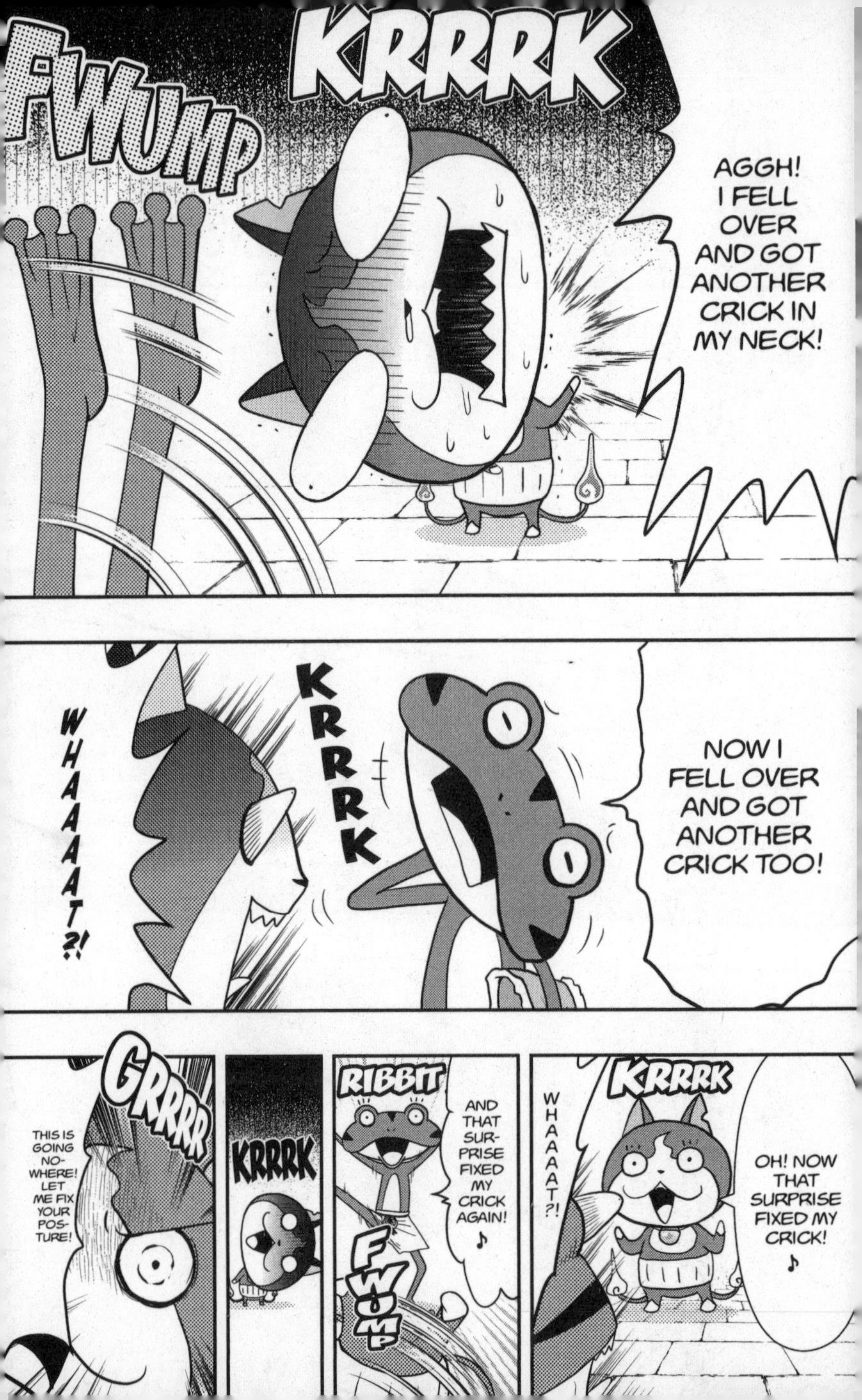
KRRRK
AGGH! I FELL OVER AND GOT ANOTHER CRICK IN MY NECK!
F-WUMP
NOW I FELL OVER AND GOT ANOTHER CRICK TOO!
KRRRK
WHAAAAAT?!
KRRRK
OH! NOW THAT SURPRISE FIXED MY CRICK! ♪
WHAAAAAT?!
RIBBIT
AND THAT SUR-PRISE FIXED MY CRICK AGAIN! ♪
FWUMP
KRRRK
GRRRR
THIS IS GOING NO-WHERE! LET ME FIX YOUR POS-TURE!

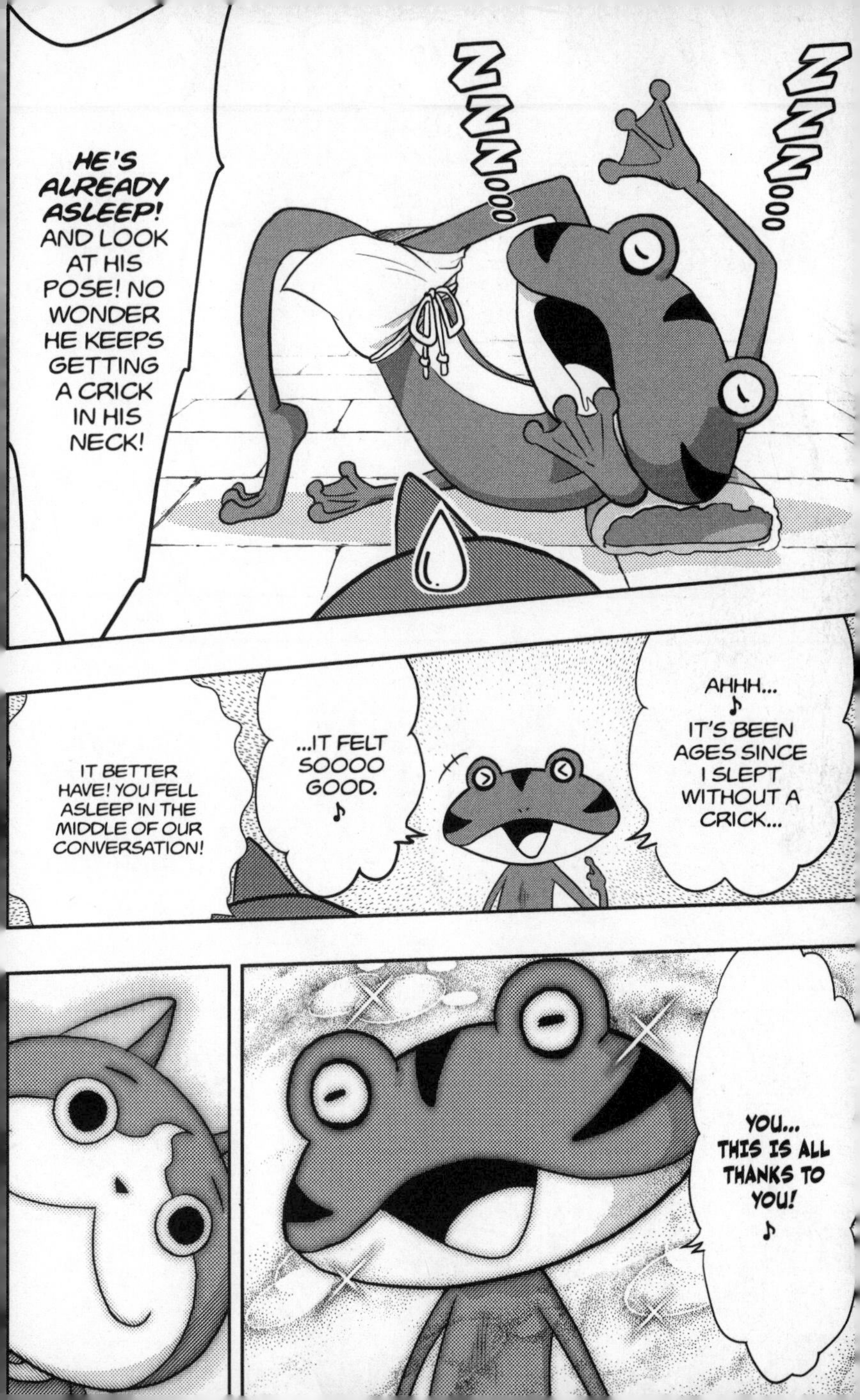
ZZZooo
ZZZooo
HE'S ALREADY ASLEEP! AND LOOK AT HIS POSE! NO WONDER HE KEEPS GETTING A CRICK IN HIS NECK!
AHHH... ♪ IT'S BEEN AGES SINCE I SLEPT WITHOUT A CRICK...
...IT FELT SOOOO GOOD. ♪
IT BETTER HAVE! YOU FELL ASLEEP IN THE MIDDLE OF OUR CONVERSATION!
YOU... THIS IS ALL THANKS TO YOU! ♪

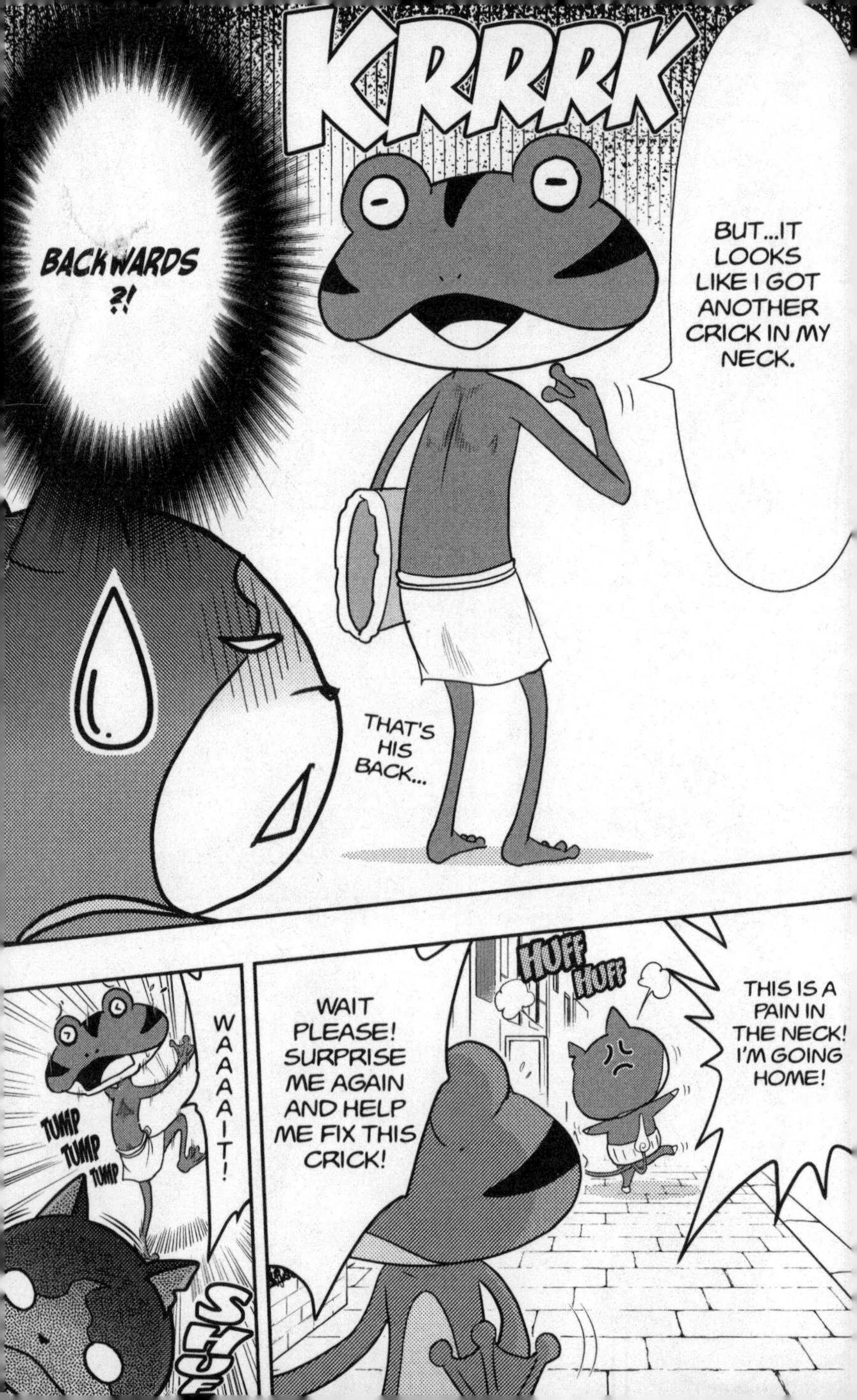
KRRRK
BUT...IT LOOKS LIKE I GOT ANOTHER CRICK IN MY NECK.
BACKWARDS ?!
THAT'S HIS BACK...
HUFF HUFF
THIS IS A PAIN IN THE NECK! I'M GOING HOME!
WAIT PLEASE! SURPRISE ME AGAIN AND HELP ME FIX THIS CRICK!
WAAAAAIT!
TUMP TUMP TUMP

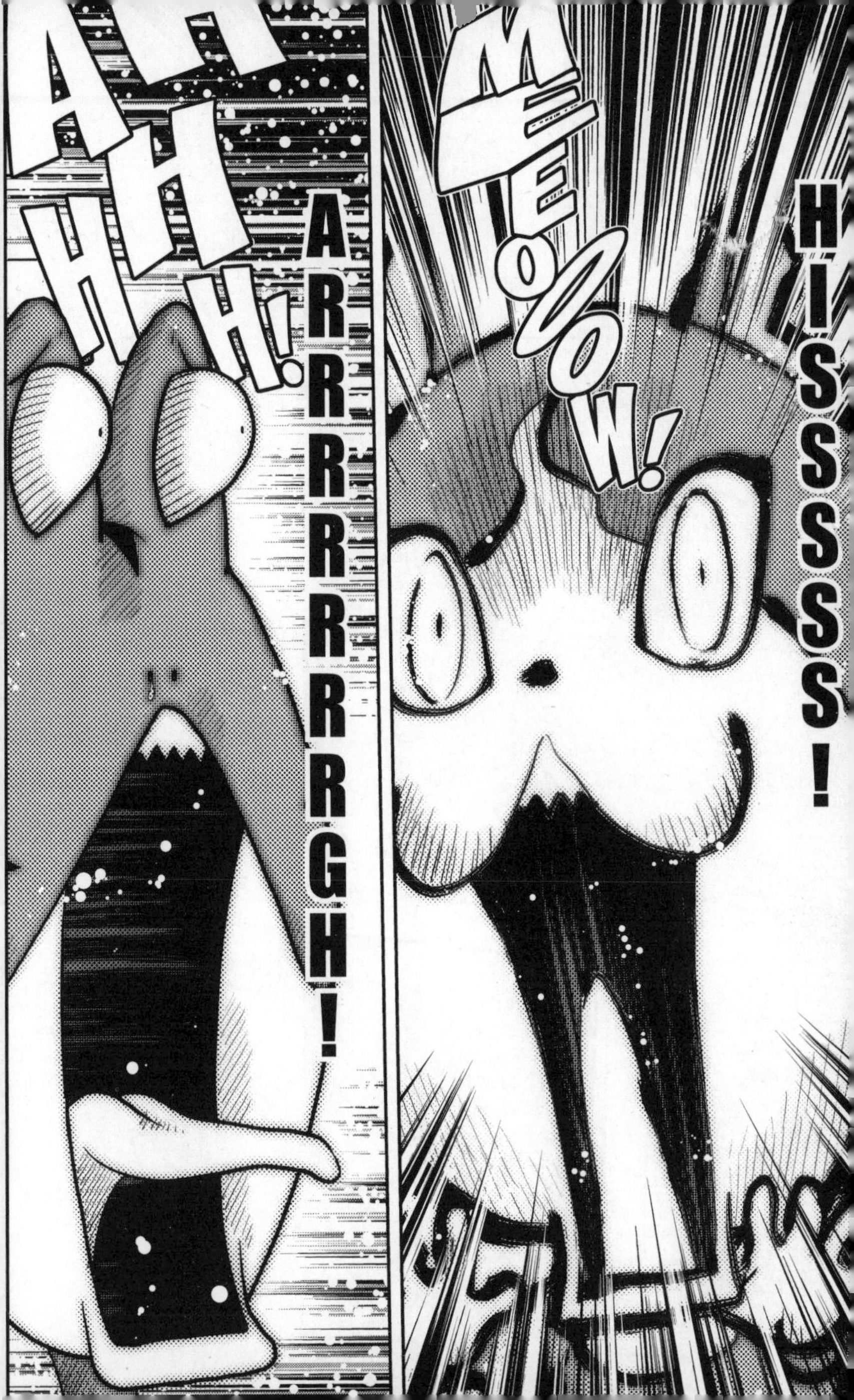
MEOOOW!
HISSSSS!
AHHHH!
ARRRRRRRGH!

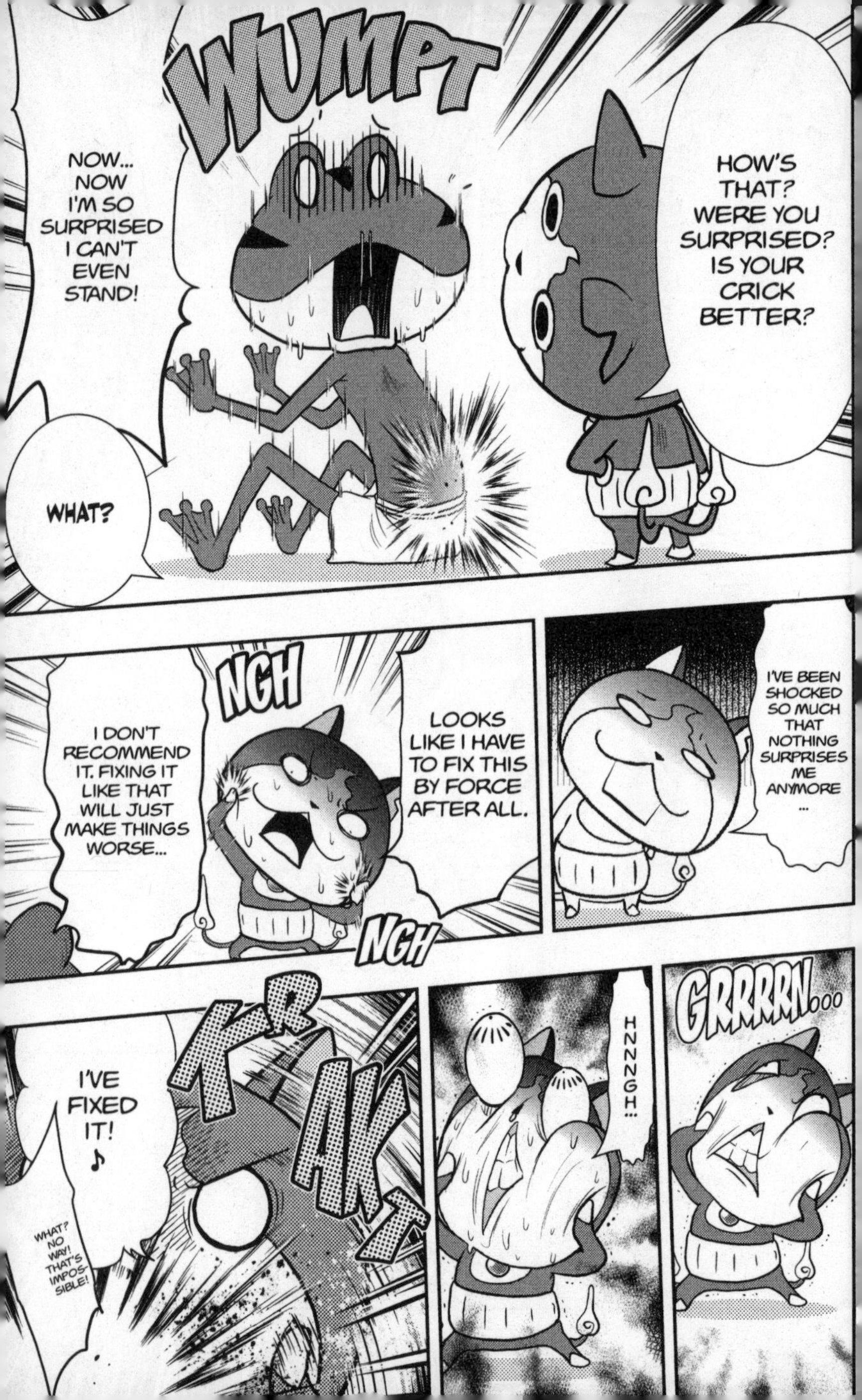
HOW'S THAT? WERE YOU SURPRISED? IS YOUR CRICK BETTER?
WUMPT
NOW... NOW I'M SO SURPRISED I CAN'T EVEN STAND!
WHAT?
I'VE BEEN SHOCKED SO MUCH THAT NOTHING SURPRISES ME ANYMORE ...
NGH
LOOKS LIKE I HAVE TO FIX THIS BY FORCE AFTER ALL.
I DON'T RECOMMEND IT. FIXING IT LIKE THAT WILL JUST MAKE THINGS WORSE...
NGH
GRRRRN...
HNNNGH!!
KRAK
I'VE FIXED IT! ♪
WHAT? NO WAY! THAT'S IMPOSSIBLE!

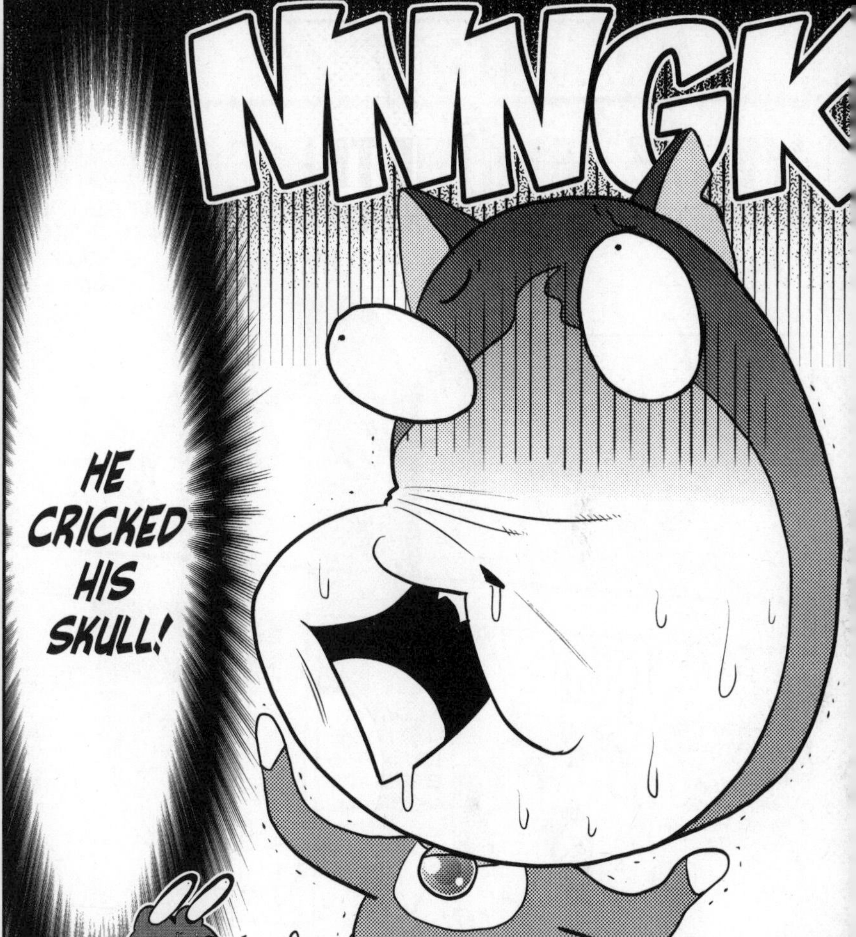
NNNGK
HE CRICKED HIS SKULL!

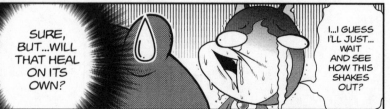

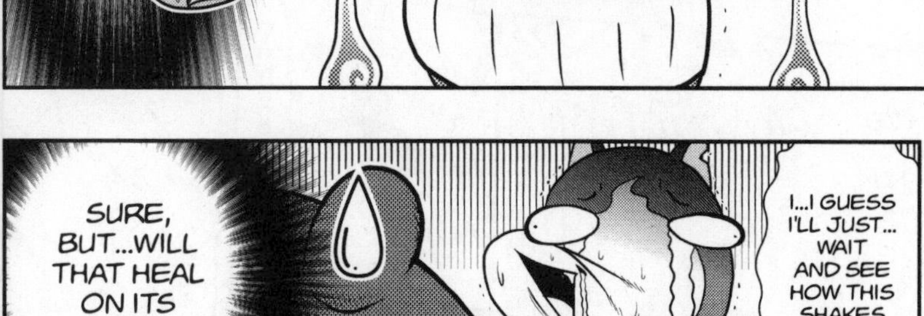
I...I GUESS I'LL JUST... WAIT AND SEE HOW THIS SHAKES OUT?
SURE, BUT...WILL THAT HEAL ON ITS OWN?

CHAPTER 90
ALWAYS OBEY THE TRAFFIC LAWS!
FEATURING STREET GUARDIAN SNARTLE

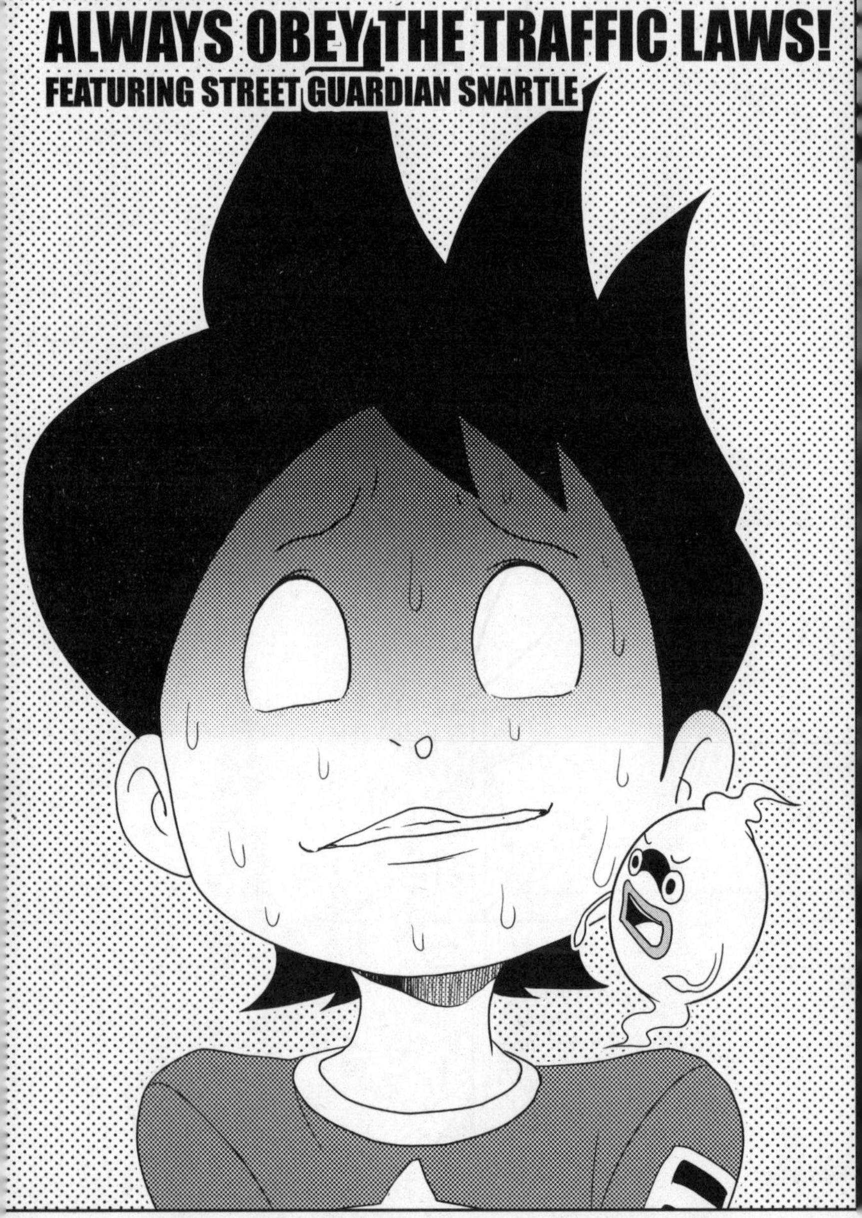

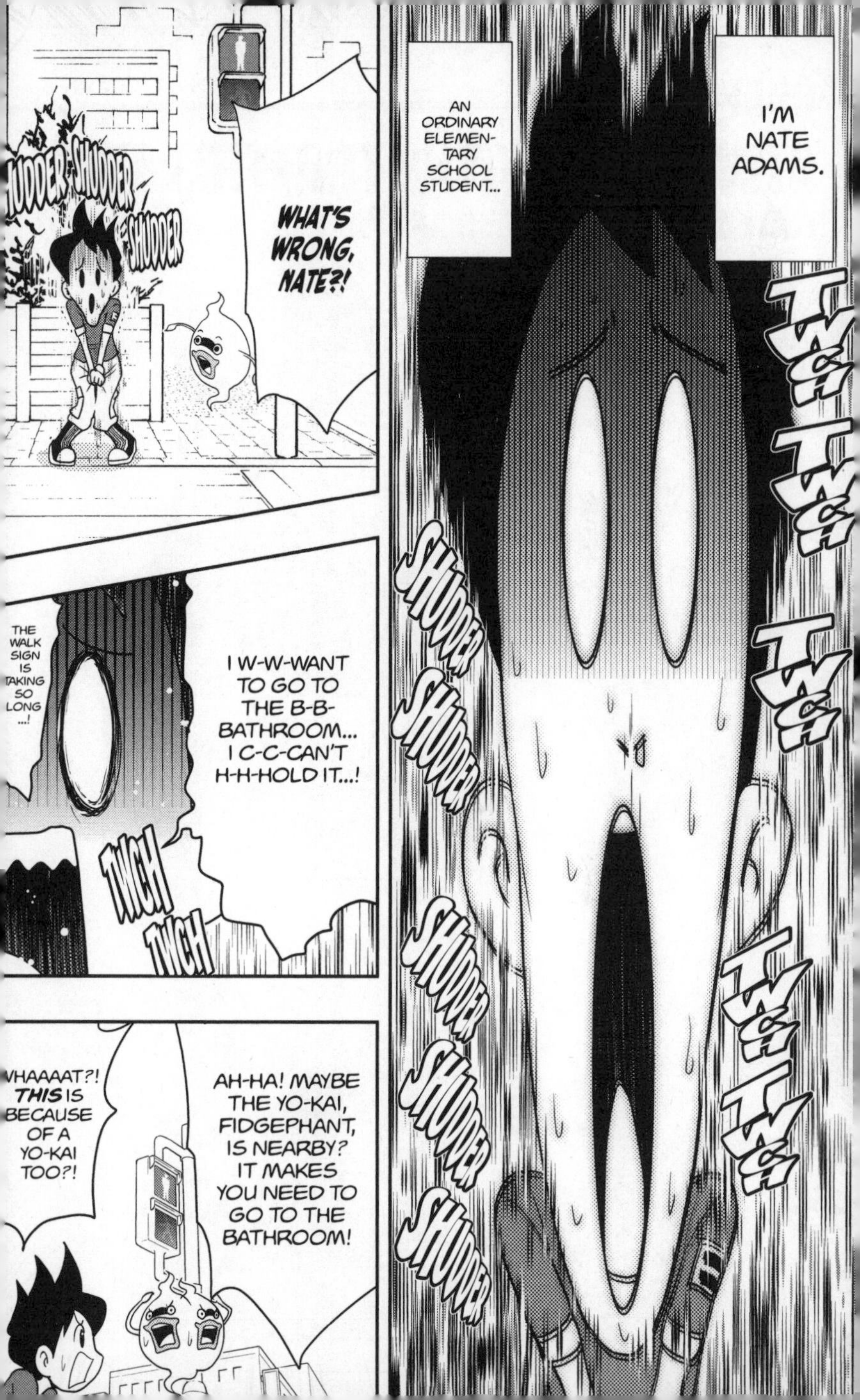
I'M NATE ADAMS.
AN ORDINARY ELEMENTARY SCHOOL STUDENT...
TWCH TWCH TWCH TWCH TWCH
SHUDDER SHUDDER SHUDDER SHUDDER SHUDDER
WHAT'S WRONG, NATE?!
SHUDDER SHUDDER SHUDDER
I W-W-WANT TO GO TO THE B-B-BATHROOM... I C-C-CAN'T H-H-HOLD IT...!
THE WALK SIGN IS TAKING SO LONG...!
TWCH TWCH
AH-HA! MAYBE THE YO-KAI, FIDGEPHANT, IS NEARBY? IT MAKES YOU NEED TO GO TO THE BATHROOM!
WHAAAAT?! THIS IS BECAUSE OF A YO-KAI TOO?!

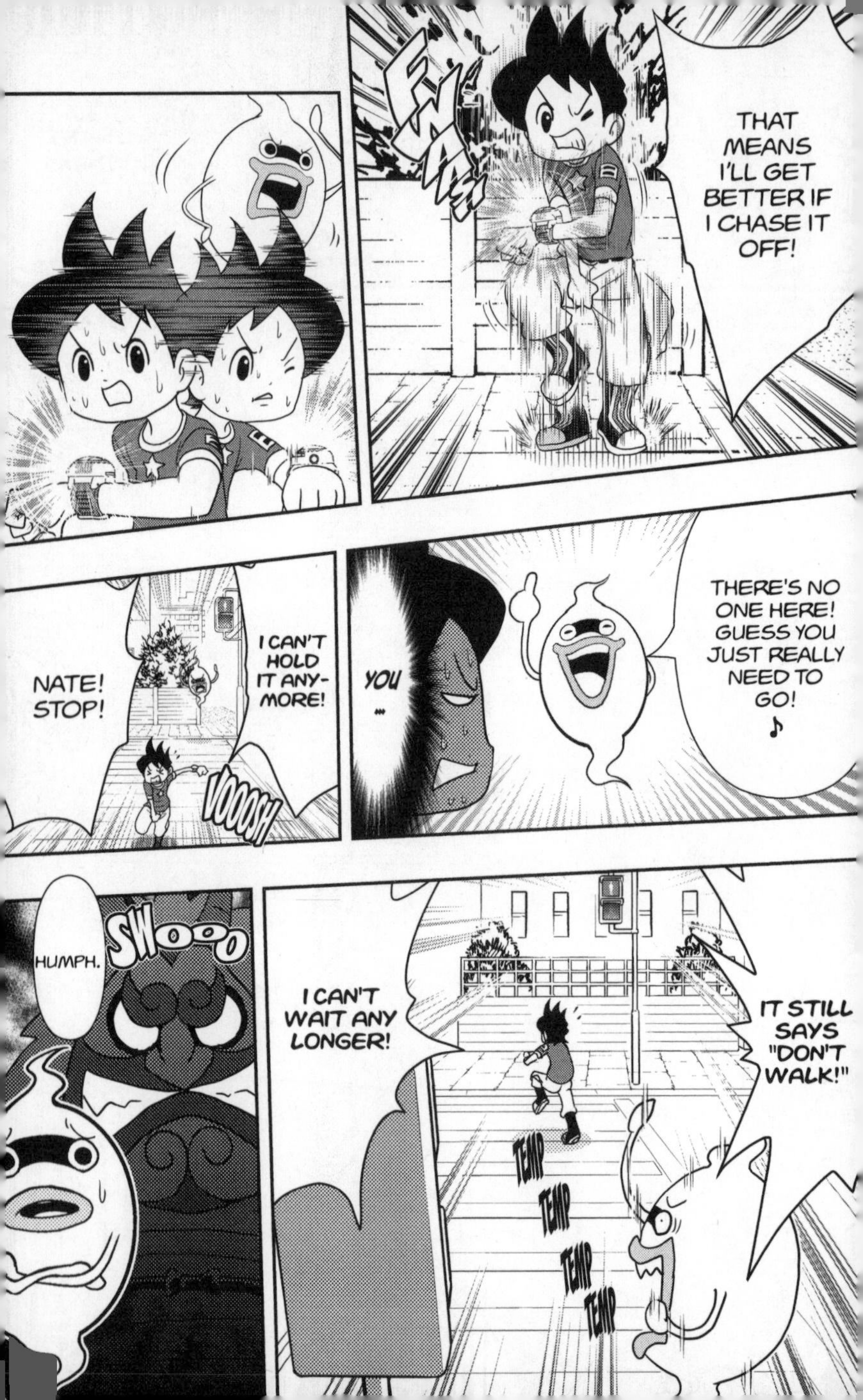
THAT MEANS I'LL GET BETTER IF I CHASE IT OFF!
THERE'S NO ONE HERE! GUESS YOU JUST REALLY NEED TO GO! ♪
YOU ...
I CAN'T HOLD IT ANY-MORE!
NATE! STOP!
VOOOSH
IT STILL SAYS "DON'T WALK!"
TEMP
TEMP
TEMP
TEMP
I CAN'T WAIT ANY LONGER!
SWOOO
HUMPH.

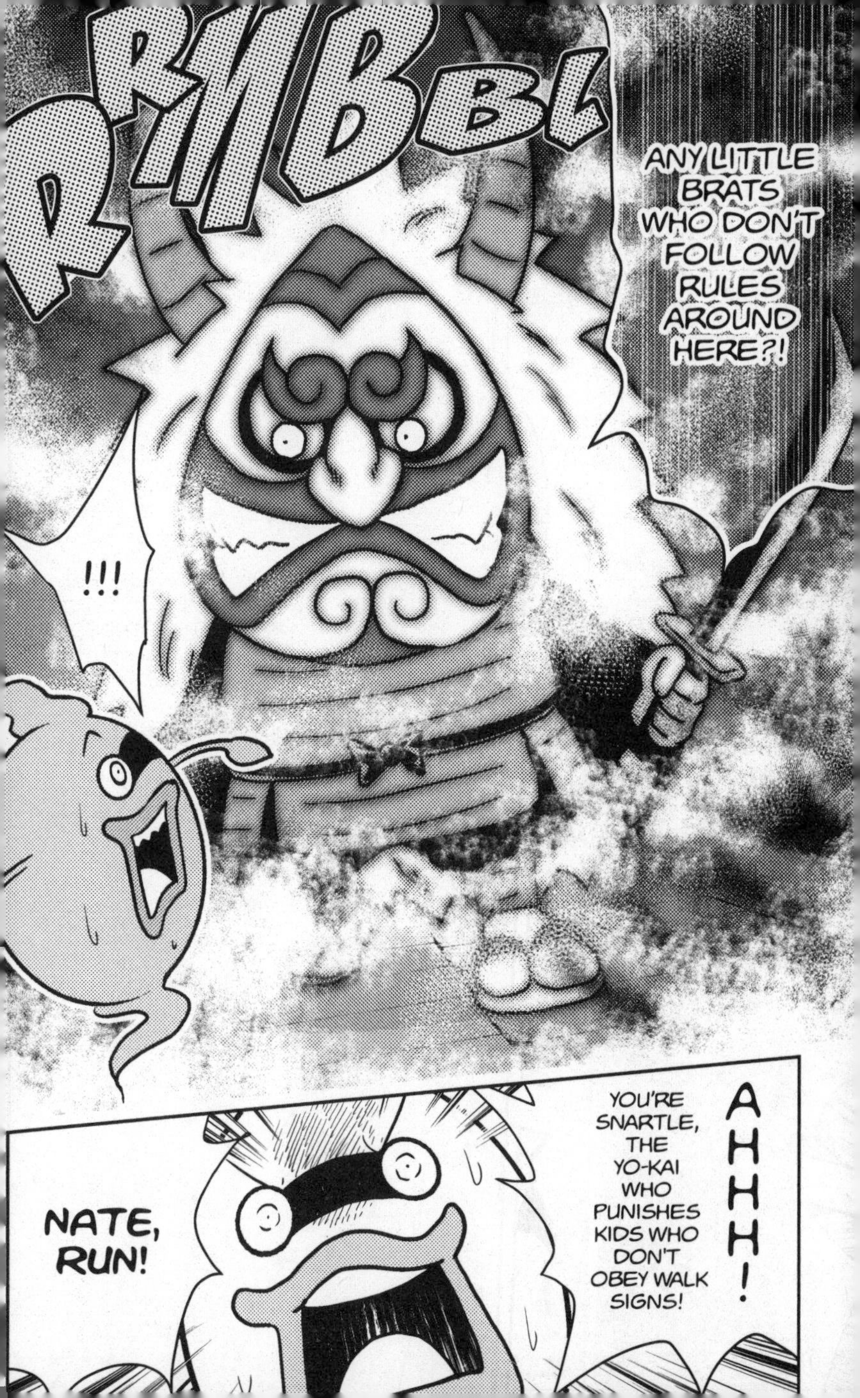
RMBBL
ANY LITTLE BRATS WHO DON'T FOLLOW RULES AROUND HERE?!
!!!
AHHH!
YOU'RE SNARTLE, THE YO-KAI WHO PUNISHES KIDS WHO DON'T OBEY WALK SIGNS!
NATE, RUN!

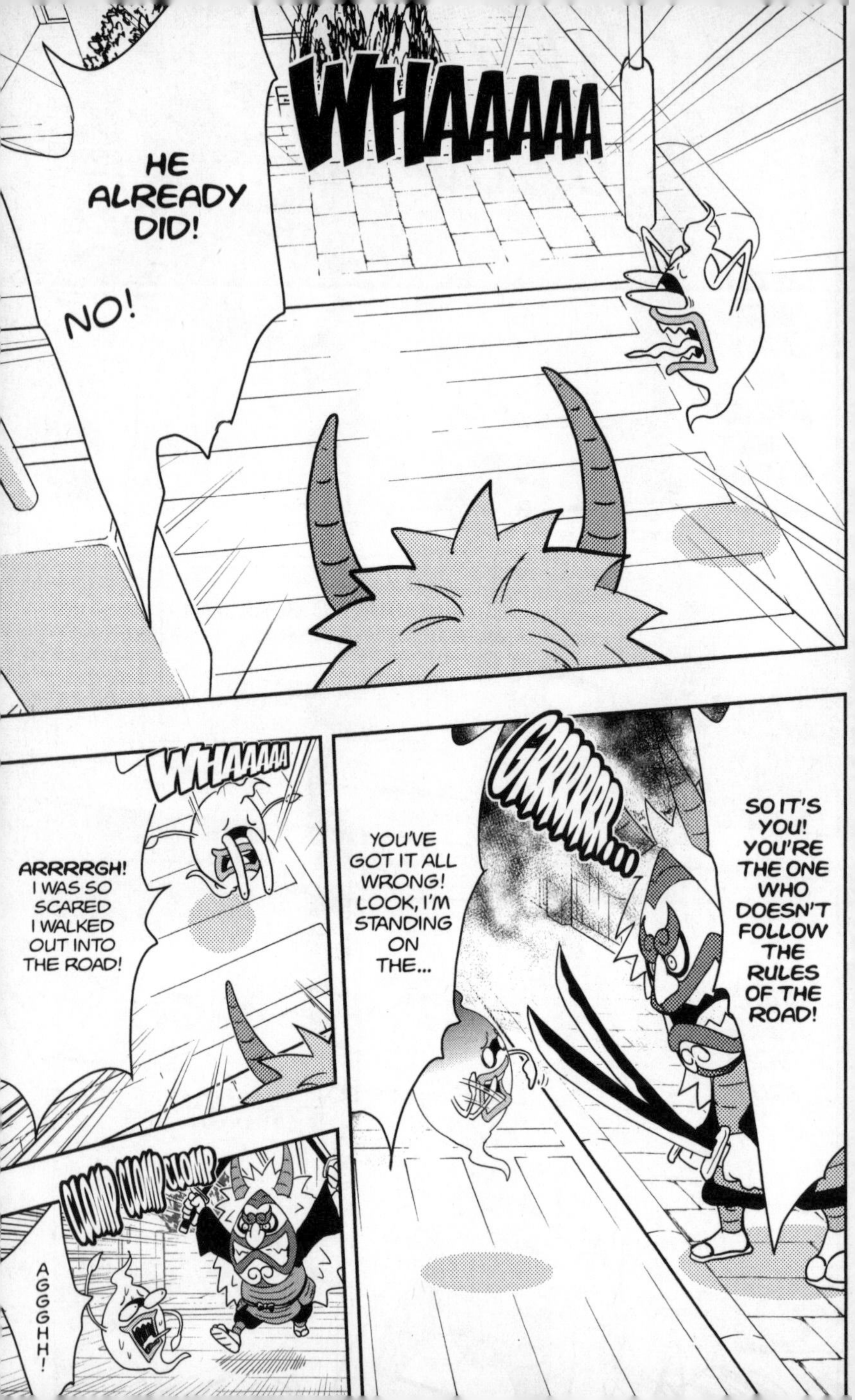
WHAAAAA
HE ALREADY DID!
NO!
GRRRRRR...
SO IT'S YOU! YOU'RE THE ONE WHO DOESN'T FOLLOW THE RULES OF THE ROAD!
YOU'VE GOT IT ALL WRONG! LOOK, I'M STANDING ON THE...
WHAAAAA
ARRRRGH! I WAS SO SCARED I WALKED OUT INTO THE ROAD!
CLOMP CLOMP CLOMP
AGGGHH!

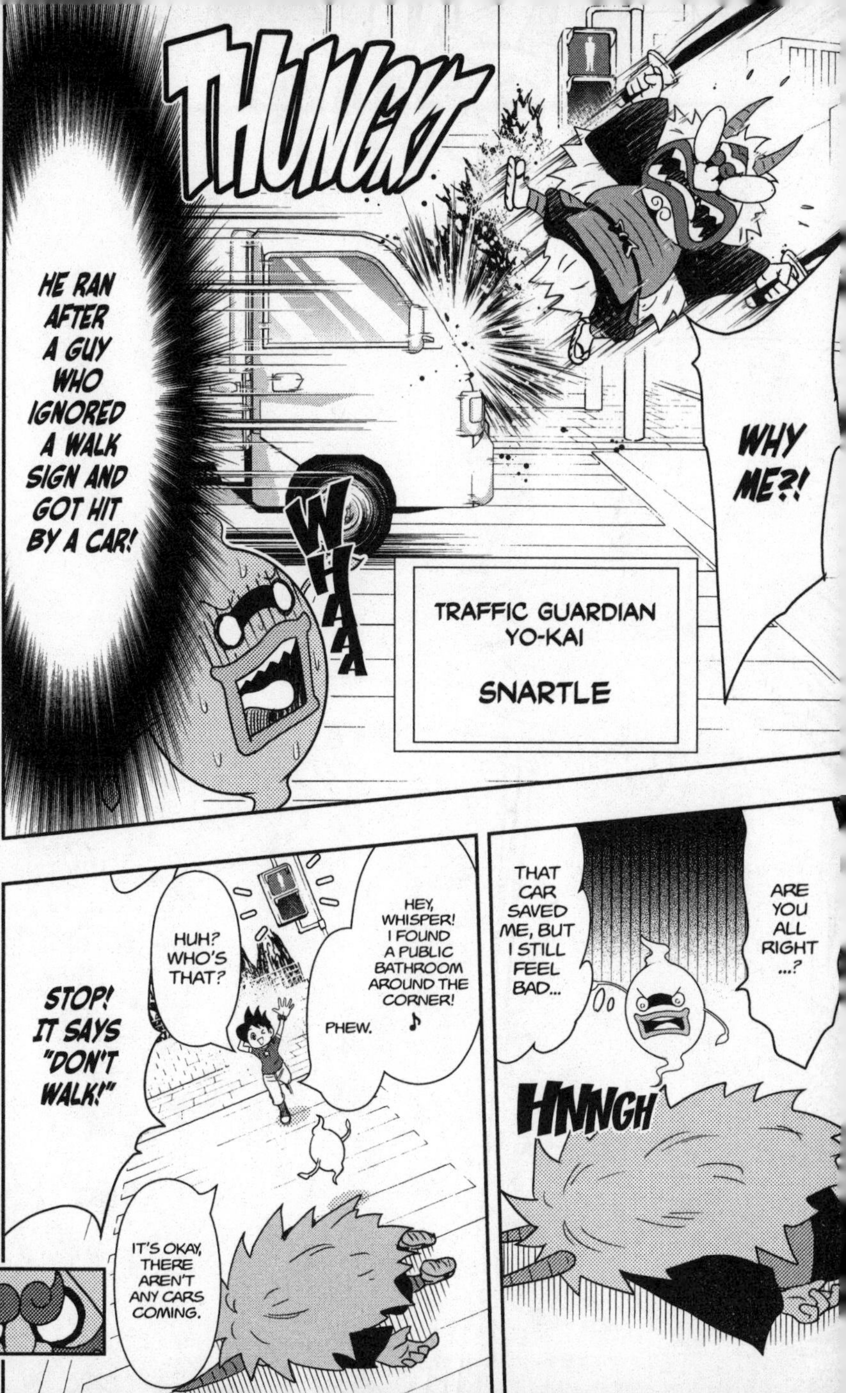
THUNCK
WHY ME?!
HE RAN AFTER A GUY WHO IGNORED A WALK SIGN AND GOT HIT BY A CAR!
TRAFFIC GUARDIAN YO-KAI
SNARTLE
WHAAAA
ARE YOU ALL RIGHT ...?
THAT CAR SAVED ME, BUT I STILL FEEL BAD...
HNNGH
HEY, WHISPER! I FOUND A PUBLIC BATHROOM AROUND THE CORNER! ♪
PHEW.
HUH? WHO'S THAT?
STOP! IT SAYS "DON'T WALK!"
IT'S OKAY, THERE AREN'T ANY CARS COMING.

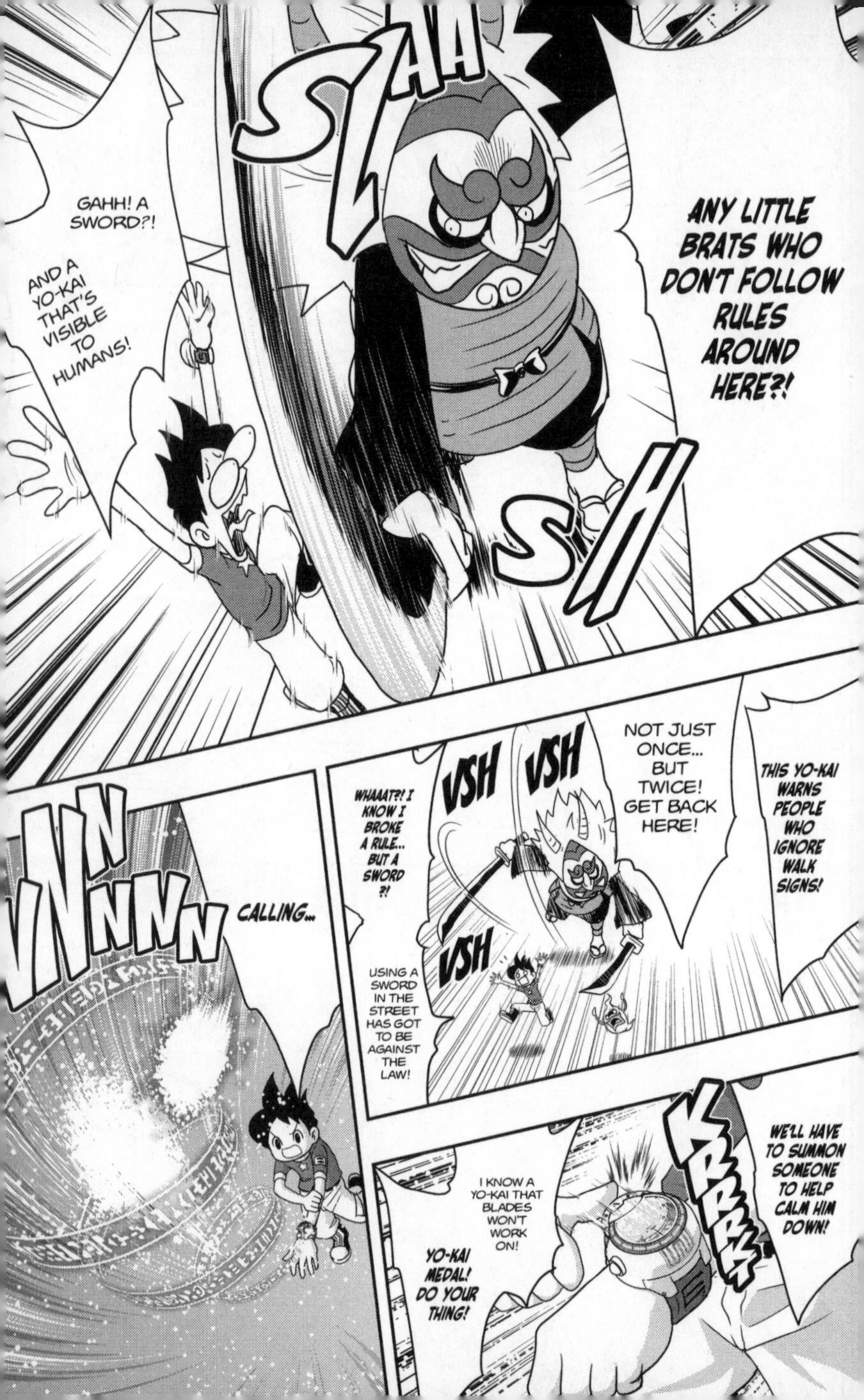
SLAA
ANY LITTLE BRATS WHO DON'T FOLLOW RULES AROUND HERE?!
SH
GAHH! A SWORD?!
AND A YO-KAI THAT'S VISIBLE TO HUMANS!
THIS YO-KAI WARNS PEOPLE WHO IGNORE WALK SIGNS!
NOT JUST ONCE... BUT TWICE! GET BACK HERE!
VSH VSH
WHAAAT?! I KNOW I BROKE A RULE... BUT A SWORD ?!
VSH
USING A SWORD IN THE STREET HAS GOT TO BE AGAINST THE LAW!
WE'LL HAVE TO SUMMON SOMEONE TO HELP CALM HIM DOWN!
KRRRK
I KNOW A YO-KAI THAT BLADES WON'T WORK ON!
YO-KAI MEDAL! DO YOUR THING!
VNNNNNN
CALLING...

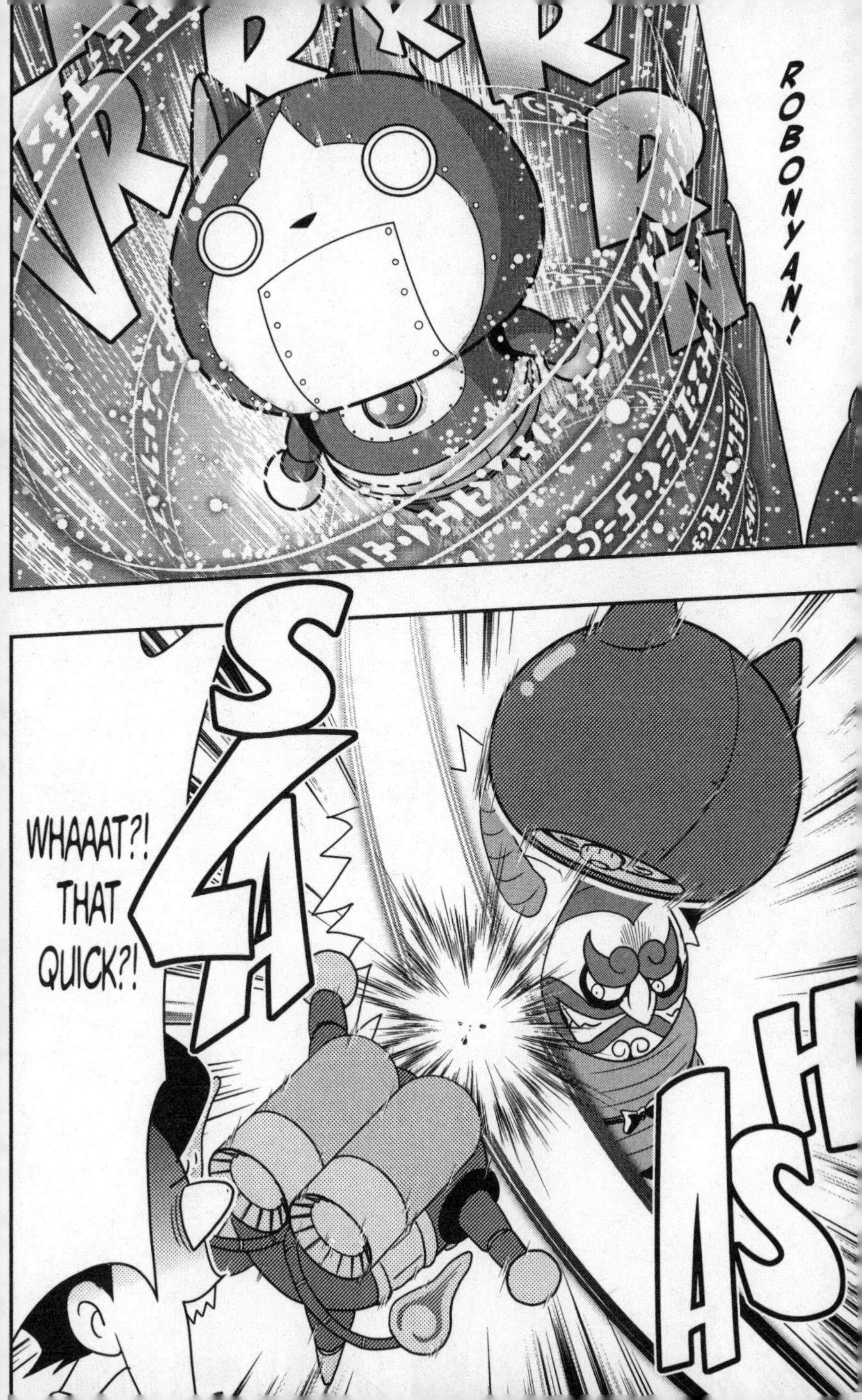
ROBONYAN!
WHAAAT?! THAT QUICK?!

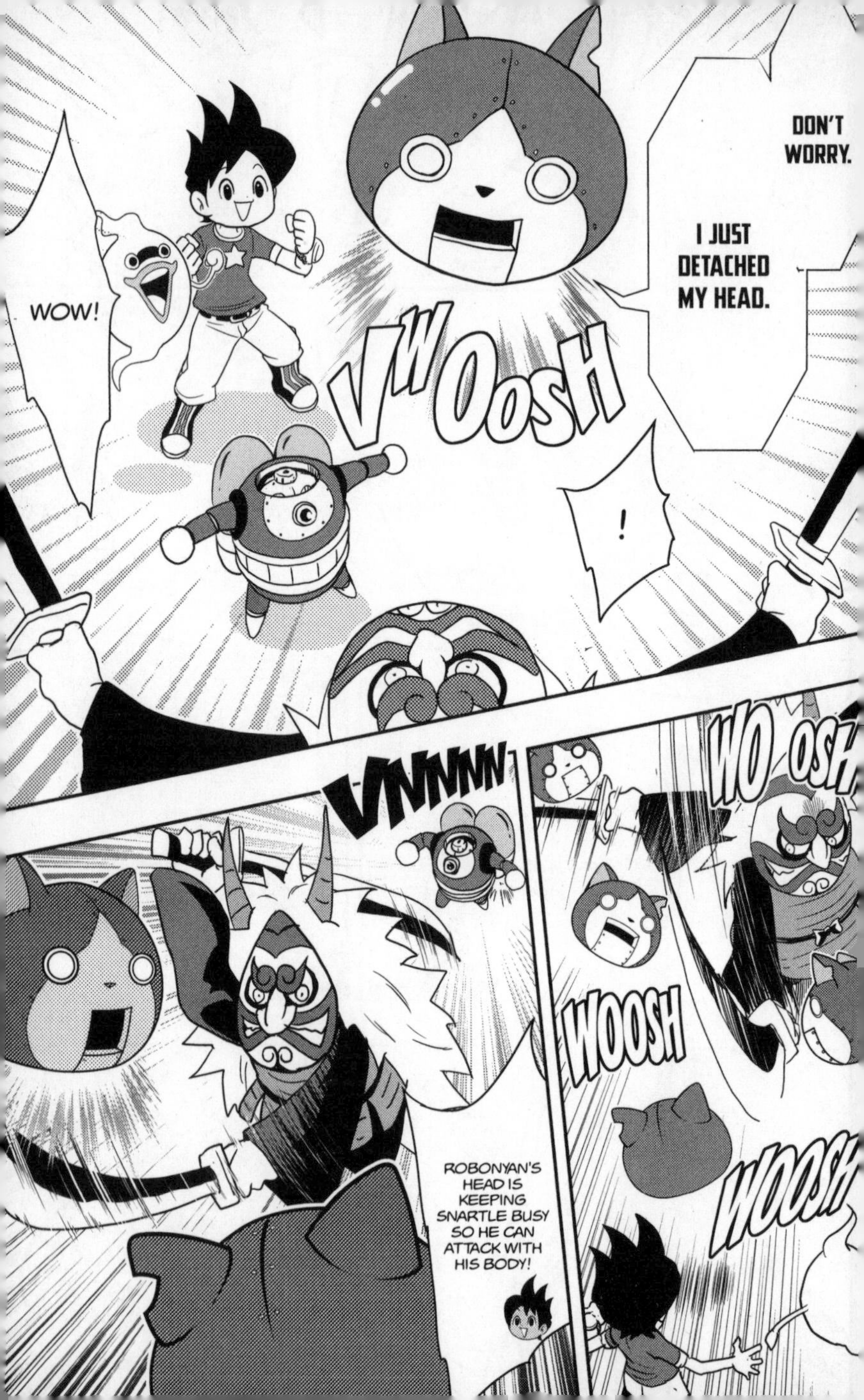
DON'T WORRY.
I JUST DETACHED MY HEAD.
VWOOSH
WOW!
!
WOOSH
WOOSH
WOOSH
VNNNN
ROBONYAN'S HEAD IS KEEPING SNARTLE BUSY SO HE CAN ATTACK WITH HIS BODY!

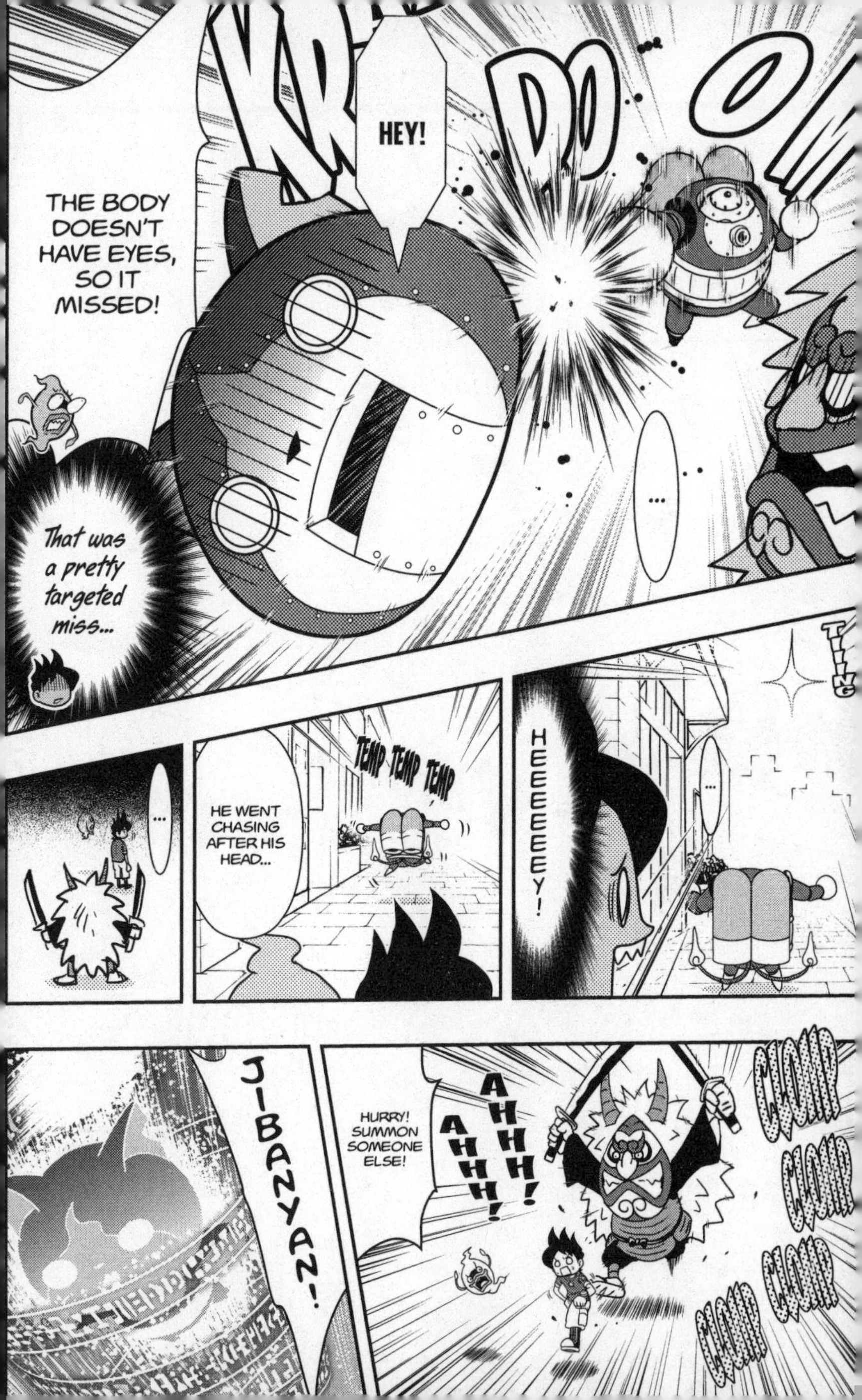
DO
HEY!
...
THE BODY DOESN'T HAVE EYES, SO IT MISSED!
That was a pretty targeted miss...
TIIING
HEEEEEEEY!
...
TEMP TEMP TEMP
HE WENT CHASING AFTER HIS HEAD...
...
CLOMP CLOMP CLOMP CLOMP CLOMP
AHHHH!
AHHHH!
HURRY! SUMMON SOMEONE ELSE!
JIBANYAN!

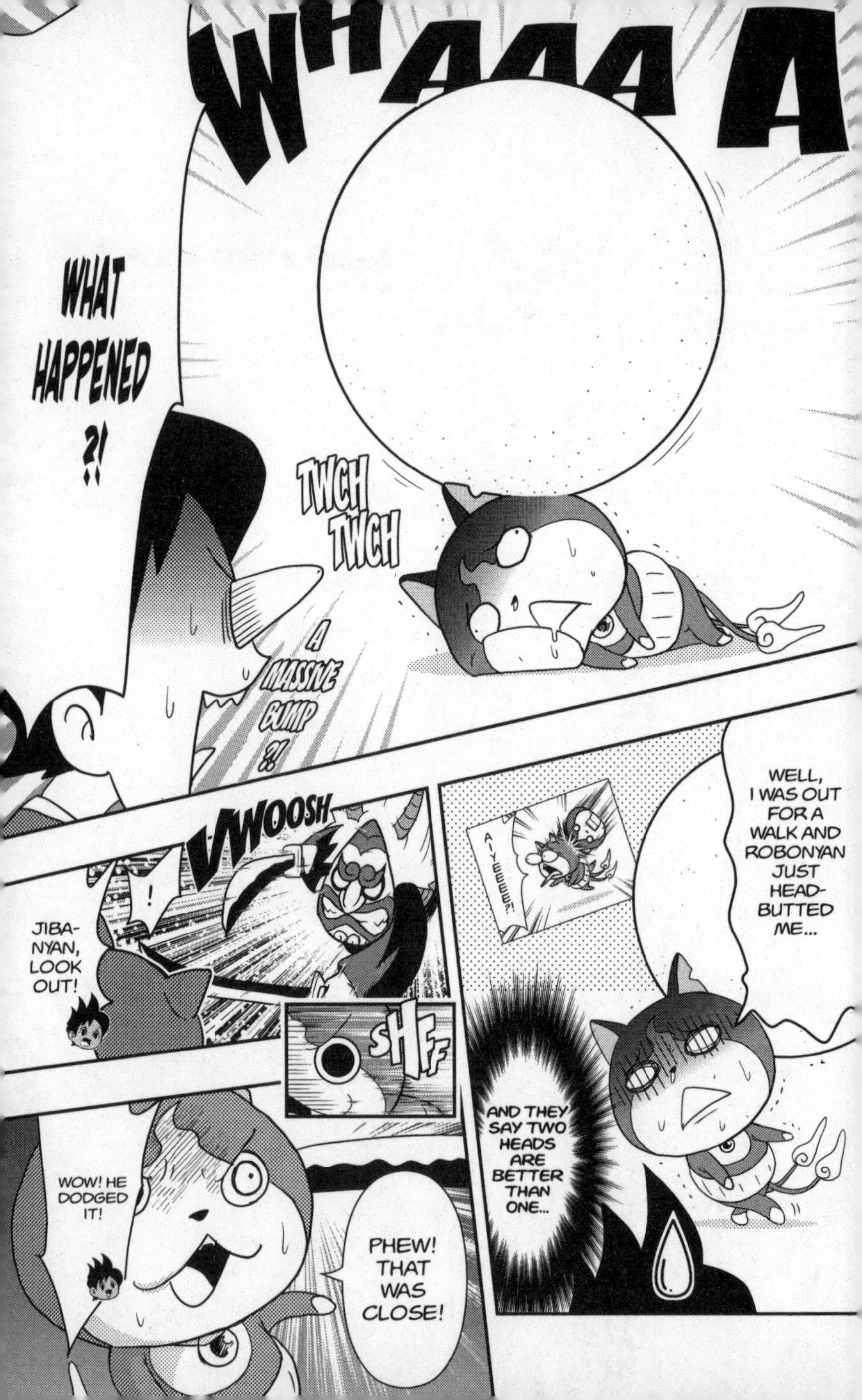
WHAAAA A
WHAT HAPPENED?!
TWCH TWCH
A MASSIVE BUMP?!
WELL, I WAS OUT FOR A WALK AND ROBONYAN JUST HEAD-BUTTED ME...
AIYEEEE?!
AND THEY SAY TWO HEADS ARE BETTER THAN ONE...
VWOOSH
!
JIBA-NYAN, LOOK OUT!
SHFF
PHEW! THAT WAS CLOSE!
WOW! HE DODGED IT!

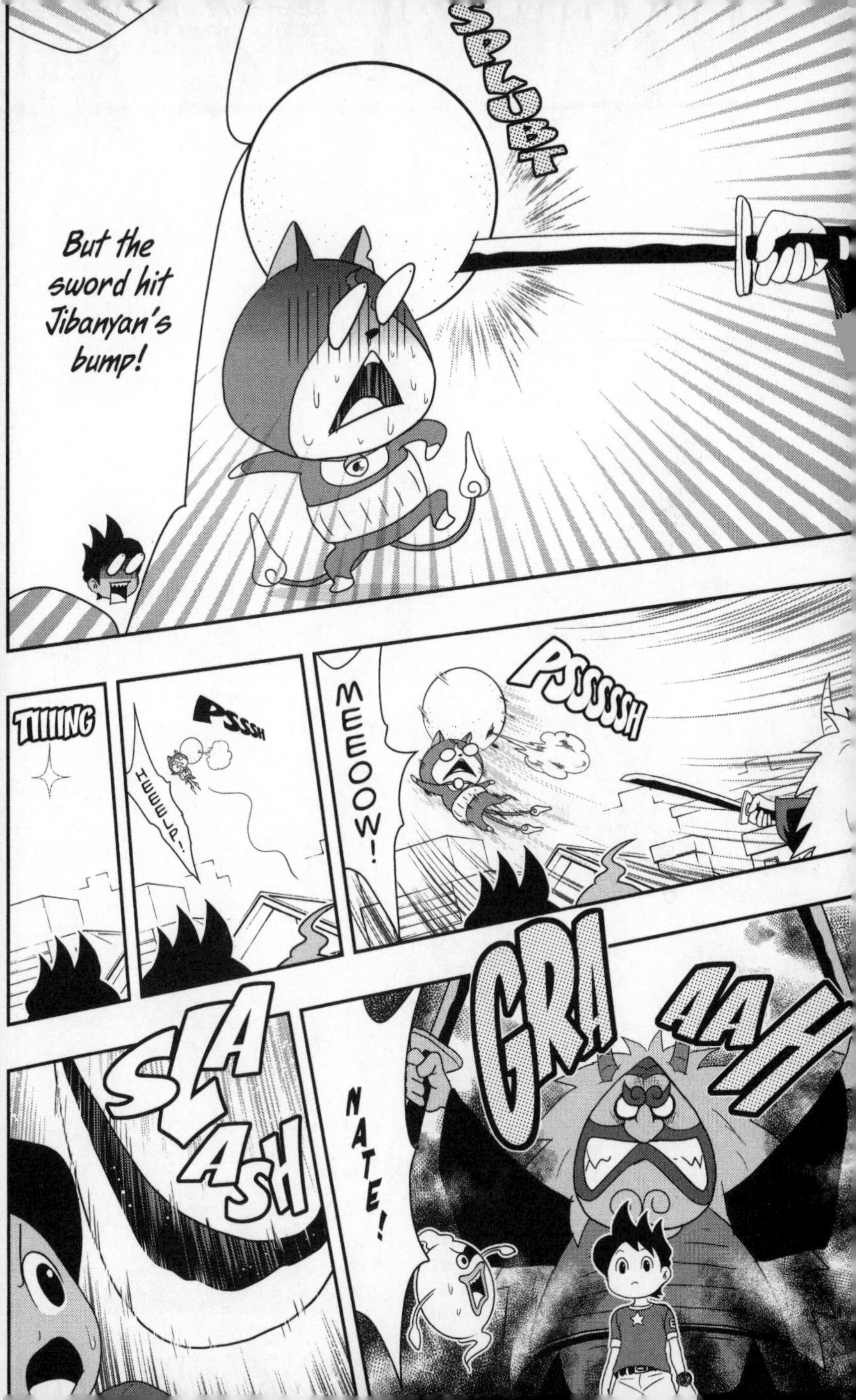
SPLUBK
But the sword hit Jibanyan's bump!
PSSSSSH
MEEOOOW!
PSSSH
HEEELP!
TIIIING
GRAAAH
NATE!
SLASH

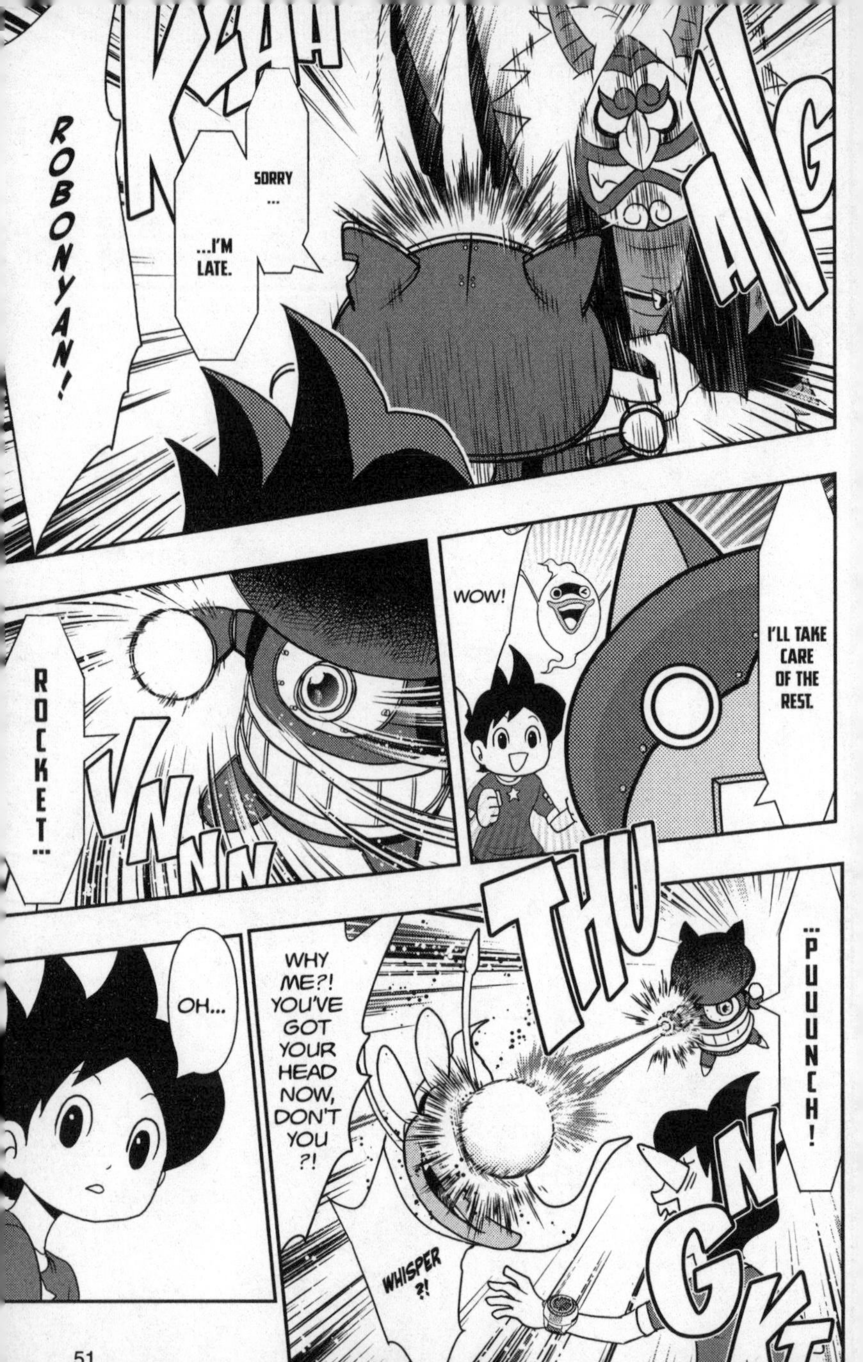
SORRY ...
...I'M LATE.
ROBONYAN!
I'LL TAKE CARE OF THE REST.
WOW!
ROCKET...
VNNNN
...PUUUNCH!
THU
WHY ME?! YOU'VE GOT YOUR HEAD NOW, DON'T YOU?!
WHISPER?!
GNKT
OH...

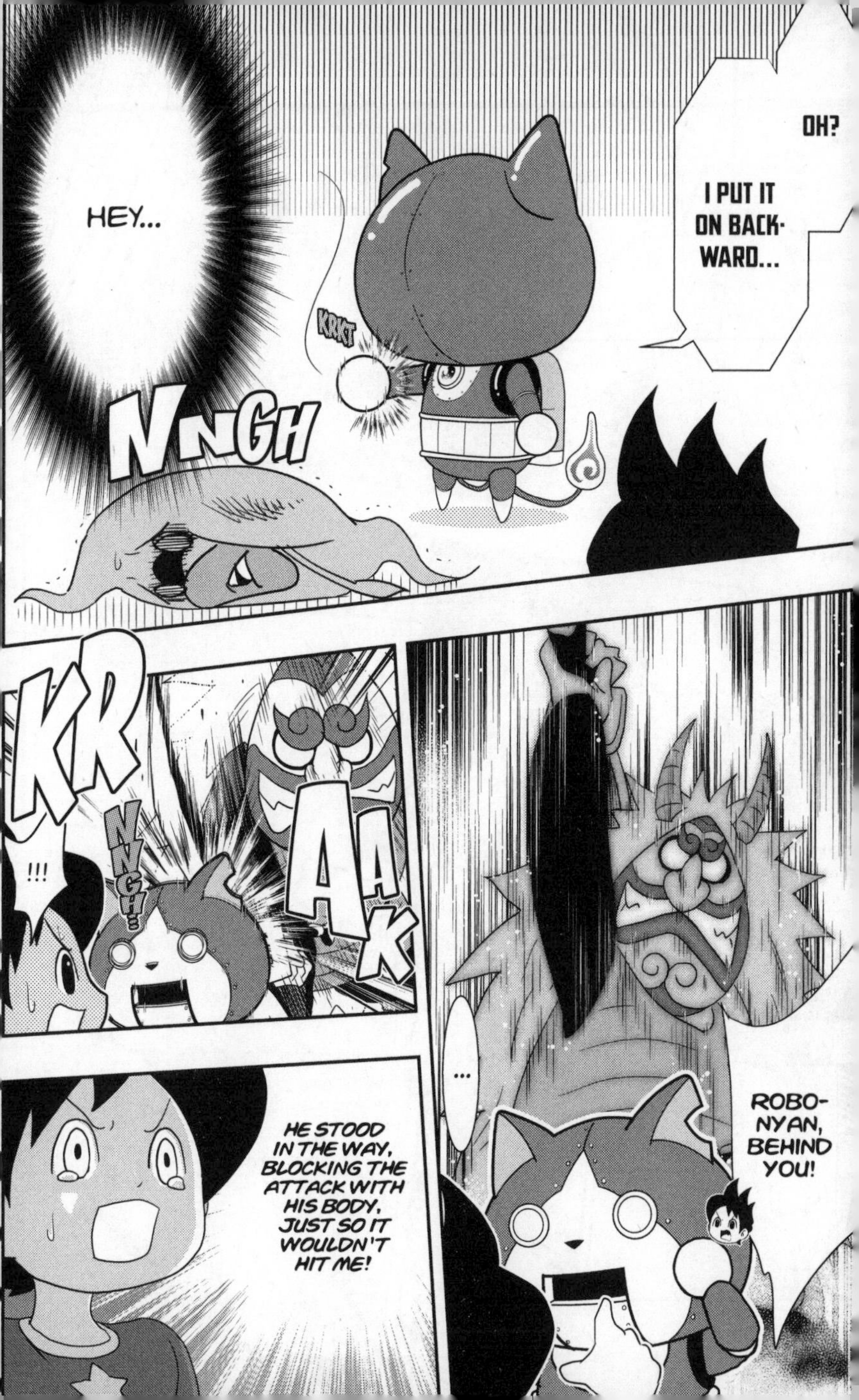
OH?
I PUT IT ON BACKWARD...
KRKT
HEY...
NNGH
...
ROBO-NYAN, BEHIND YOU!
KRAAK
NNGH!!
!!!
HE STOOD IN THE WAY, BLOCKING THE ATTACK WITH HIS BODY, JUST SO IT WOULDN'T HIT ME!

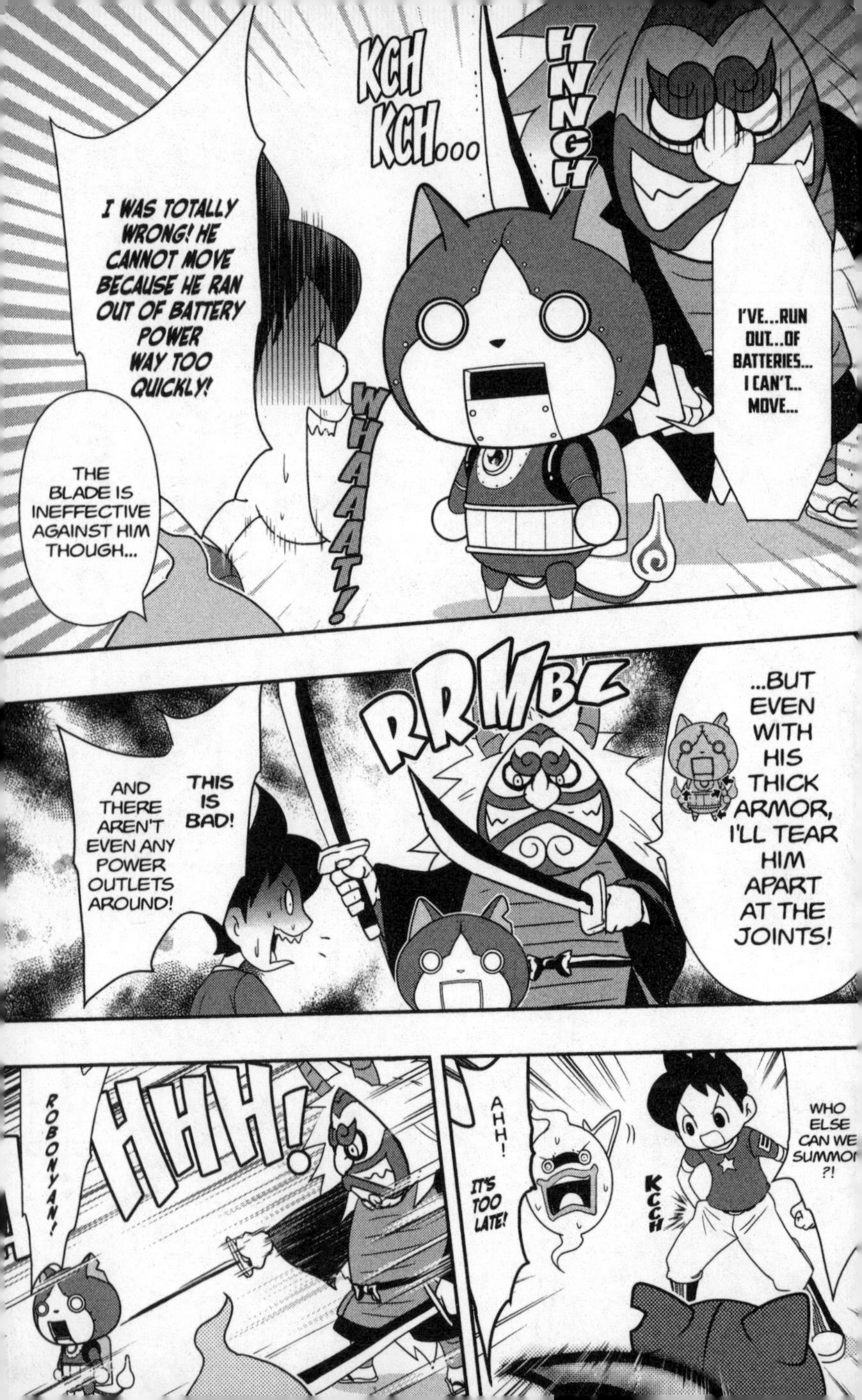
HNNNGH
KCH KCH...
I'VE...RUN OUT...OF BATTERIES... I CAN'T... MOVE...
I WAS TOTALLY WRONG! HE CANNOT MOVE BECAUSE HE RAN OUT OF BATTERY POWER WAY TOO QUICKLY!
WHAAAAT!
THE BLADE IS INEFFECTIVE AGAINST HIM THOUGH...
...BUT EVEN WITH HIS THICK ARMOR, I'LL TEAR HIM APART AT THE JOINTS!
RRMBL
THIS IS BAD!
AND THERE AREN'T EVEN ANY POWER OUTLETS AROUND!
WHO ELSE CAN WE SUMMO ?!
KCCH
AHH!
IT'S TOO LATE!
HHH!
ROBONYAN!

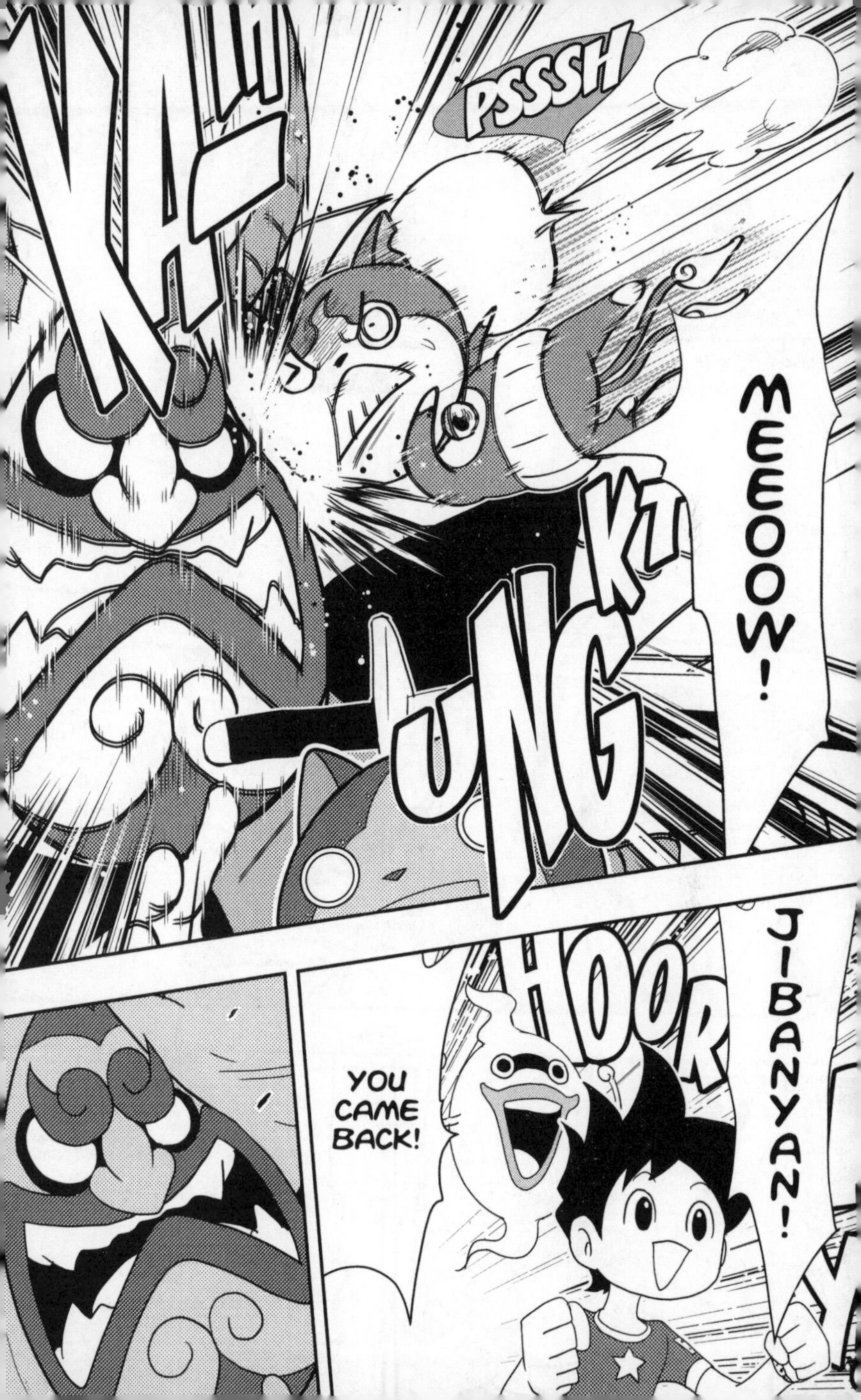
PSSSH
MEEOOW!
KTUNG
YAH-
JIBANYAN!
HOOR
YOU CAME BACK!

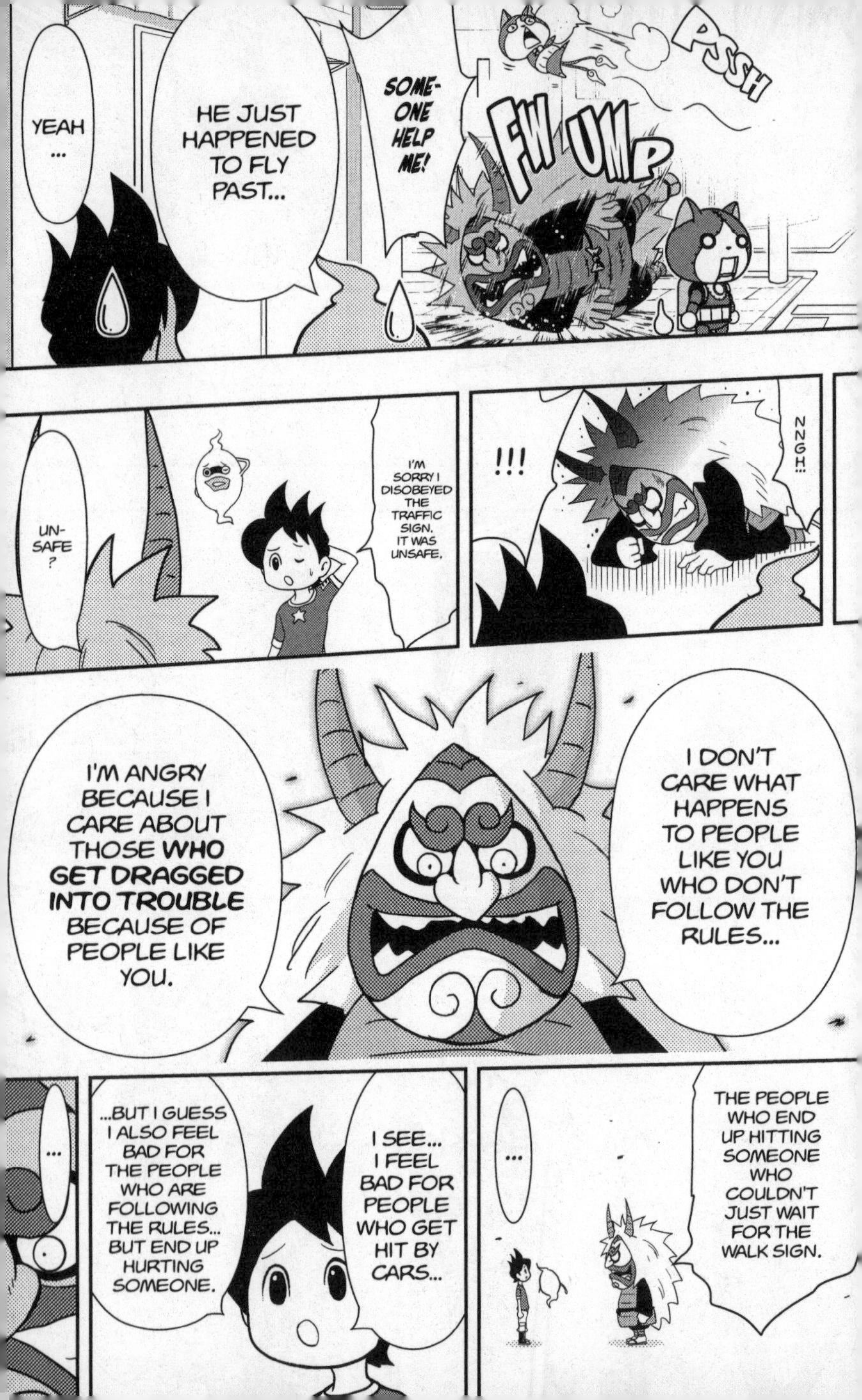
PSSH
FWUMP
SOMEONE HELP ME!
HE JUST HAPPENED TO FLY PAST...
YEAH...
NNGH...
!!!
I'M SORRY I DISOBEYED THE TRAFFIC SIGN. IT WAS UNSAFE.
UNSAFE?
I DON'T CARE WHAT HAPPENS TO PEOPLE LIKE YOU WHO DON'T FOLLOW THE RULES...
I'M ANGRY BECAUSE I CARE ABOUT THOSE **WHO GET DRAGGED INTO TROUBLE** BECAUSE OF PEOPLE LIKE YOU.
THE PEOPLE WHO END UP HITTING SOMEONE WHO COULDN'T JUST WAIT FOR THE WALK SIGN.
...
I SEE... I FEEL BAD FOR PEOPLE WHO GET HIT BY CARS...
...BUT I GUESS I ALSO FEEL BAD FOR THE PEOPLE WHO ARE FOLLOWING THE RULES... BUT END UP HURTING SOMEONE.
...

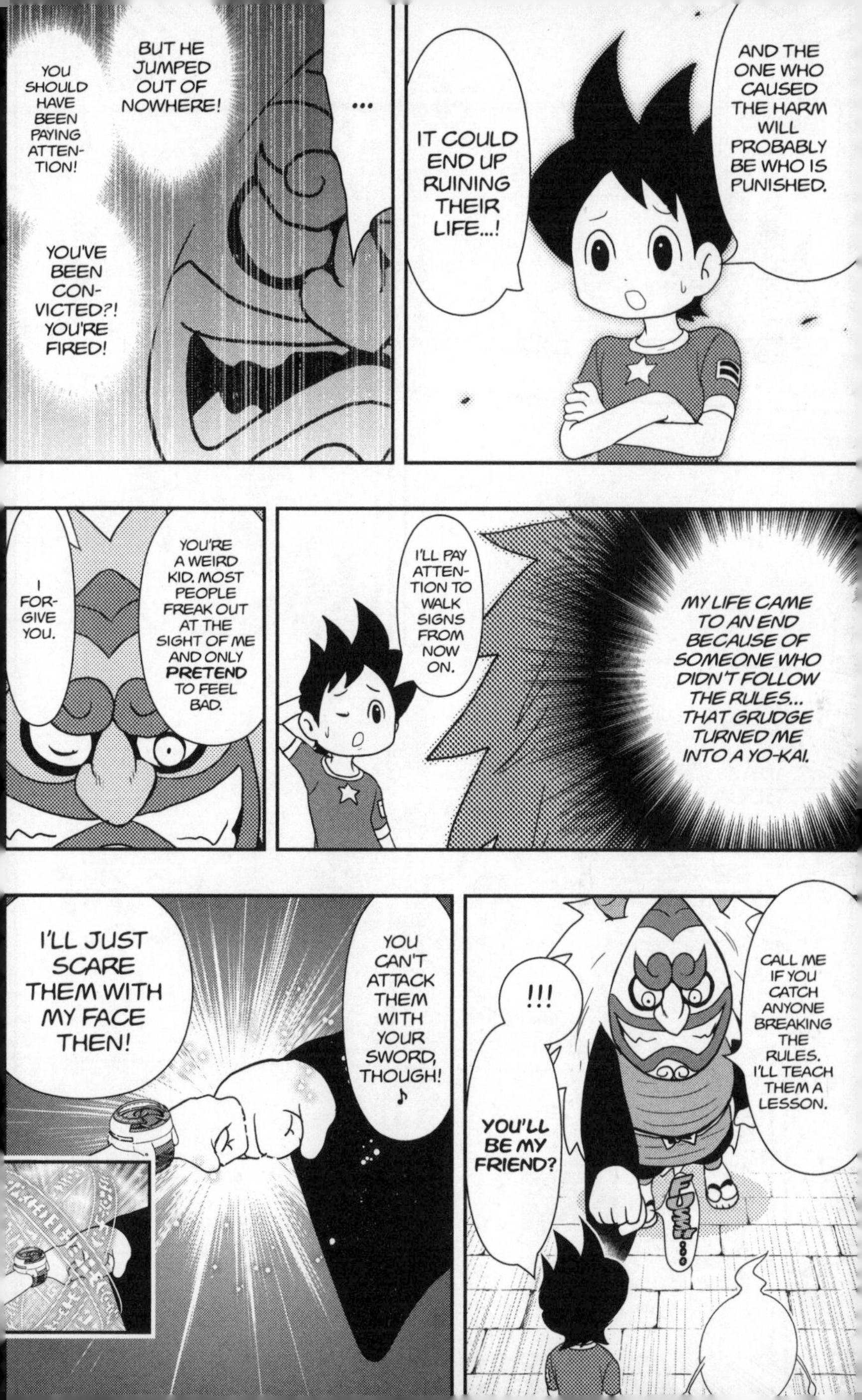
AND THE ONE WHO CAUSED THE HARM WILL PROBABLY BE WHO IS PUNISHED.
IT COULD END UP RUINING THEIR LIFE...!
...
BUT HE JUMPED OUT OF NOWHERE!
YOU SHOULD HAVE BEEN PAYING ATTENTION!
YOU'VE BEEN CONVICTED?! YOU'RE FIRED!
MY LIFE CAME TO AN END BECAUSE OF SOMEONE WHO DIDN'T FOLLOW THE RULES... THAT GRUDGE TURNED ME INTO A YO-KAI.
I'LL PAY ATTENTION TO WALK SIGNS FROM NOW ON.
YOU'RE A WEIRD KID. MOST PEOPLE FREAK OUT AT THE SIGHT OF ME AND ONLY **PRETEND** TO FEEL BAD.
I FORGIVE YOU.
CALL ME IF YOU CATCH ANYONE BREAKING THE RULES. I'LL TEACH THEM A LESSON.
!!!
YOU'LL BE MY FRIEND?
YOU CAN'T ATTACK THEM WITH YOUR SWORD, THOUGH! ♪
I'LL JUST SCARE THEM WITH MY FACE THEN!

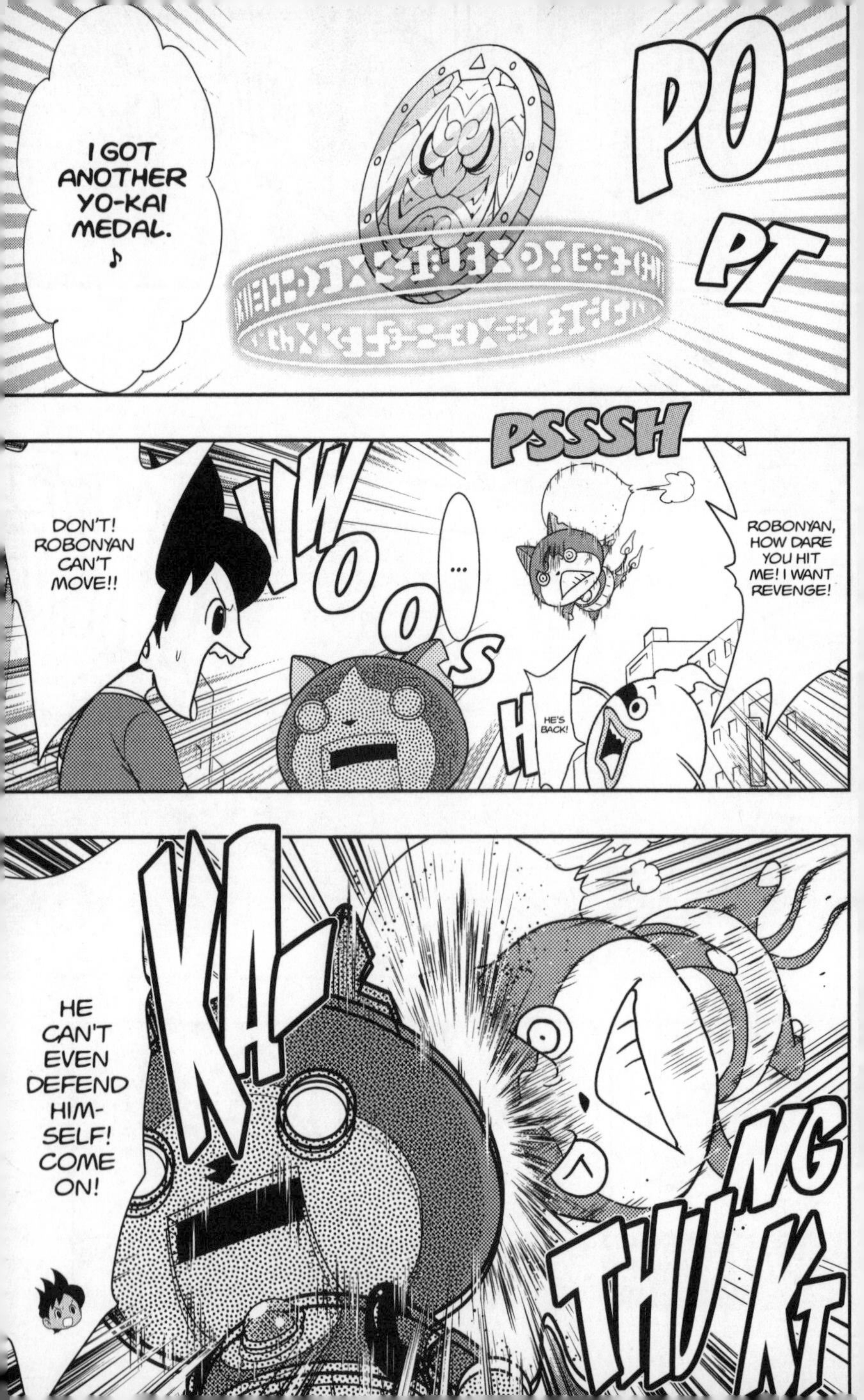
POPT
I GOT ANOTHER YO-KAI MEDAL. ♪
PSSSH
ROBONYAN, HOW DARE YOU HIT ME! I WANT REVENGE!
...
WHOOOSH
HE'S BACK!
DON'T! ROBONYAN CAN'T MOVE!!
NG
THUKT
KA-
HE CAN'T EVEN DEFEND HIM-SELF! COME ON!

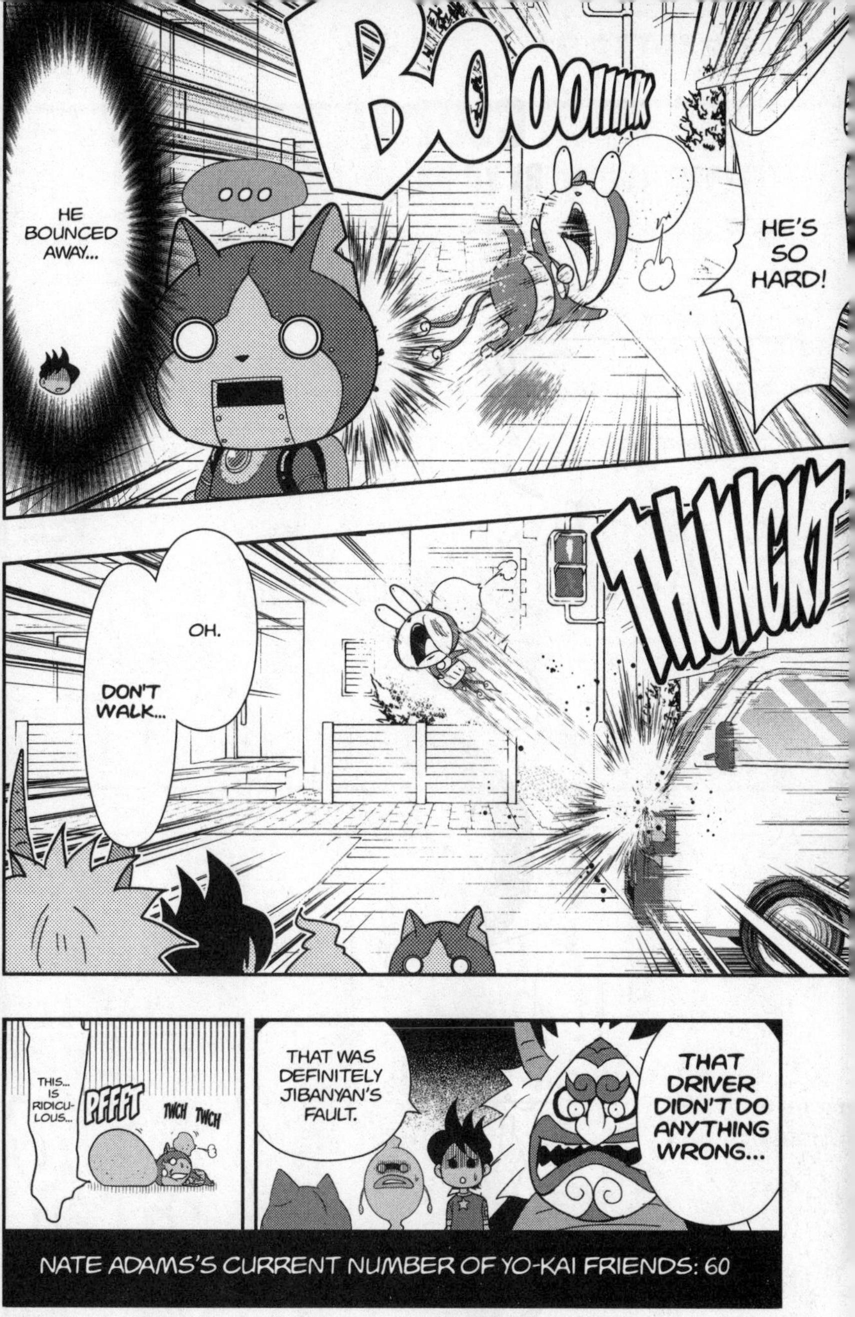

HE'S SO HARD!
BOOOIIIINK
...
HE BOUNCED AWAY...
THUNCK!
OH.
DON'T WALK...
THAT DRIVER DIDN'T DO ANYTHING WRONG...
THAT WAS DEFINITELY JIBANYAN'S FAULT.
THIS... IS RIDICULOUS...
PFFFT
TWCH TWCH
NATE ADAMS'S CURRENT NUMBER OF YO-KAI FRIENDS: 60

CHAPTER 91
THE HAIR CLUB FOR YO-KAI!
FEATURING FURRY YO-KAI FURGUS

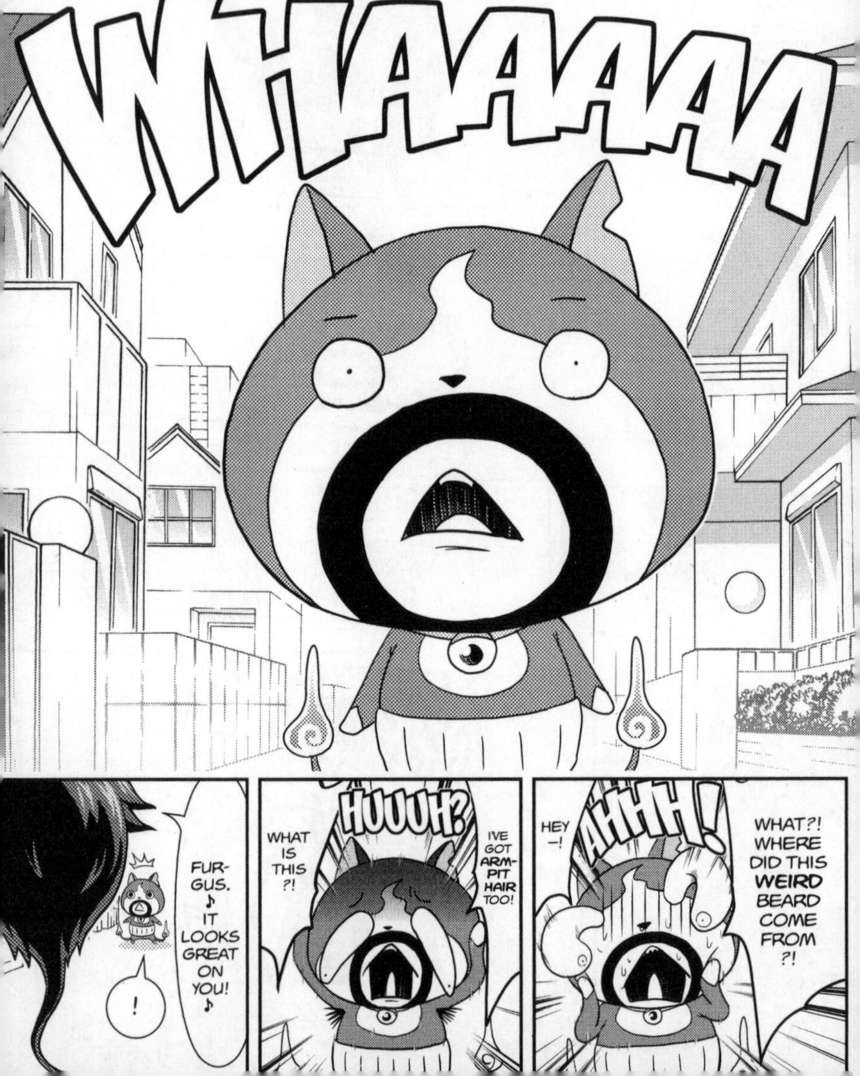
WHAAAAA
WHAT?! WHERE DID THIS WEIRD BEARD COME FROM?!
AHHH!
HEY—!
I'VE GOT ARMPIT HAIR TOO!
HUUUH?
WHAT IS THIS?!
FURGUS. ♪ IT LOOKS GREAT ON YOU! ♪
!

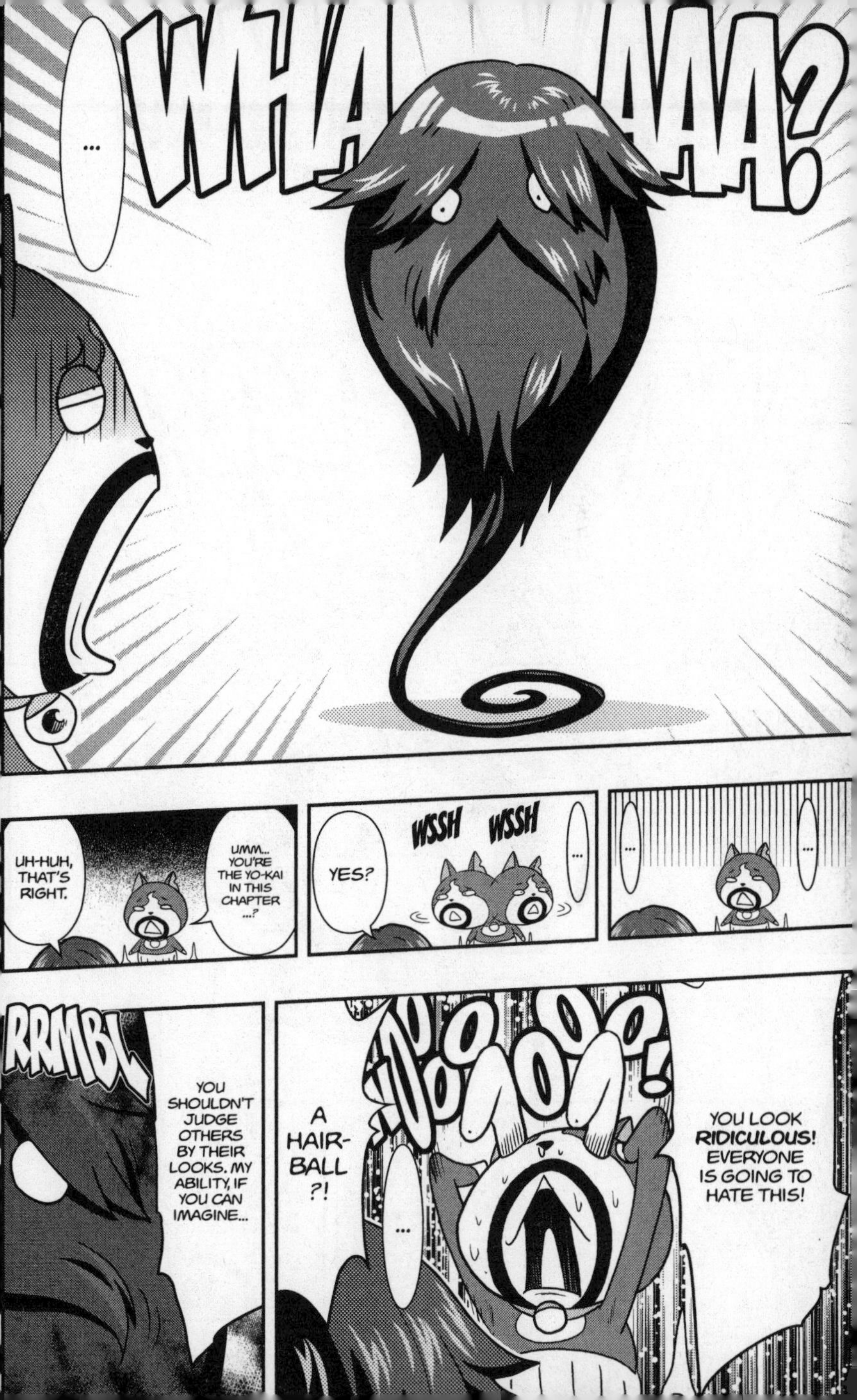
WHA AAA?
...
...
...
...
WSSH WSSH
YES?
UMM... YOU'RE THE YO-KAI IN THIS CHAPTER ...?
UH-HUH, THAT'S RIGHT.
YOU LOOK **RIDICULOUS!** EVERYONE IS GOING TO HATE THIS!
A HAIR-BALL ?!
...
RRMBL
YOU SHOULDN'T JUDGE OTHERS BY THEIR LOOKS. MY ABILITY, IF YOU CAN IMAGINE...

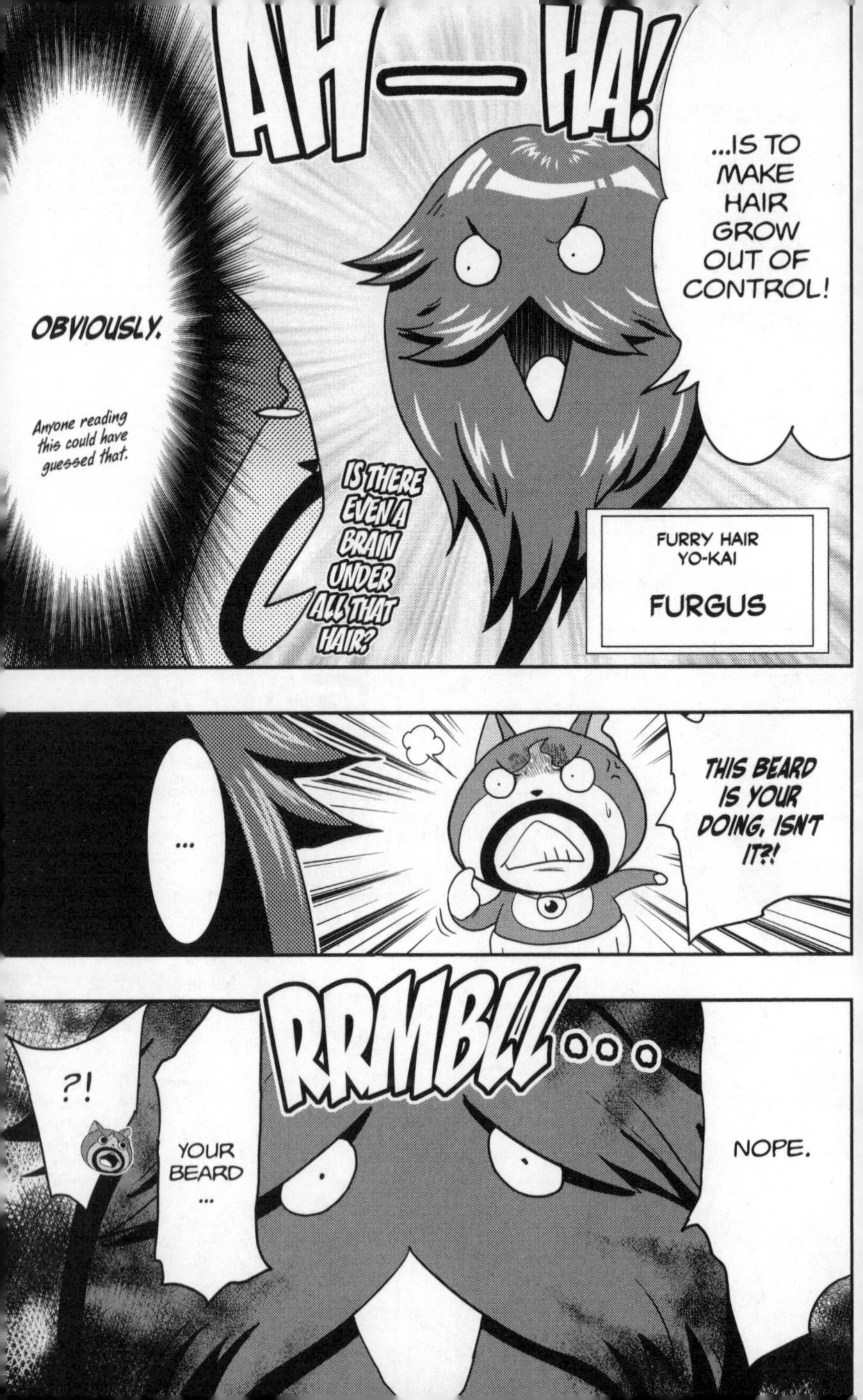
...IS TO MAKE HAIR GROW OUT OF CONTROL!
AH—HA!
FURRY HAIR YO-KAI
FURGUS
IS THERE EVEN A BRAIN UNDER ALL THAT HAIR?
OBVIOUSLY.
Anyone reading this could have guessed that.
THIS BEARD IS YOUR DOING, ISN'T IT?!
...
NOPE.
RRMBLL...
YOUR BEARD ...
?!

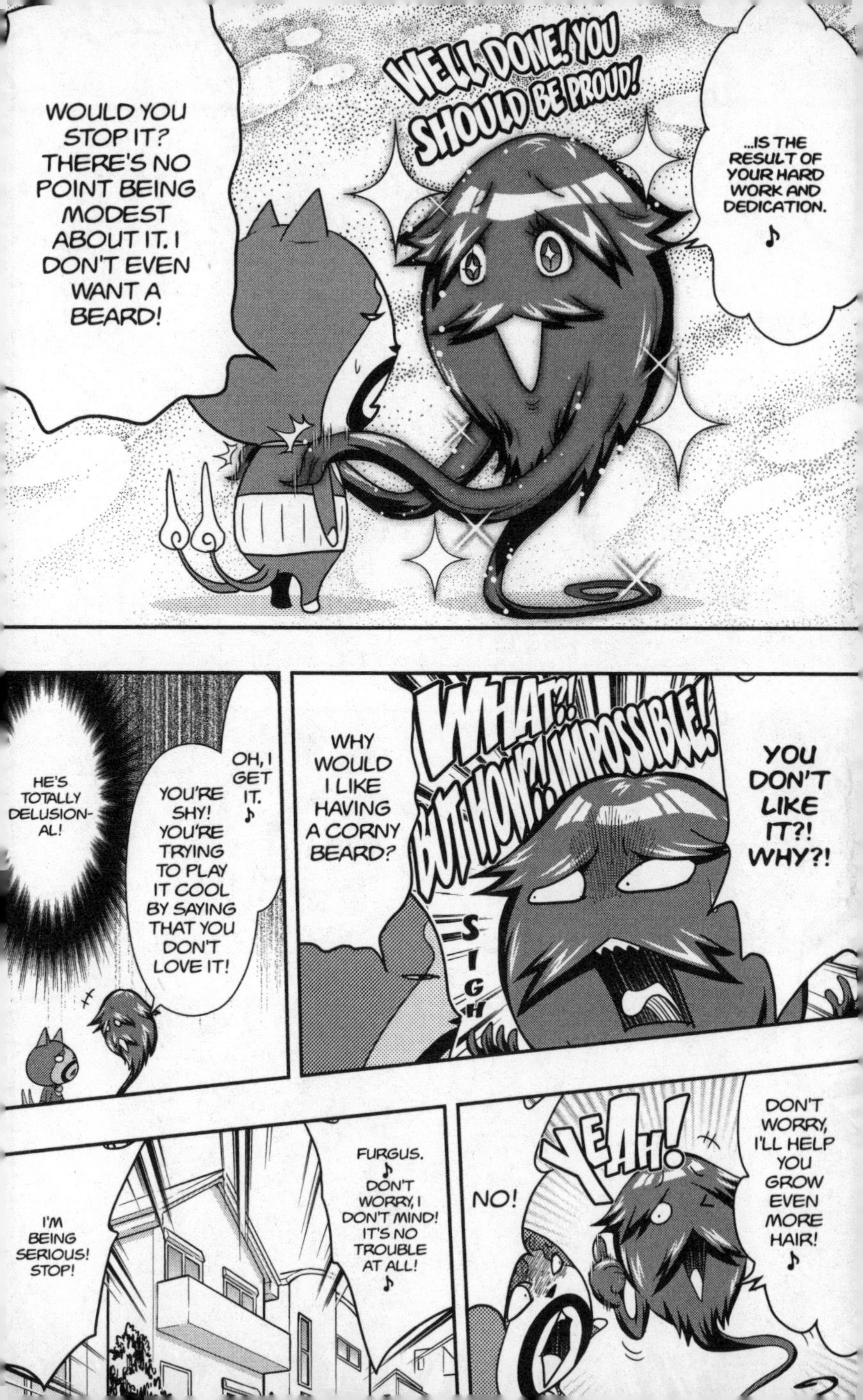
...IS THE RESULT OF YOUR HARD WORK AND DEDICATION. ♪
WELL DONE! YOU SHOULD BE PROUD!
WOULD YOU STOP IT? THERE'S NO POINT BEING MODEST ABOUT IT. I DON'T EVEN WANT A BEARD!
YOU DON'T LIKE IT?! WHY?!
WHAT?! BUT HOW?! IMPOSSIBLE!
WHY WOULD I LIKE HAVING A CORNY BEARD?
SIGH
OH, I GET IT. ♪
YOU'RE SHY! YOU'RE TRYING TO PLAY IT COOL BY SAYING THAT YOU DON'T LOVE IT!
HE'S TOTALLY DELUSIONAL!
DON'T WORRY, I'LL HELP YOU GROW EVEN MORE HAIR! ♪
YEAH!
NO!
FURGUS. ♪ DON'T WORRY, I DON'T MIND! IT'S NO TROUBLE AT ALL! ♪
I'M BEING SERIOUS! STOP!

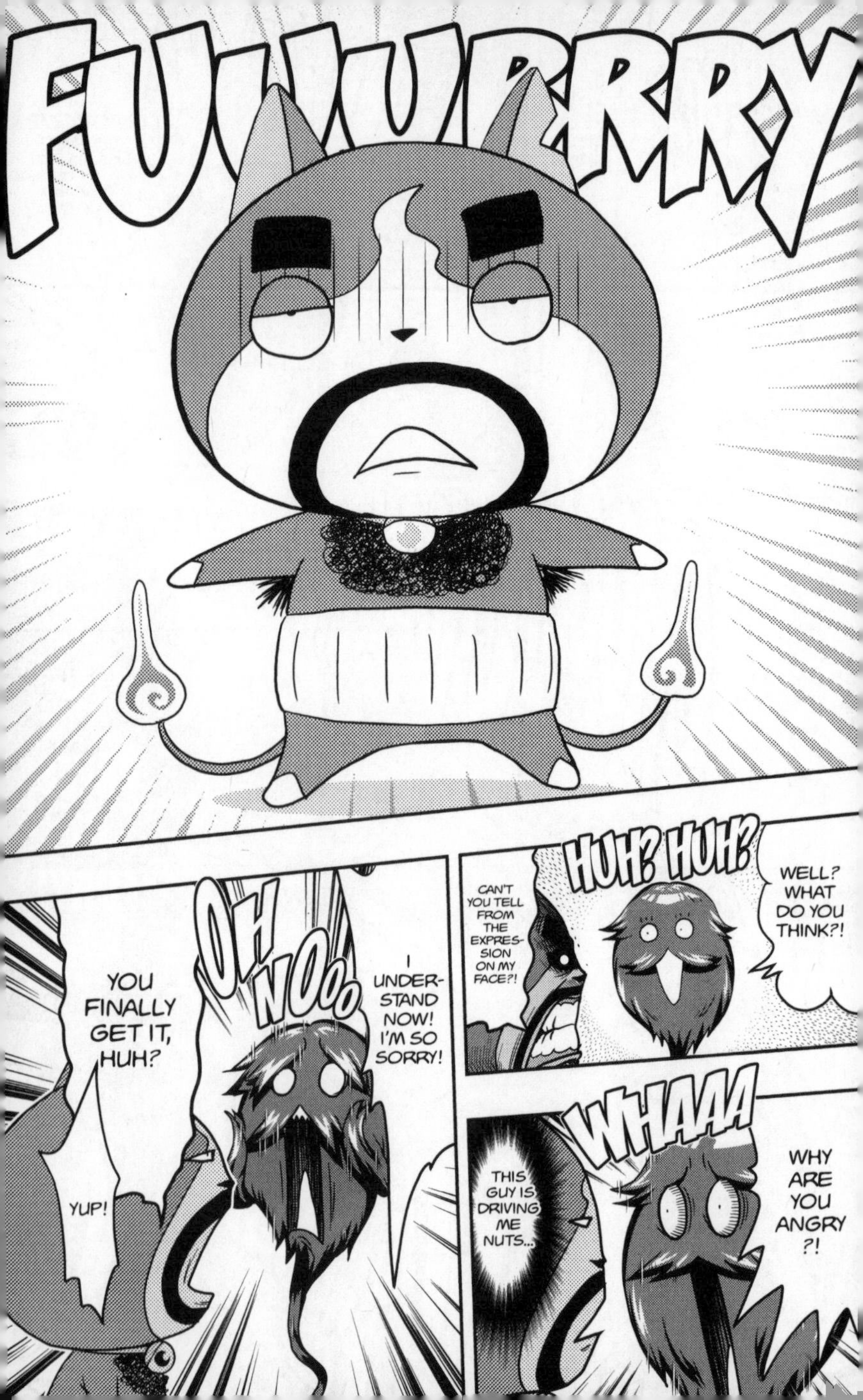
FUUURRRY
HUH? HUH?
WELL? WHAT DO YOU THINK?!
CAN'T YOU TELL FROM THE EXPRES-SION ON MY FACE?!
WHAAA
WHY ARE YOU ANGRY ?!
THIS GUY IS DRIVING ME NUTS...
I UNDER-STAND NOW! I'M SO SORRY!
OH NOooo
YOU FINALLY GET IT, HUH?
YUP!

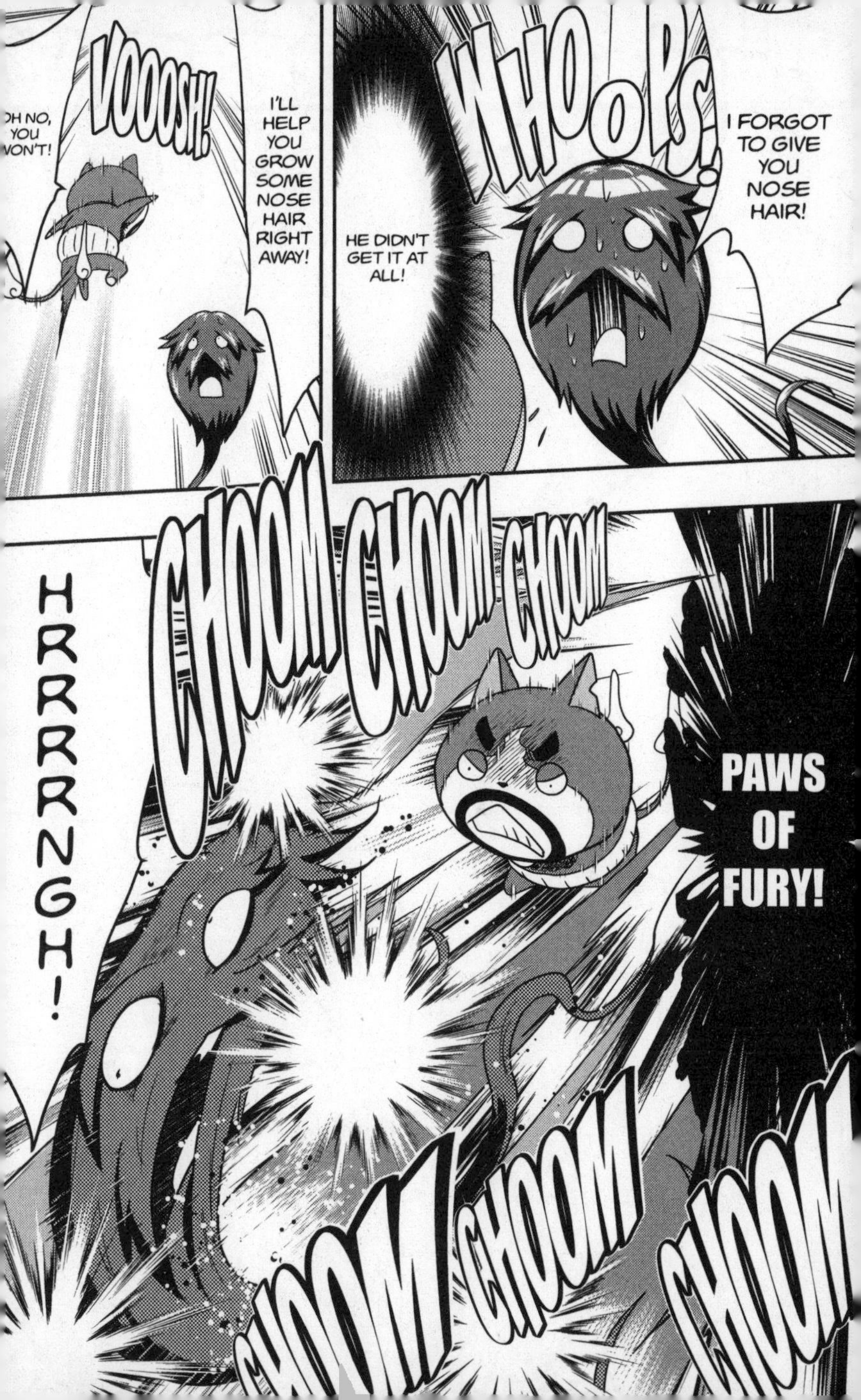
WHOOPS!
I FORGOT TO GIVE YOU NOSE HAIR!
HE DIDN'T GET IT AT ALL!
I'LL HELP YOU GROW SOME NOSE HAIR RIGHT AWAY!
VOOOSH!
OH NO, YOU WON'T!
CHOOM CHOOM CHOOM
PAWS OF FURY!
HRRRRNGH!
CHOOM CHOOM CHOOM

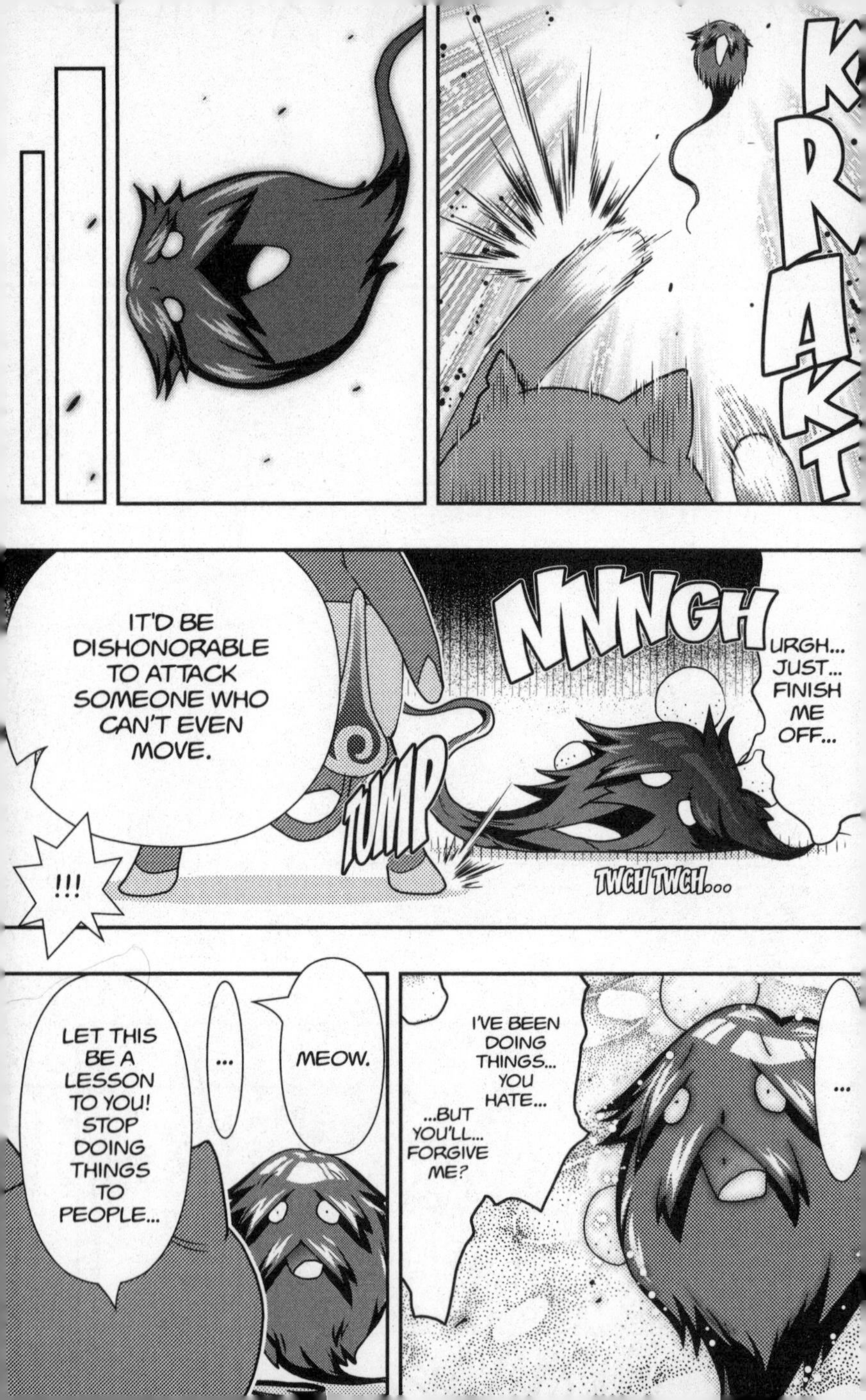
KRAKT
NNNGH
URGH... JUST... FINISH ME OFF...
TWCH TWCH...
TUMP
IT'D BE DISHONORABLE TO ATTACK SOMEONE WHO CAN'T EVEN MOVE.
!!!
...
I'VE BEEN DOING THINGS... YOU HATE...
...BUT YOU'LL... FORGIVE ME?
MEOW.
...
LET THIS BE A LESSON TO YOU! STOP DOING THINGS TO PEOPLE...

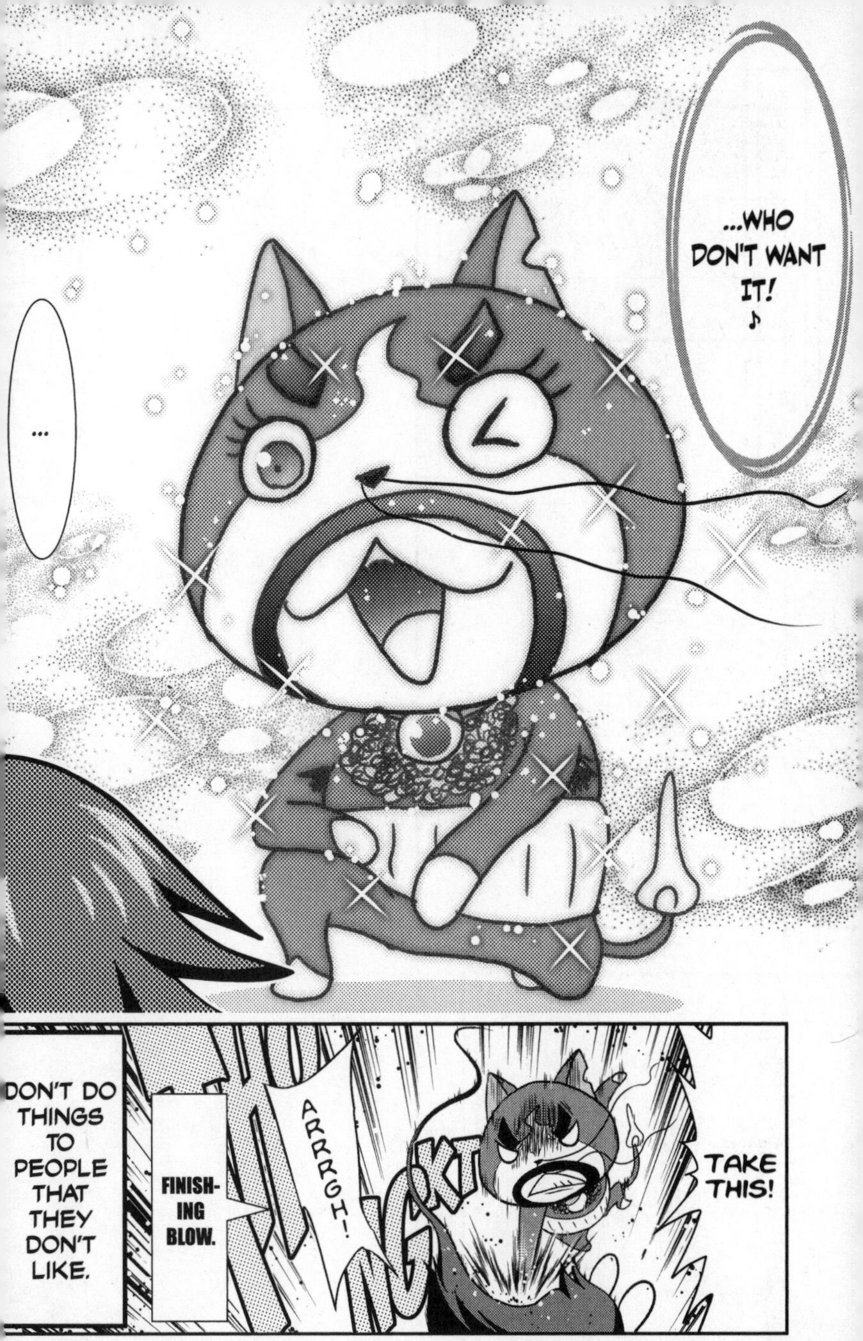
...WHO DON'T WANT IT! ♪
...
TAKE THIS!
ARRRGH!
FINISHING BLOW.
DON'T DO THINGS TO PEOPLE THAT THEY DON'T LIKE.

HAIR REMOVAL

GRNNN
I'LL JUST PULL THIS NOSE HAIR OUT!
IT'S NO USE! I GAVE IT EXCEPTIONALLY STRONG ROOTS!
HNNGH
I'LL GET IT OUT NO MATTER WHAT!
IT'LL NEVER WORK!
SHOOPT
IMPOSSIBLE!
HOORAY!
WSSH
HE PULLED OFF HIS NOSE TOO!

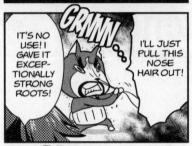

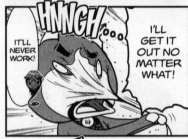

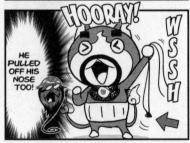

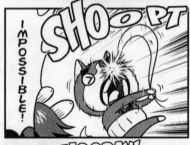

CHAPTER 92
ANGER IS INFECTIOUS!
FEATURING ANGER YO-KAI HISSFIT

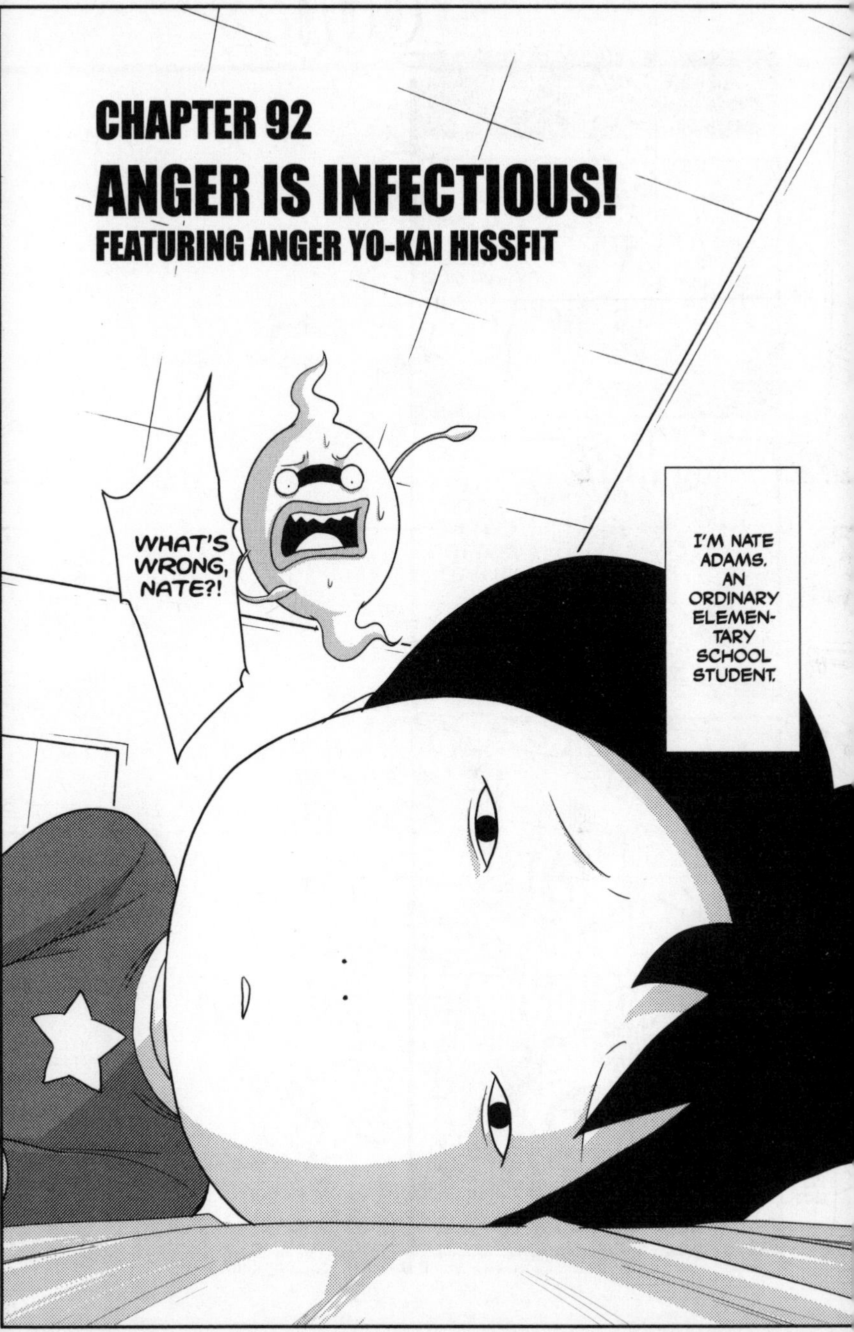
I'M NATE ADAMS. AN ORDINARY ELEMEN-TARY SCHOOL STUDENT.
WHAT'S WRONG, NATE?!

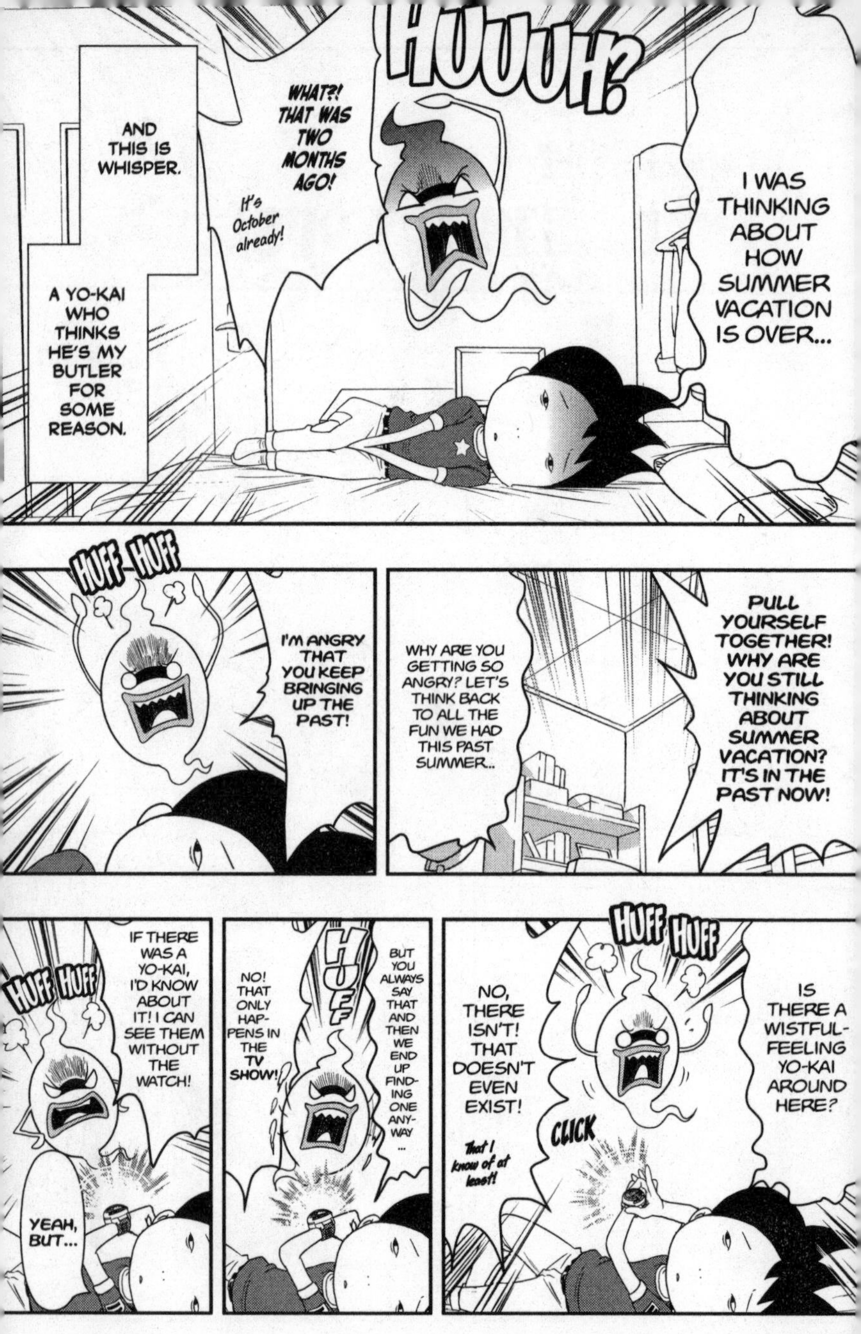
I WAS THINKING ABOUT HOW SUMMER VACATION IS OVER...
HUUUUH?
WHAT?! THAT WAS TWO MONTHS AGO!
It's October already!
AND THIS IS WHISPER.
A YO-KAI WHO THINKS HE'S MY BUTLER FOR SOME REASON.
PULL YOURSELF TOGETHER! WHY ARE YOU STILL THINKING ABOUT SUMMER VACATION? IT'S IN THE PAST NOW!
WHY ARE YOU GETTING SO ANGRY? LET'S THINK BACK TO ALL THE FUN WE HAD THIS PAST SUMMER...
HUFF HUFF
I'M ANGRY THAT YOU KEEP BRINGING UP THE PAST!
HUFF HUFF
IS THERE A WISTFUL-FEELING YO-KAI AROUND HERE?
CLICK
NO, THERE ISN'T! THAT DOESN'T EVEN EXIST!
That I know of at least!
BUT YOU ALWAYS SAY THAT AND THEN WE END UP FINDING ONE ANYWAY...
HUFF
NO! THAT ONLY HAPPENS IN THE TV SHOW!
IF THERE WAS A YO-KAI, I'D KNOW ABOUT IT! I CAN SEE THEM WITHOUT THE WATCH!
HUFF HUFF
YEAH, BUT...

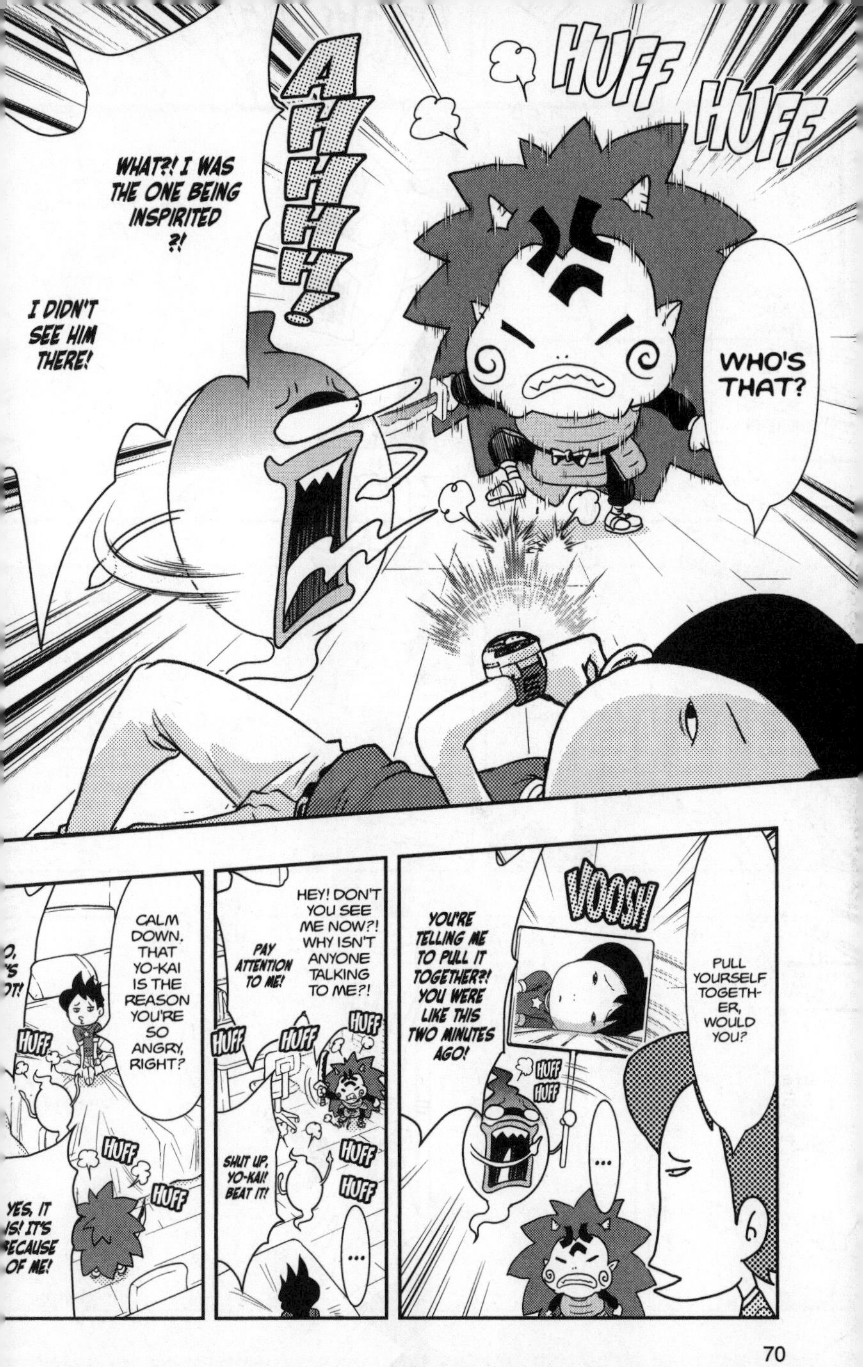
HUFF HUFF
WHO'S THAT?
AHHHHH!
WHAT?! I WAS THE ONE BEING INSPIRITED?!
I DIDN'T SEE HIM THERE!
PULL YOURSELF TOGETH-ER, WOULD YOU?
VOOSH
YOU'RE TELLING ME TO PULL IT TOGETHER?! YOU WERE LIKE THIS TWO MINUTES AGO!
HUFF HUFF
...
HEY! DON'T YOU SEE ME NOW?! WHY ISN'T ANYONE TALKING TO ME?!
PAY ATTENTION TO ME!
HUFF
HUFF
HUFF
HUFF
HUFF
SHUT UP, YO-KAI! BEAT IT!
...
CALM DOWN. THAT YO-KAI IS THE REASON YOU'RE SO ANGRY, RIGHT?
HUFF
HUFF
HUFF
YES, IT IS! IT'S ECAUSE OF ME!

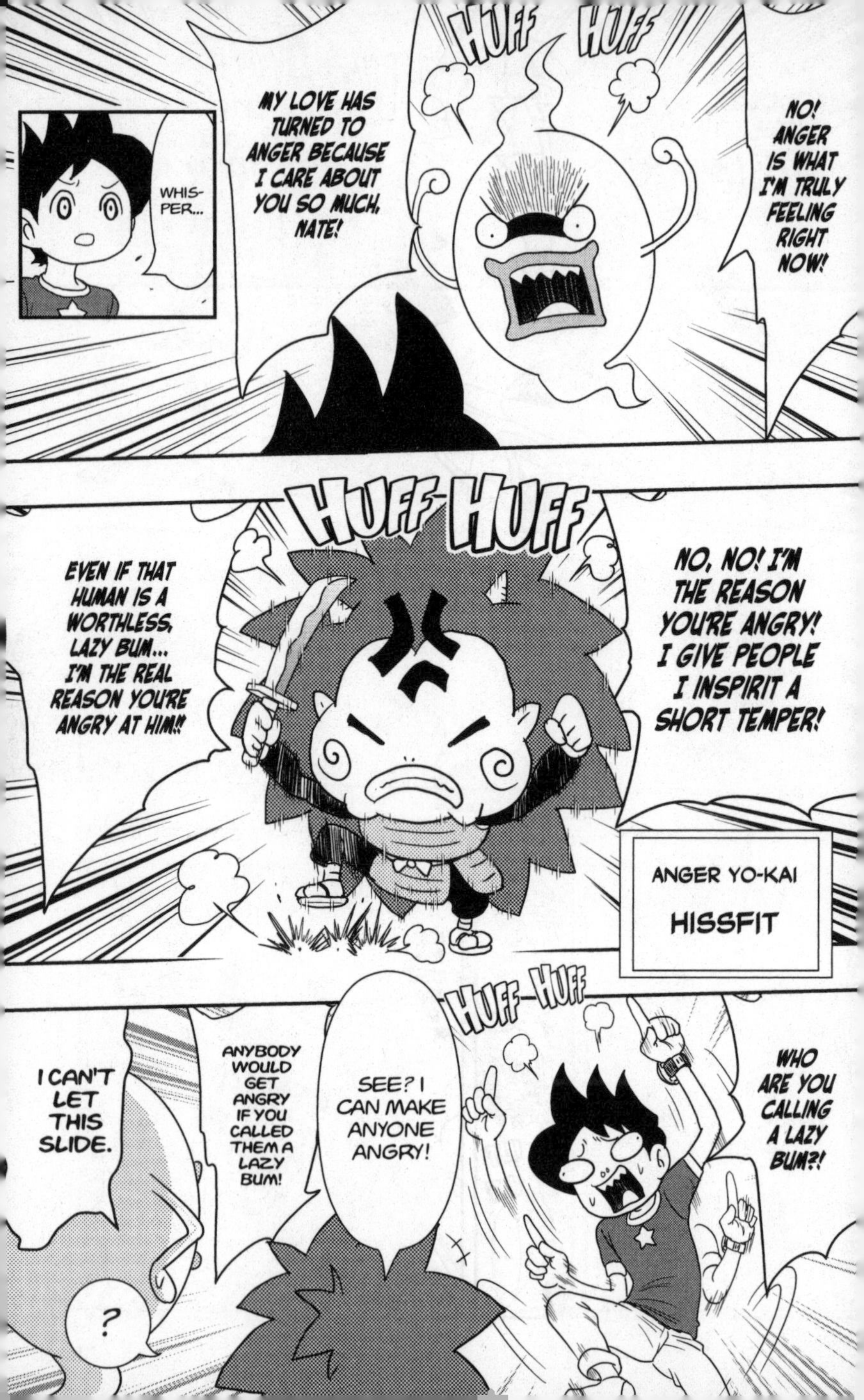
HUFF HUFF
NO! ANGER IS WHAT I'M TRULY FEELING RIGHT NOW!
MY LOVE HAS TURNED TO ANGER BECAUSE I CARE ABOUT YOU SO MUCH, NATE!
WHISPER...
HUFF-HUFF
NO, NO! I'M THE REASON YOU'RE ANGRY! I GIVE PEOPLE I INSPIRIT A SHORT TEMPER!
EVEN IF THAT HUMAN IS A WORTHLESS, LAZY BUM... I'M THE REAL REASON YOU'RE ANGRY AT HIM!!
ANGER YO-KAI
HISSFIT
HUFF-HUFF
WHO ARE YOU CALLING A LAZY BUM?!
SEE? I CAN MAKE ANYONE ANGRY!
ANYBODY WOULD GET ANGRY IF YOU CALLED THEM A LAZY BUM!
I CAN'T LET THIS SLIDE.
?

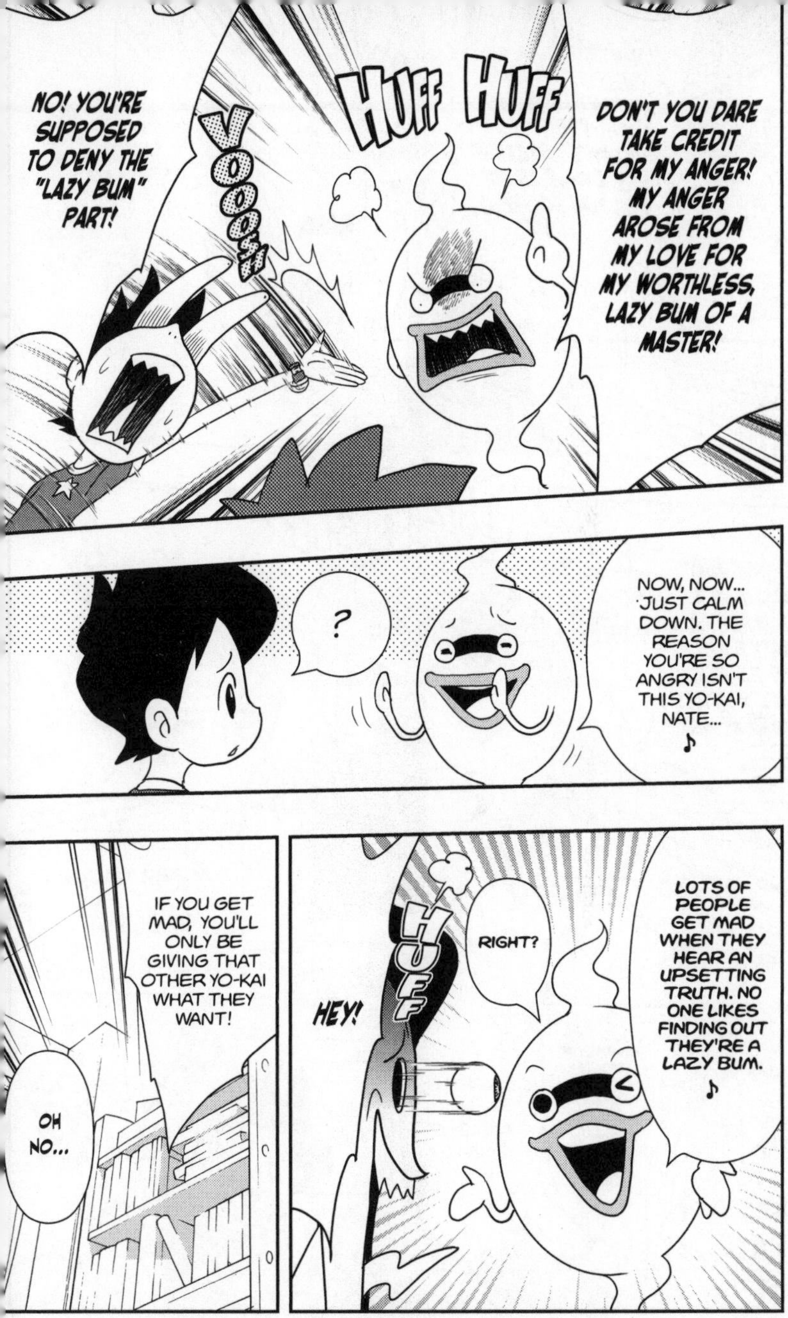
DON'T YOU DARE TAKE CREDIT FOR MY ANGER! MY ANGER AROSE FROM MY LOVE FOR MY WORTHLESS, LAZY BUM OF A MASTER!
HUFF HUFF
NO! YOU'RE SUPPOSED TO DENY THE "LAZY BUM" PART!
VOOOM!
NOW, NOW... JUST CALM DOWN. THE REASON YOU'RE SO ANGRY ISN'T THIS YO-KAI, NATE... ♪
?
LOTS OF PEOPLE GET MAD WHEN THEY HEAR AN UPSETTING TRUTH. NO ONE LIKES FINDING OUT THEY'RE A LAZY BUM. ♪
RIGHT?
HUFF
HEY!
IF YOU GET MAD, YOU'LL ONLY BE GIVING THAT OTHER YO-KAI WHAT THEY WANT!
OH NO...

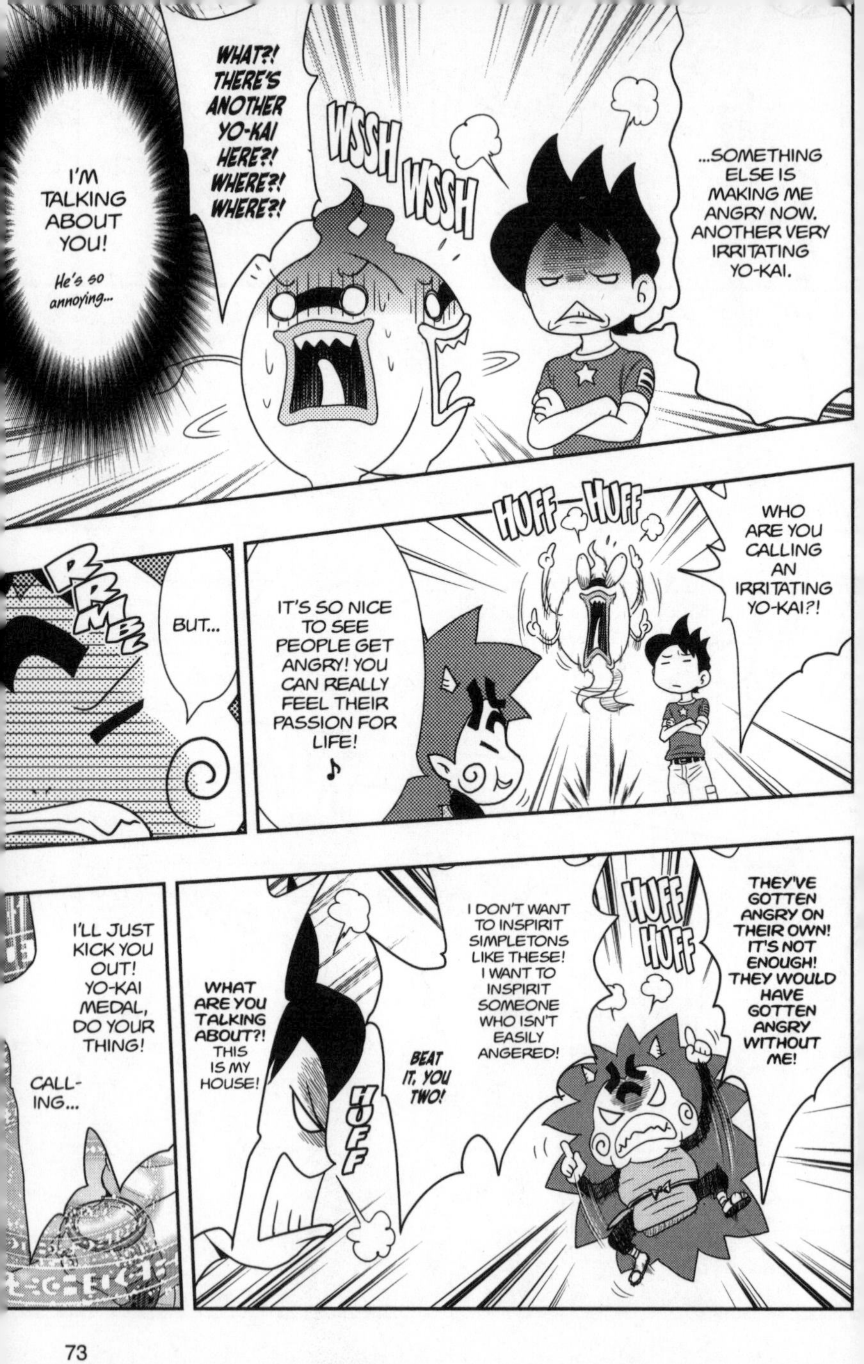
...SOMETHING ELSE IS MAKING ME ANGRY NOW. ANOTHER VERY IRRITATING YO-KAI.
WHAT?! THERE'S ANOTHER YO-KAI HERE?! WHERE?! WHERE?!
WSSH WSSH
I'M TALKING ABOUT YOU!
He's so annoying...
WHO ARE YOU CALLING AN IRRITATING YO-KAI?!
HUFF HUFF
IT'S SO NICE TO SEE PEOPLE GET ANGRY! YOU CAN REALLY FEEL THEIR PASSION FOR LIFE! ♪
BUT...
RRMBL
THEY'VE GOTTEN ANGRY ON THEIR OWN! IT'S NOT ENOUGH! THEY WOULD HAVE GOTTEN ANGRY WITHOUT ME!
HUFF HUFF
I DON'T WANT TO INSPIRIT SIMPLETONS LIKE THESE! I WANT TO INSPIRIT SOMEONE WHO ISN'T EASILY ANGERED!
BEAT IT, YOU TWO!
WHAT ARE YOU TALKING ABOUT?! THIS IS MY HOUSE!
HUFF
I'LL JUST KICK YOU OUT! YO-KAI MEDAL, DO YOUR THING!
CALLING...

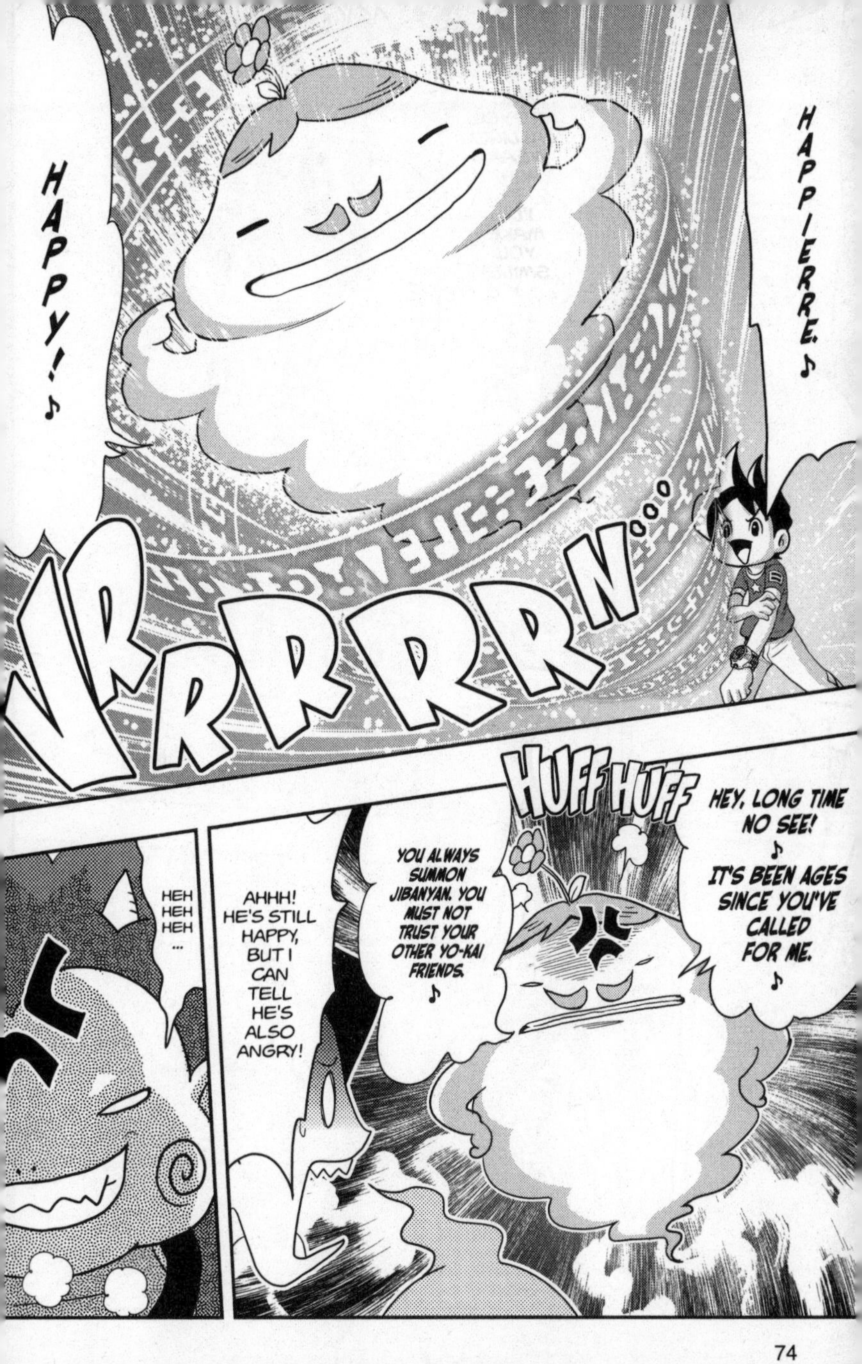
HAPPIERRE.♪
HAPPY!!♪
VRRRRRN...
HUFF HUFF
HEY, LONG TIME NO SEE! ♪ IT'S BEEN AGES SINCE YOU'VE CALLED FOR ME. ♪
YOU ALWAYS SUMMON JIBANYAN. YOU MUST NOT TRUST YOUR OTHER YO-KAI FRIENDS. ♪
AHHH! HE'S STILL HAPPY, BUT I CAN TELL HE'S ALSO ANGRY!
HEH HEH HEH ...

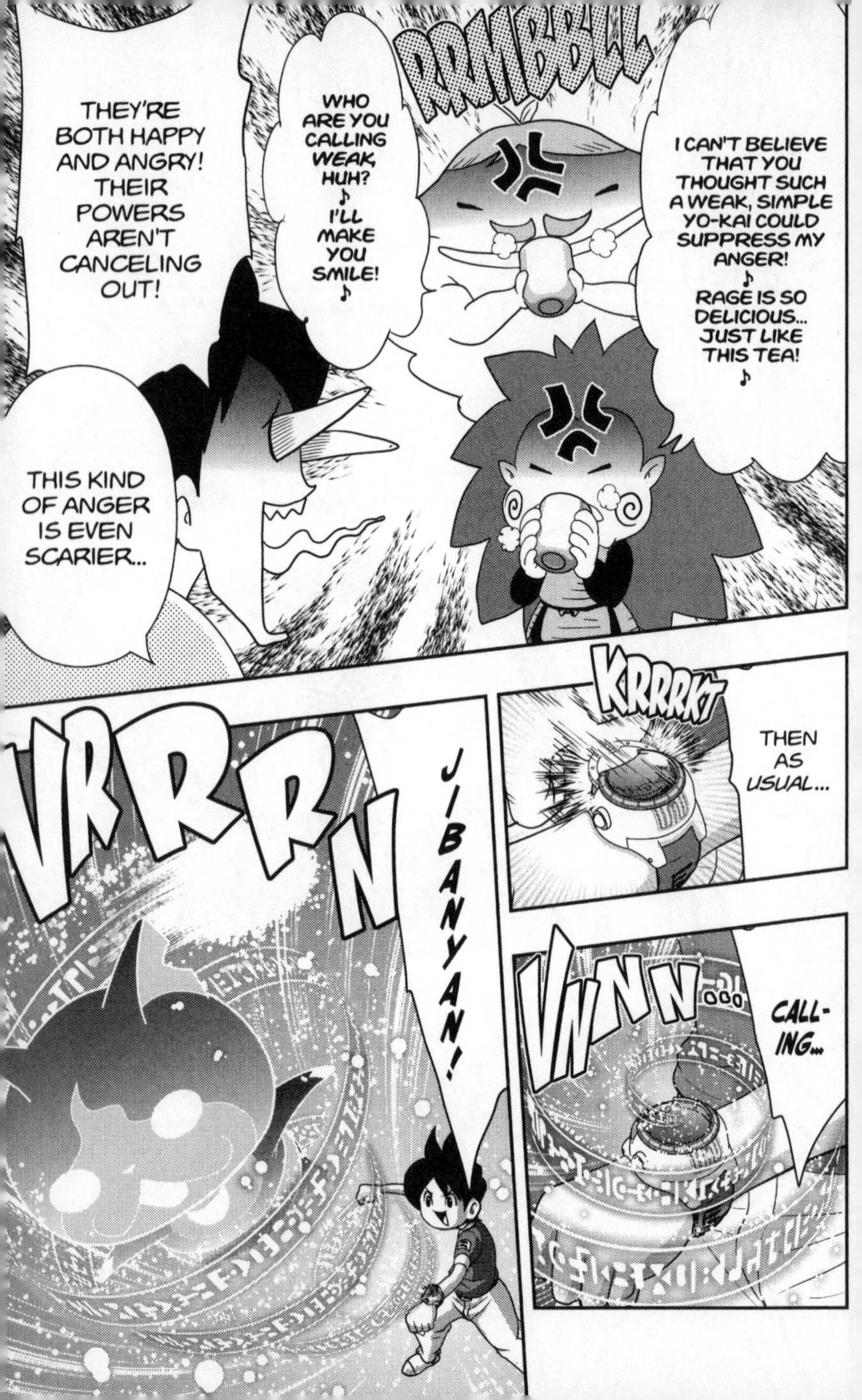
RRMBBLL
I CAN'T BELIEVE THAT YOU THOUGHT SUCH A WEAK, SIMPLE YO-KAI COULD SUPPRESS MY ANGER! ♪ RAGE IS SO DELICIOUS... JUST LIKE THIS TEA! ♪
WHO ARE YOU CALLING WEAK, HUH? ♪ I'LL MAKE YOU SMILE! ♪
THEY'RE BOTH HAPPY AND ANGRY! THEIR POWERS AREN'T CANCELING OUT!
THIS KIND OF ANGER IS EVEN SCARIER...
KRRRKT
THEN AS USUAL...
VNNN...
CALL-ING...
JIBANYAN!
VRRRN

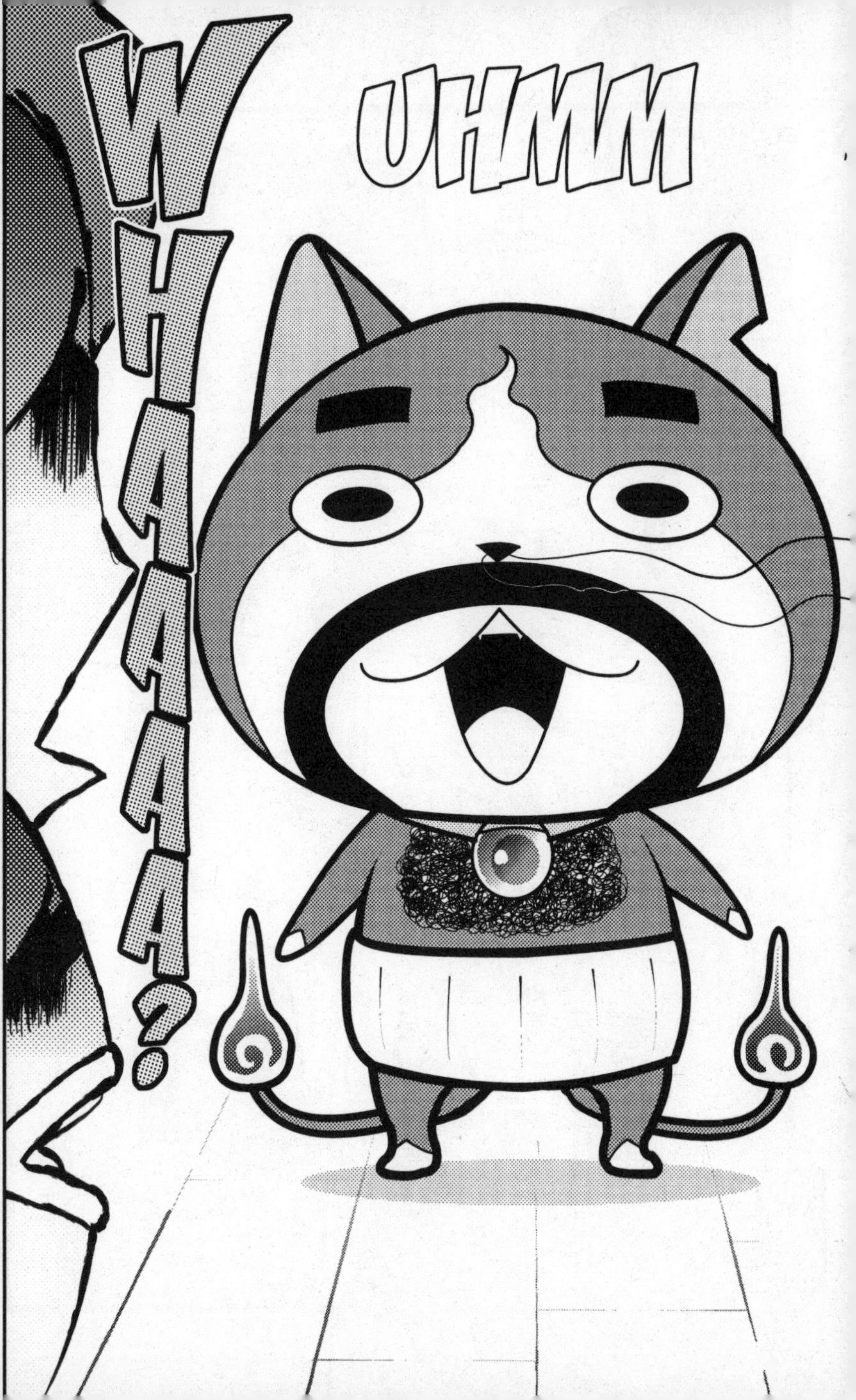
UHMM
WHAAAAA?

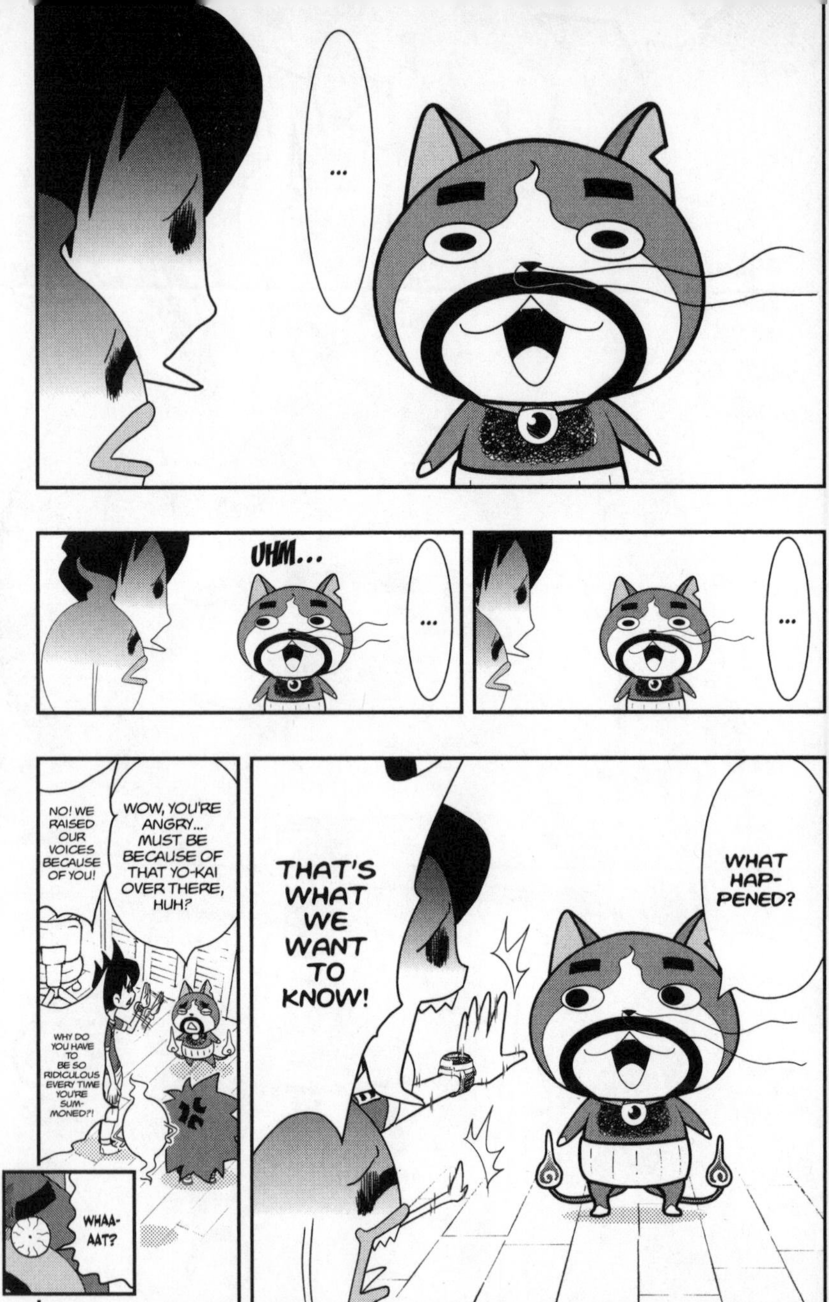

...
...
UHM...
...
WHAT HAP-PENED?
THAT'S WHAT WE WANT TO KNOW!
WOW, YOU'RE ANGRY... MUST BE BECAUSE OF THAT YO-KAI OVER THERE, HUH?
NO! WE RAISED OUR VOICES BECAUSE OF YOU!
WHY DO YOU HAVE TO BE SO RIDICULOUS EVERY TIME YOU'RE SUM-MONED?!
WHAA-AAT?

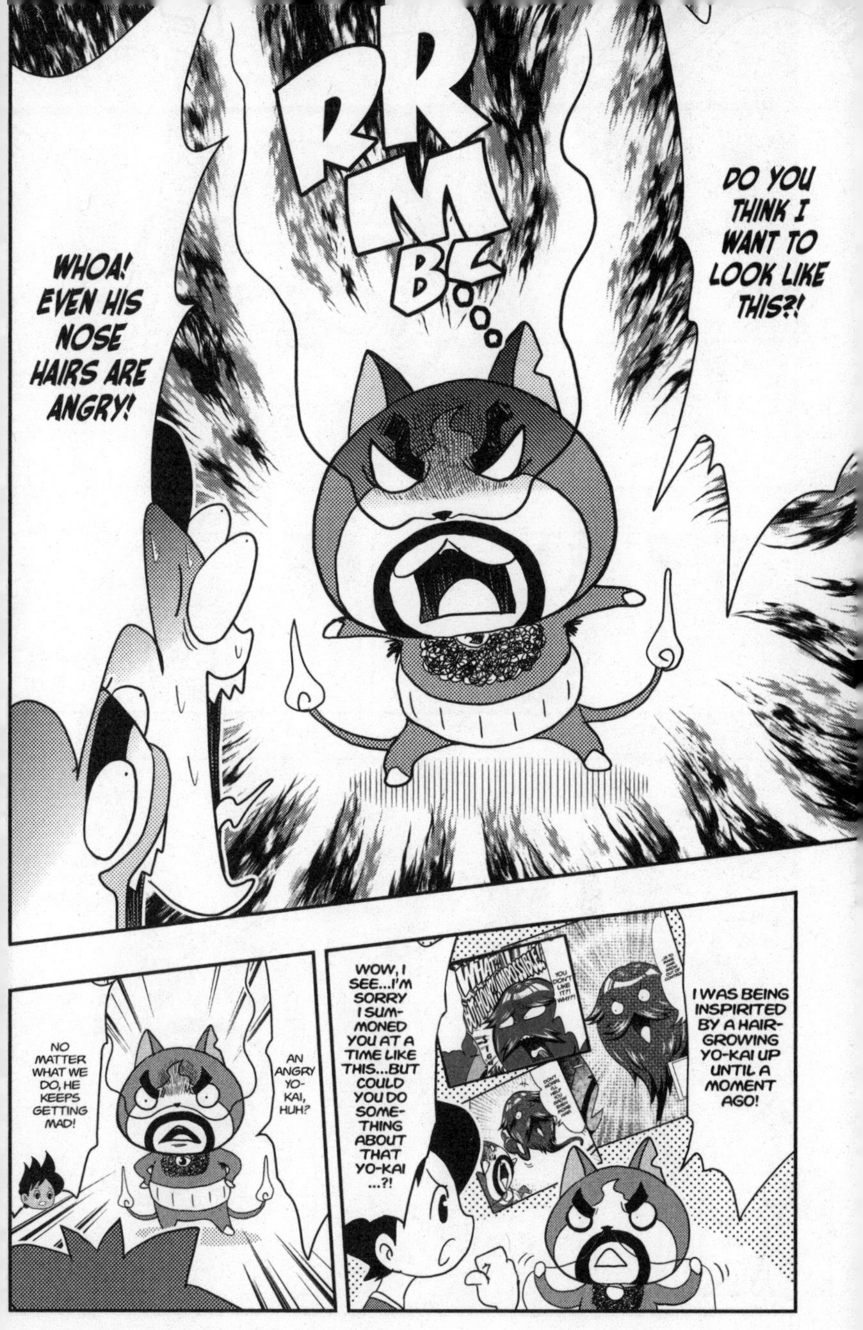
RRMBL
DO YOU THINK I WANT TO LOOK LIKE THIS?!
WHOA! EVEN HIS NOSE HAIRS ARE ANGRY!
I WAS BEING INSPIRITED BY A HAIR-GROWING YO-KAI UP UNTIL A MOMENT AGO!
WOW, I SEE...I'M SORRY I SUMMONED YOU AT A TIME LIKE THIS...BUT COULD YOU DO SOMETHING ABOUT THAT YO-KAI ...?!
AN ANGRY YO-KAI, HUH?
NO MATTER WHAT WE DO, HE KEEPS GETTING MAD!

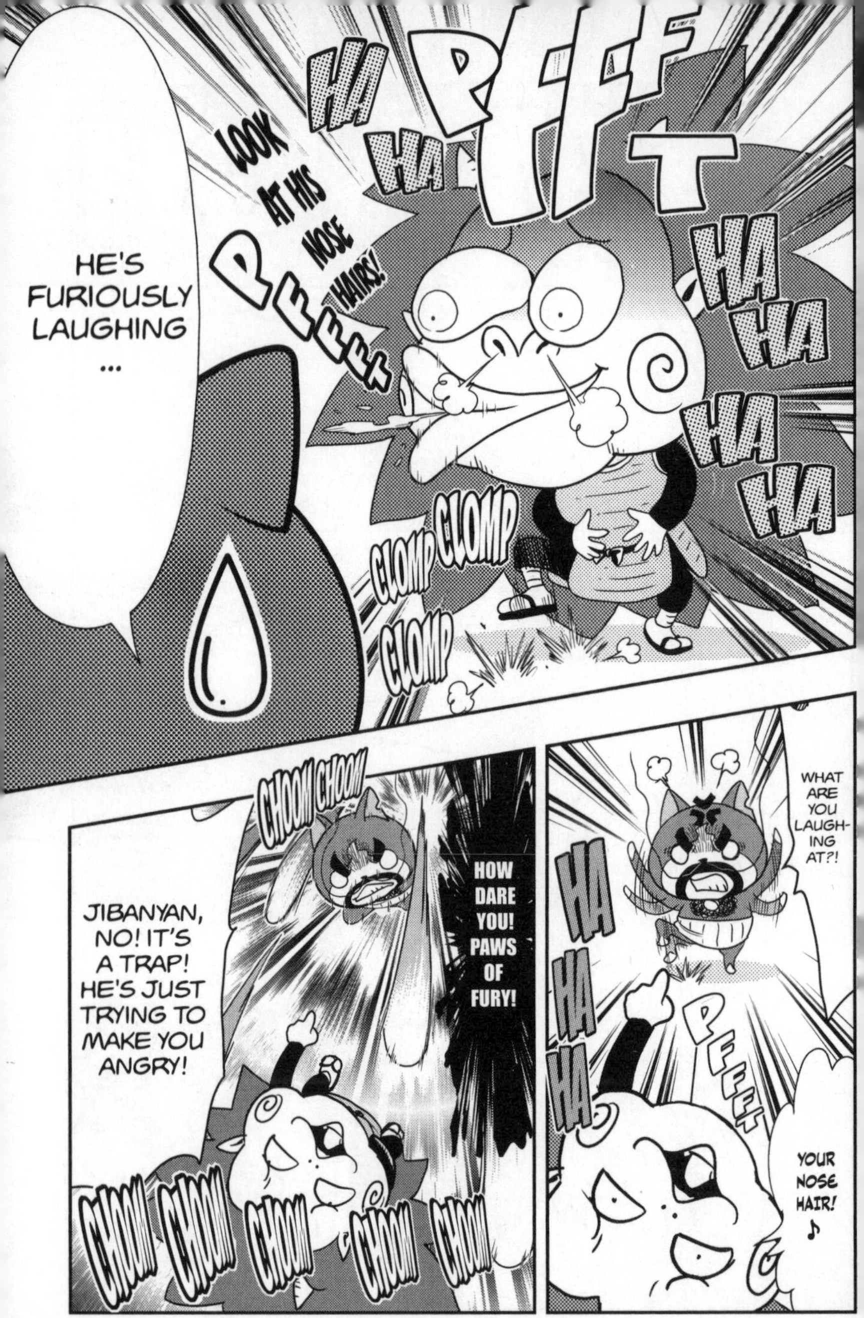
PFFFFT
HA HA
HA HA HA HA HA HA
LOOK AT HIS NOSE HAIRS!
PFFFT
HE'S FURIOUSLY LAUGHING ...
CLOMP CLOMP
CLOMP
CLOMP
WHAT ARE YOU LAUGH-ING AT?!
HA HA HA
PFFFT
YOUR NOSE HAIR! ♪
CHOOM CHOOM
HOW DARE YOU! PAWS OF FURY!
JIBANYAN, NO! IT'S A TRAP! HE'S JUST TRYING TO MAKE YOU ANGRY!
CHOOM CHOOM CHOOM CHOOM CHOOM

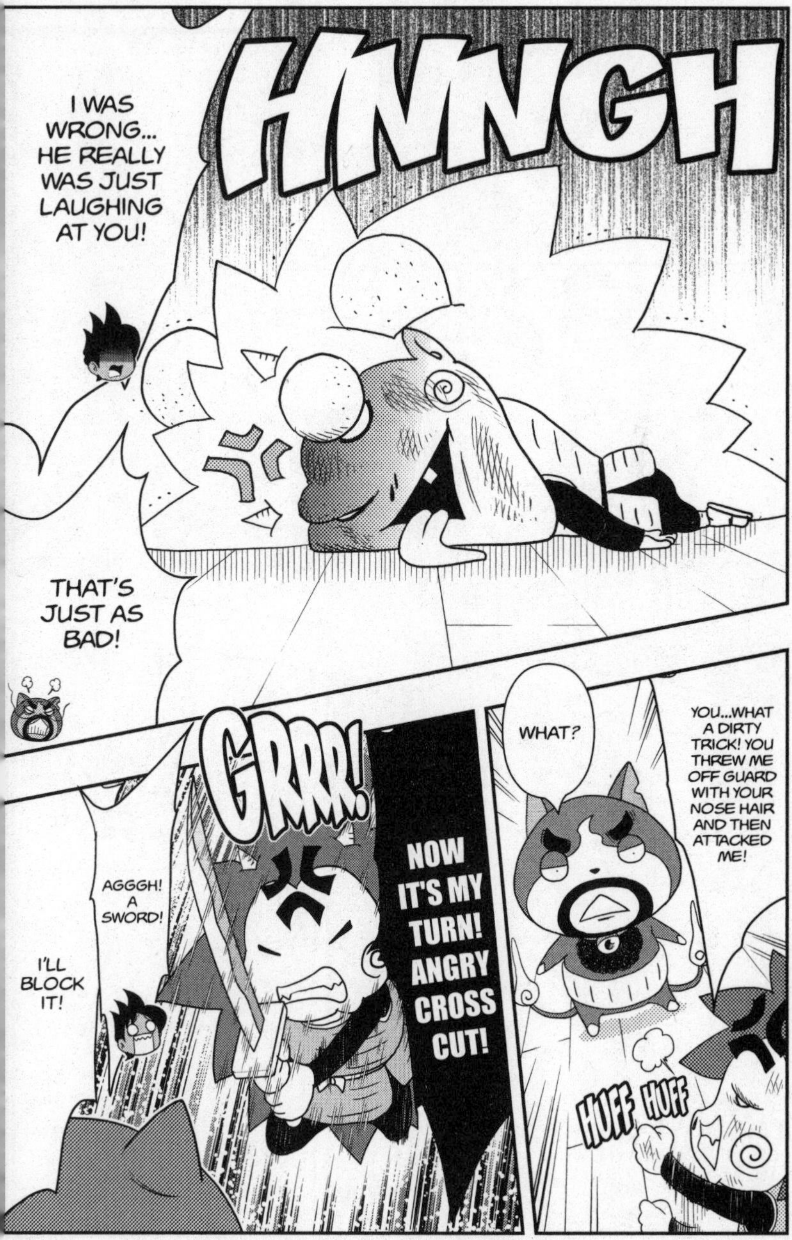
HNNGH
I WAS WRONG... HE REALLY WAS JUST LAUGHING AT YOU!
THAT'S JUST AS BAD!
YOU...WHAT A DIRTY TRICK! YOU THREW ME OFF GUARD WITH YOUR NOSE HAIR AND THEN ATTACKED ME!
WHAT?
HUFF HUFF
GRRR!
NOW IT'S MY TURN! ANGRY CROSS CUT!
AGGGH! A SWORD!
I'LL BLOCK IT!

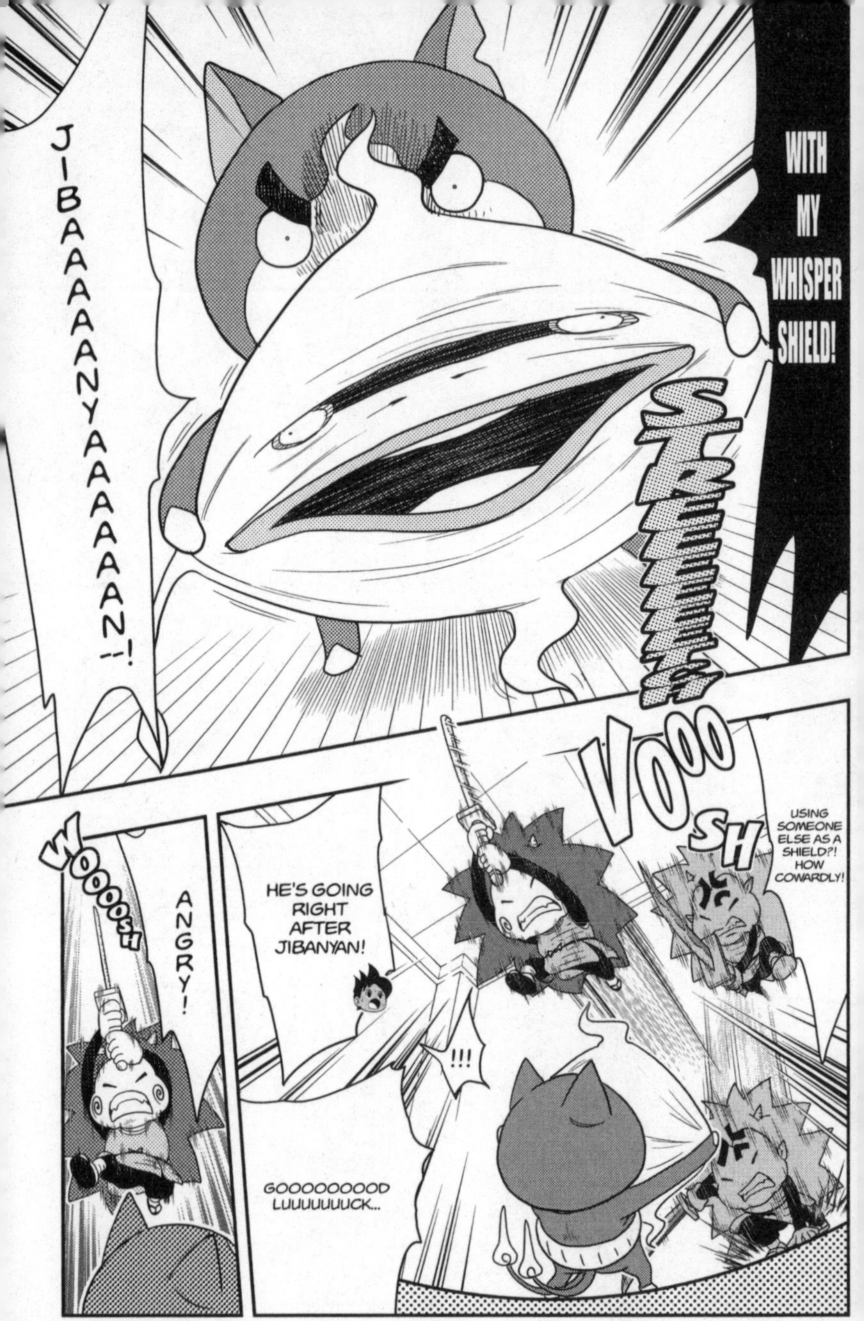
WITH MY WHISPER SHIELD!
JIBAAAAANYAAAAAAAN--!
VOOOSH
USING SOMEONE ELSE AS A SHIELD?! HOW COWARDLY!
HE'S GOING RIGHT AFTER JIBANYAN!
!!!
GOOOOOOOOD LUUUUUUUCK...
WOOOOOSH
ANGRY!

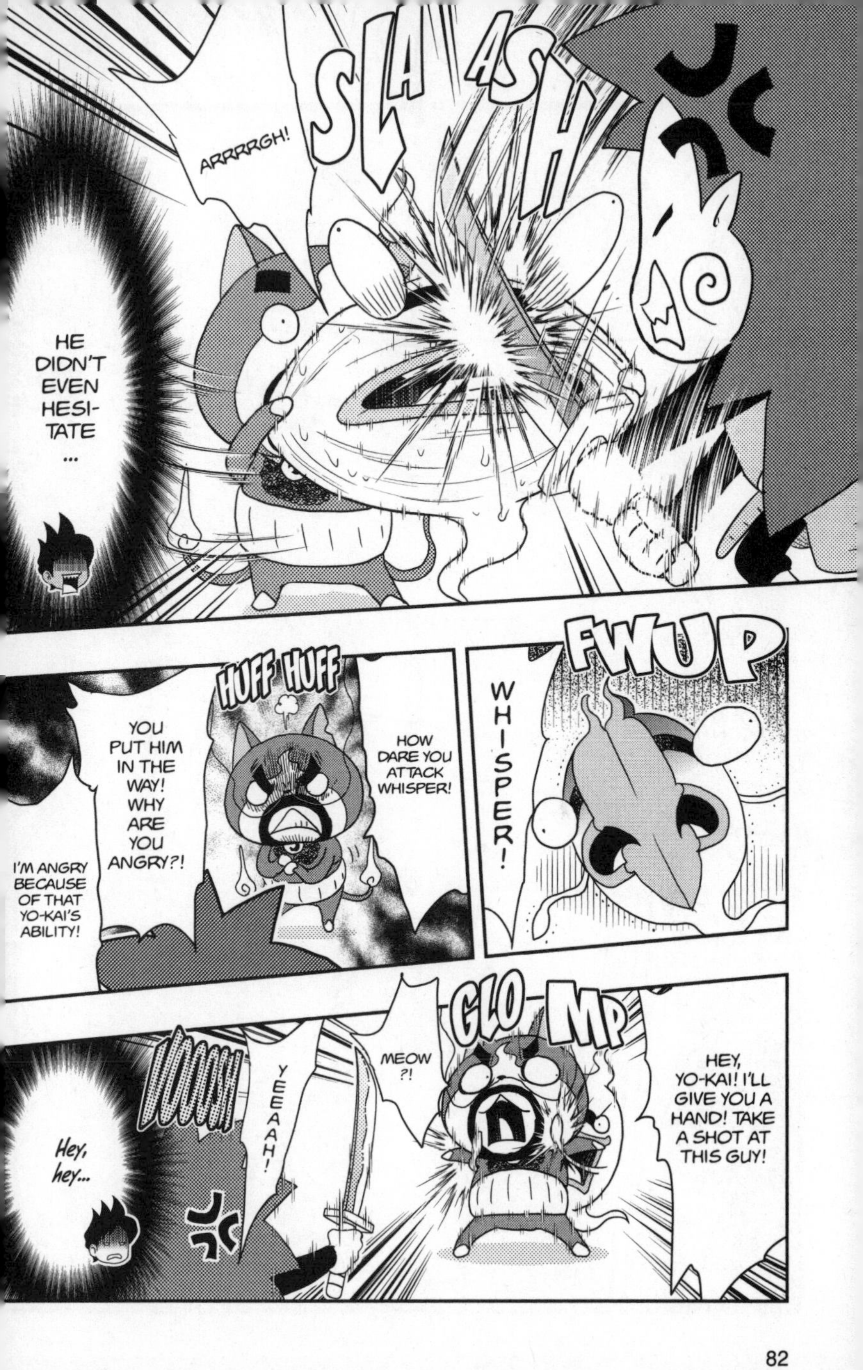
SLASH
ARRRRGH!
HE DIDN'T EVEN HESI-TATE...
FWUP
WHISPER!
HUFF HUFF
HOW DARE YOU ATTACK WHISPER!
YOU PUT HIM IN THE WAY! WHY ARE YOU ANGRY?!
I'M ANGRY BECAUSE OF THAT YO-KAI'S ABILITY!
HEY, YO-KAI! I'LL GIVE YOU A HAND! TAKE A SHOT AT THIS GUY!
GLOMP
MEOW?!
YEEAAH!
VOOOSH
Hey, hey...

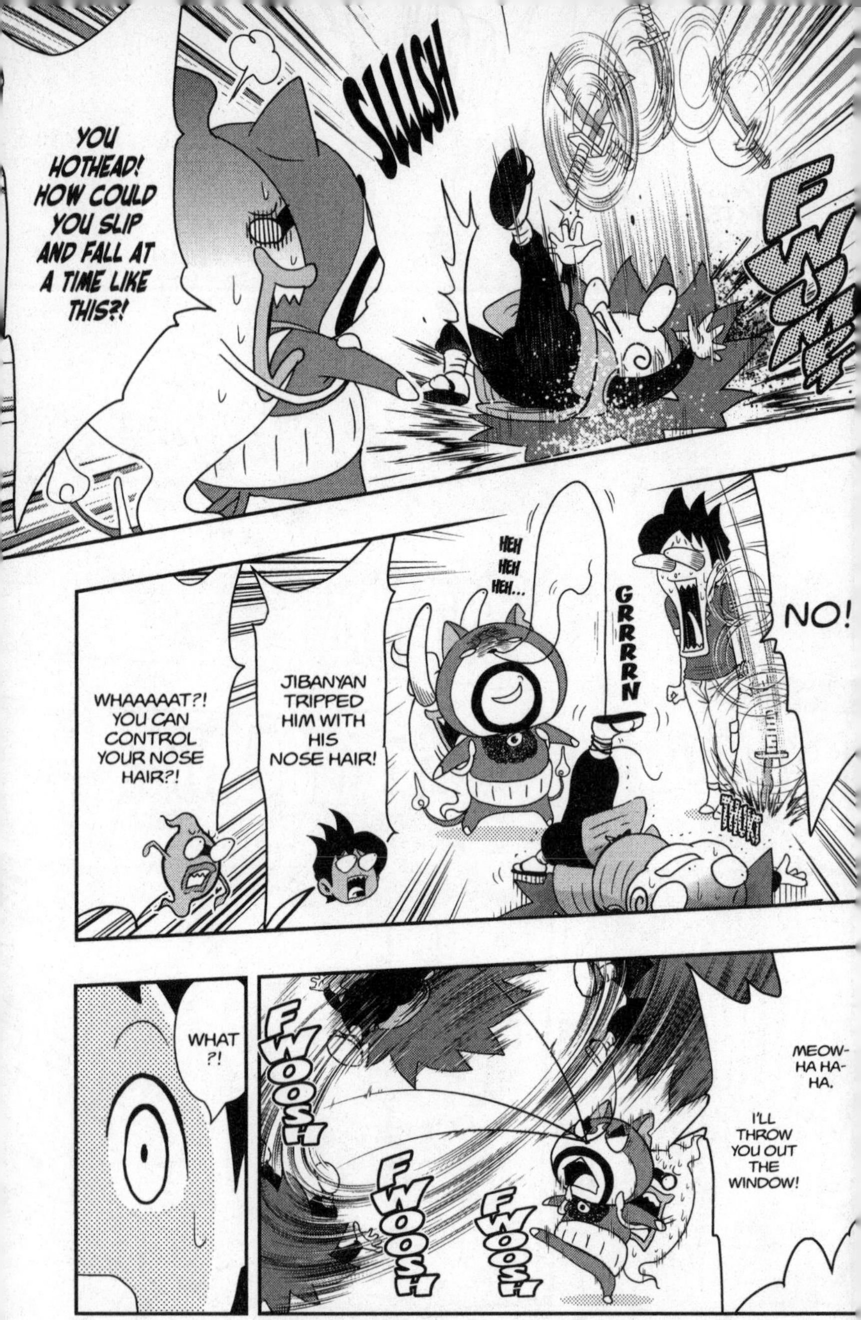
FWUMP
SLISH
YOU HOTHEAD! HOW COULD YOU SLIP AND FALL AT A TIME LIKE THIS?!
NO!
GRRRRN
HEH HEH HEH...
THUNK
JIBANYAN TRIPPED HIM WITH HIS NOSE HAIR!
WHAAAAAT?! YOU CAN CONTROL YOUR NOSE HAIR?!
MEOW-HA HA-HA.
I'LL THROW YOU OUT THE WINDOW!
FWOOSH
FWOOSH
FWOOSH
WHAT?!

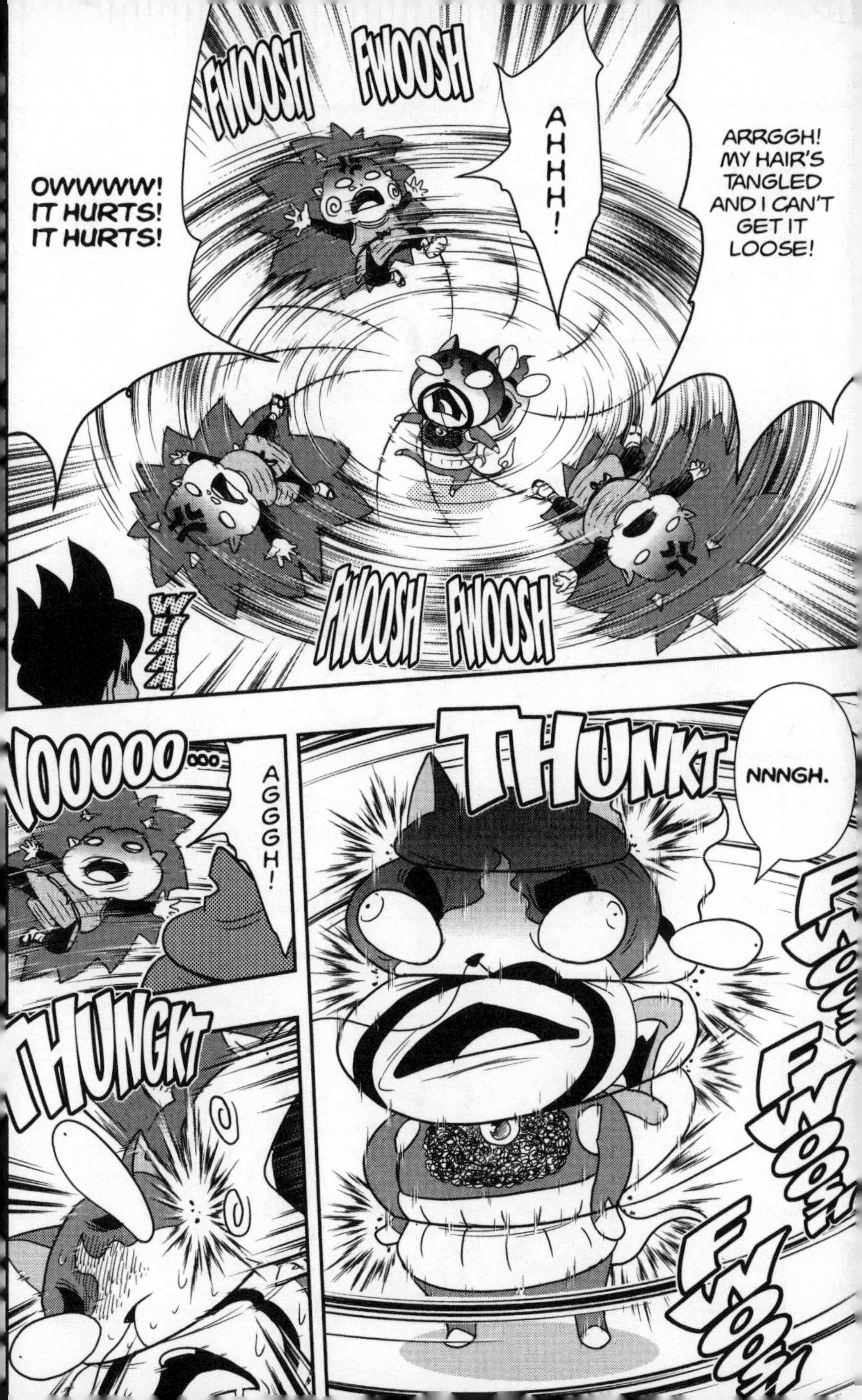
ARRGGH! MY HAIR'S TANGLED AND I CAN'T GET IT LOOSE!
AHHH!
FWOOSH FWOOSH
OWWWW! IT HURTS! IT HURTS!
FWOOSH FWOOSH
THUNKT
NNNGH.
AGGGH!
THUNGKT

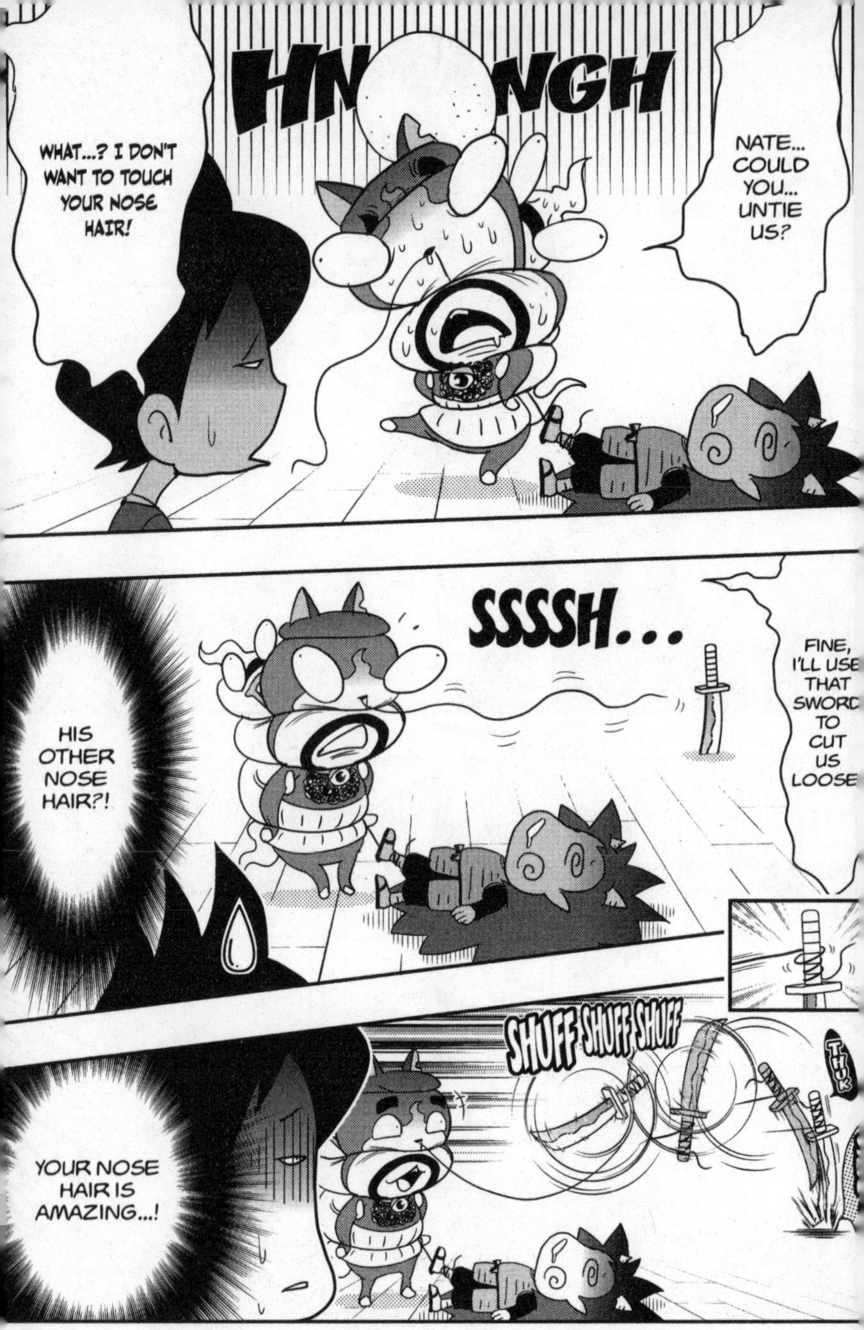

NATE... COULD YOU... UNTIE US?
HN NGH
WHAT...? I DON'T WANT TO TOUCH YOUR NOSE HAIR!
FINE, I'LL USE THAT SWORD TO CUT US LOOSE
SSSSH...
HIS OTHER NOSE HAIR?!
THUK
SHUFF SHUFF SHUFF
YOUR NOSE HAIR IS AMAZING...!

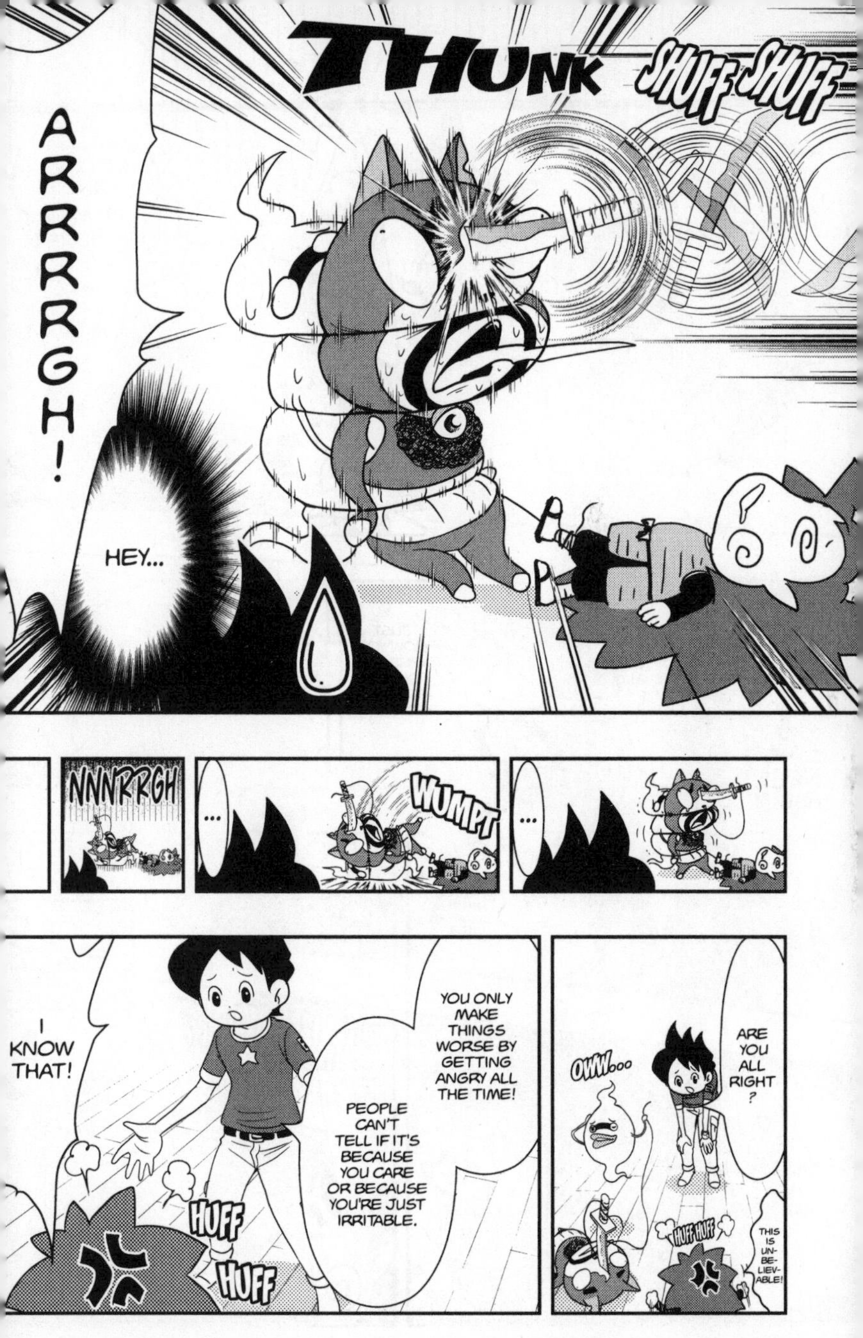
SHUFF SHUFF
THUNK
ARRRRRGH!
HEY...
...
...
WUMPT
NNNRRGH
ARE YOU ALL RIGHT?
OWWooo
HUFF HUFF
THIS IS UN-BE-LIEV-ABLE!
YOU ONLY MAKE THINGS WORSE BY GETTING ANGRY ALL THE TIME!
PEOPLE CAN'T TELL IF IT'S BECAUSE YOU CARE OR BECAUSE YOU'RE JUST IRRITABLE.
I KNOW THAT!
HUFF
HUFF

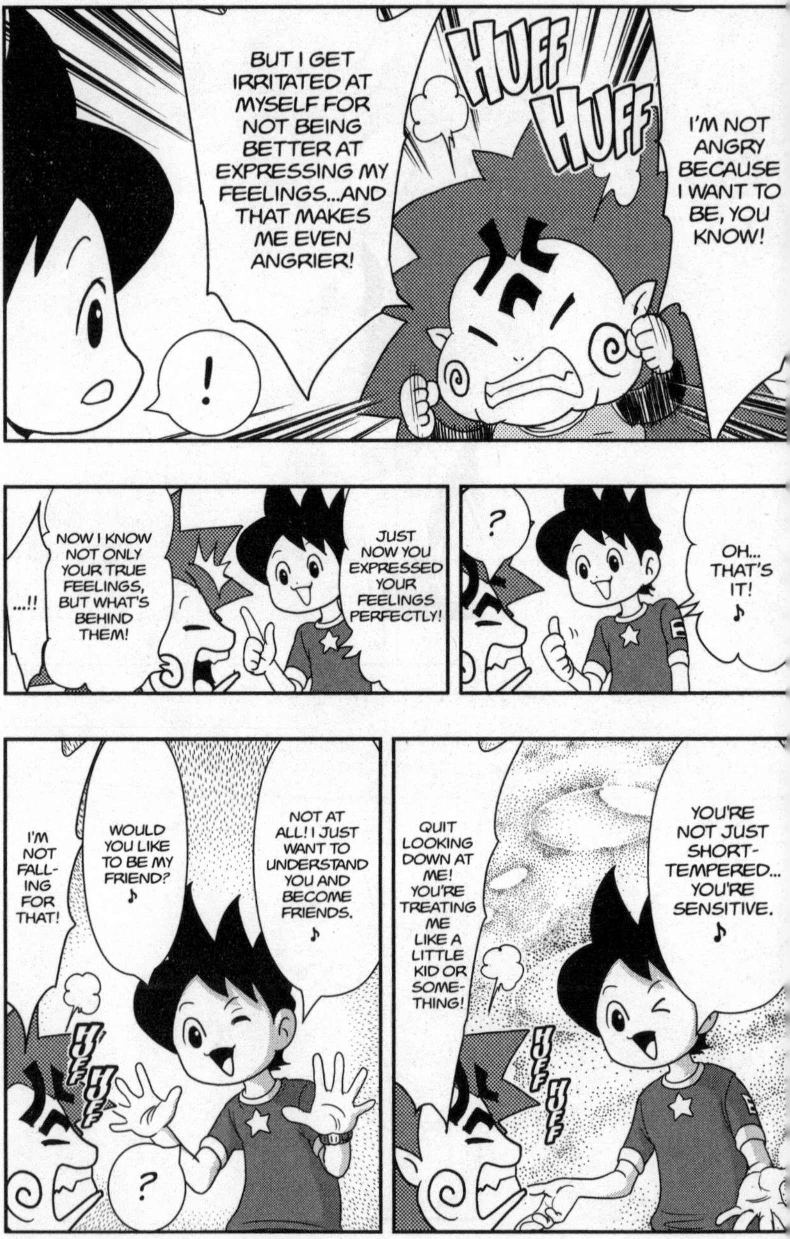
I'M NOT ANGRY BECAUSE I WANT TO BE, YOU KNOW!
HUFF HUFF
BUT I GET IRRITATED AT MYSELF FOR NOT BEING BETTER AT EXPRESSING MY FEELINGS...AND THAT MAKES ME EVEN ANGRIER!
!
OH... THAT'S IT! ♪
?
JUST NOW YOU EXPRESSED YOUR FEELINGS PERFECTLY!
NOW I KNOW NOT ONLY YOUR TRUE FEELINGS, BUT WHAT'S BEHIND THEM!
...!!
YOU'RE NOT JUST SHORT-TEMPERED... YOU'RE SENSITIVE. ♪
QUIT LOOKING DOWN AT ME! YOU'RE TREATING ME LIKE A LITTLE KID OR SOME-THING!
HUFF HUFF
NOT AT ALL! I JUST WANT TO UNDERSTAND YOU AND BECOME FRIENDS. ♪
WOULD YOU LIKE TO BE MY FRIEND? ♪
I'M NOT FALL-ING FOR THAT!
HUFF HUFF
?

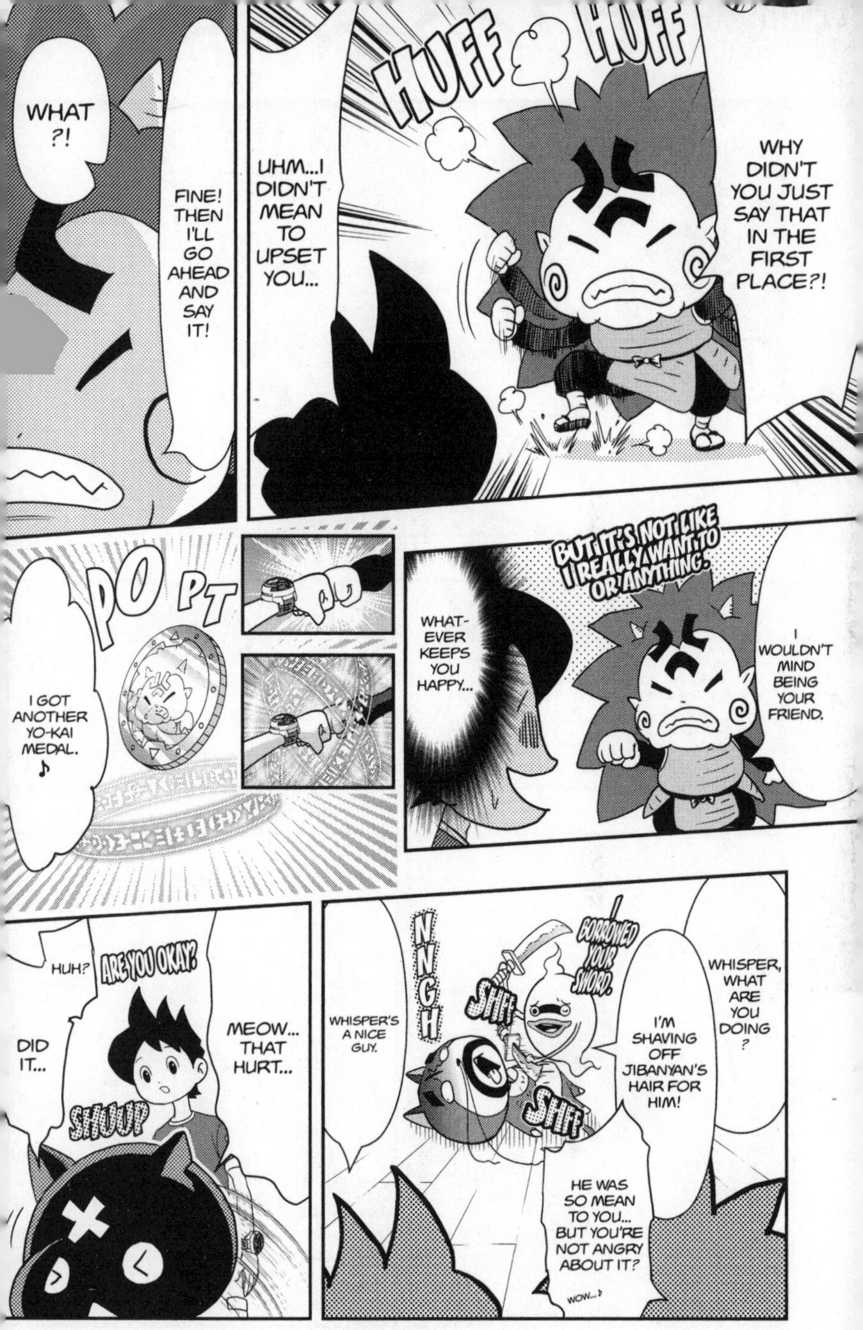
HUFF HUFF
WHY DIDN'T YOU JUST SAY THAT IN THE FIRST PLACE?!
UHM...I DIDN'T MEAN TO UPSET YOU...
FINE! THEN I'LL GO AHEAD AND SAY IT!
WHAT?!
BUT IT'S NOT LIKE I REALLY WANT TO OR ANYTHING.
I WOULDN'T MIND BEING YOUR FRIEND.
WHATEVER KEEPS YOU HAPPY...
POPT
I GOT ANOTHER YO-KAI MEDAL. ♪
WHISPER, WHAT ARE YOU DOING?
I'M SHAVING OFF JIBANYAN'S HAIR FOR HIM!
I BORROWED YOUR SWORD.
SHFF
NNGH
SHFF
WHISPER'S A NICE GUY.
HE WAS SO MEAN TO YOU... BUT YOU'RE NOT ANGRY ABOUT IT?
WOW...♪
MEOW... THAT HURT...
ARE YOU OKAY?
HUH?
DID IT...
SHUUP

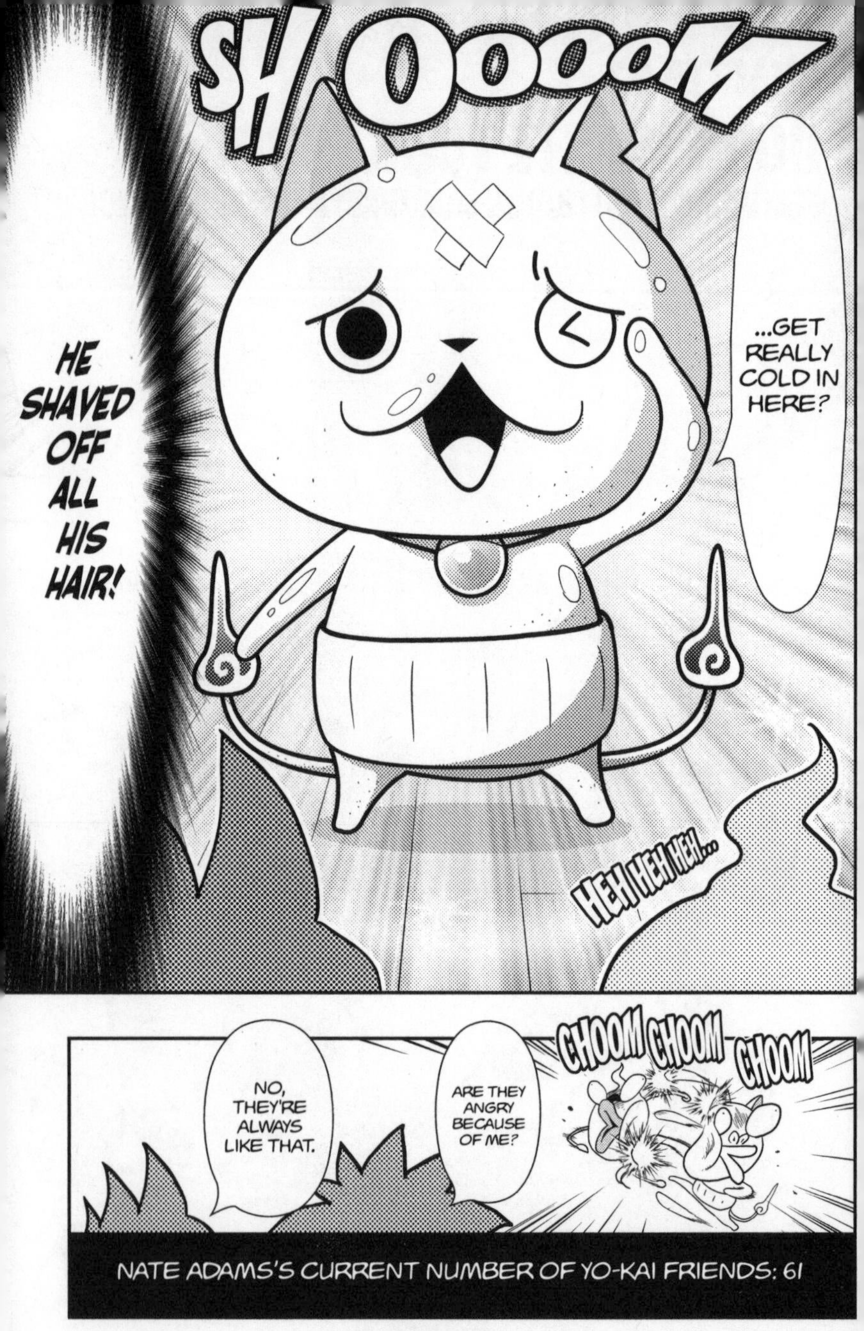
SHOOOOM
...GET REALLY COLD IN HERE?
HEH HEH HEH...
HE SHAVED OFF ALL HIS HAIR!
CHOOM CHOOM CHOOM
ARE THEY ANGRY BECAUSE OF ME?
NO, THEY'RE ALWAYS LIKE THAT.
NATE ADAMS'S CURRENT NUMBER OF YO-KAI FRIENDS: 61

CHAPTER 93

DON'T WASTE YOUR FOOD!

FEATURING MYSTERIOUS SAMURAI YO-KAI SLICENRICE

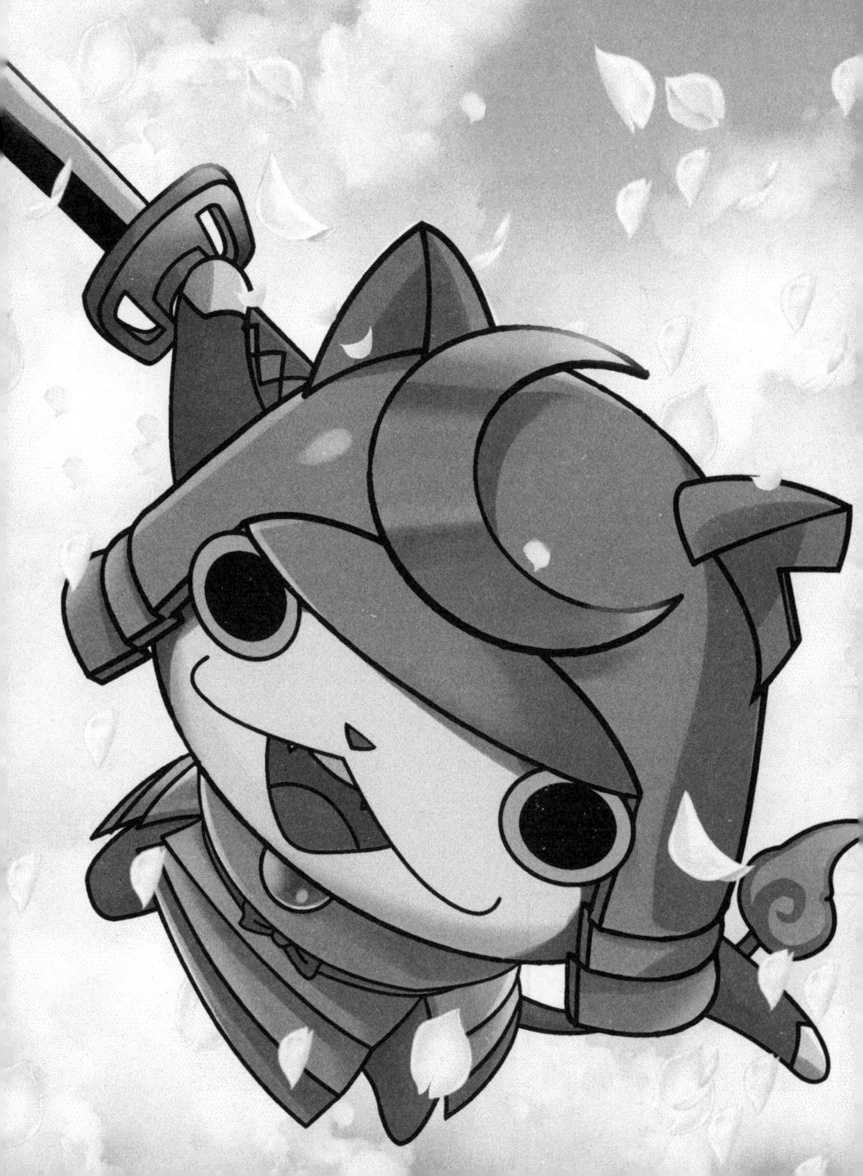

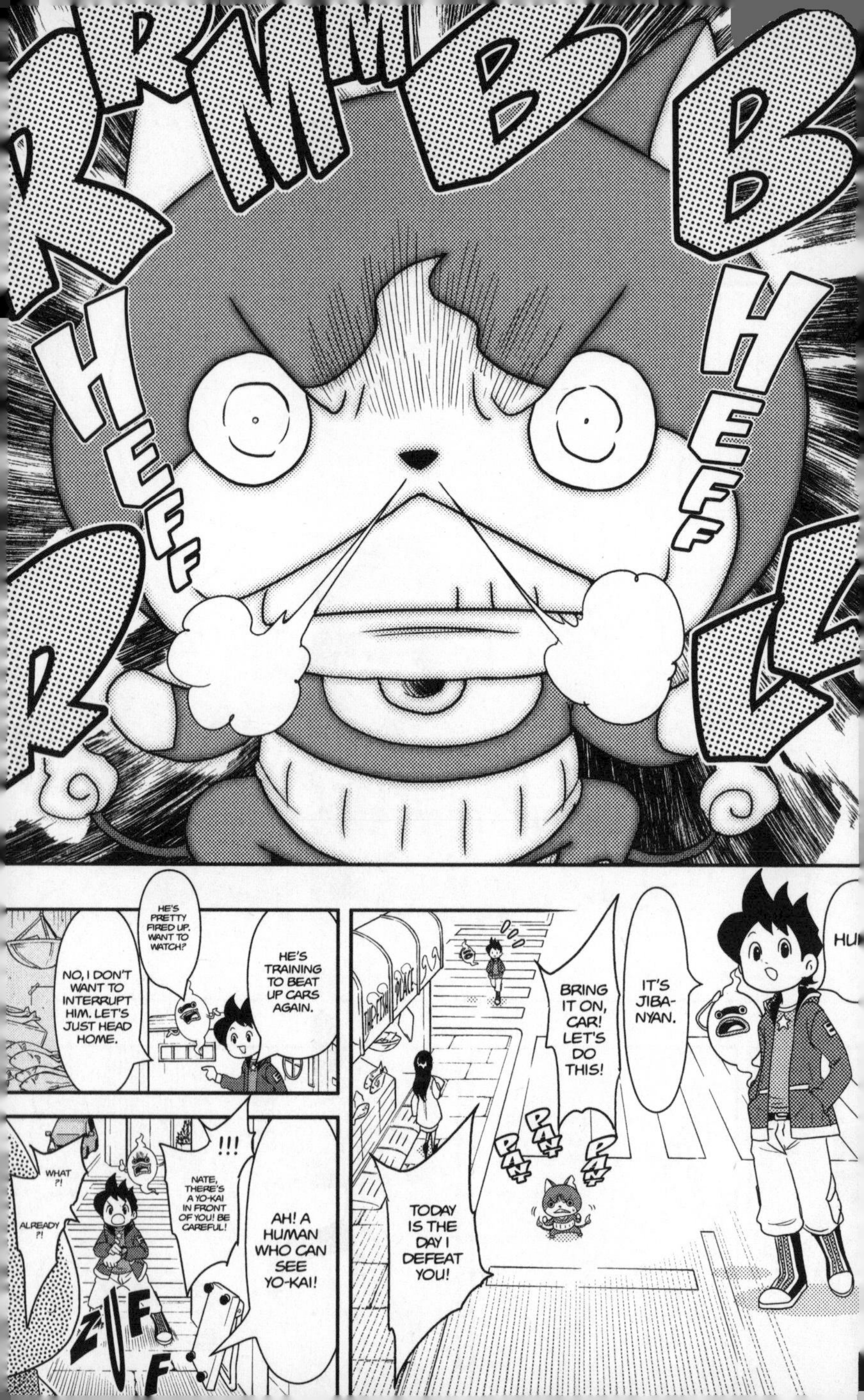
HEFF
HEFF
HU
IT'S JIBA-NYAN.
BRING IT ON, CAR! LET'S DO THIS!
PANT
PANT
PANT
TODAY IS THE DAY I DEFEAT YOU!
HE'S TRAINING TO BEAT UP CARS AGAIN.
HE'S PRETTY FIRED UP. WANT TO WATCH?
NO, I DON'T WANT TO INTERRUPT HIM. LET'S JUST HEAD HOME.
AH! A HUMAN WHO CAN SEE YO-KAI!
NATE, THERE'S A YO-KAI IN FRONT OF YOU! BE CAREFUL!
!!!
WHAT?!
ALREADY?!
ZIFF
F

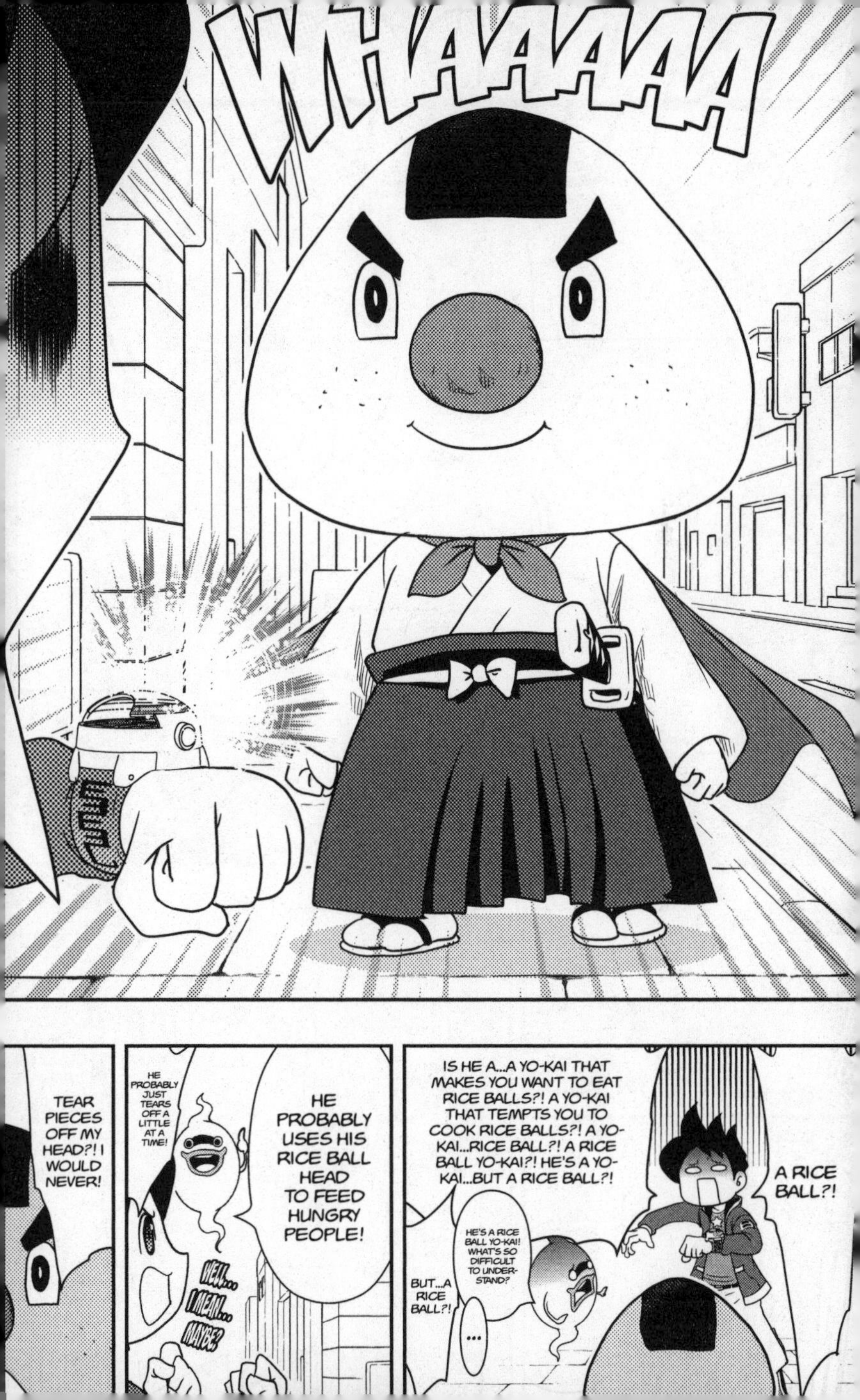
WHAAAAAA
A RICE BALL?!
IS HE A...A YO-KAI THAT MAKES YOU WANT TO EAT RICE BALLS?! A YO-KAI THAT TEMPTS YOU TO COOK RICE BALLS?! A YO-KAI...RICE BALL?! A RICE BALL YO-KAI?! HE'S A YO-KAI...BUT A RICE BALL?!
HE'S A RICE BALL YO-KAI! WHAT'S SO DIFFICULT TO UNDERSTAND?
BUT...A RICE BALL?!
...
HE PROBABLY USES HIS RICE BALL HEAD TO FEED HUNGRY PEOPLE!
HE PROBABLY JUST TEARS OFF A LITTLE AT A TIME!
WELL... I MEAN... MAYBE?
TEAR PIECES OFF MY HEAD?! I WOULD NEVER!

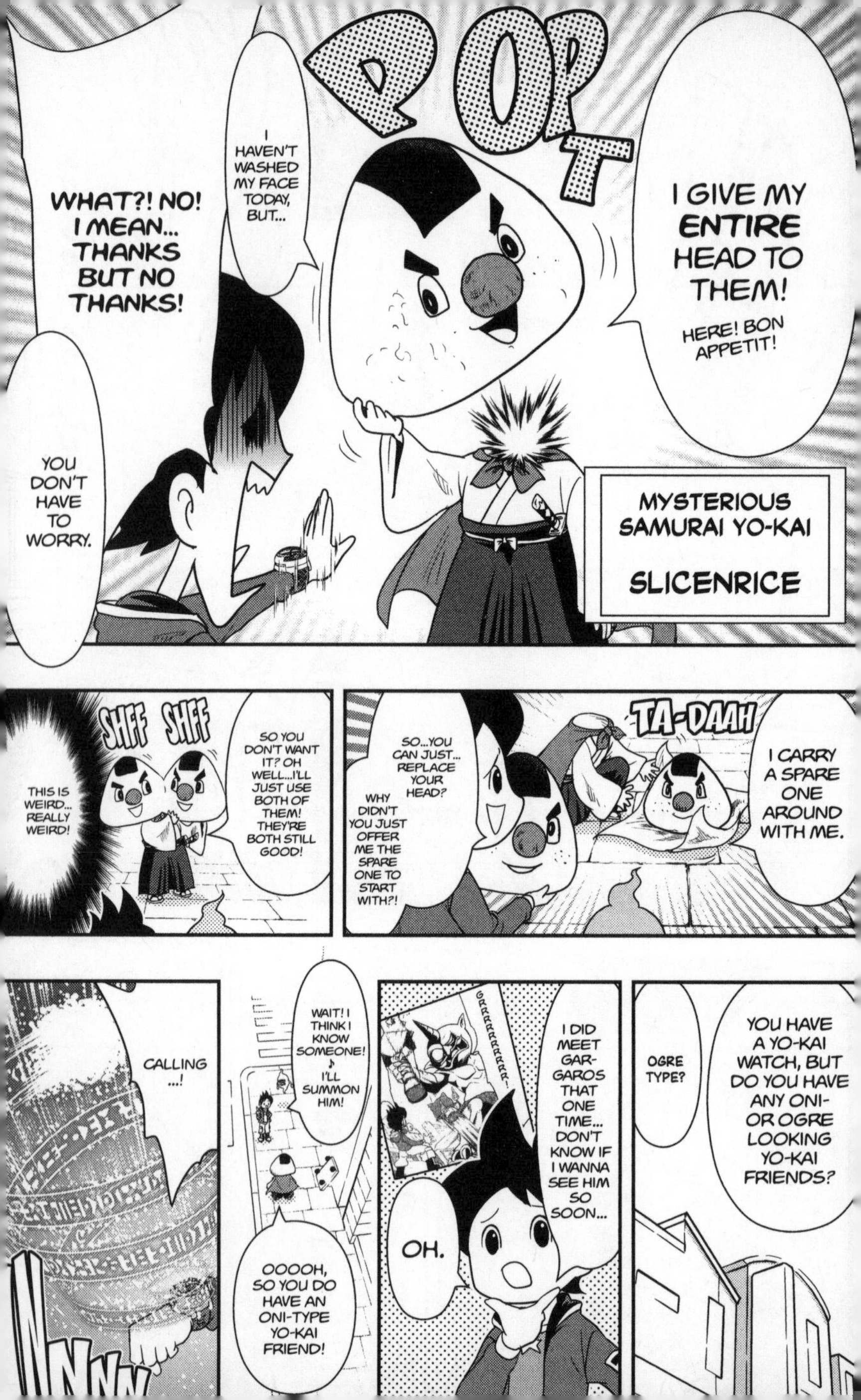
POP
I GIVE MY ENTIRE HEAD TO THEM!
HERE! BON APPETIT!
I HAVEN'T WASHED MY FACE TODAY, BUT...
WHAT?! NO! I MEAN... THANKS BUT NO THANKS!
MYSTERIOUS SAMURAI YO-KAI
SLICENRICE
YOU DON'T HAVE TO WORRY.
TA-DAAH
I CARRY A SPARE ONE AROUND WITH ME.
SO...YOU CAN JUST... REPLACE YOUR HEAD?
WHY DIDN'T YOU JUST OFFER ME THE SPARE ONE TO START WITH?!
SHFF SHFF
SO YOU DON'T WANT IT? OH WELL...I'LL JUST USE BOTH OF THEM! THEY'RE BOTH STILL GOOD!
THIS IS WEIRD... REALLY WEIRD!
YOU HAVE A YO-KAI WATCH, BUT DO YOU HAVE ANY ONI- OR OGRE LOOKING YO-KAI FRIENDS?
OGRE TYPE?
GRRRRRRRRRR-
I DID MEET GAR-GAROS THAT ONE TIME... DON'T KNOW IF I WANNA SEE HIM SO SOON...
OH.
WAIT! I THINK I KNOW SOMEONE! ♪ I'LL SUMMON HIM!
OOOOH, SO YOU DO HAVE AN ONI-TYPE YO-KAI FRIEND!
CALLING ...!
NNNN

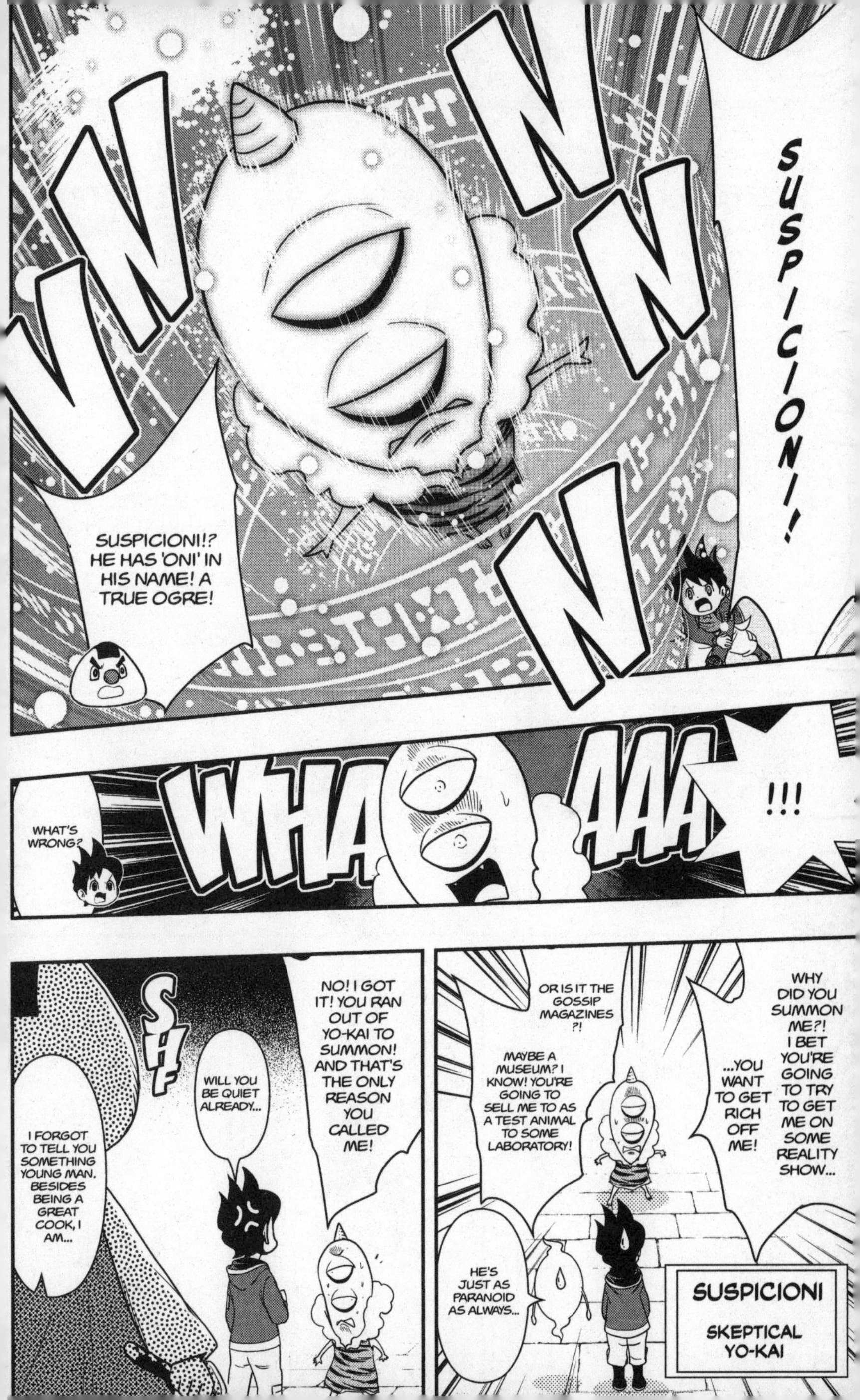
SUSPICIONI!
VWNNNN
SUSPICIONI!? HE HAS 'ONI' IN HIS NAME! A TRUE OGRE!
WHAAAA!!!
WHAT'S WRONG?
WHY DID YOU SUMMON ME?! I BET YOU'RE GOING TO TRY TO GET ME ON SOME REALITY SHOW...
...YOU WANT TO GET RICH OFF ME!
OR IS IT THE GOSSIP MAGAZINES?!
MAYBE A MUSEUM? I KNOW! YOU'RE GOING TO SELL ME TO AS A TEST ANIMAL TO SOME LABORATORY!
SUSPICIONI
SKEPTICAL YO-KAI
HE'S JUST AS PARANOID AS ALWAYS...
NO! I GOT IT! YOU RAN OUT OF YO-KAI TO SUMMON! AND THAT'S THE ONLY REASON YOU CALLED ME!
WILL YOU BE QUIET ALREADY...
SHF
I FORGOT TO TELL YOU SOMETHING YOUNG MAN. BESIDES BEING A GREAT COOK, I AM...

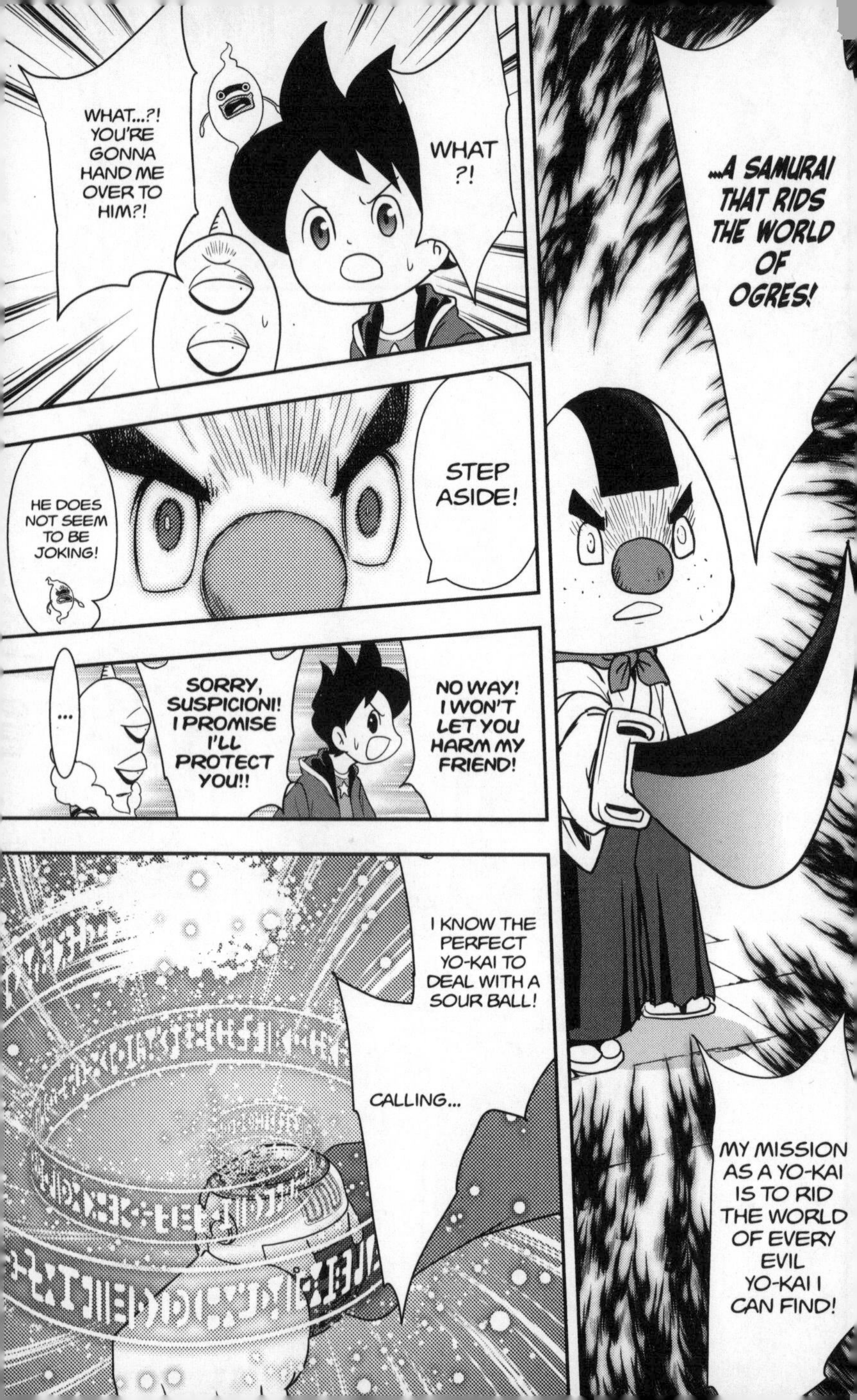
...A SAMURAI THAT RIDS THE WORLD OF OGRES!
MY MISSION AS A YO-KAI IS TO RID THE WORLD OF EVERY EVIL YO-KAI I CAN FIND!
WHAT ?!
WHAT...?! YOU'RE GONNA HAND ME OVER TO HIM?!
STEP ASIDE!
HE DOES NOT SEEM TO BE JOKING!
NO WAY! I WON'T LET YOU HARM MY FRIEND!
SORRY, SUSPICIONI! I PROMISE I'LL PROTECT YOU!!
...
I KNOW THE PERFECT YO-KAI TO DEAL WITH A SOUR BALL!
CALLING...

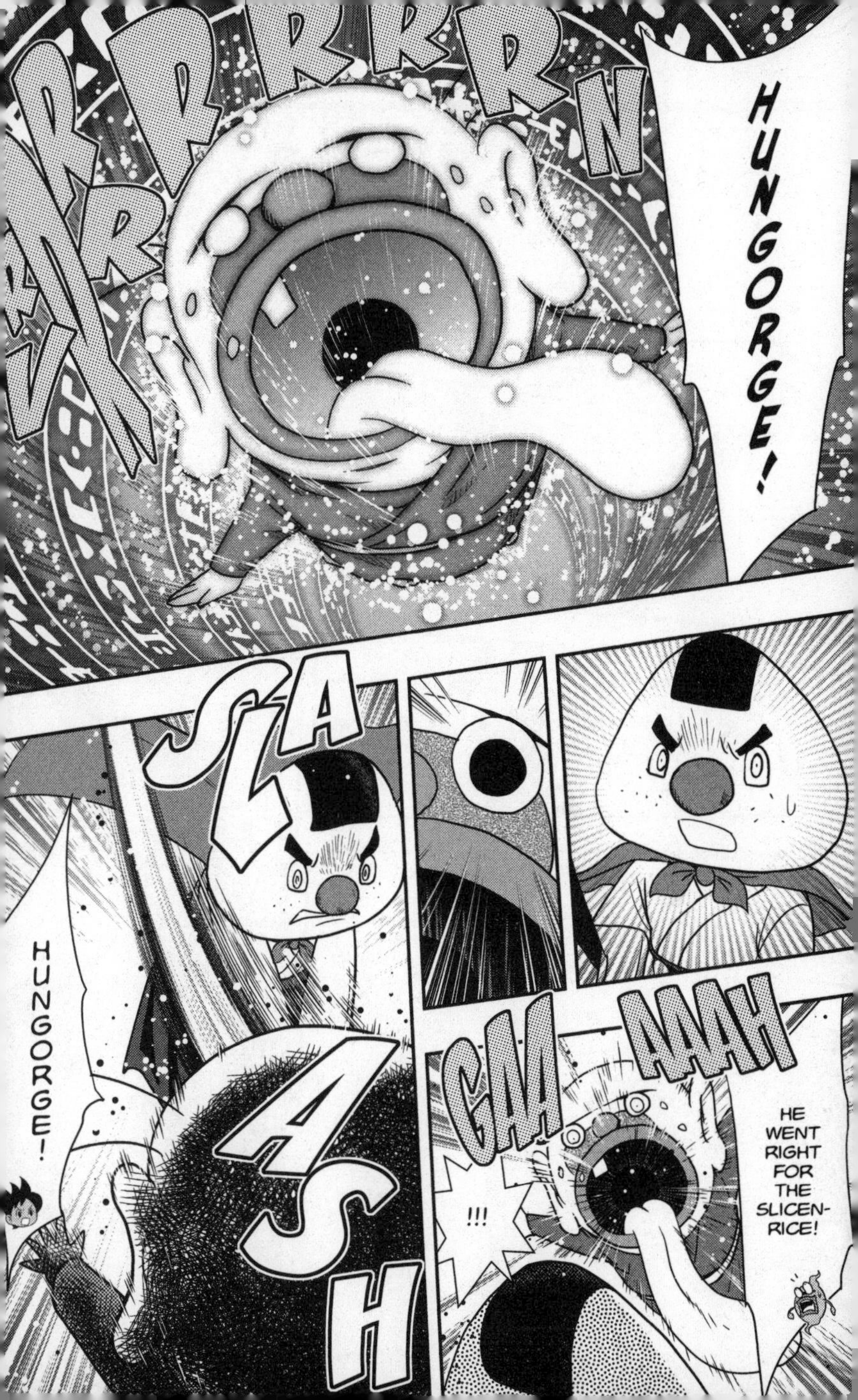
HUNGORGE!
RRRRRRRN
SLASH
HUNGORGE!
HE WENT RIGHT FOR THE SLICEN-RICE!
GAA-AAAH
!!!

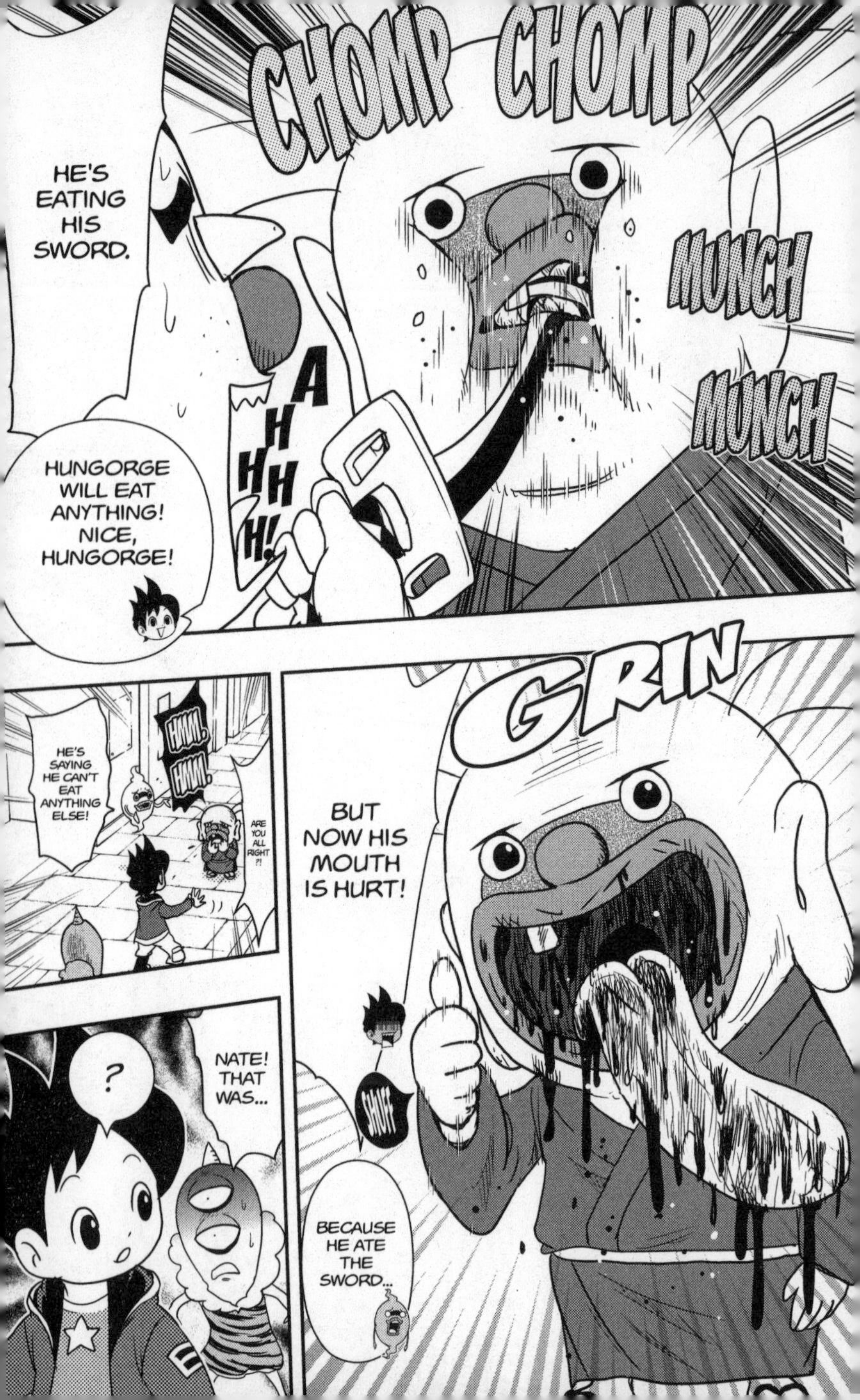
CHOMP CHOMP
MUNCH MUNCH
HE'S EATING HIS SWORD.
AHHHHH!
HUNGORGE WILL EAT ANYTHING! NICE, HUNGORGE!
GRIN
BUT NOW HIS MOUTH IS HURT!
SNIFF
BECAUSE HE ATE THE SWORD...
HMM. HMM.
ARE YOU ALL RIGHT?!
HE'S SAYING HE CAN'T EAT ANYTHING ELSE!
NATE! THAT WAS...
?

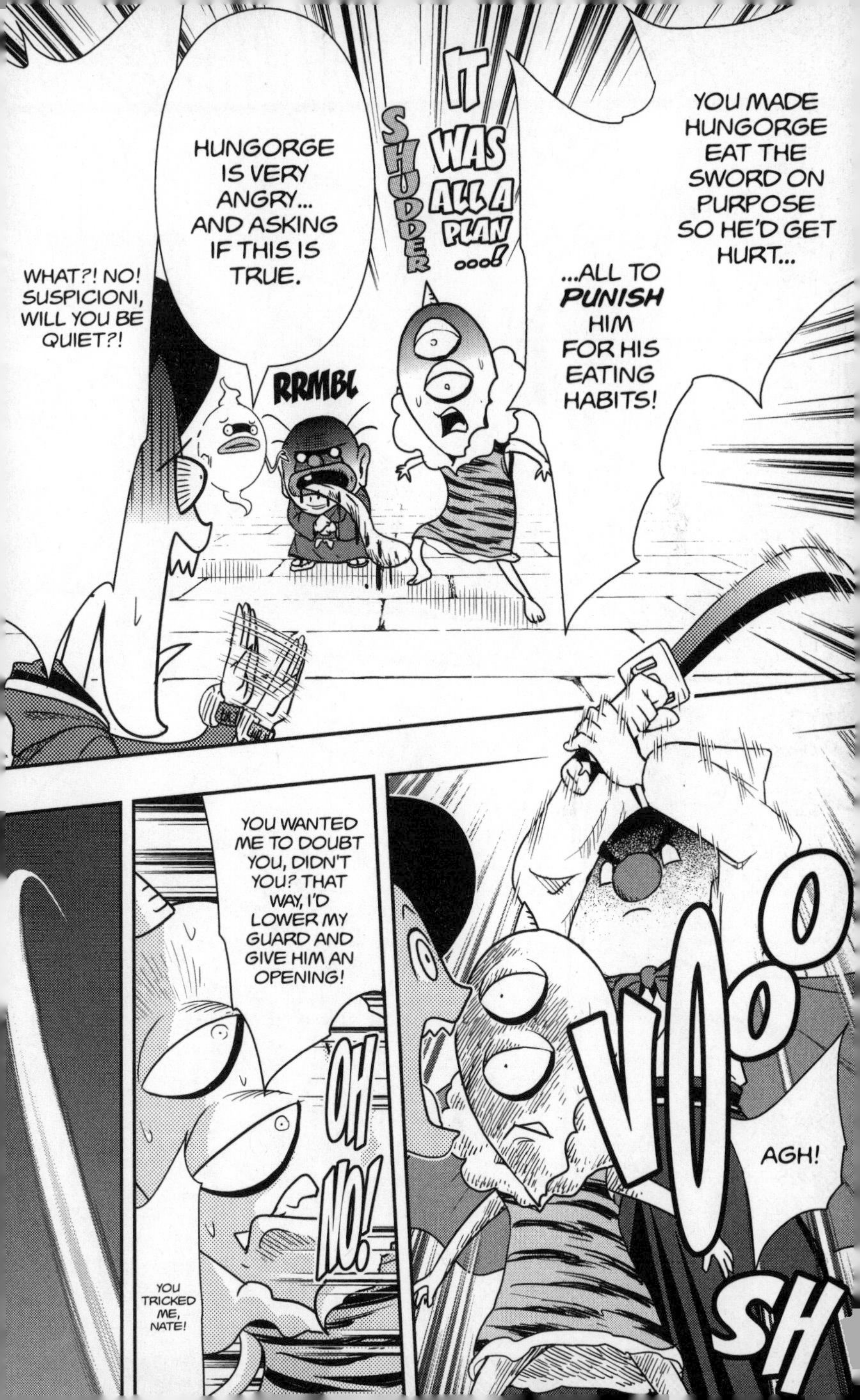

YOU MADE HUNGORGE EAT THE SWORD ON PURPOSE SO HE'D GET HURT...
...ALL TO **PUNISH** HIM FOR HIS EATING HABITS!
IT WAS ALL A PLAN ooo!
SHUDDER
HUNGORGE IS VERY ANGRY... AND ASKING IF THIS IS TRUE.
RRMBL
WHAT?! NO! SUSPICIONI, WILL YOU BE QUIET?!
AGH!
VOOOO
SH
YOU WANTED ME TO DOUBT YOU, DIDN'T YOU? THAT WAY, I'D LOWER MY GUARD AND GIVE HIM AN OPENING!
OH NO!
YOU TRICKED ME, NATE!

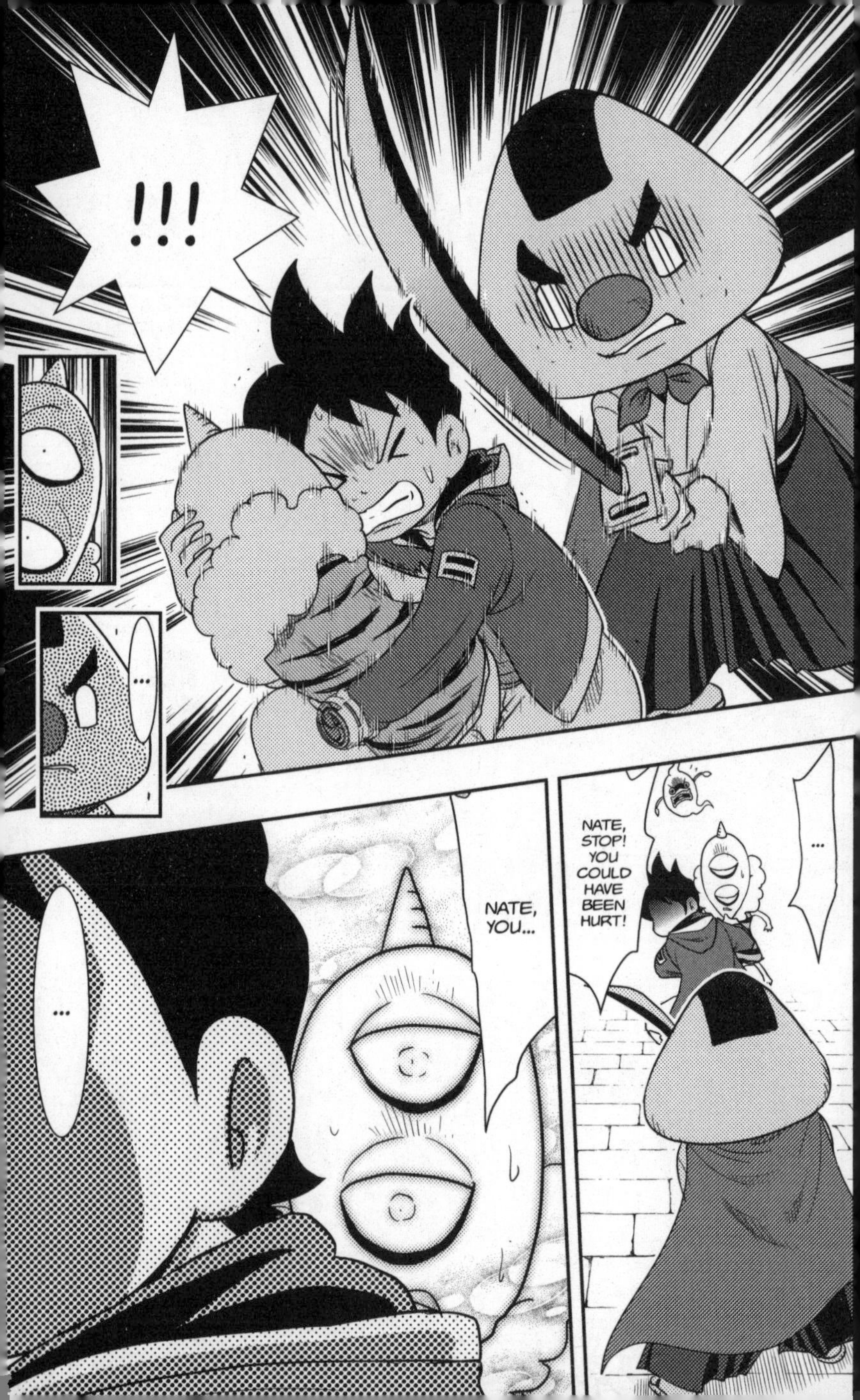
!!!
...
...
NATE, STOP! YOU COULD HAVE BEEN HURT!
NATE, YOU...
...

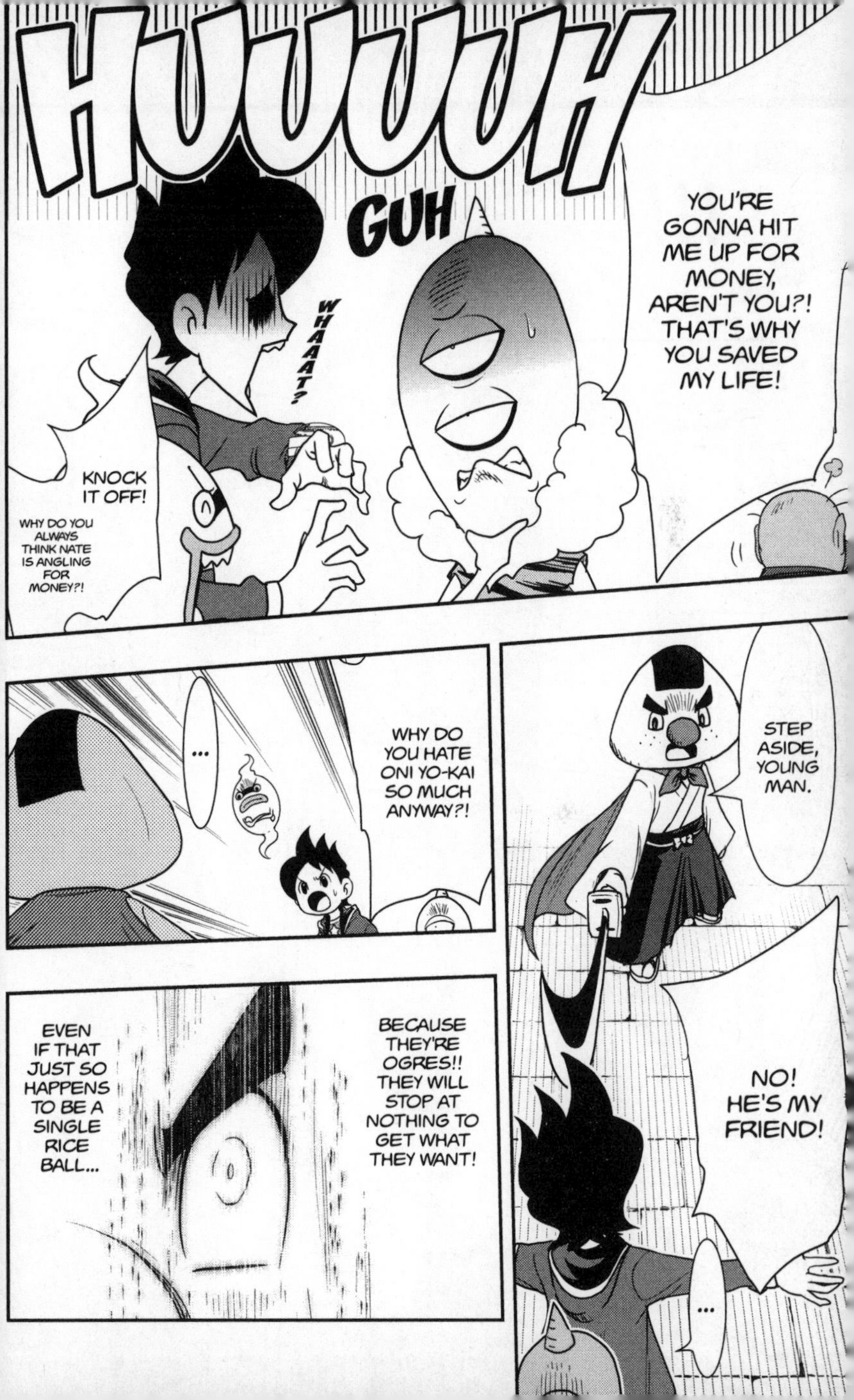
HUUUUH
YOU'RE GONNA HIT ME UP FOR MONEY, AREN'T YOU?! THAT'S WHY YOU SAVED MY LIFE!
GUH
WHAAAT?
KNOCK IT OFF!
WHY DO YOU ALWAYS THINK NATE IS ANGLING FOR MONEY?!
STEP ASIDE, YOUNG MAN.
NO! HE'S MY FRIEND!
...
WHY DO YOU HATE ONI YO-KAI SO MUCH ANYWAY?!
...
BECAUSE THEY'RE OGRES!! THEY WILL STOP AT NOTHING TO GET WHAT THEY WANT!
EVEN IF THAT JUST SO HAPPENS TO BE A SINGLE RICE BALL...

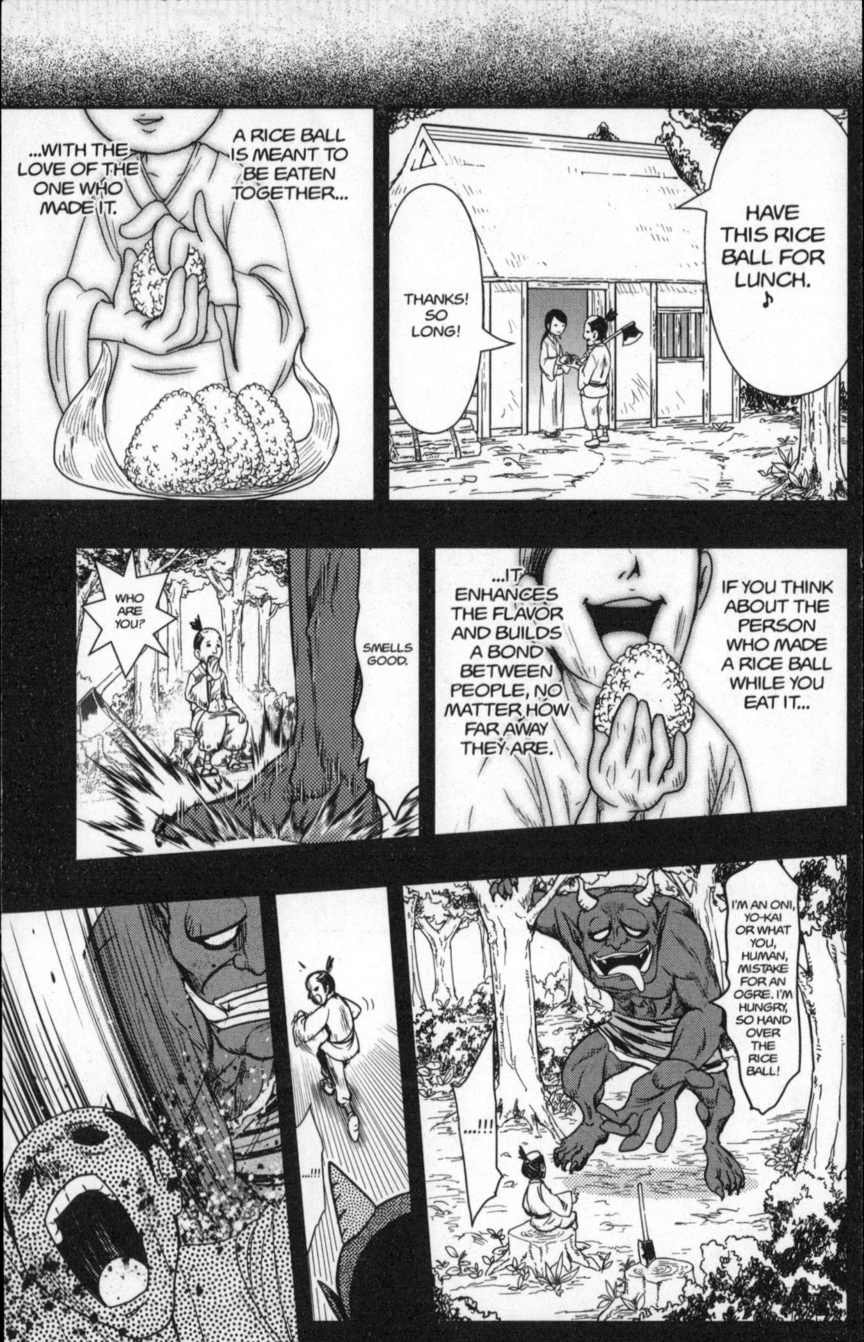
HAVE THIS RICE BALL FOR LUNCH. ♪
THANKS! SO LONG!
A RICE BALL IS MEANT TO BE EATEN TOGETHER...
...WITH THE LOVE OF THE ONE WHO MADE IT.
IF YOU THINK ABOUT THE PERSON WHO MADE A RICE BALL WHILE YOU EAT IT...
...IT ENHANCES THE FLAVOR AND BUILDS A BOND BETWEEN PEOPLE, NO MATTER HOW FAR AWAY THEY ARE.
SMELLS GOOD.
WHO ARE YOU?
I'M AN ONI, YO-KAI OR WHAT YOU, HUMAN, MISTAKE FOR AN OGRE. I'M HUNGRY, SO HAND OVER THE RICE BALL!
...!!!
...!!!

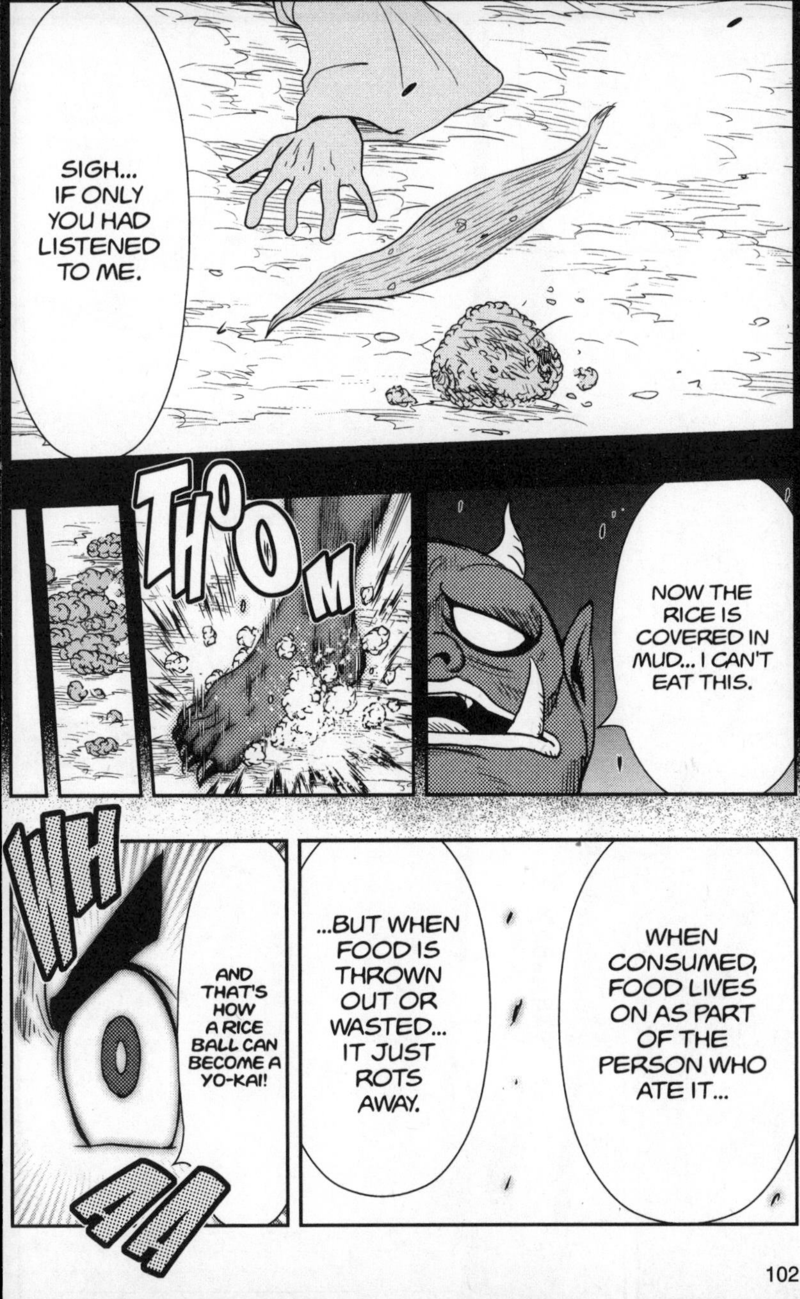
SIGH... IF ONLY YOU HAD LISTENED TO ME.
NOW THE RICE IS COVERED IN MUD... I CAN'T EAT THIS.
THOOM
WHEN CONSUMED, FOOD LIVES ON AS PART OF THE PERSON WHO ATE IT...
...BUT WHEN FOOD IS THROWN OUT OR WASTED... IT JUST ROTS AWAY.
AND THAT'S HOW A RICE BALL CAN BECOME A YO-KAI!
WHOAA

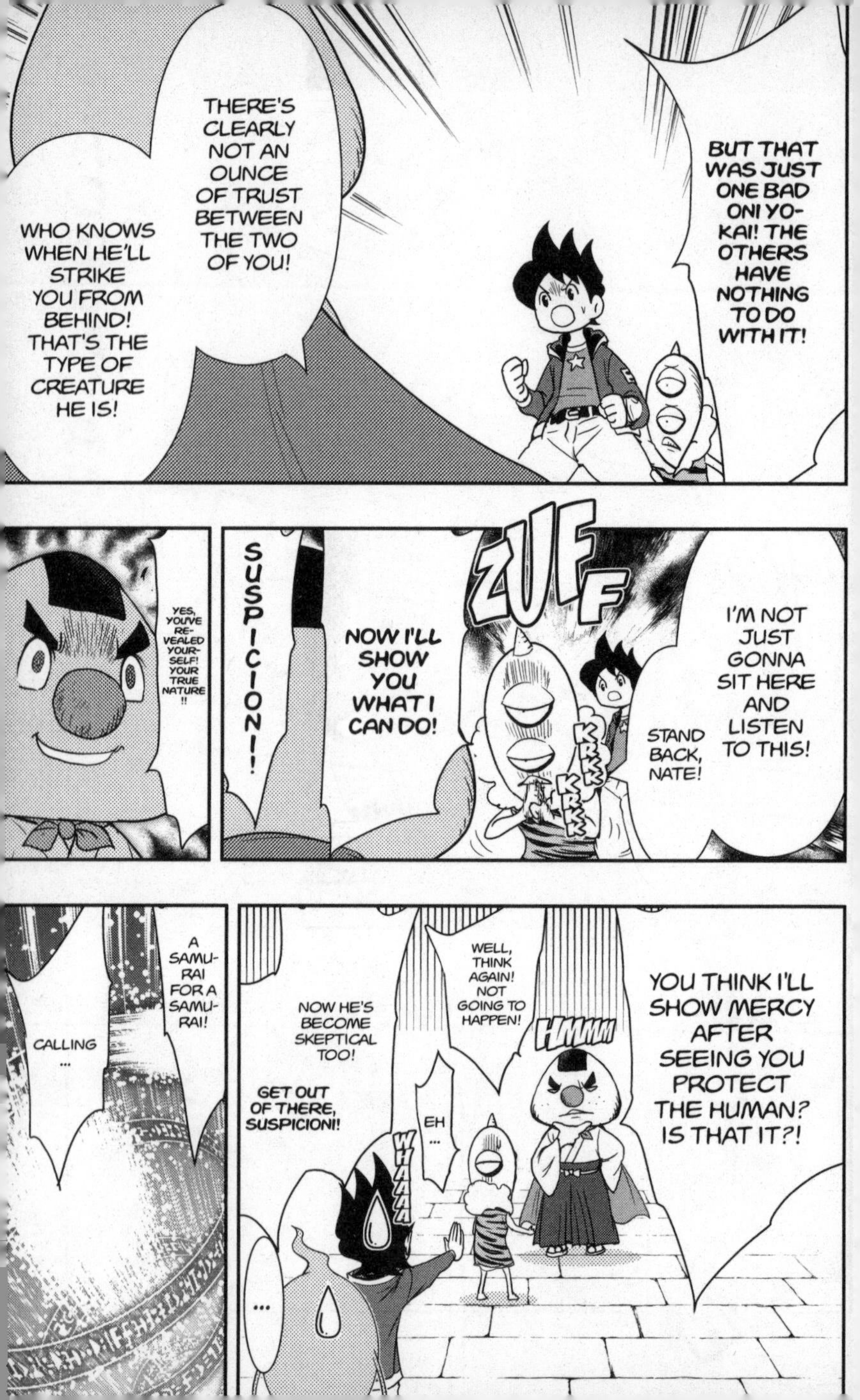
BUT THAT WAS JUST ONE BAD ONI YO-KAI! THE OTHERS HAVE NOTHING TO DO WITH IT!
THERE'S CLEARLY NOT AN OUNCE OF TRUST BETWEEN THE TWO OF YOU!
WHO KNOWS WHEN HE'LL STRIKE YOU FROM BEHIND! THAT'S THE TYPE OF CREATURE HE IS!
I'M NOT JUST GONNA SIT HERE AND LISTEN TO THIS!
STAND BACK, NATE!
ZUFF
KRKK KRKK
NOW I'LL SHOW YOU WHAT I CAN DO!
SUSPICION!!
YES, YOU'VE REVEALED YOURSELF! YOUR TRUE NATURE!!
YOU THINK I'LL SHOW MERCY AFTER SEEING YOU PROTECT THE HUMAN? IS THAT IT?!
HMMM
WELL, THINK AGAIN! NOT GOING TO HAPPEN!
NOW HE'S BECOME SKEPTICAL TOO!
EH ...
WHAAAA
GET OUT OF THERE, SUSPICIONI!
...
A SAMURAI FOR A SAMURAI!
CALLING ...

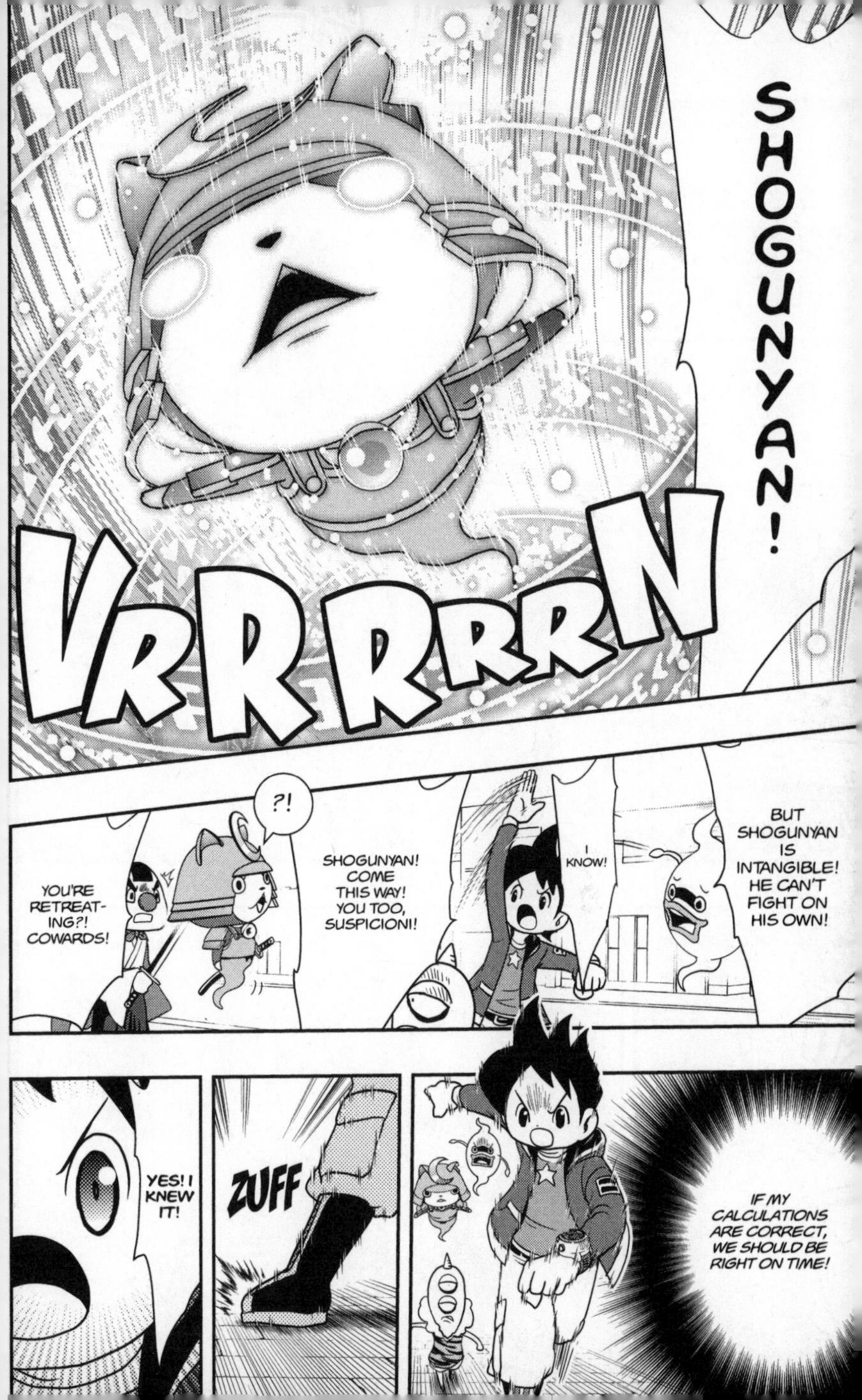
SHOGUNYAN!
VRRRRRN
BUT SHOGUNYAN IS INTANGIBLE! HE CAN'T FIGHT ON HIS OWN!
I KNOW!
SHOGUNYAN! COME THIS WAY! YOU TOO, SUSPICIONI!
?!
YOU'RE RETREAT-ING?! COWARDS!
IF MY CALCULATIONS ARE CORRECT, WE SHOULD BE RIGHT ON TIME!
ZUFF
YES! I KNEW IT!

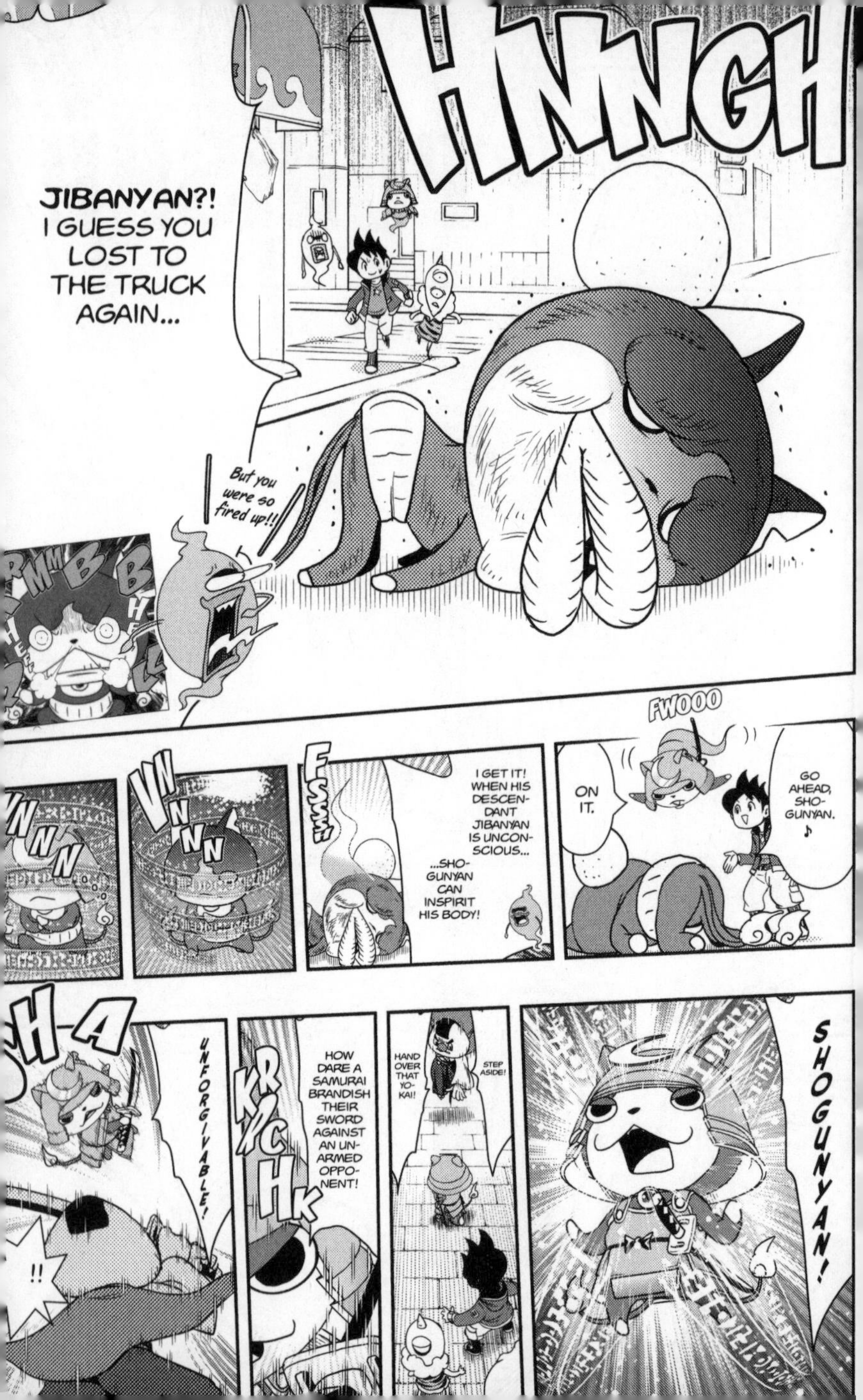
HNNNGH
JIBANYAN?! I GUESS YOU LOST TO THE TRUCK AGAIN...
But you were so fired up!!
FWOOO
GO AHEAD, SHOGUNYAN. ♪
ON IT.
I GET IT! WHEN HIS DESCENDANT JIBANYAN IS UNCONSCIOUS...
...SHOGUNYAN CAN INSPIRIT HIS BODY!
FSSSH
VNNNN
VNNNN
SHOGUNYAN!
STEP ASIDE!
HAND OVER THAT YO-KAI!
HOW DARE A SAMURAI BRANDISH THEIR SWORD AGAINST AN UNARMED OPPONENT!
KRKCHK
UNFORGIVABLE!
!!

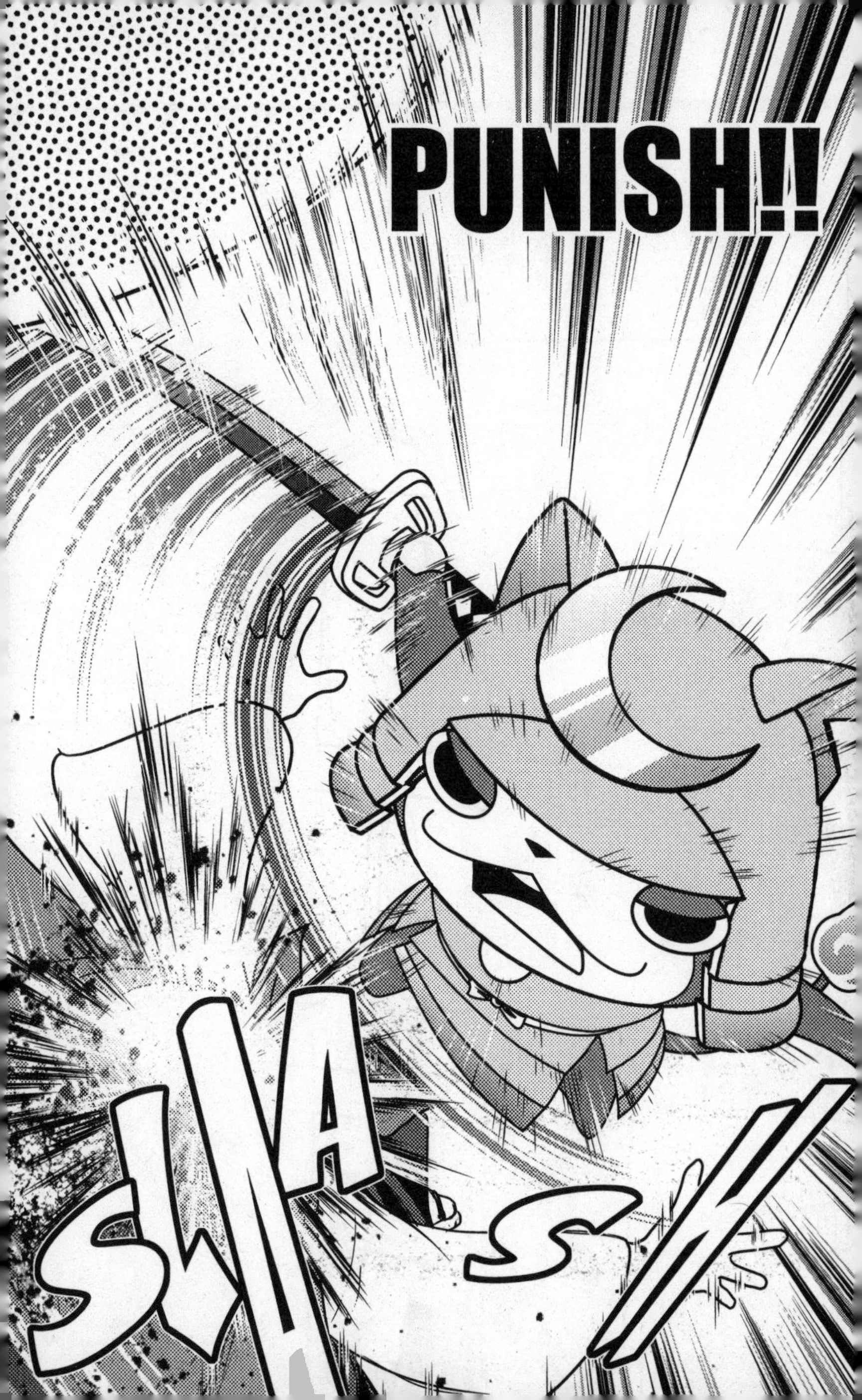
PUNISH!!
SLASH

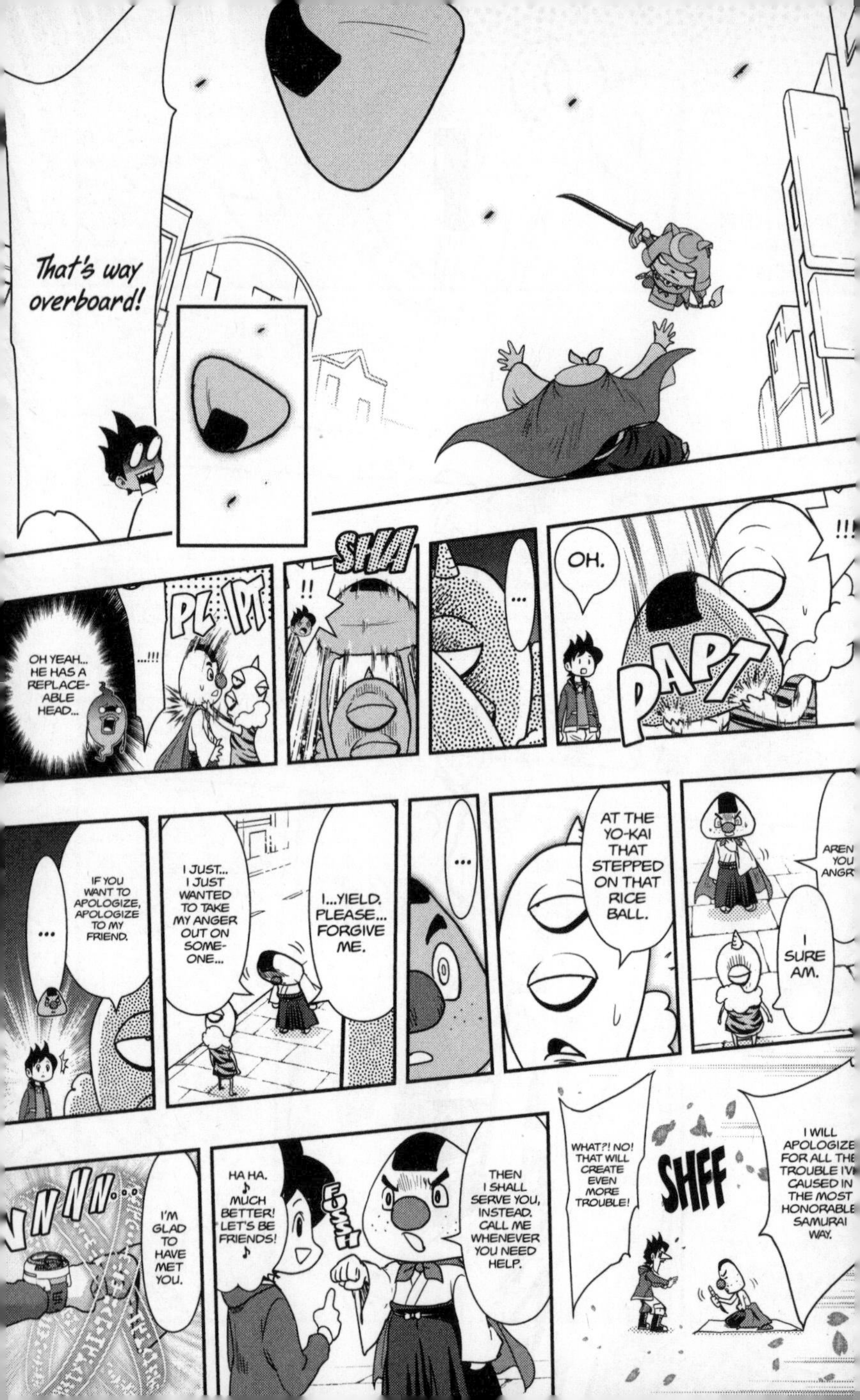
That's way overboard!
!!!
PAPT
OH.
...
SHA
!!
PLIPT
...!!!
OH YEAH... HE HAS A REPLACE-ABLE HEAD...
AREN YOU ANGR
I SURE AM.
AT THE YO-KAI THAT STEPPED ON THAT RICE BALL.
...
I...YIELD. PLEASE... FORGIVE ME.
I JUST... I JUST WANTED TO TAKE MY ANGER OUT ON SOME-ONE...
IF YOU WANT TO APOLOGIZE, APOLOGIZE TO MY FRIEND.
...
I WILL APOLOGIZE FOR ALL THE TROUBLE I'V CAUSED IN THE MOST HONORABLE SAMURAI WAY.
SHFF
WHAT?! NO! THAT WILL CREATE EVEN MORE TROUBLE!
THEN I SHALL SERVE YOU, INSTEAD. CALL ME WHENEVER YOU NEED HELP.
HA HA. ♪ MUCH BETTER! LET'S BE FRIENDS! ♪
I'M GLAD TO HAVE MET YOU.

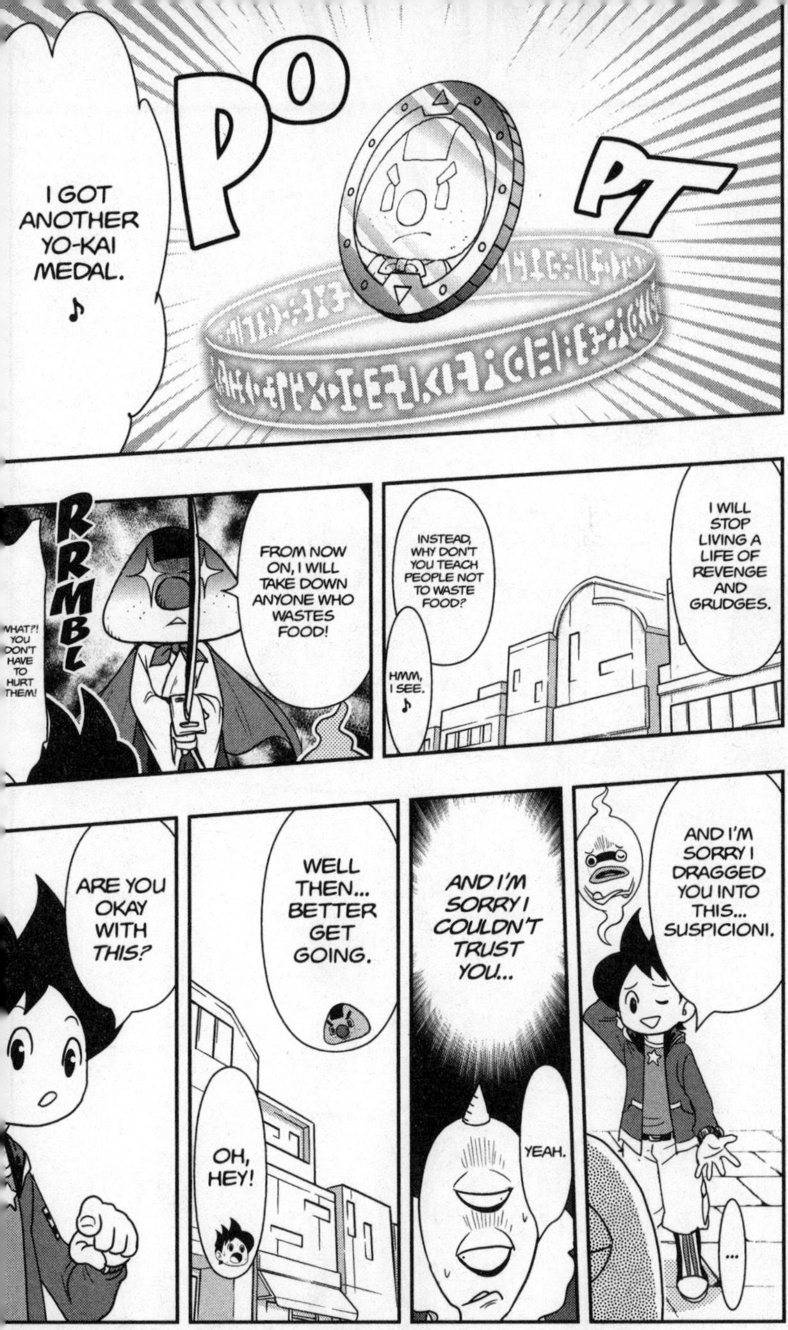
POOPT
I GOT ANOTHER YO-KAI MEDAL. ♪
I WILL STOP LIVING A LIFE OF REVENGE AND GRUDGES.
INSTEAD, WHY DON'T YOU TEACH PEOPLE NOT TO WASTE FOOD?
HMM, I SEE. ♪
FROM NOW ON, I WILL TAKE DOWN ANYONE WHO WASTES FOOD!
RRMBL
WHAT?! YOU DON'T HAVE TO HURT THEM!
AND I'M SORRY I DRAGGED YOU INTO THIS... SUSPICIONI.
...
AND I'M SORRY I COULDN'T TRUST YOU...
YEAH.
WELL THEN... BETTER GET GOING.
OH, HEY!
ARE YOU OKAY WITH THIS?

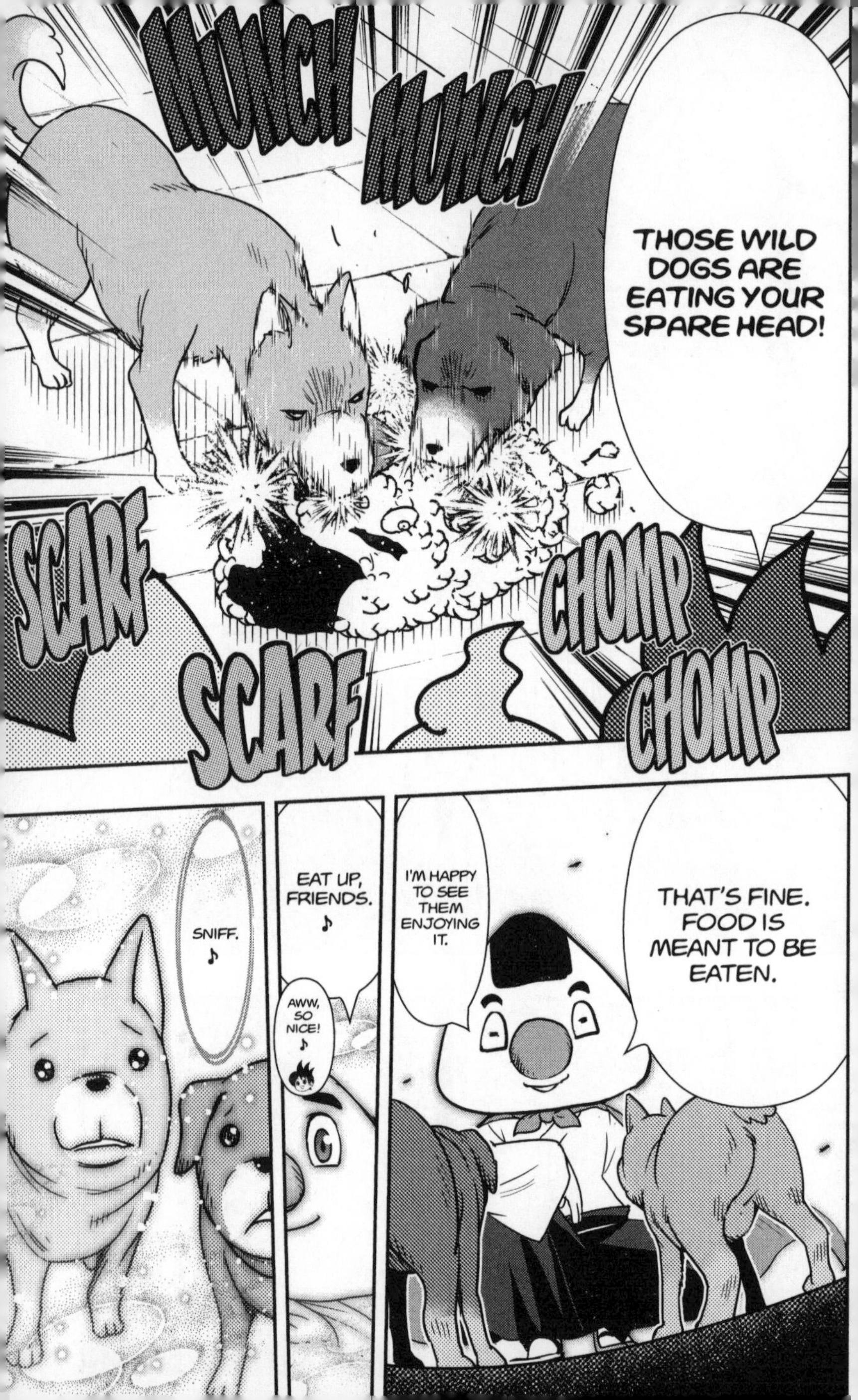
THOSE WILD DOGS ARE EATING YOUR SPARE HEAD!
MUNCH MUNCH
CHOMP CHOMP
SCARF SCARF
THAT'S FINE. FOOD IS MEANT TO BE EATEN.
I'M HAPPY TO SEE THEM ENJOYING IT.
EAT UP, FRIENDS. ♪
AWW, SO NICE! ♪
SNIFF. ♪

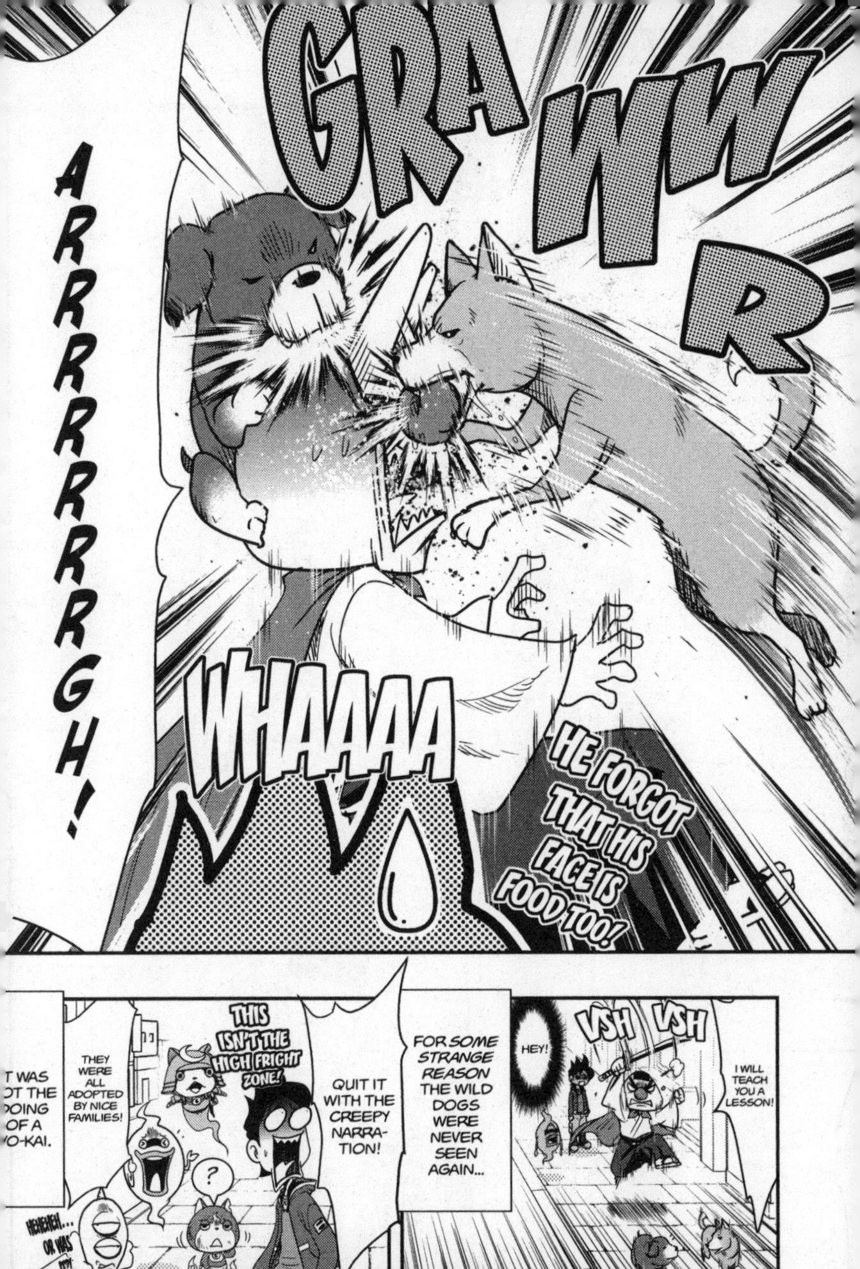
GRAWWR
ARRRRRRRRRGH!
WHAAAA
HE FORGOT THAT HIS FACE IS FOOD TOO!
I WILL TEACH YOU A LESSON!
VSH VSH
HEY!
FOR SOME STRANGE REASON THE WILD DOGS WERE NEVER SEEN AGAIN...
QUIT IT WITH THE CREEPY NARRATION!
THIS ISN'T THE HIGH FRIGHT ZONE!
THEY WERE ALL ADOPTED BY NICE FAMILIES!
?
HEHEHEH... OR WAS IT?!
T WAS OT THE DOING OF A O-KAI.

NATE ADAMS'S CURRENT NUMBER OF YO-KAI FRIENDS: 62

CHAPTER 94
DRENCHED IN YOU-KNOW-WHAT!
FEATURING WETTING YO-KAI FIDGEPHANT

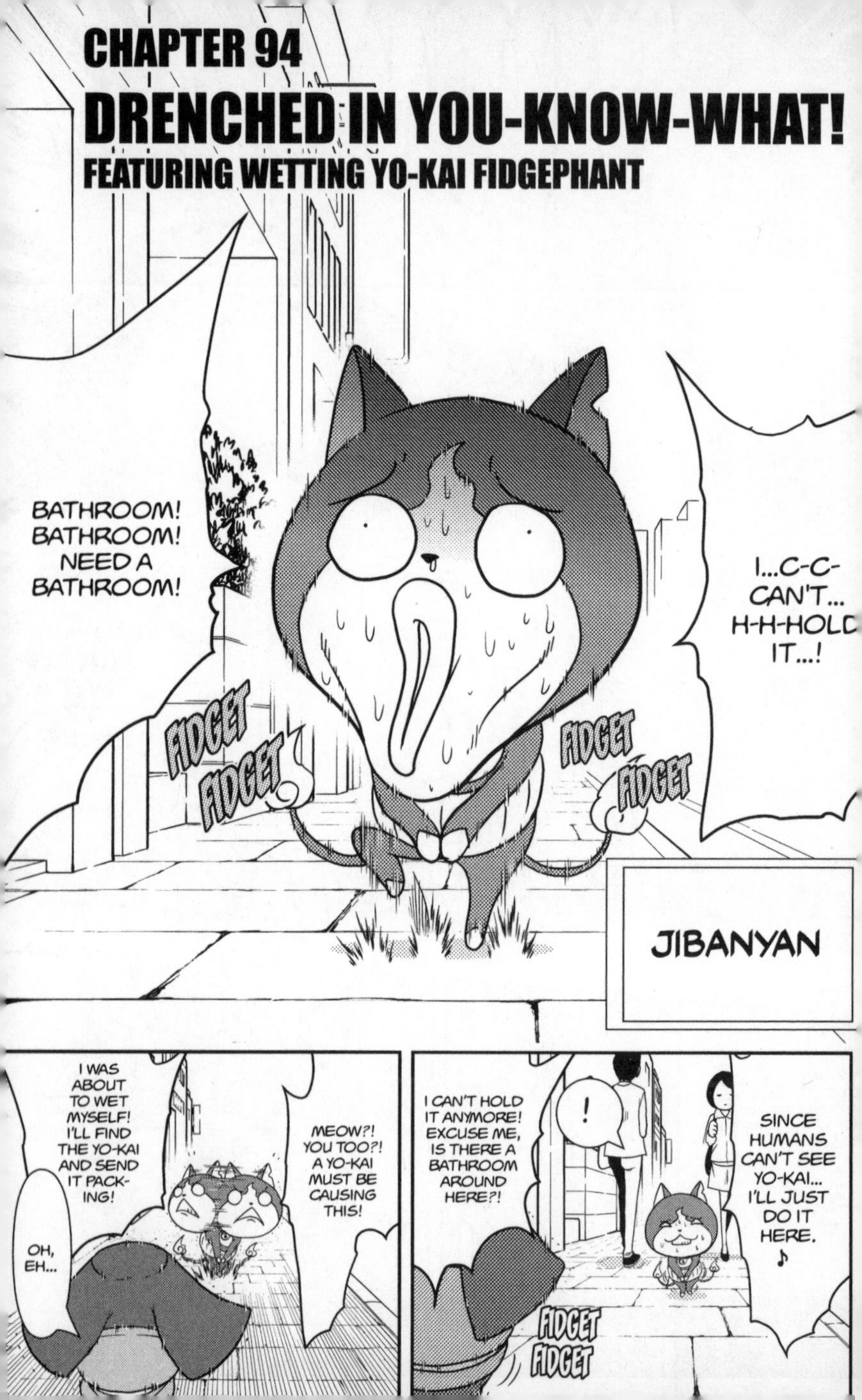
I...C-C-CAN'T... H-H-HOLD IT...!
BATHROOM! BATHROOM! NEED A BATHROOM!
FIDGET FIDGET
FIDGET FIDGET
JIBANYAN
SINCE HUMANS CAN'T SEE YO-KAI... I'LL JUST DO IT HERE. ♪
!
I CAN'T HOLD IT ANYMORE! EXCUSE ME, IS THERE A BATHROOM AROUND HERE?!
FIDGET FIDGET
MEOW?! YOU TOO?! A YO-KAI MUST BE CAUSING THIS!
I WAS ABOUT TO WET MYSELF! I'LL FIND THE YO-KAI AND SEND IT PACK-ING!
OH, EH...

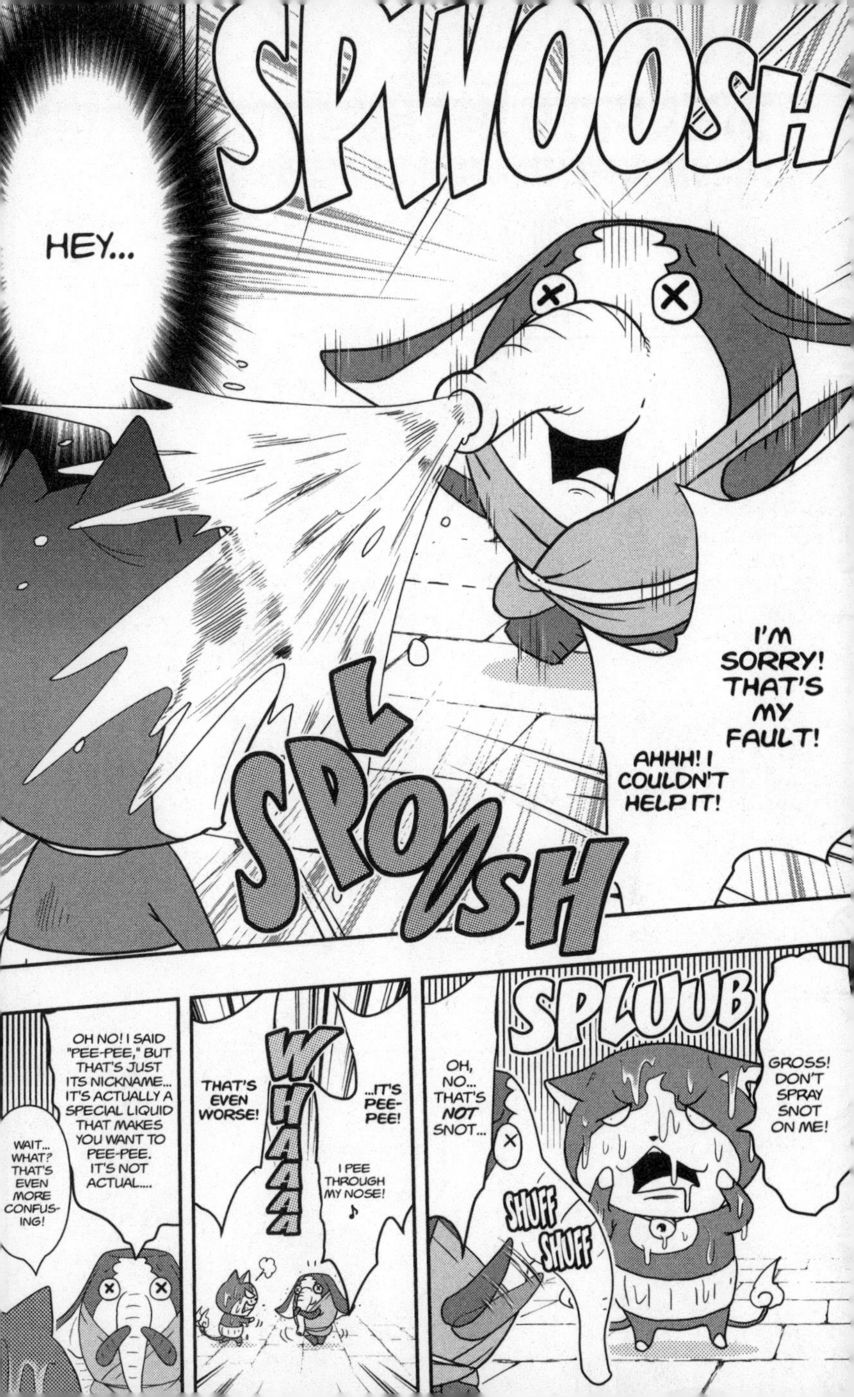
SPWOOSH
HEY...
I'M SORRY! THAT'S MY FAULT!
AHHH! I COULDN'T HELP IT!
SPLOOSH
SPLUUB
GROSS! DON'T SPRAY SNOT ON ME!
OH, NO... THAT'S NOT SNOT...
SHUFF SHUFF
...IT'S PEE-PEE!
WHAAAAA
THAT'S EVEN WORSE!
I PEE THROUGH MY NOSE! ♪
OH NO! I SAID "PEE-PEE," BUT THAT'S JUST ITS NICKNAME... IT'S ACTUALLY A SPECIAL LIQUID THAT MAKES YOU WANT TO PEE-PEE. IT'S NOT ACTUAL....
WAIT... WHAT? THAT'S EVEN MORE CONFUS-ING!

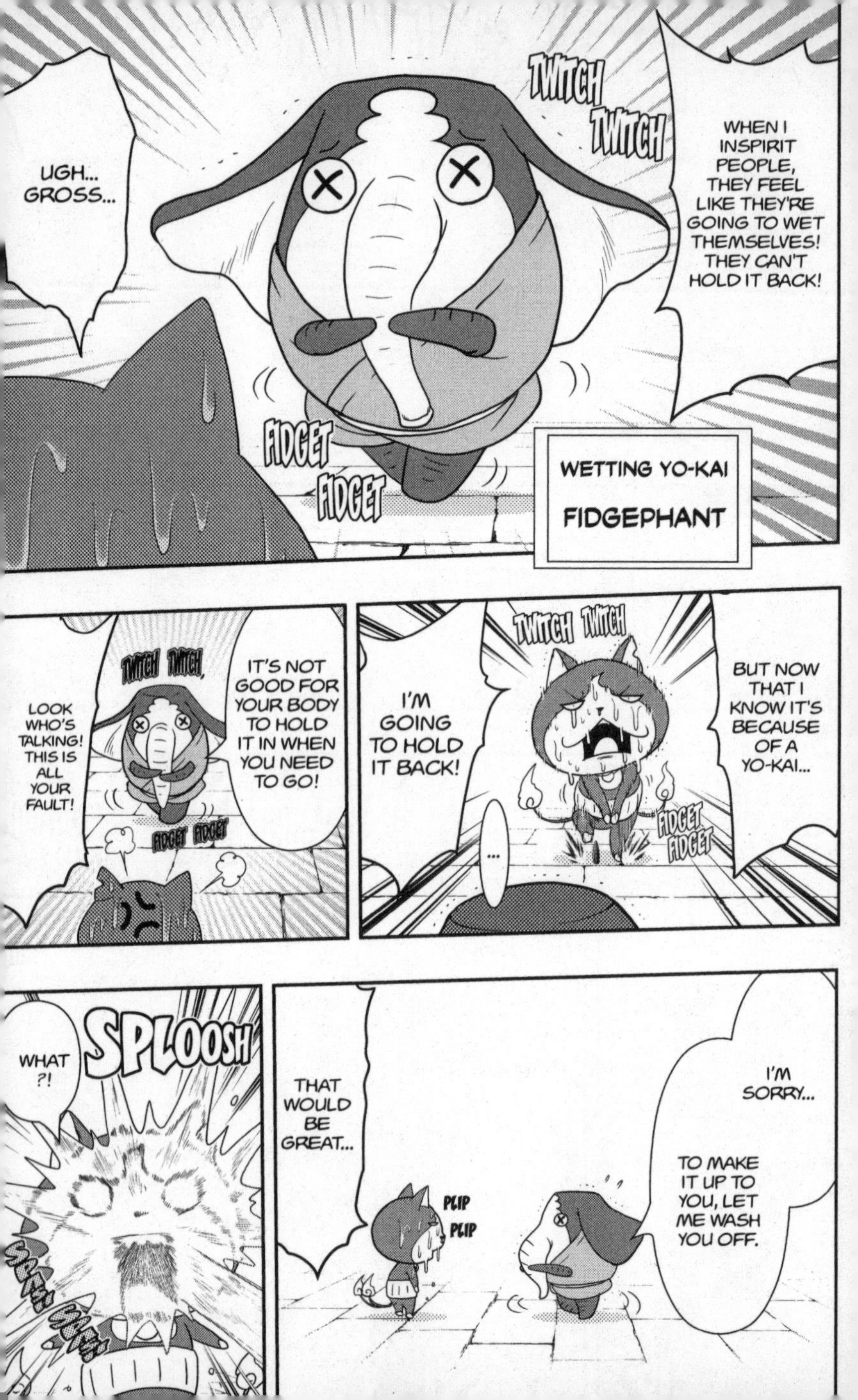
WHEN I INSPIRIT PEOPLE, THEY FEEL LIKE THEY'RE GOING TO WET THEMSELVES! THEY CAN'T HOLD IT BACK!
TWITCH TWITCH
UGH... GROSS...
WETTING YO-KAI
FIDGEPHANT
FIDGET FIDGET
BUT NOW THAT I KNOW IT'S BECAUSE OF A YO-KAI...
TWITCH TWITCH
I'M GOING TO HOLD IT BACK!
FIDGET FIDGET
...
IT'S NOT GOOD FOR YOUR BODY TO HOLD IT IN WHEN YOU NEED TO GO!
TWITCH TWITCH,
LOOK WHO'S TALKING! THIS IS ALL YOUR FAULT!
FIDGET FIDGET
I'M SORRY...
TO MAKE IT UP TO YOU, LET ME WASH YOU OFF.
THAT WOULD BE GREAT...
PLIP PLIP
SPLOOSH
WHAT ?!

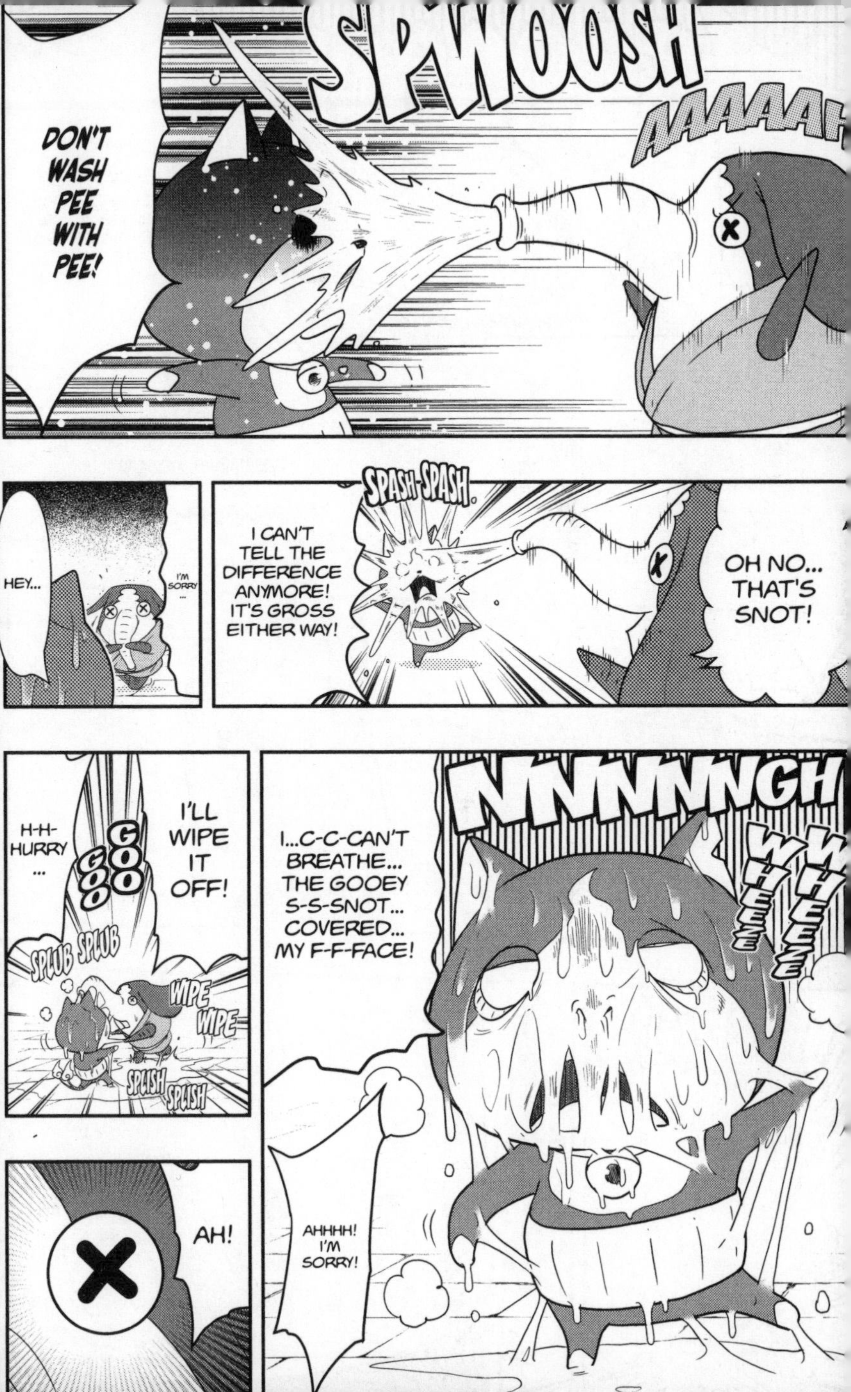
SPWOOSH
AAAAAH
DON'T WASH PEE WITH PEE!
SPASH-SPASH
OH NO... THAT'S SNOT!
I CAN'T TELL THE DIFFERENCE ANYMORE! IT'S GROSS EITHER WAY!
I'M SORRY...
HEY...
NNNNNGH
WHEEZE WHEEZE
I...C-C-CAN'T BREATHE... THE GOOEY S-S-SNOT... COVERED... MY F-F-FACE!
AHHHH! I'M SORRY!
I'LL WIPE IT OFF!
GOO GOO
H-H-HURRY...
SPLUB SPLUB
WIPE WIPE
SPLISH SPLISH
AH!

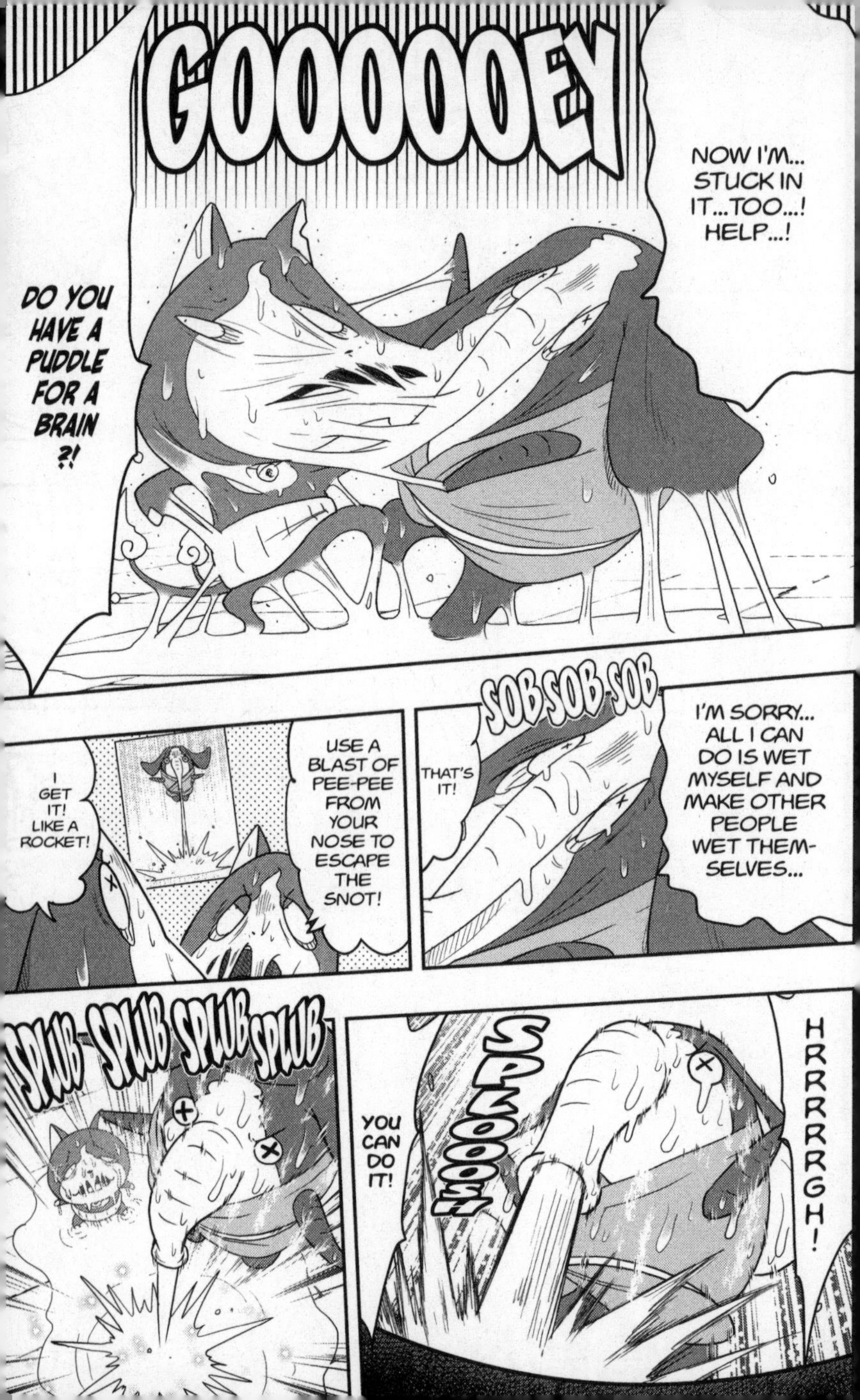
GOOOOOEY
NOW I'M... STUCK IN IT...TOO...! HELP...!
DO YOU HAVE A PUDDLE FOR A BRAIN ?!
SOB SOB SOB
I'M SORRY... ALL I CAN DO IS WET MYSELF AND MAKE OTHER PEOPLE WET THEMSELVES...
THAT'S IT!
USE A BLAST OF PEE-PEE FROM YOUR NOSE TO ESCAPE THE SNOT!
I GET IT! LIKE A ROCKET!
HRRRRRGH!
SPLOOOOSH!
YOU CAN DO IT!
SPLUB-SPLUB SPLUB SPLUB

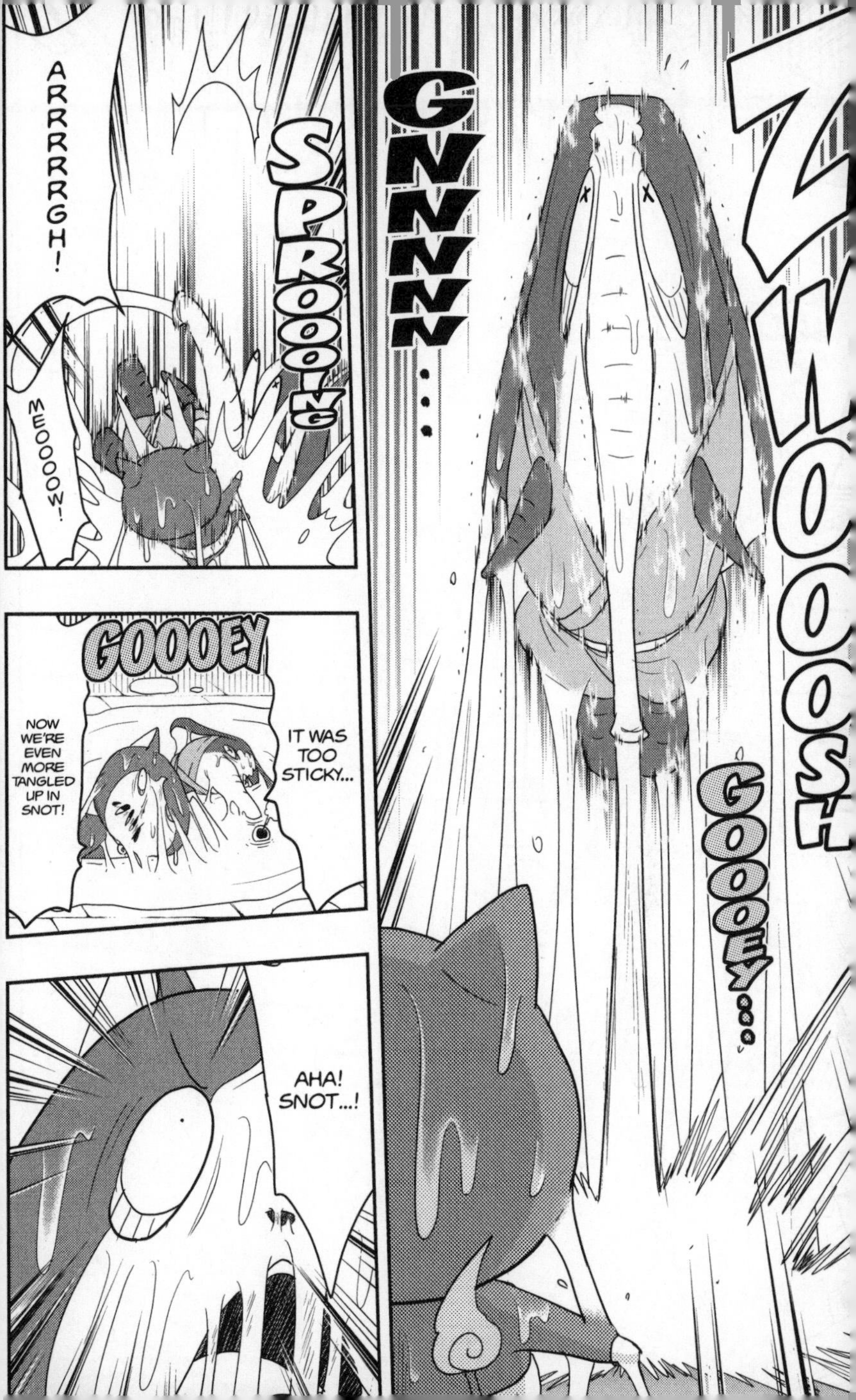
ZWOOOSH
GNNNN...
GOOOEY...
SPROOOING
ARRRRRGH!
MEOOOOW!
GOOOEY
IT WAS TOO STICKY...
NOW WE'RE EVEN MORE TANGLED UP IN SNOT!
AHA! SNOT...!

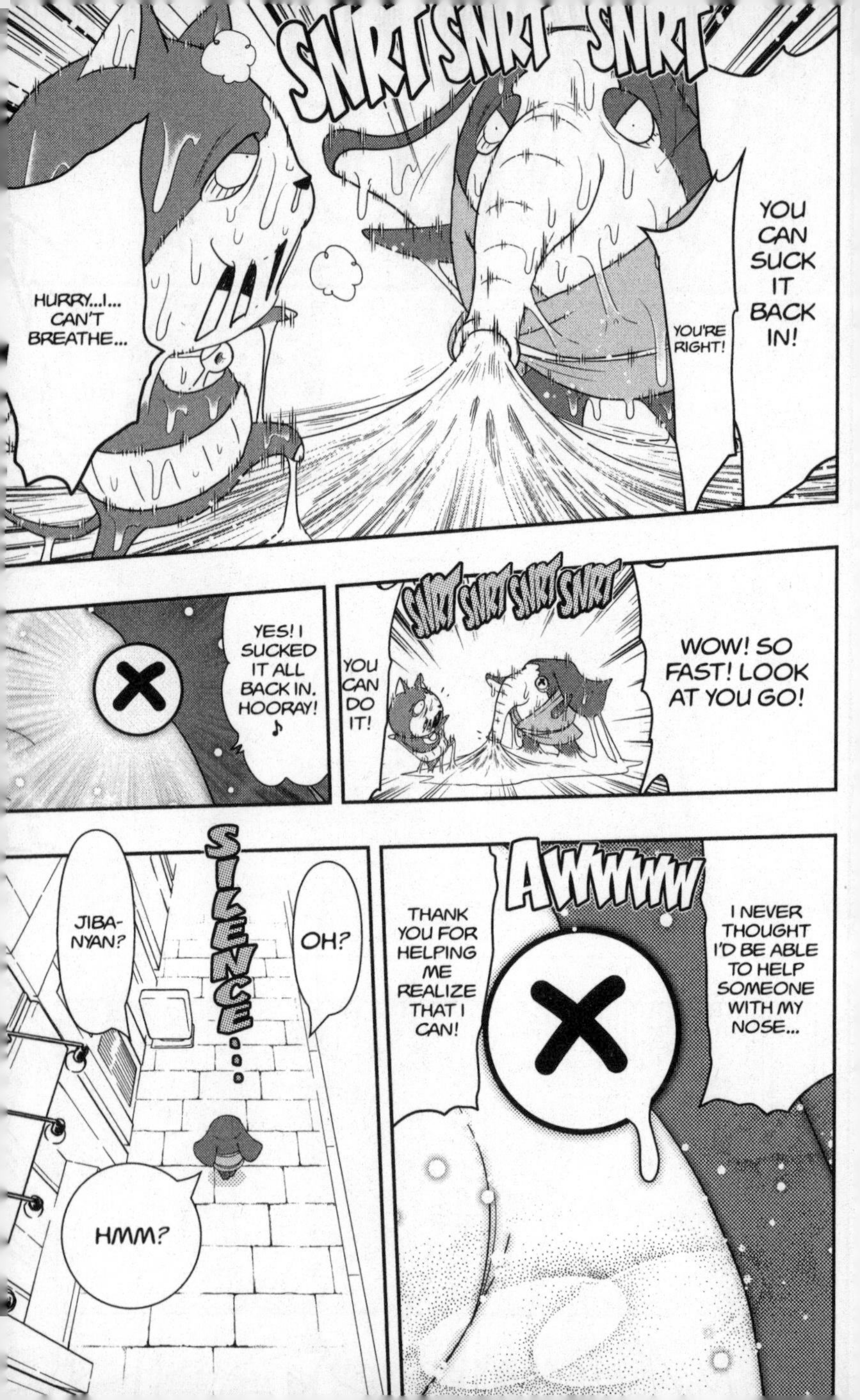
SNRT SNRT SNRT
YOU CAN SUCK IT BACK IN!
YOU'RE RIGHT!
HURRY...I... CAN'T BREATHE...
WOW! SO FAST! LOOK AT YOU GO!
SNRT SNRT SNRT SNRT
YOU CAN DO IT!
YES! I SUCKED IT ALL BACK IN. HOORAY! ♪
AWWWWW
I NEVER THOUGHT I'D BE ABLE TO HELP SOMEONE WITH MY NOSE...
THANK YOU FOR HELPING ME REALIZE THAT I CAN!
SILENCE...
OH?
JIBA-NYAN?
HMM?

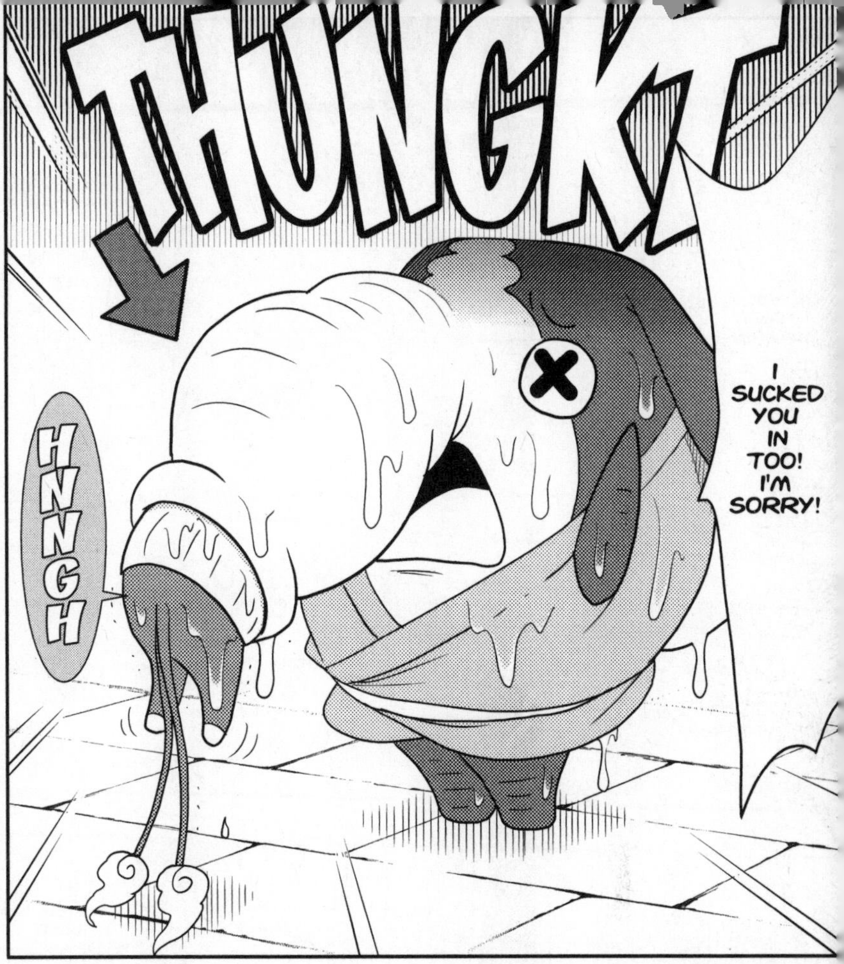
THUNK!
I SUCKED YOU IN TOO! I'M SORRY!
HNNGH

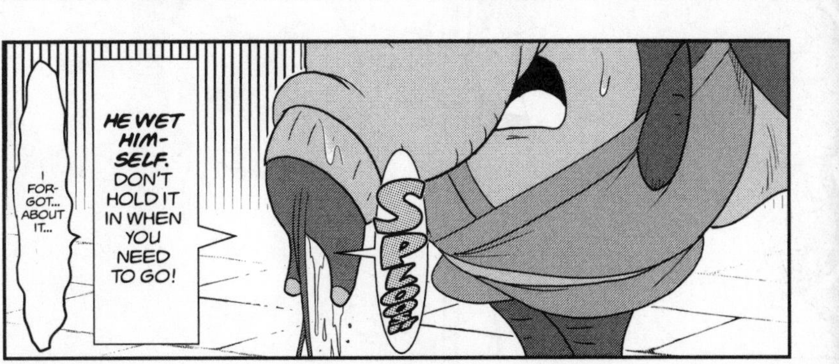
SPLOOSH
HE WET HIMSELF. DON'T HOLD IT IN WHEN YOU NEED TO GO!
I FORGOT... ABOUT IT...

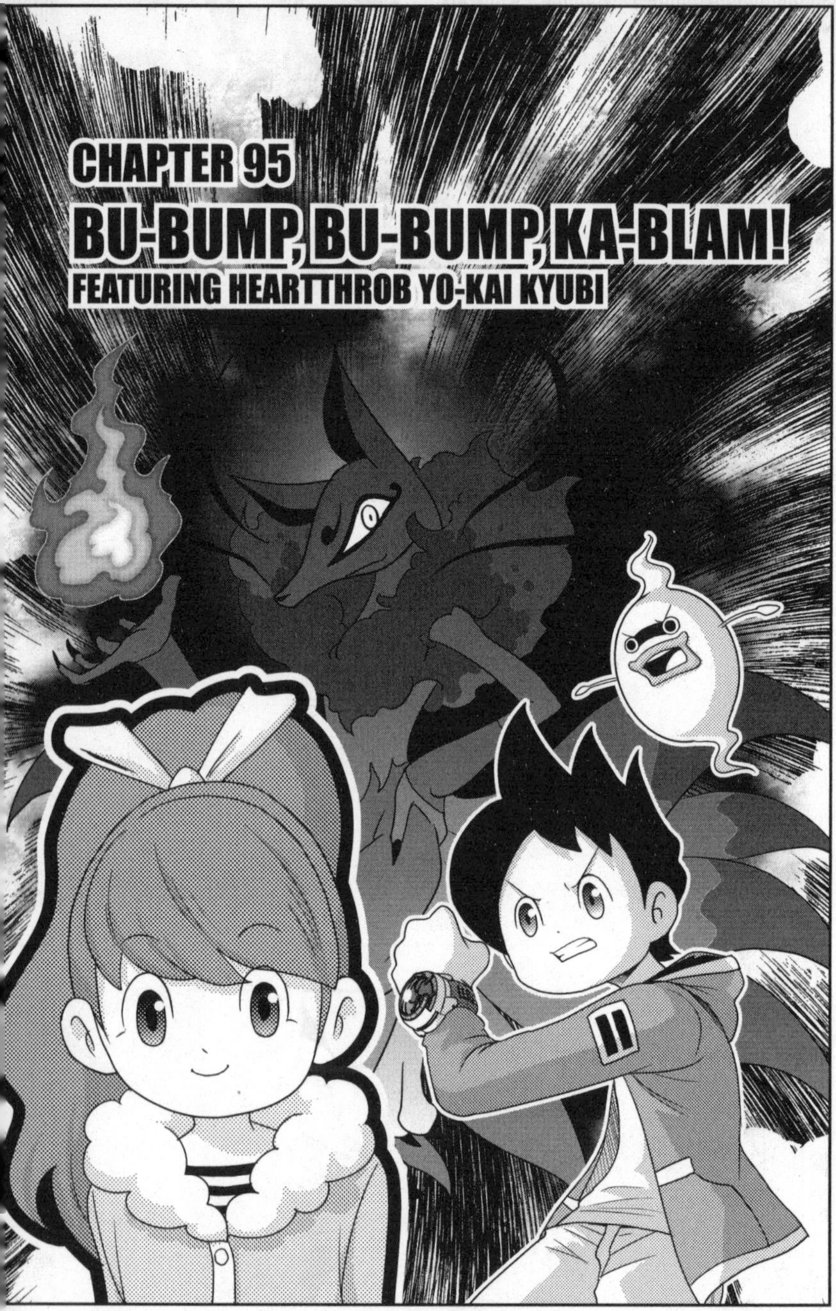
CHAPTER 95
BU-BUMP, BU-BUMP, KA-BLAM!
FEATURING HEARTTHROB YO-KAI KYUBI

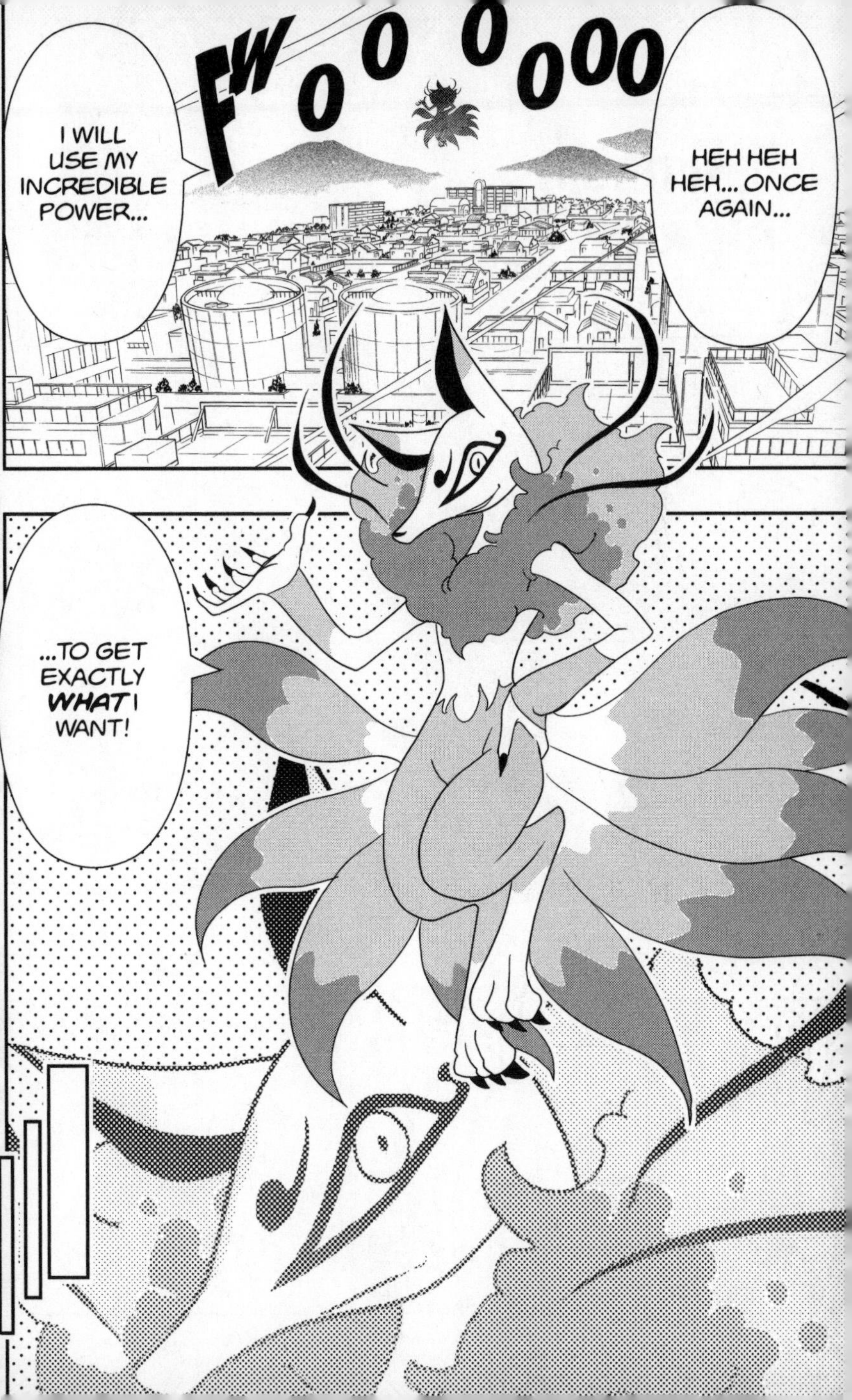
HEH HEH HEH... ONCE AGAIN...
FWOOOOOO
I WILL USE MY INCREDIBLE POWER...
...TO GET EXACTLY WHAT I WANT!

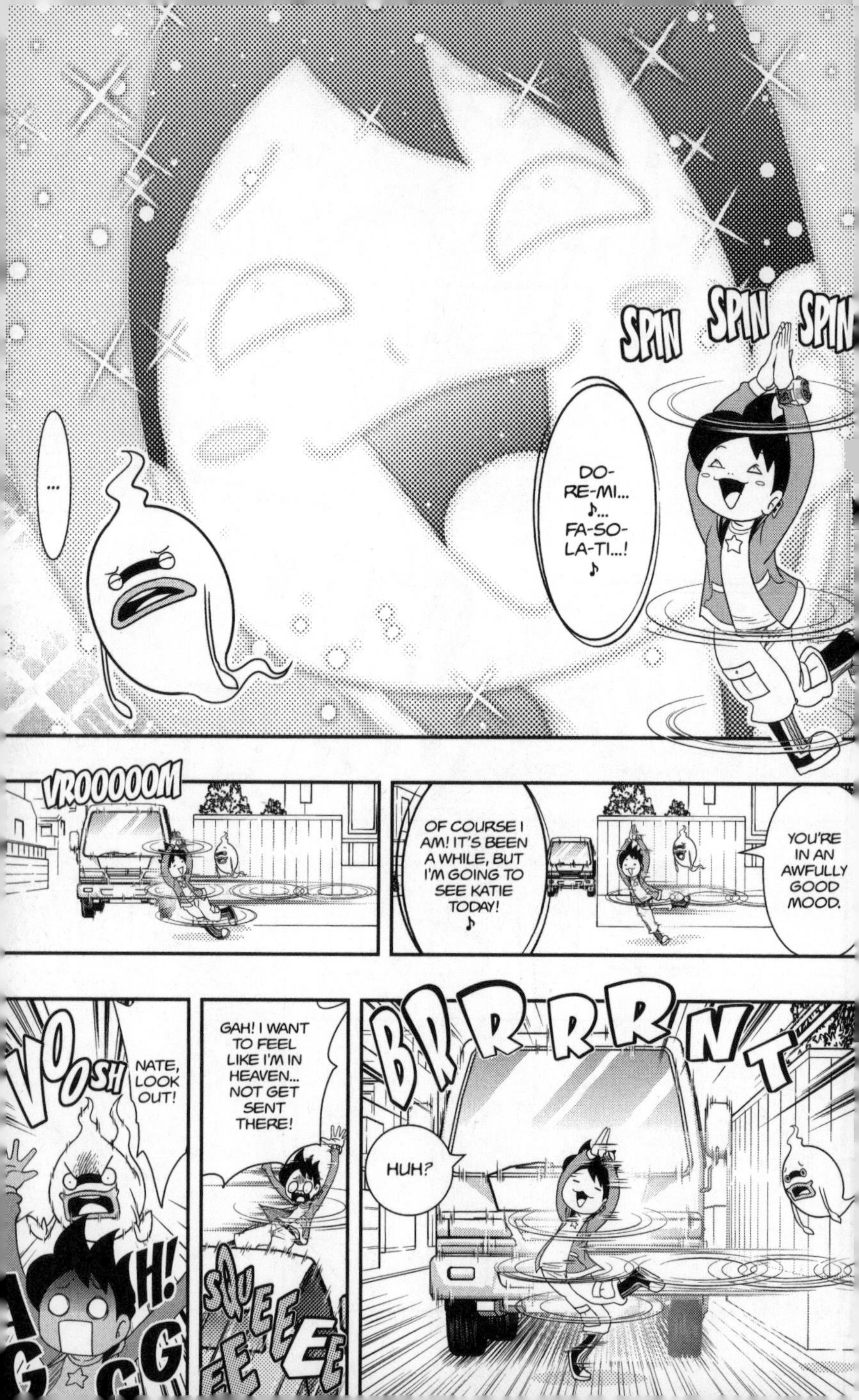
SPIN SPIN SPIN
DO-RE-MI... ♪... FA-SO-LA-TI...! ♪
...
YOU'RE IN AN AWFULLY GOOD MOOD.
OF COURSE I AM! IT'S BEEN A WHILE, BUT I'M GOING TO SEE KATIE TODAY! ♪
VROOOOOM
BRRRRNT
HUH?
GAH! I WANT TO FEEL LIKE I'M IN HEAVEN... NOT GET SENT THERE!
SQUEEEEEE
VOOSH
NATE, LOOK OUT!

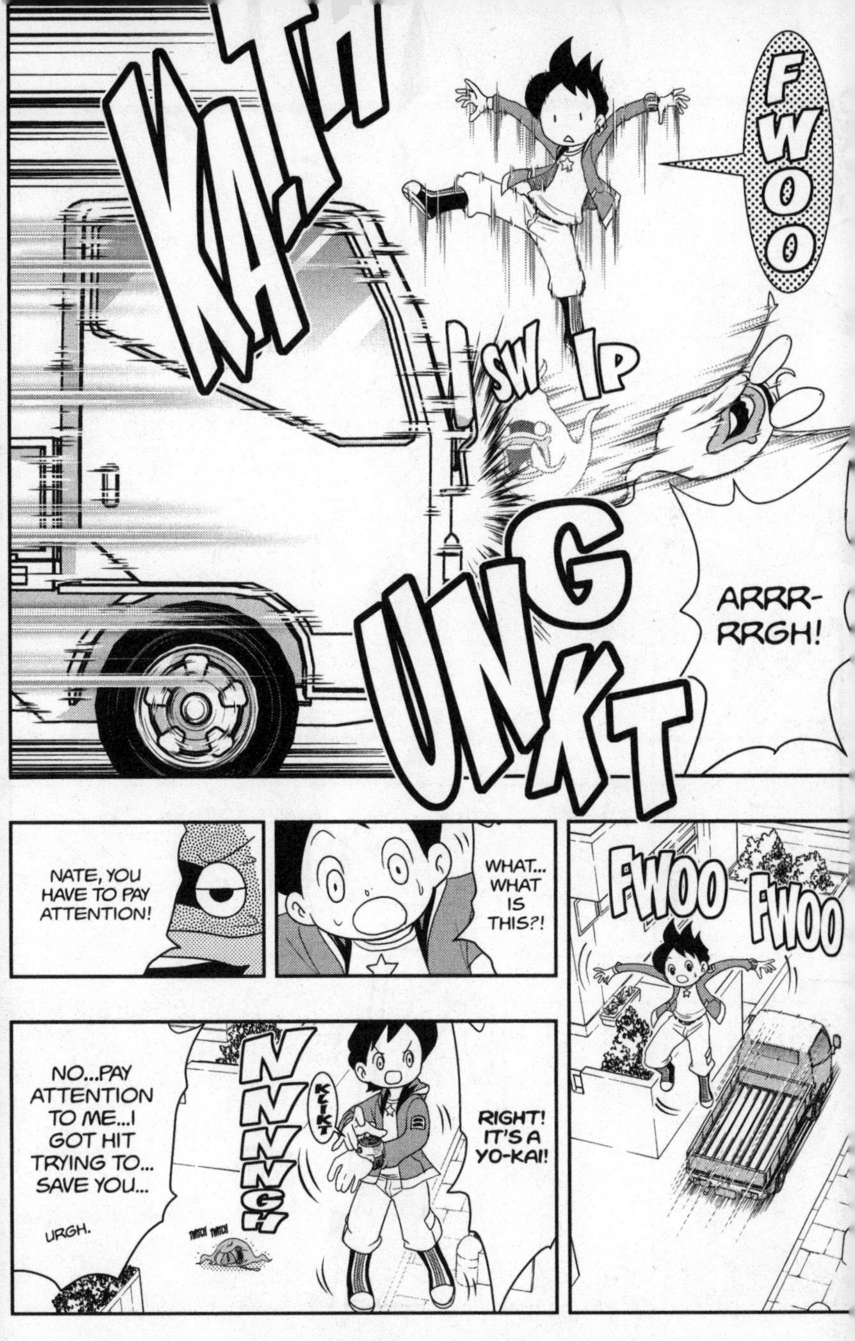

FWOO
SW IP
UNG
KT
ARRR-RRGH!
FWOO
FWOO
WHAT... WHAT IS THIS?!
NATE, YOU HAVE TO PAY ATTENTION!
RIGHT! IT'S A YO-KAI!
NNNNNGH
KLIK
NO...PAY ATTENTION TO ME...I GOT HIT TRYING TO... SAVE YOU...
URGH.
TWITCH TWITCH

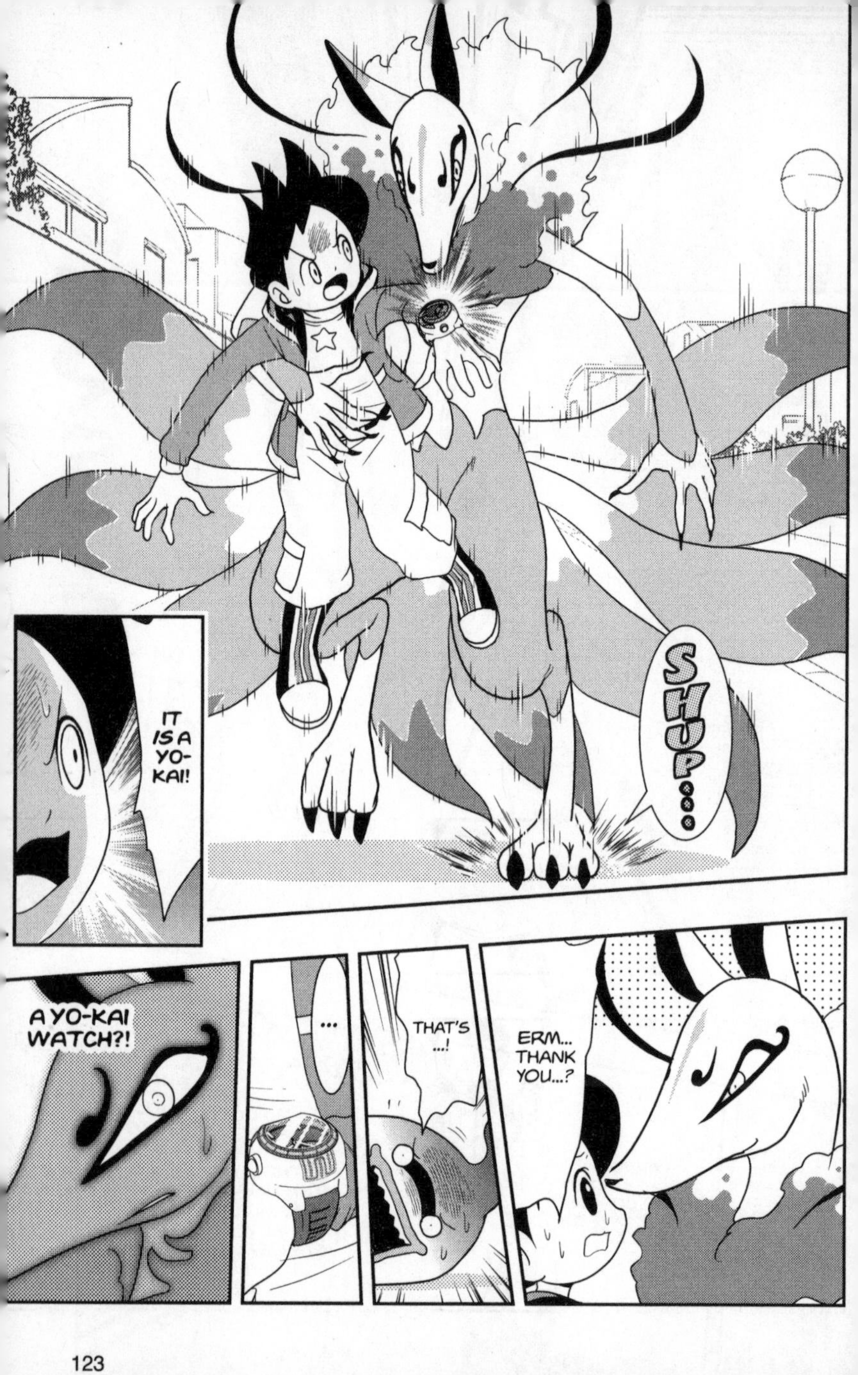
SHUP...
IT IS A YO-KAI!
ERM... THANK YOU...?
THAT'S ...!
...
A YO-KAI WATCH?!

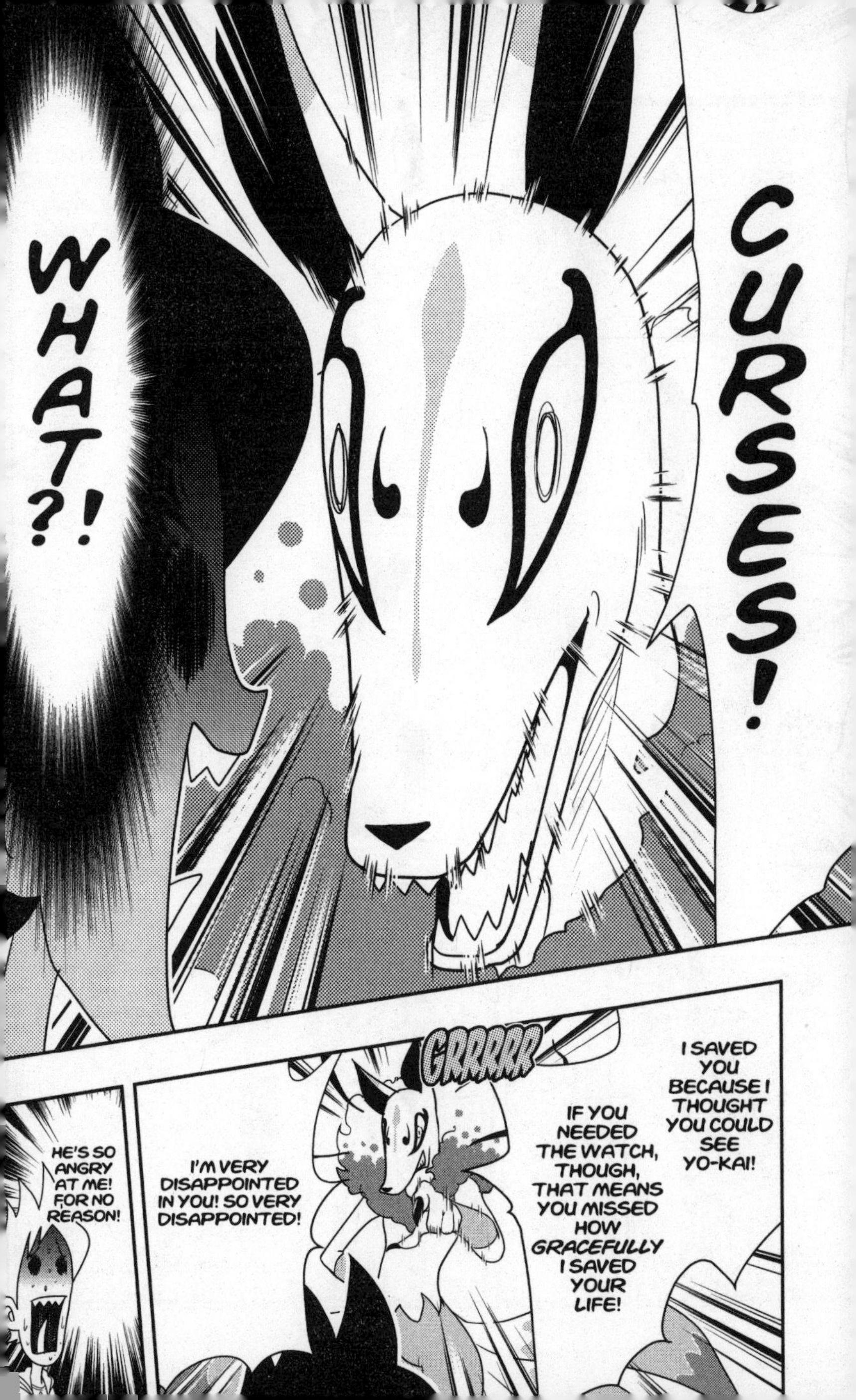
CURSES!
WHAT?!
GRRRRR
I SAVED YOU BECAUSE I THOUGHT YOU COULD SEE YO-KAI!
IF YOU NEEDED THE WATCH, THOUGH, THAT MEANS YOU MISSED HOW GRACEFULLY I SAVED YOUR LIFE!
I'M VERY DISAPPOINTED IN YOU! SO VERY DISAPPOINTED!
HE'S SO ANGRY AT ME! FOR NO REASON!

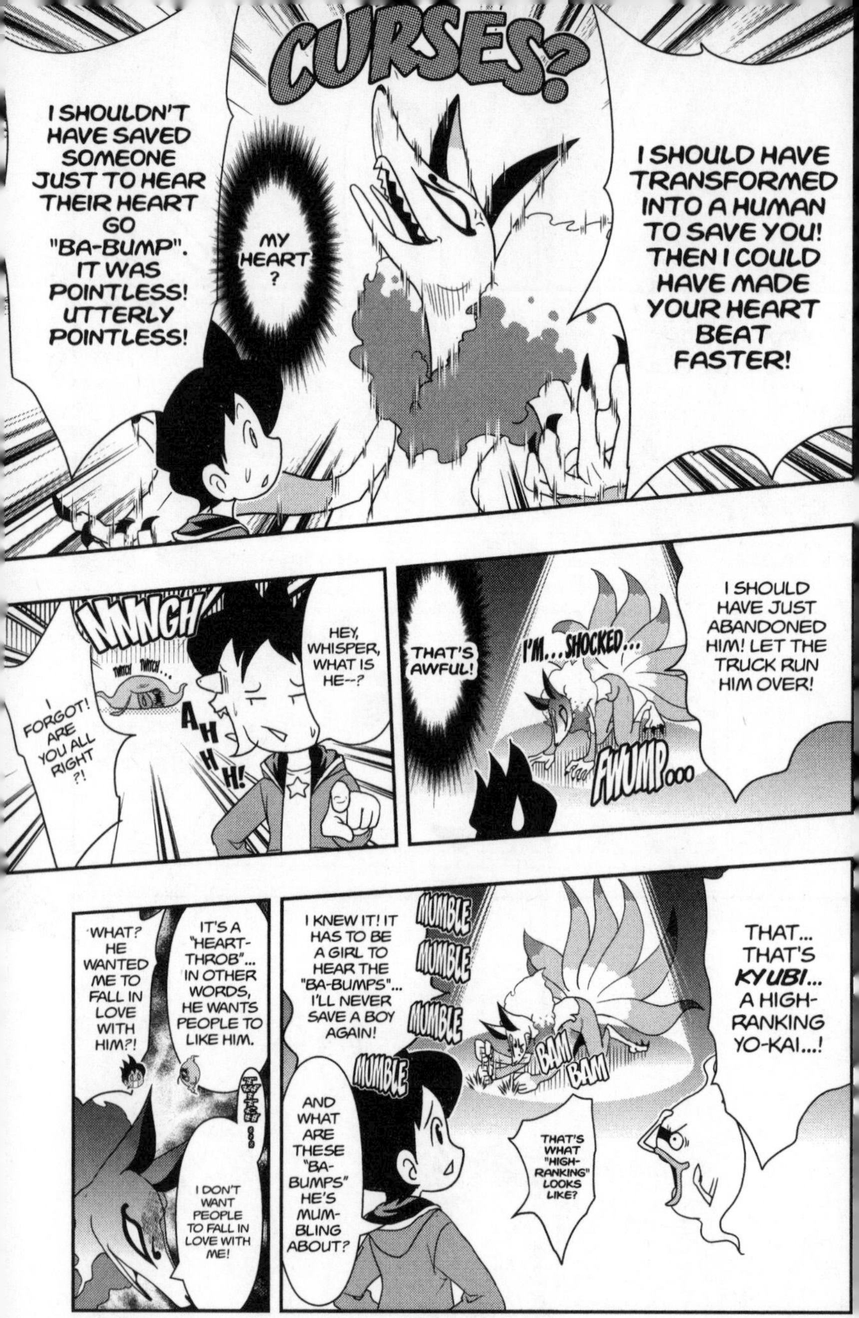
CURSES?!
I SHOULD HAVE TRANSFORMED INTO A HUMAN TO SAVE YOU! THEN I COULD HAVE MADE YOUR HEART BEAT FASTER!
I SHOULDN'T HAVE SAVED SOMEONE JUST TO HEAR THEIR HEART GO "BA-BUMP". IT WAS POINTLESS! UTTERLY POINTLESS!
MY HEART?
I SHOULD HAVE JUST ABANDONED HIM! LET THE TRUCK RUN HIM OVER!
I'M...SHOCKED...
THAT'S AWFUL!
FWUMP...
HEY, WHISPER, WHAT IS HE--?
MMNGH
TWITCH TWITCH...
AHHH!
I FORGOT! ARE YOU ALL RIGHT?!
THAT... THAT'S KYUBI... A HIGH-RANKING YO-KAI...!
MUMBLE
MUMBLE
MUMBLE
I KNEW IT! IT HAS TO BE A GIRL TO HEAR THE "BA-BUMPS"... I'LL NEVER SAVE A BOY AGAIN!
BAM
BAM
THAT'S WHAT "HIGH-RANKING" LOOKS LIKE?
MUMBLE
AND WHAT ARE THESE "BA-BUMPS" HE'S MUMBLING ABOUT?
IT'S A "HEART-THROB"... IN OTHER WORDS, HE WANTS PEOPLE TO LIKE HIM.
WHAT? HE WANTED ME TO FALL IN LOVE WITH HIM?!
I DON'T WANT PEOPLE TO FALL IN LOVE WITH ME!

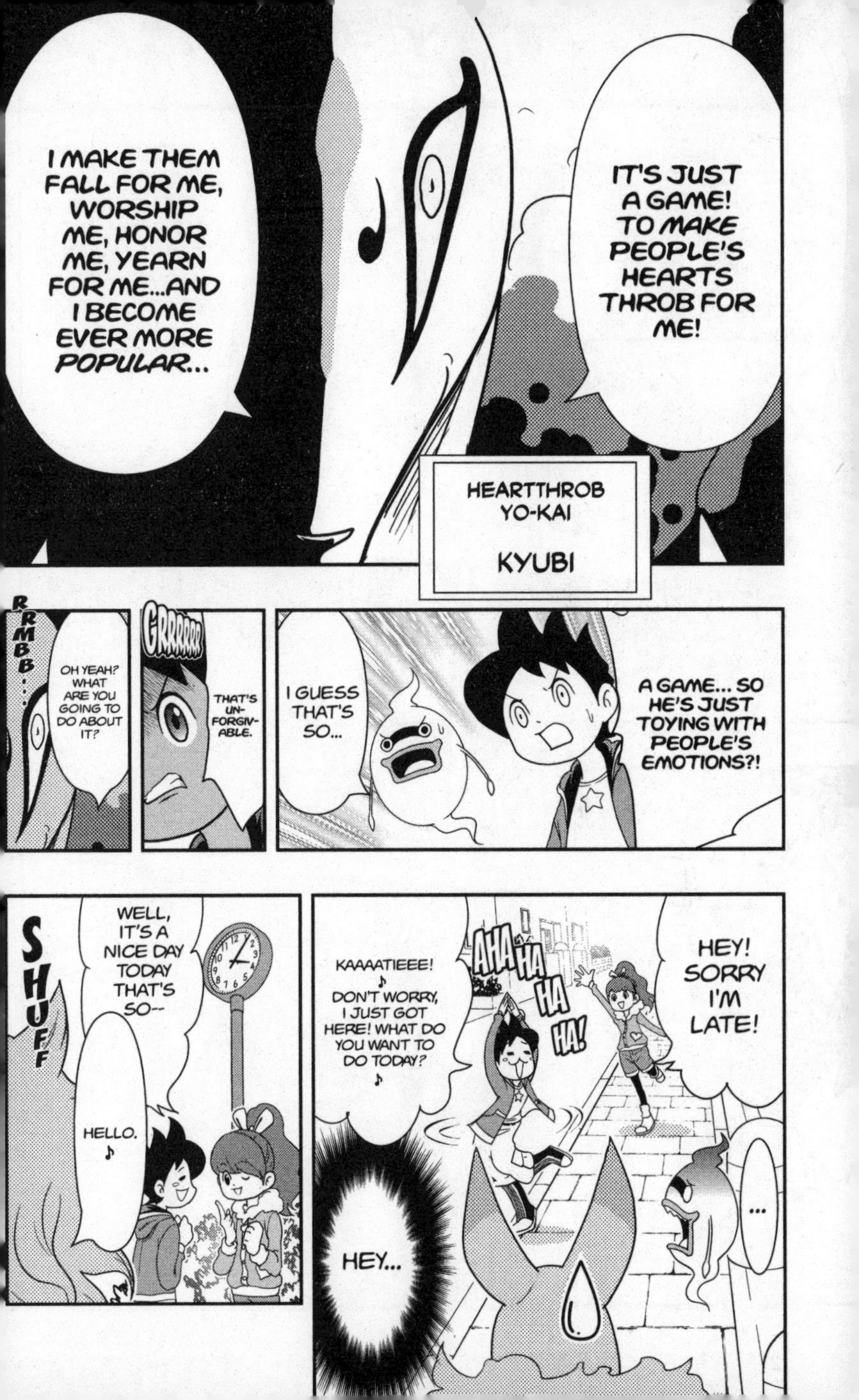
IT'S JUST A GAME! TO MAKE PEOPLE'S HEARTS THROB FOR ME!
I MAKE THEM FALL FOR ME, WORSHIP ME, HONOR ME, YEARN FOR ME...AND I BECOME EVER MORE *POPULAR*...
HEARTTHROB YO-KAI
KYUBI
A GAME... SO HE'S JUST TOYING WITH PEOPLE'S EMOTIONS?!
I GUESS THAT'S SO...
GRRRRRR
THAT'S UN-FORGIV-ABLE.
RRMBB...
OH YEAH? WHAT ARE YOU GOING TO DO ABOUT IT?
HEY! SORRY I'M LATE!
AHAHAHAHA!
KAAAATIEEE! ♪ DON'T WORRY, I JUST GOT HERE! WHAT DO YOU WANT TO DO TODAY? ♪
...
HEY...
WELL, IT'S A NICE DAY TODAY THAT'S SO--
SHUFF
HELLO. ♪

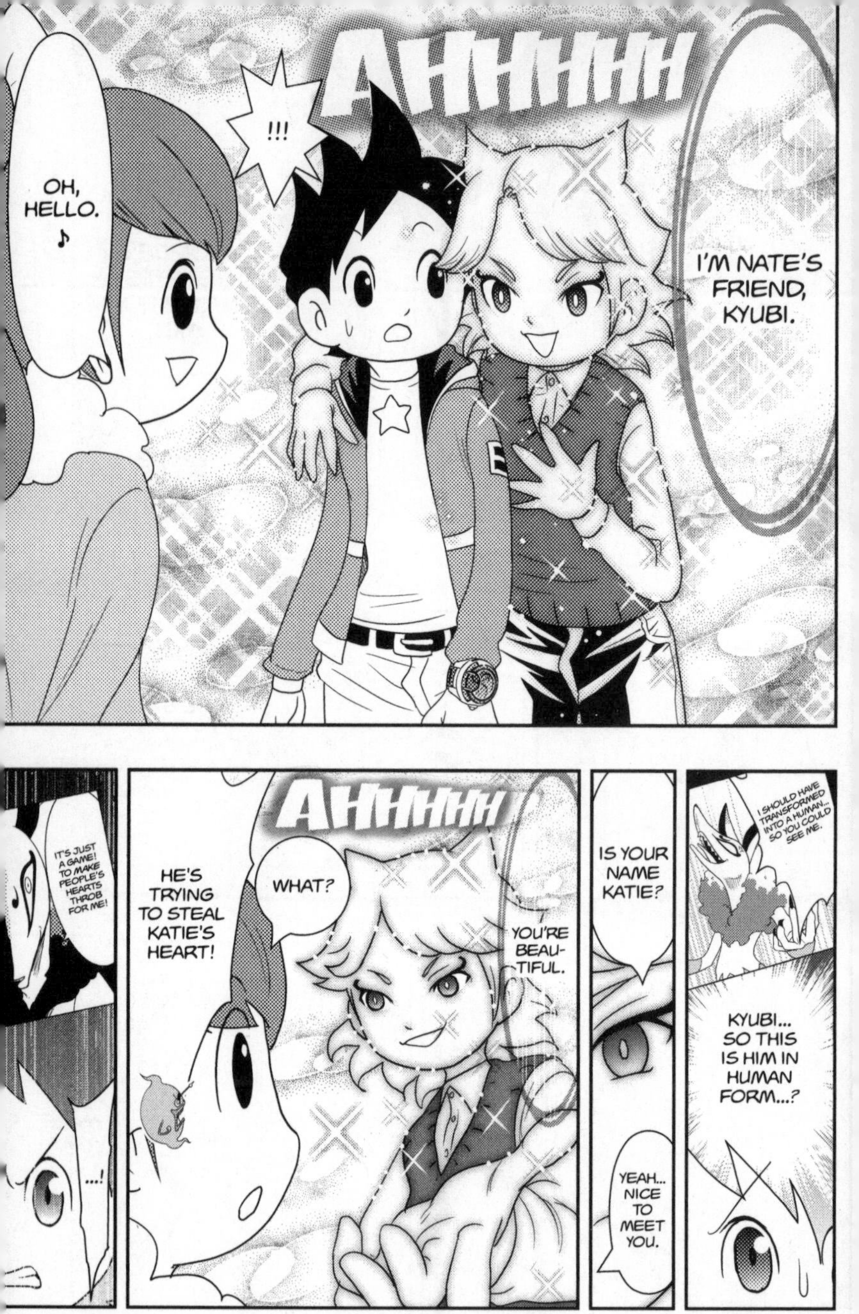
AHHHHHH
I'M NATE'S FRIEND, KYUBI.
!!!
OH, HELLO. ♪
I SHOULD HAVE TRANSFORMED INTO A HUMAN... SO YOU COULD SEE ME.
KYUBI... SO THIS IS HIM IN HUMAN FORM...?
IS YOUR NAME KATIE?
YEAH... NICE TO MEET YOU.
AHHHHHH
YOU'RE BEAU-TIFUL.
WHAT?
HE'S TRYING TO STEAL KATIE'S HEART!
IT'S JUST A GAME! TO MAKE PEOPLE'S HEARTS THROB FOR ME!
...!

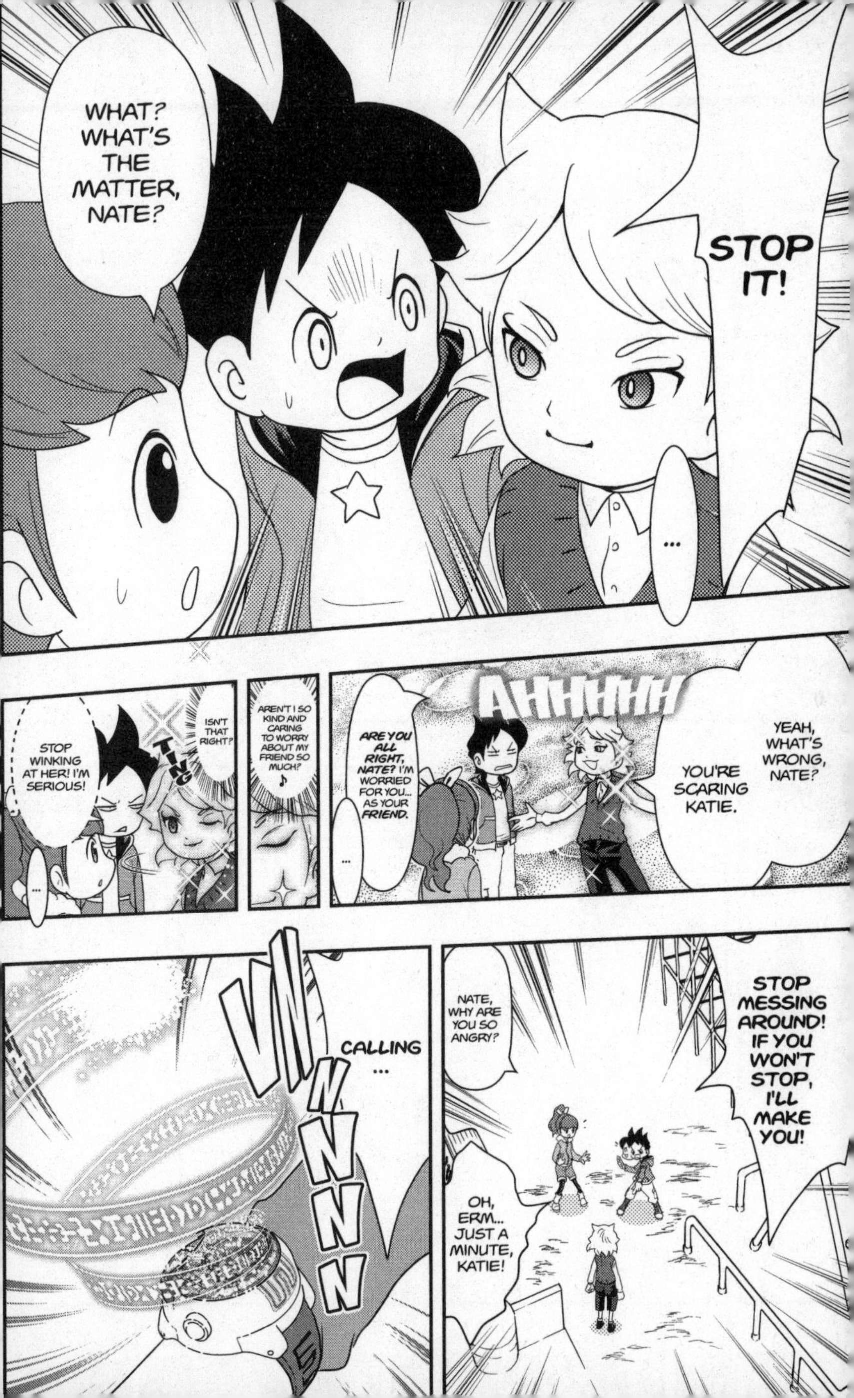
STOP IT!
WHAT? WHAT'S THE MATTER, NATE?
...
YEAH, WHAT'S WRONG, NATE?
YOU'RE SCARING KATIE.
AHHHHHH
ARE YOU ALL RIGHT, NATE? I'M WORRIED FOR YOU... AS YOUR FRIEND.
...
AREN'T I SO KIND AND CARING TO WORRY ABOUT MY FRIEND SO MUCH? ♪
ISN'T THAT RIGHT?
TING
STOP WINKING AT HER! I'M SERIOUS!
...
STOP MESSING AROUND! IF YOU WON'T STOP, I'LL MAKE YOU!
NATE, WHY ARE YOU SO ANGRY?
OH, ERM... JUST A MINUTE, KATIE!
CALLING ...
VVNNNNNN

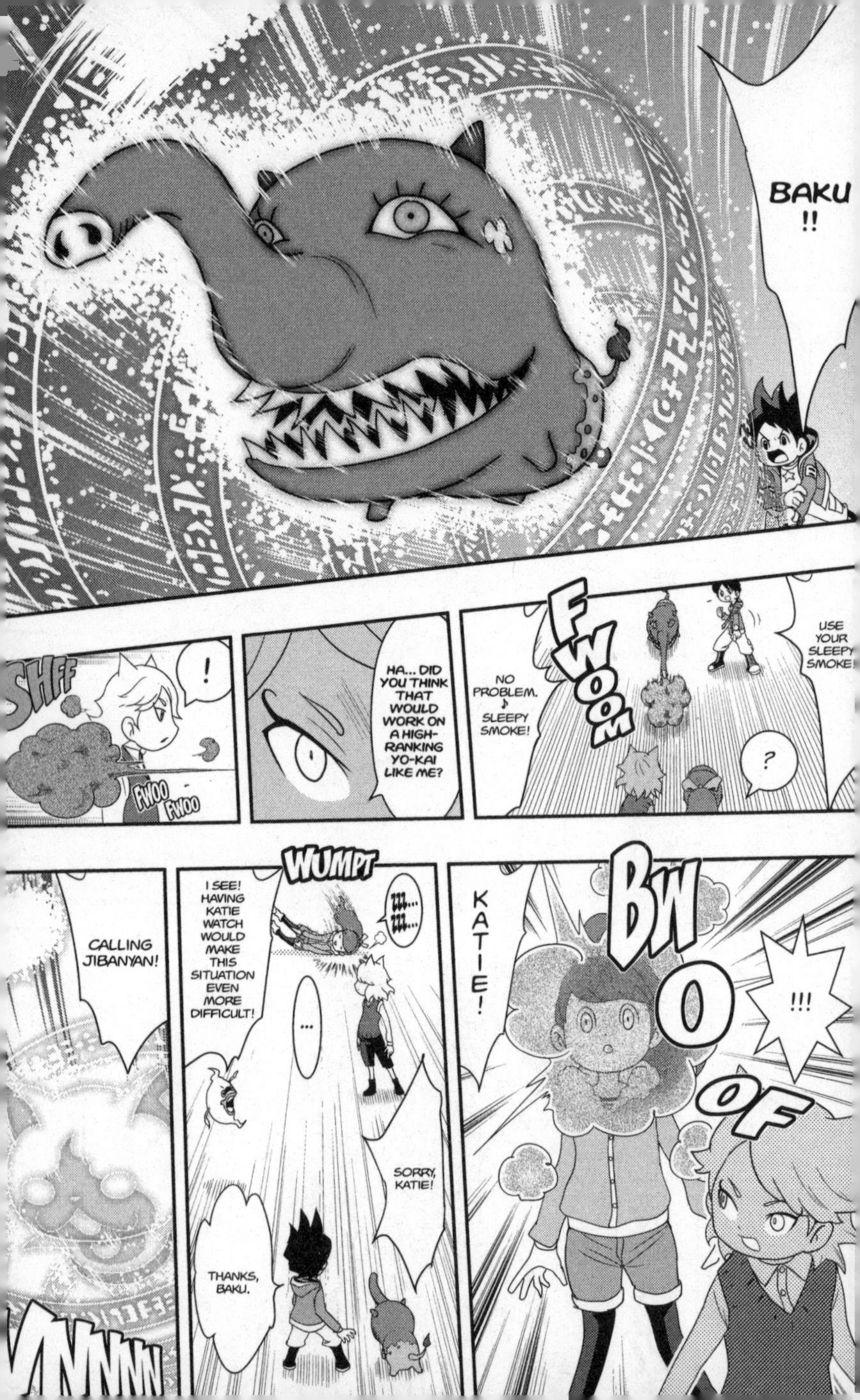
BAKU !!
USE YOUR SLEEPY SMOKE!
FWOOM
NO PROBLEM. ♪ SLEEPY SMOKE!
?
HA... DID YOU THINK THAT WOULD WORK ON A HIGH-RANKING YO-KAI LIKE ME?
!
SHFF
FWOO FWOO
BWOOF
KATIE!
!!!
WUMPT
I SEE! HAVING KATIE WATCH WOULD MAKE THIS SITUATION EVEN MORE DIFFICULT!
ZZZ... ZZZ...
...
SORRY, KATIE!
THANKS, BAKU.
CALLING JIBANYAN!
VNNNNN

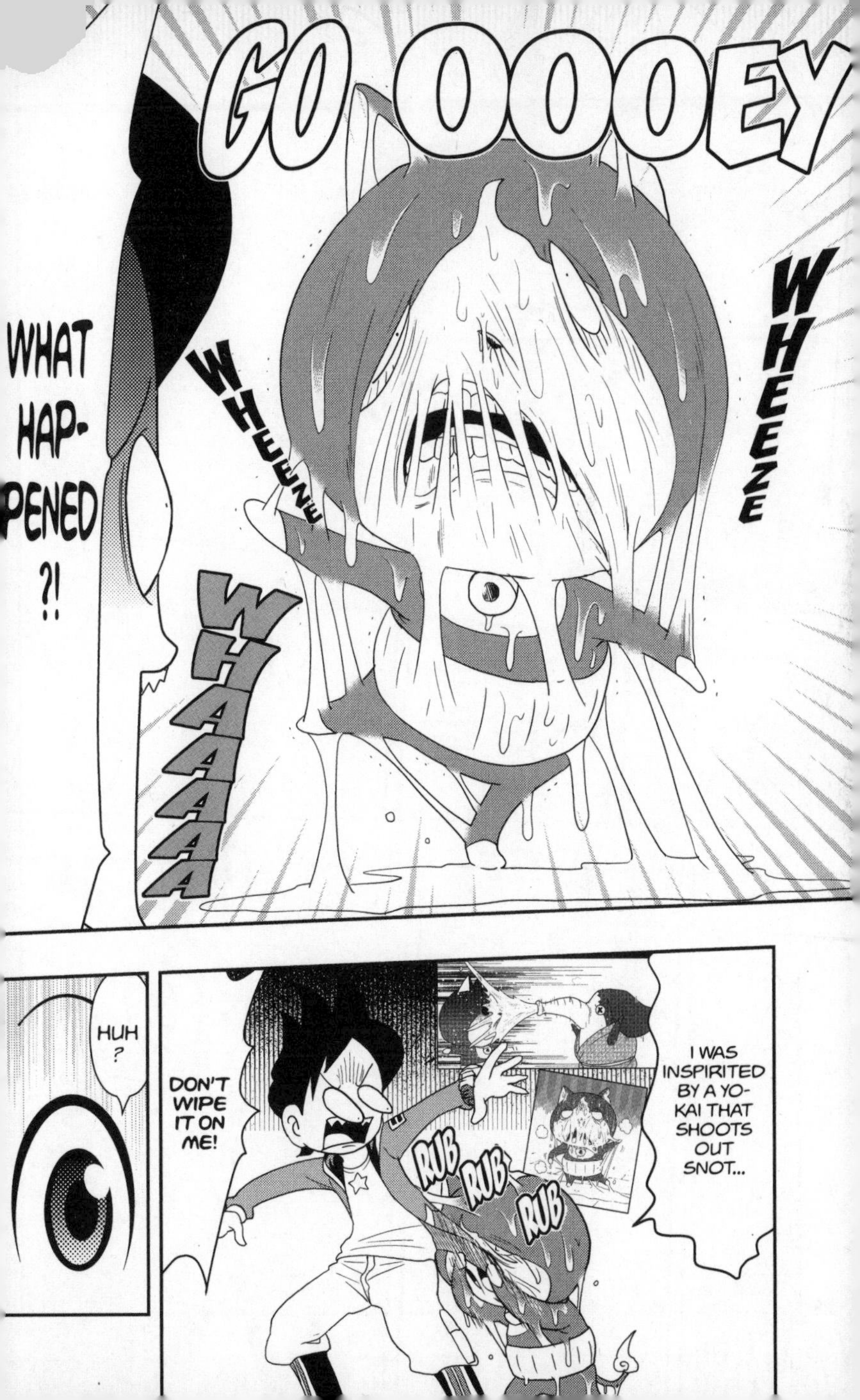
GO OOOEY
WHEEZE
WHEEZE
WHAAAAAA
WHAT HAP-PENED ?!
I WAS INSPIRITED BY A YO-KAI THAT SHOOTS OUT SNOT...
DON'T WIPE IT ON ME!
RUB
RUB
RUB
HUH ?

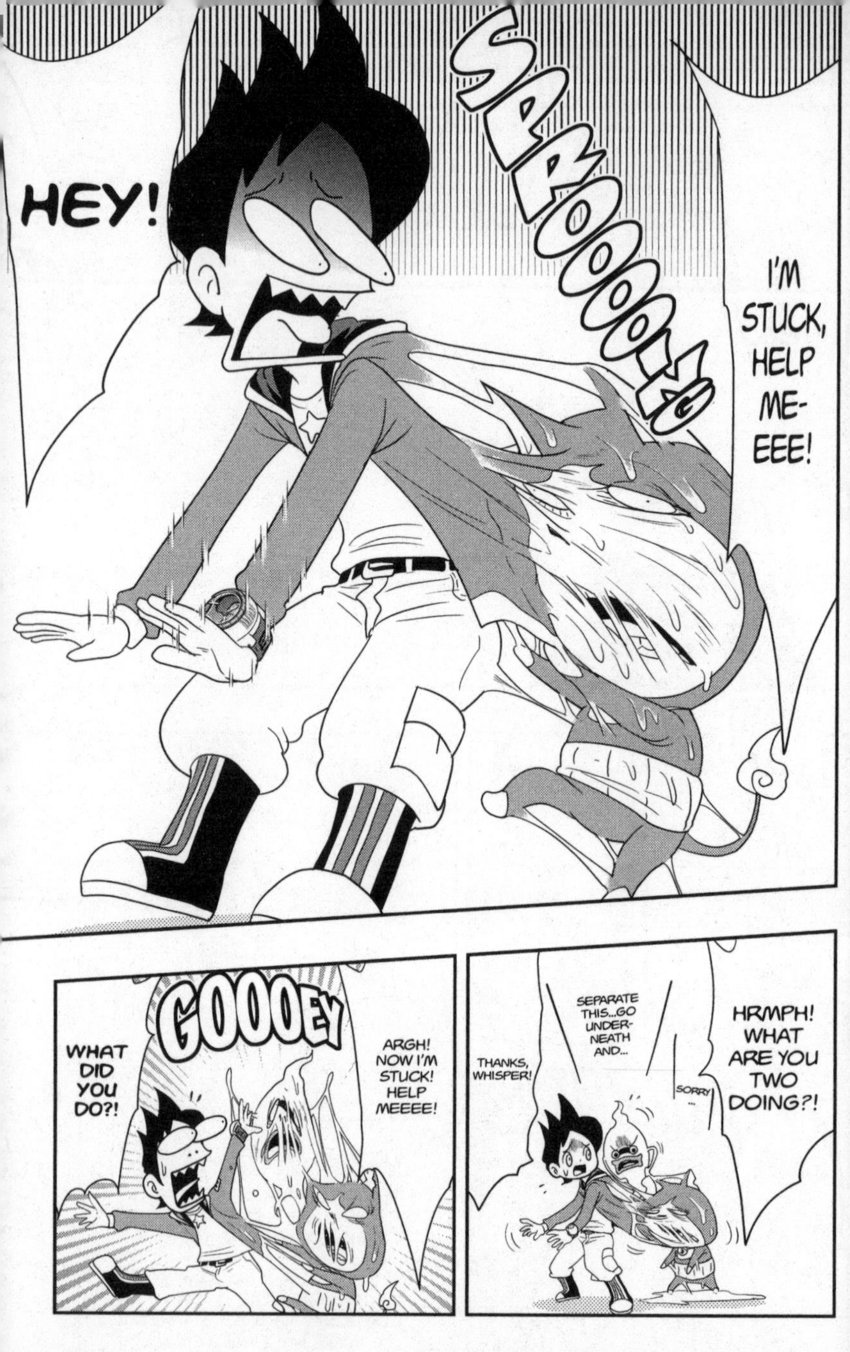
I'M STUCK, HELP ME-EEE!
SPROOOOOING
HEY!
HRMPH! WHAT ARE YOU TWO DOING?!
SEPARATE THIS...GO UNDER-NEATH AND...
SORRY...
THANKS, WHISPER!
ARGH! NOW I'M STUCK! HELP MEEEE!
GOOOEY
WHAT DID YOU DO?!

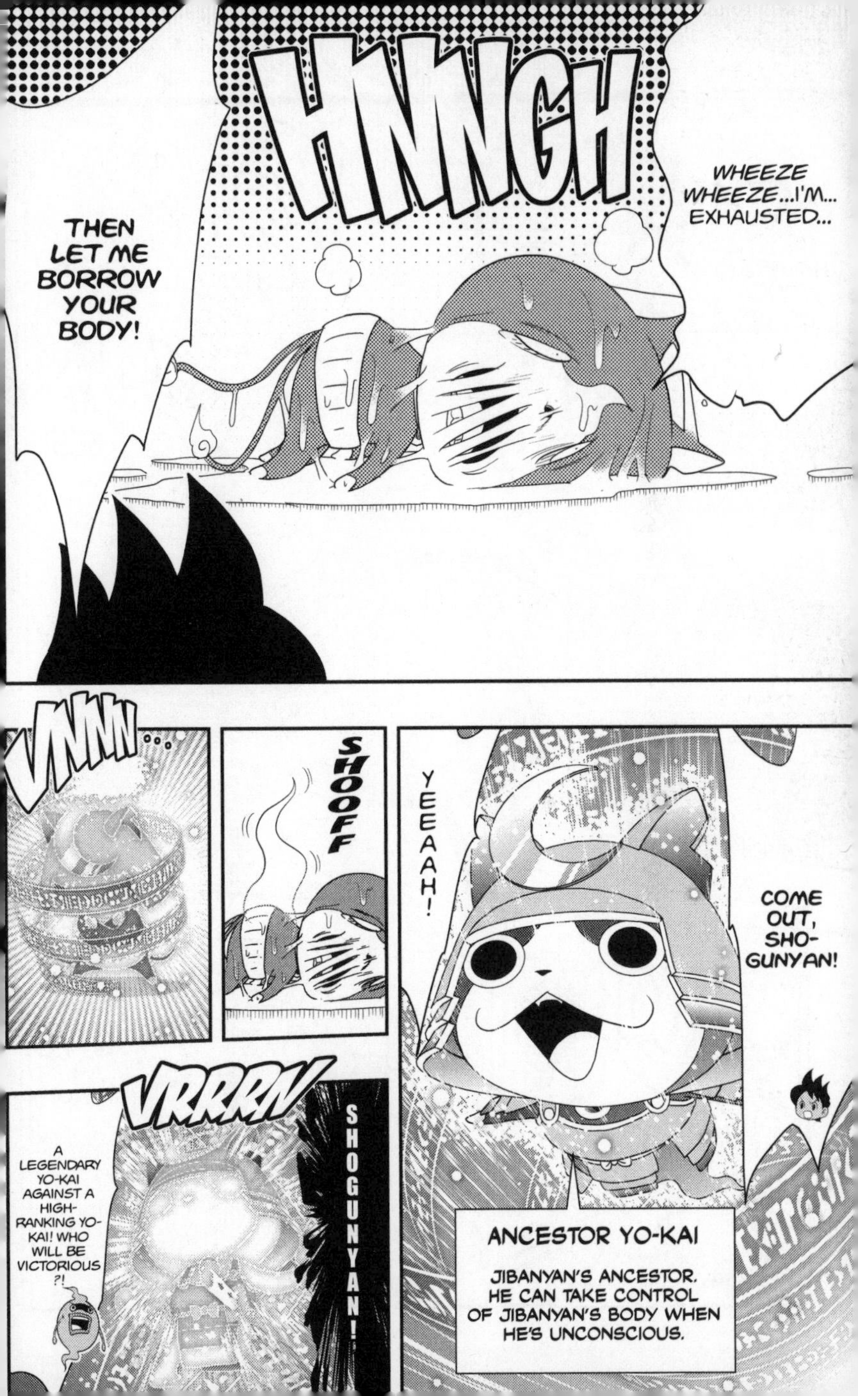
HNNNGH
WHEEZE WHEEZE...I'M... EXHAUSTED...
THEN LET ME BORROW YOUR BODY!
COME OUT, SHO-GUNYAN!
YEEAAAH!
ANCESTOR YO-KAI
JIBANYAN'S ANCESTOR. HE CAN TAKE CONTROL OF JIBANYAN'S BODY WHEN HE'S UNCONSCIOUS.
SHOOFF
VNNNN...
VRRRN
SHOGUNYAN!
A LEGENDARY YO-KAI AGAINST A HIGH-RANKING YO-KAI! WHO WILL BE VICTORIOUS?!

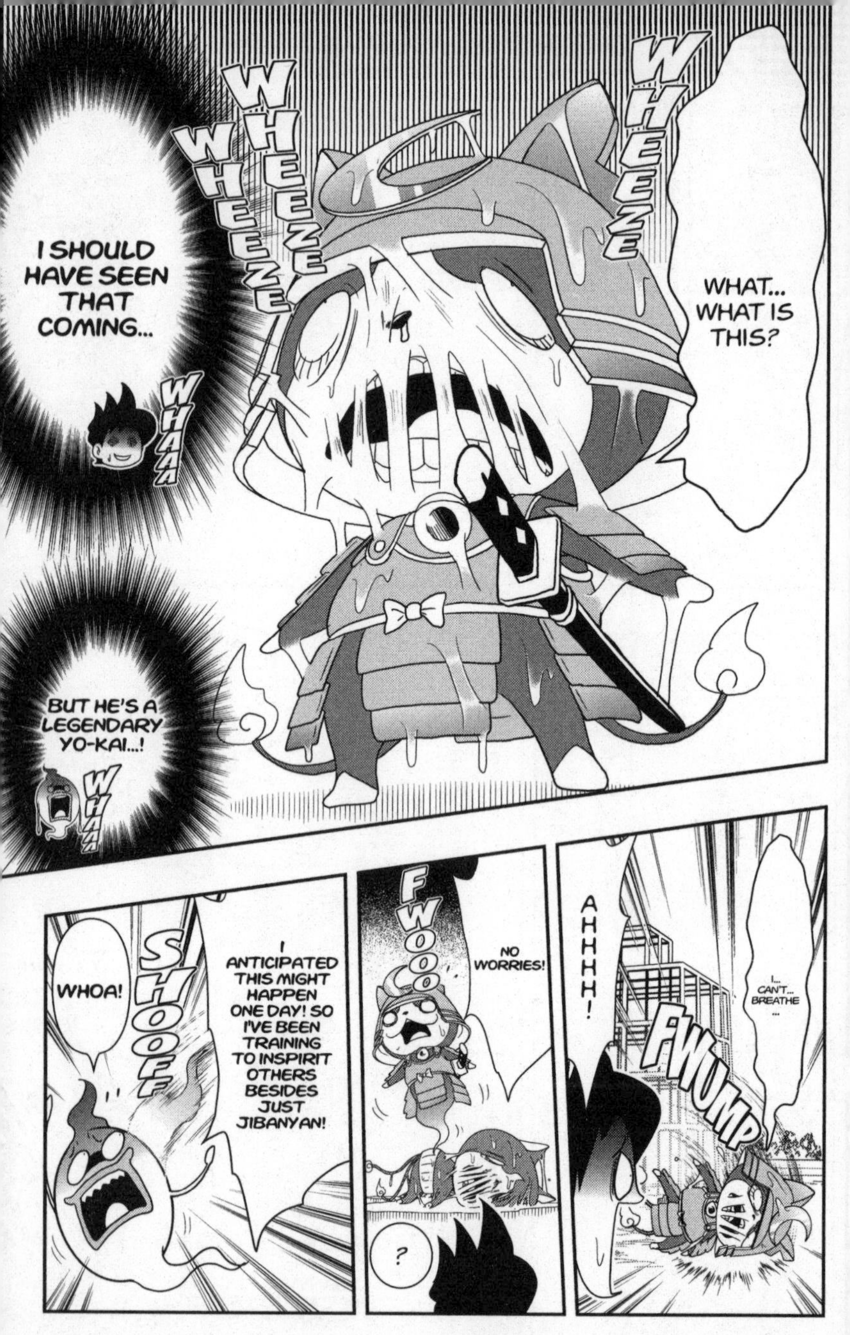
WHEEZE
WHAT... WHAT IS THIS?
WHEEZE
WHEEZE
I SHOULD HAVE SEEN THAT COMING...
WHAAA
BUT HE'S A LEGENDARY YO-KAI...!
WHAAA
I... CAN'T... BREATHE ...
FWUMP
AHHHH!
NO WORRIES!
FWOOO
?
I ANTICIPATED THIS MIGHT HAPPEN ONE DAY! SO I'VE BEEN TRAINING TO INSPIRIT OTHERS BESIDES JUST JIBANYAN!
SHOOFF
WHOA!

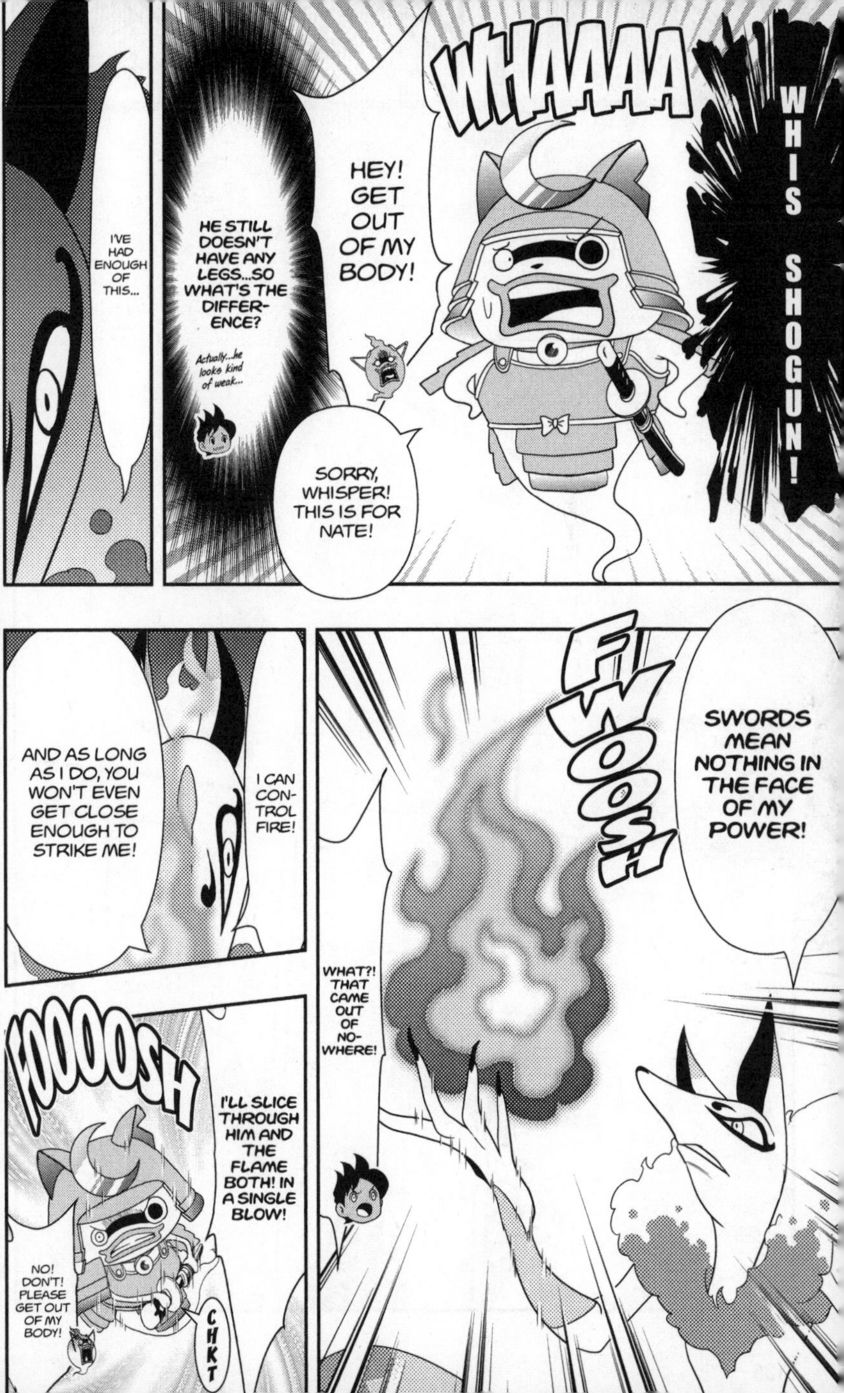
WHIS SHOGUN!
WHAAAAA
HEY! GET OUT OF MY BODY!
SORRY, WHISPER! THIS IS FOR NATE!
HE STILL DOESN'T HAVE ANY LEGS...SO WHAT'S THE DIFFER-ENCE?
Actually...he looks kind of weak...
I'VE HAD ENOUGH OF THIS...
SWORDS MEAN NOTHING IN THE FACE OF MY POWER!
FWOOOSH
WHAT?! THAT CAME OUT OF NO-WHERE!
I CAN CON-TROL FIRE!
AND AS LONG AS I DO, YOU WON'T EVEN GET CLOSE ENOUGH TO STRIKE ME!
FOOOOSH
I'LL SLICE THROUGH HIM AND THE FLAME BOTH! IN A SINGLE BLOW!
CHKT
NO! DON'T! PLEASE GET OUT OF MY BODY!

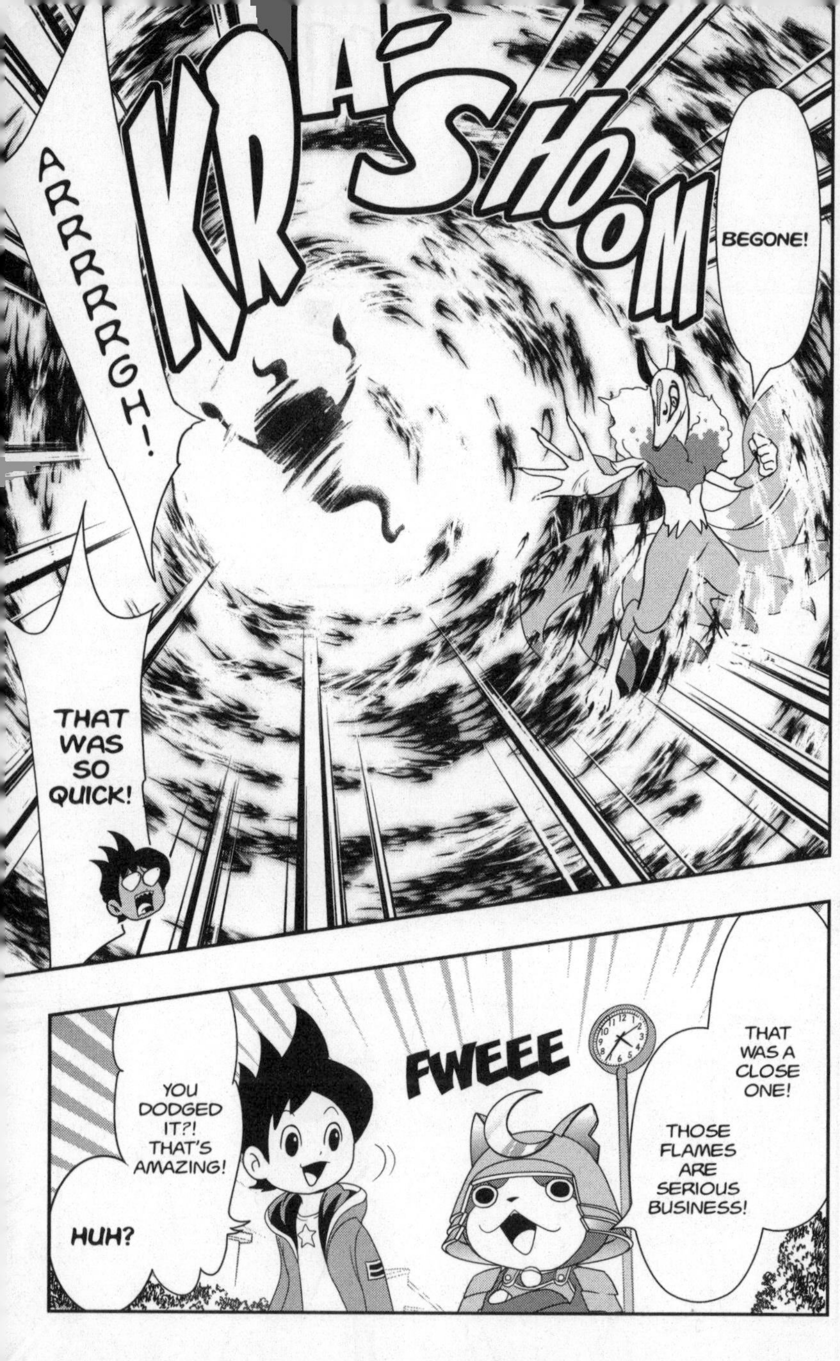
BEGONE!
KRA-SHOOM
ARRRRRGH!
THAT WAS SO QUICK!
THAT WAS A CLOSE ONE!
THOSE FLAMES ARE SERIOUS BUSINESS!
FWEEE
YOU DODGED IT?! THAT'S AMAZING!
HUH?

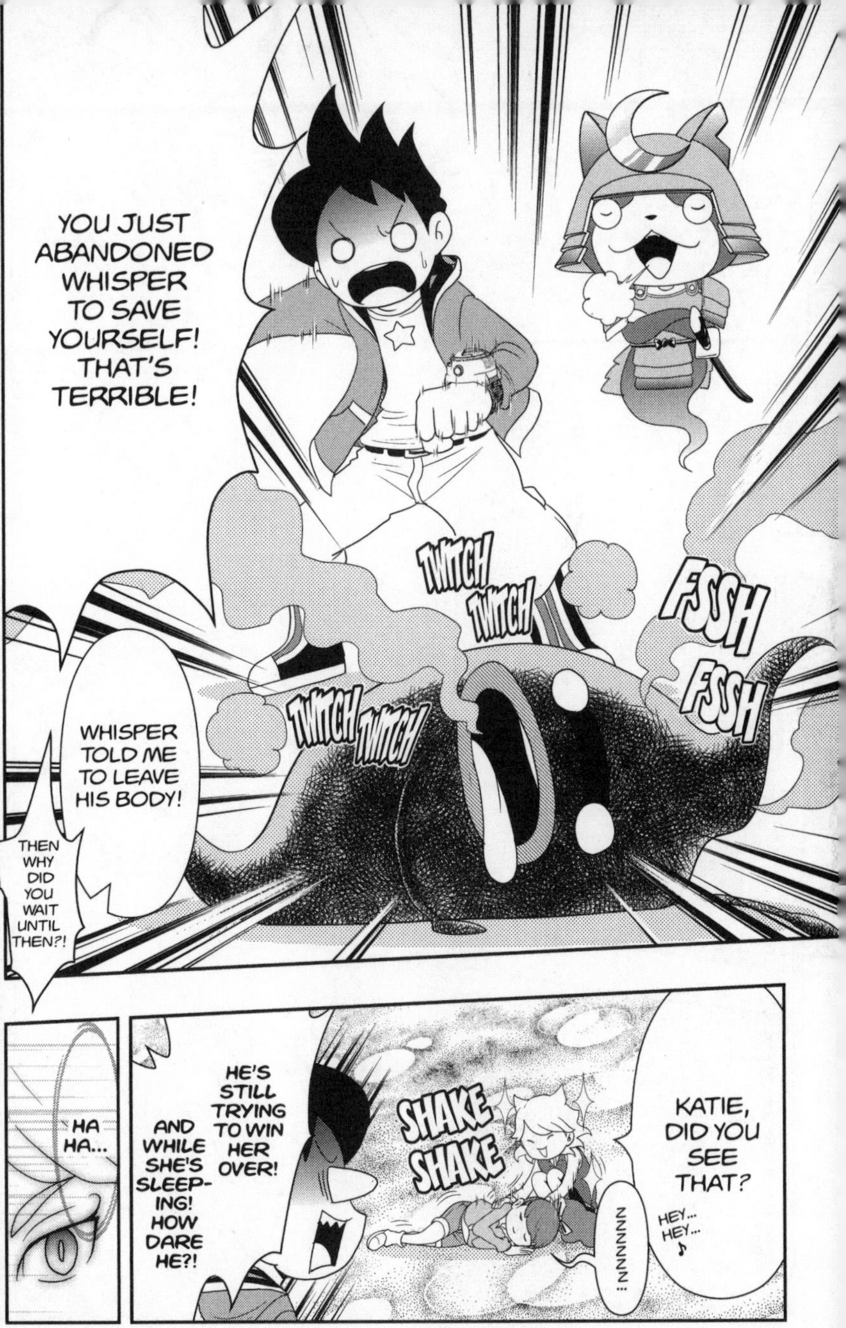
YOU JUST ABANDONED WHISPER TO SAVE YOURSELF! THAT'S TERRIBLE!
FSSH
FSSH
TWITCH TWITCH
TWITCH TWITCH
WHISPER TOLD ME TO LEAVE HIS BODY!
THEN WHY DID YOU WAIT UNTIL THEN?!
KATIE, DID YOU SEE THAT?
HEY... HEY... ♪
ZZZZZZ...
SHAKE SHAKE
HE'S STILL TRYING TO WIN HER OVER!
AND WHILE SHE'S SLEEP-ING! HOW DARE HE?!
HA HA...

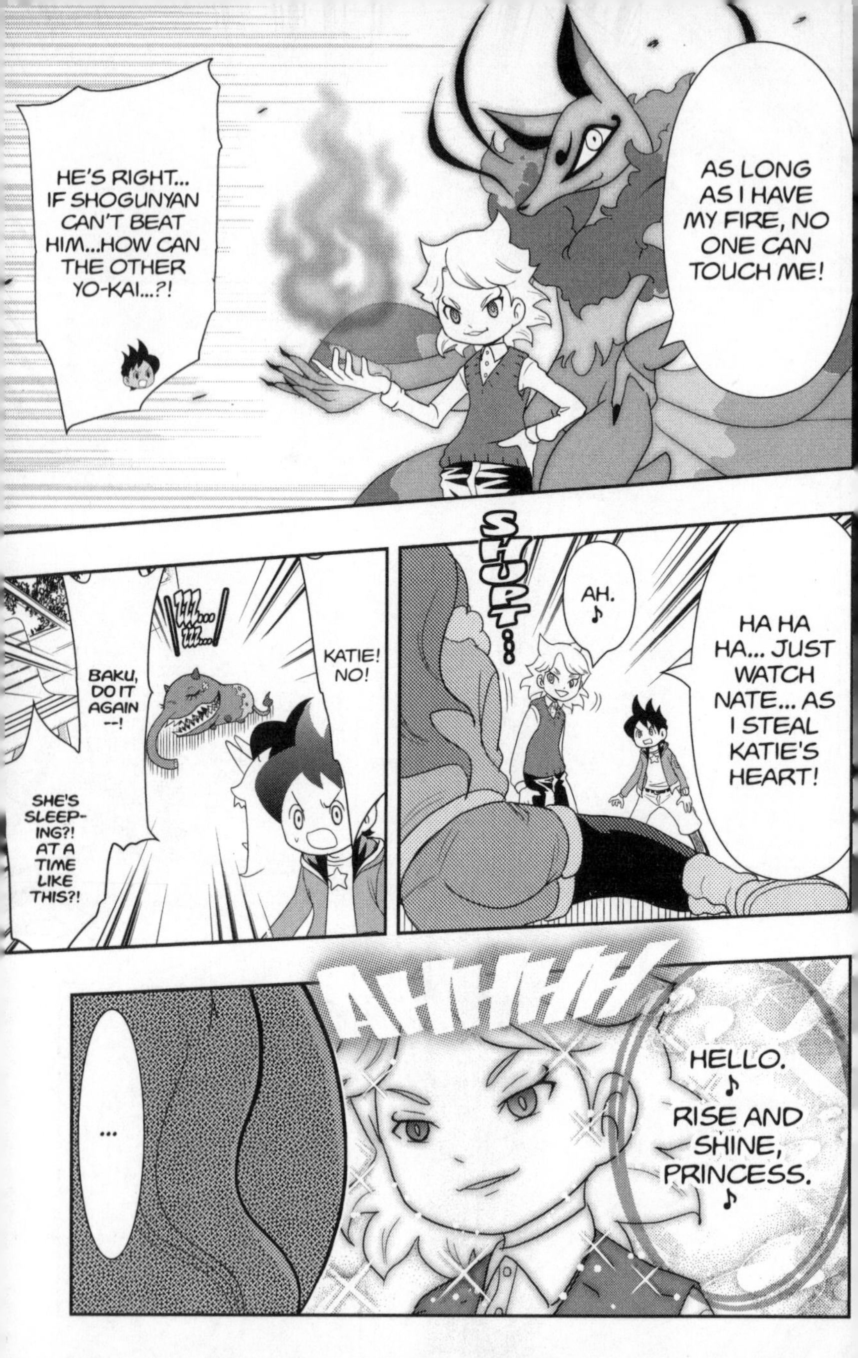
AS LONG AS I HAVE MY FIRE, NO ONE CAN TOUCH ME!
HE'S RIGHT... IF SHOGUNYAN CAN'T BEAT HIM...HOW CAN THE OTHER YO-KAI...?!
SHUPT...
AH. ♪
HA HA HA... JUST WATCH NATE... AS I STEAL KATIE'S HEART!
KATIE! NO!
ZZZ... ZZZ...
BAKU, DO IT AGAIN --!
SHE'S SLEEP-ING?! AT A TIME LIKE THIS?!
AHHHH
HELLO. ♪ RISE AND SHINE, PRINCESS. ♪
...

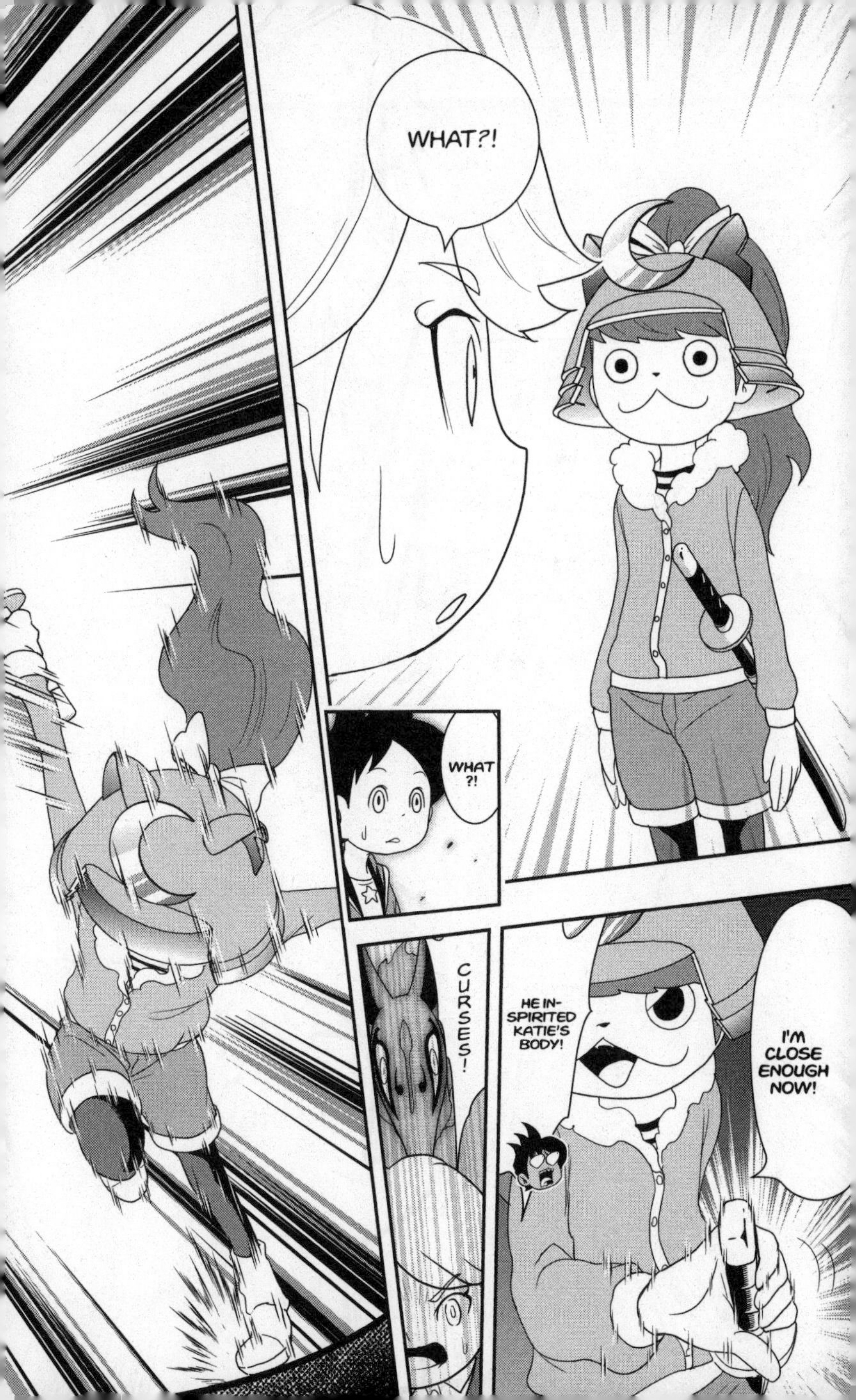
WHAT?!
WHAT ?!
I'M CLOSE ENOUGH NOW!
HE IN-SPIRITED KATIE'S BODY!
CURSES!

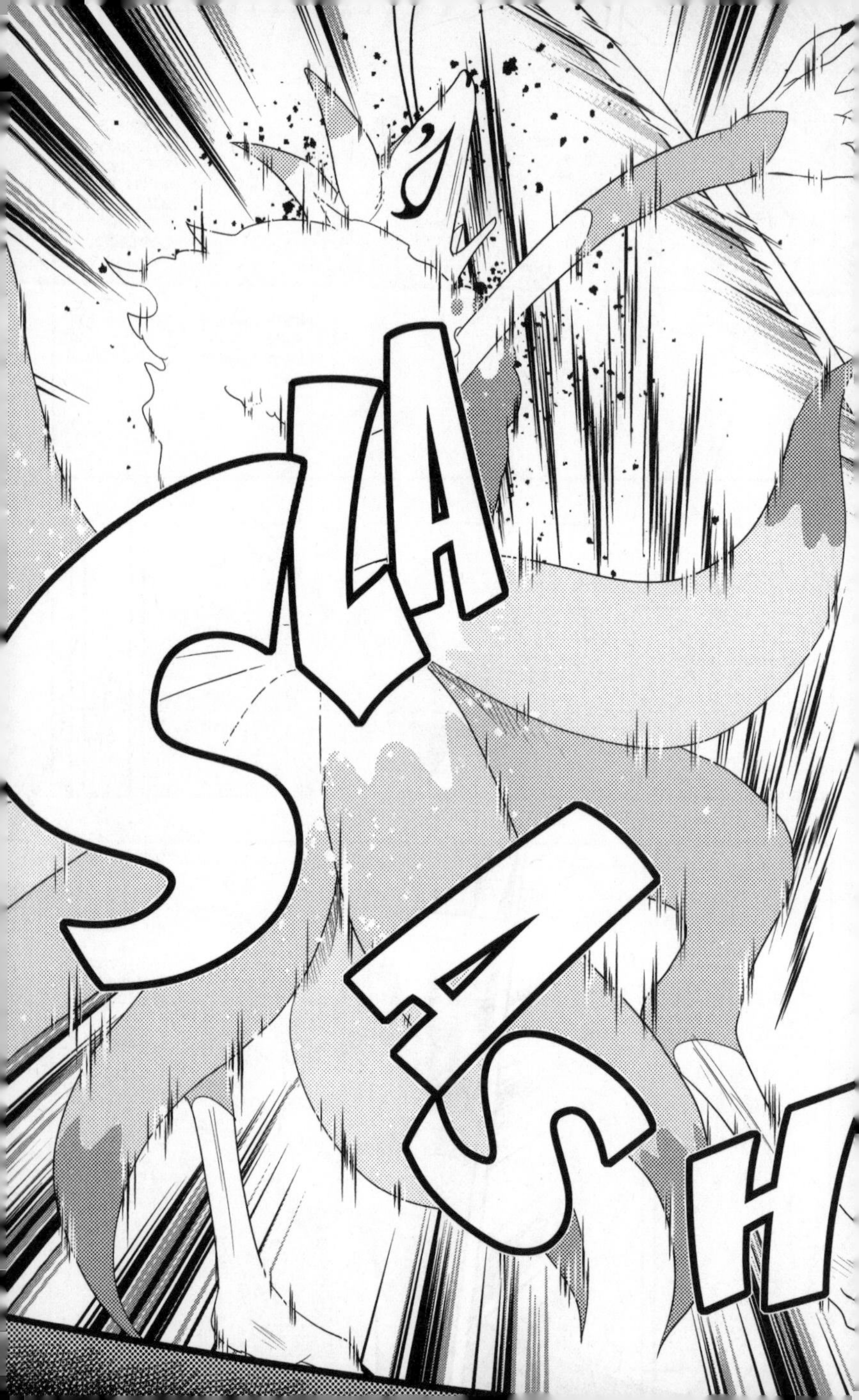
SLASH

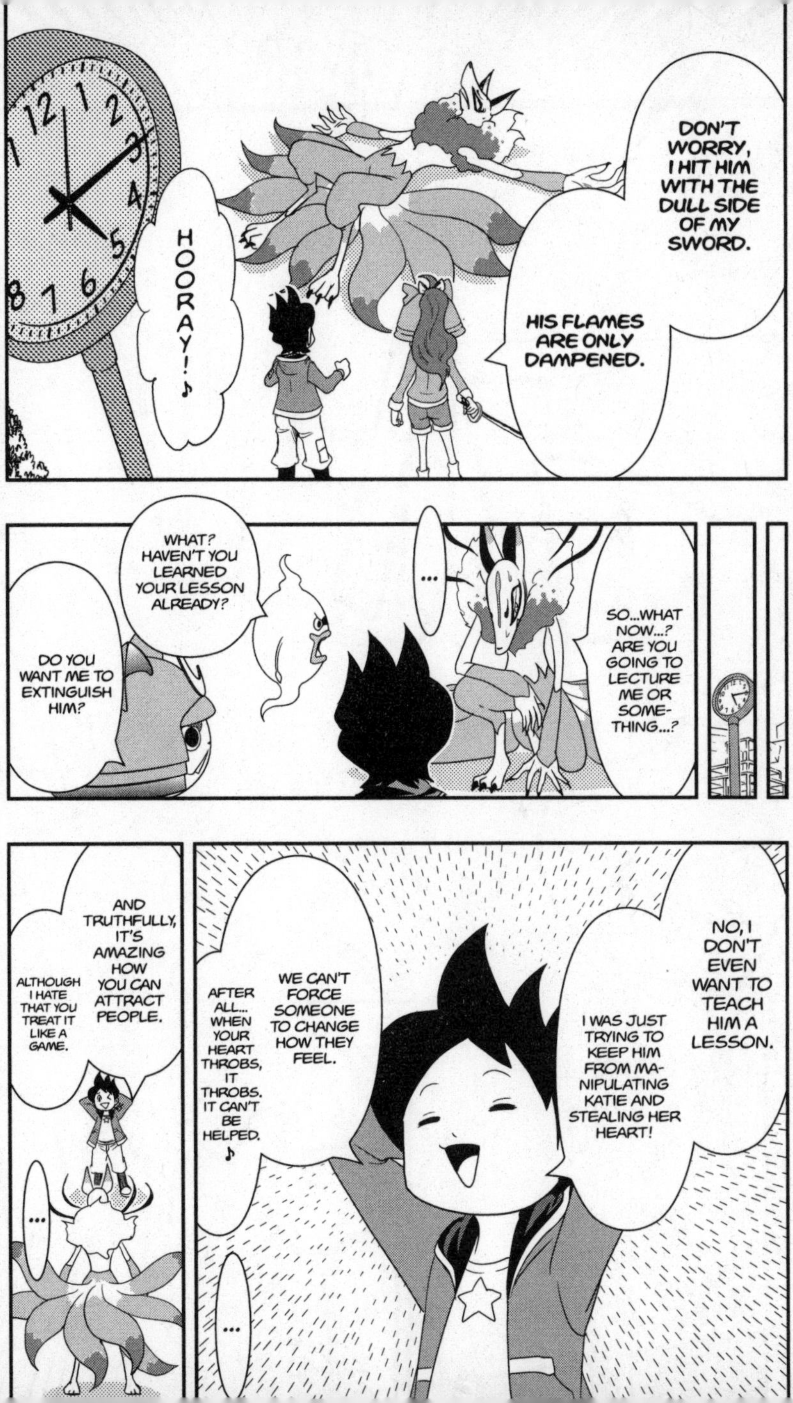
DON'T WORRY, I HIT HIM WITH THE DULL SIDE OF MY SWORD.
HIS FLAMES ARE ONLY DAMPENED.
HOORAY!♪
SO...WHAT NOW...? ARE YOU GOING TO LECTURE ME OR SOME-THING...?
...
WHAT? HAVEN'T YOU LEARNED YOUR LESSON ALREADY?
DO YOU WANT ME TO EXTINGUISH HIM?
NO, I DON'T EVEN WANT TO TEACH HIM A LESSON.
I WAS JUST TRYING TO KEEP HIM FROM MA-NIPULATING KATIE AND STEALING HER HEART!
WE CAN'T FORCE SOMEONE TO CHANGE HOW THEY FEEL.
AFTER ALL... WHEN YOUR HEART THROBS, IT THROBS. IT CAN'T BE HELPED. ♪
...
AND TRUTHFULLY, IT'S AMAZING HOW YOU CAN ATTRACT PEOPLE.
ALTHOUGH I HATE THAT YOU TREAT IT LIKE A GAME.
...

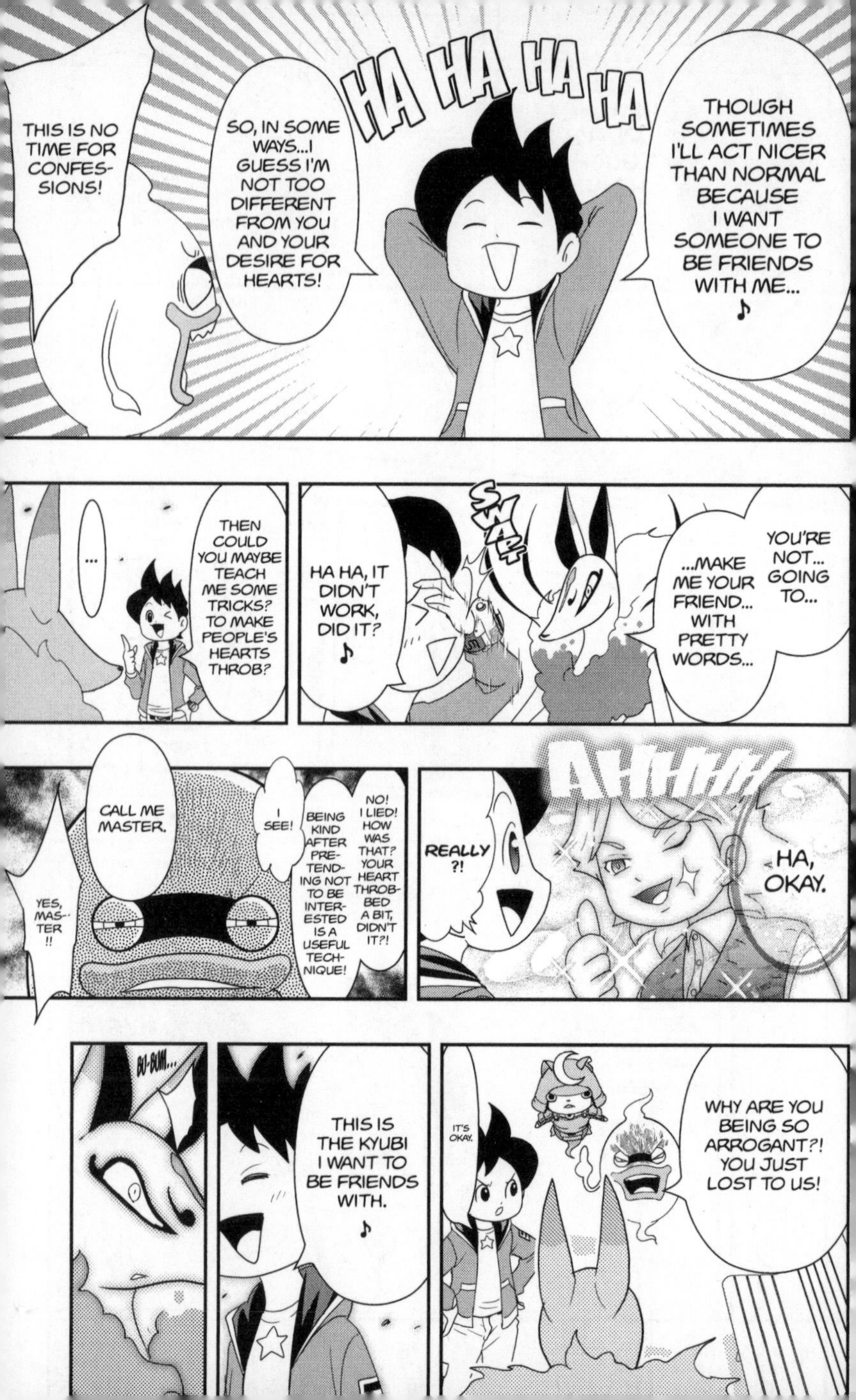
THOUGH SOMETIMES I'LL ACT NICER THAN NORMAL BECAUSE I WANT SOMEONE TO BE FRIENDS WITH ME... ♪
HA HA HA HA
SO, IN SOME WAYS...I GUESS I'M NOT TOO DIFFERENT FROM YOU AND YOUR DESIRE FOR HEARTS!
THIS IS NO TIME FOR CONFES- SIONS!
YOU'RE NOT... GOING TO...
...MAKE ME YOUR FRIEND... WITH PRETTY WORDS...
SWAP
HA HA, IT DIDN'T WORK, DID IT? ♪
THEN COULD YOU MAYBE TEACH ME SOME TRICKS? TO MAKE PEOPLE'S HEARTS THROB?
...
AHHH
HA, OKAY.
REALLY ?!
NO! I LIED! HOW WAS THAT? YOUR HEART THROB- BED A BIT, DIDN'T IT?!
BEING KIND AFTER PRE- TEND- ING NOT TO BE INTER- ESTED IS A USEFUL TECH- NIQUE!
I SEE!
CALL ME MASTER.
YES, MAS- TER !!
WHY ARE YOU BEING SO ARROGANT?! YOU JUST LOST TO US!
IT'S OKAY.
THIS IS THE KYUBI I WANT TO BE FRIENDS WITH. ♪
BU-BUM...

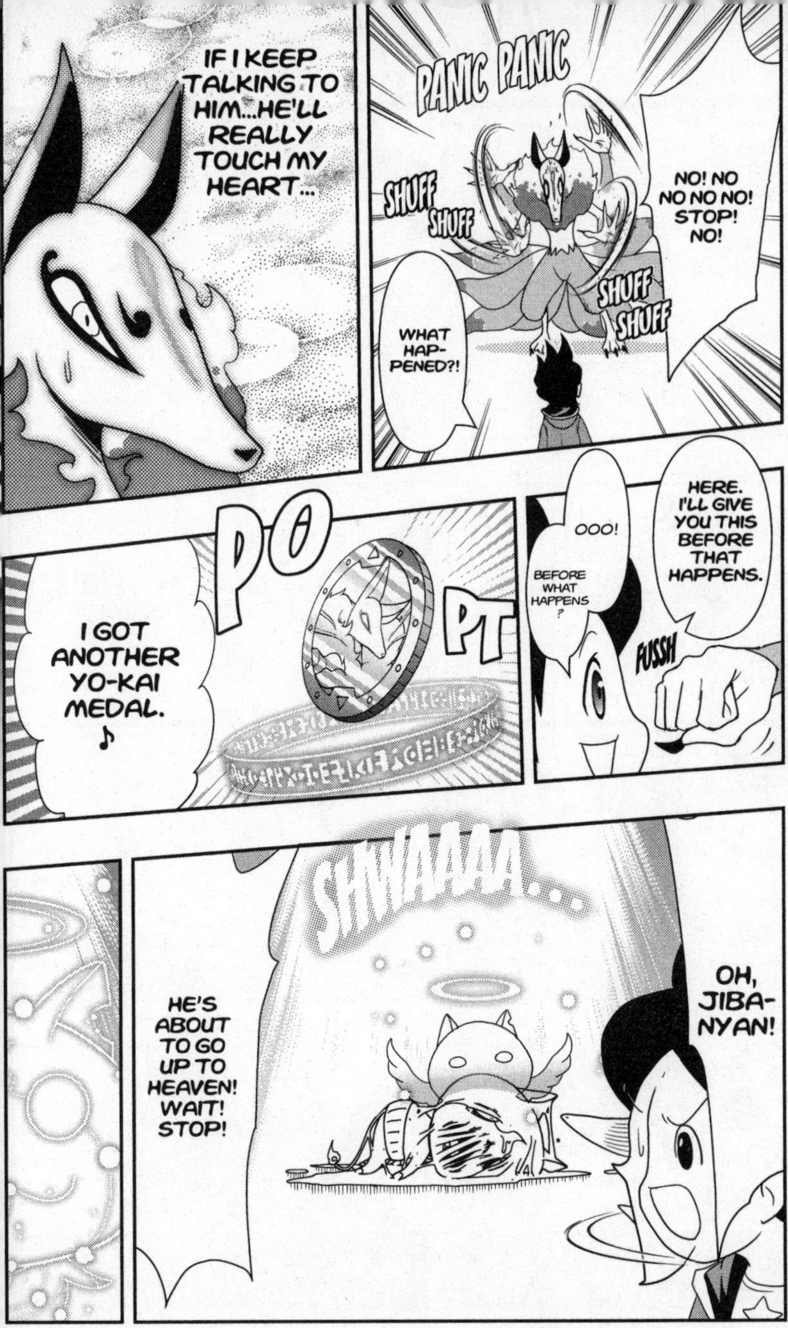
PANIC PANIC
SHUFF SHUFF
NO! NO NO NO NO! STOP! NO!
SHUFF SHUFF
WHAT HAP-PENED?!
IF I KEEP TALKING TO HIM...HE'LL REALLY TOUCH MY HEART...
HERE. I'LL GIVE YOU THIS BEFORE THAT HAPPENS.
OOO!
BEFORE WHAT HAPPENS?
FUSSH
PO PT
I GOT ANOTHER YO-KAI MEDAL. ♪
SHWAAAA...
OH, JIBA-NYAN!
HE'S ABOUT TO GO UP TO HEAVEN! WAIT! STOP!

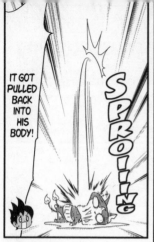

MEOW.
GOOOEY...
THE SNOT IS STUCK ON HIS SOUL TOO!
SPROIIING
IT GOT PULLED BACK INTO HIS BODY!
MEOW... THAT WAS CLOSE... I WAS ALMOST DONE FOR..
ZZZ... ZZZ...
SHUP...
NOR-MALLY, HE'D HAVE BEEN DONE FOR!
...
WHEEZE WHEEZE
OH... KATIE!
WOW, IT'S GOTTEN LATE! I NEED TO GET HOME. SEE YOU LATER, NATE!
WHAAAAAA
WHAT?! NO! WE DIDN'T EVEN HAVE TIME TO HANG OUT!

NATE ADAMS'S CURRENT NUMBER OF YO-KAI FRIENDS: 63

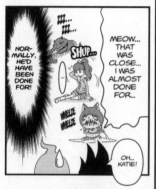

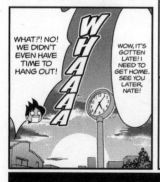

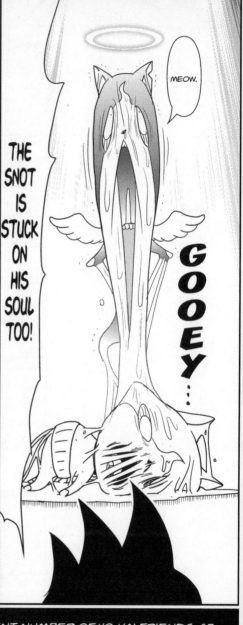

SHOGUN KATIE

FWEEE
SHOGUNYAN, INSPIRIT KATIE AND BRING HER BACK!!
NO PRO-BLEM!
TEMP TEMP TEMP
SHUP
EXCUSE ME, KATIE.
ALLOW ME TO BORROW YOUR BODY FOR JUST A MOMENT PLEASE...
TEMP TEMP TEMP
I'M SORRY, NATE! LET'S HANG OUT FOR A LITTLE LONGER! ♪
HURRAY!
TEMP TEMP TEMP
KATIE! ♪
HAHA HA HA
AHH! NEVER-MIND!

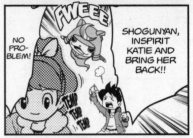

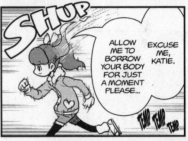

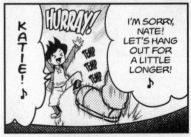

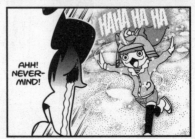

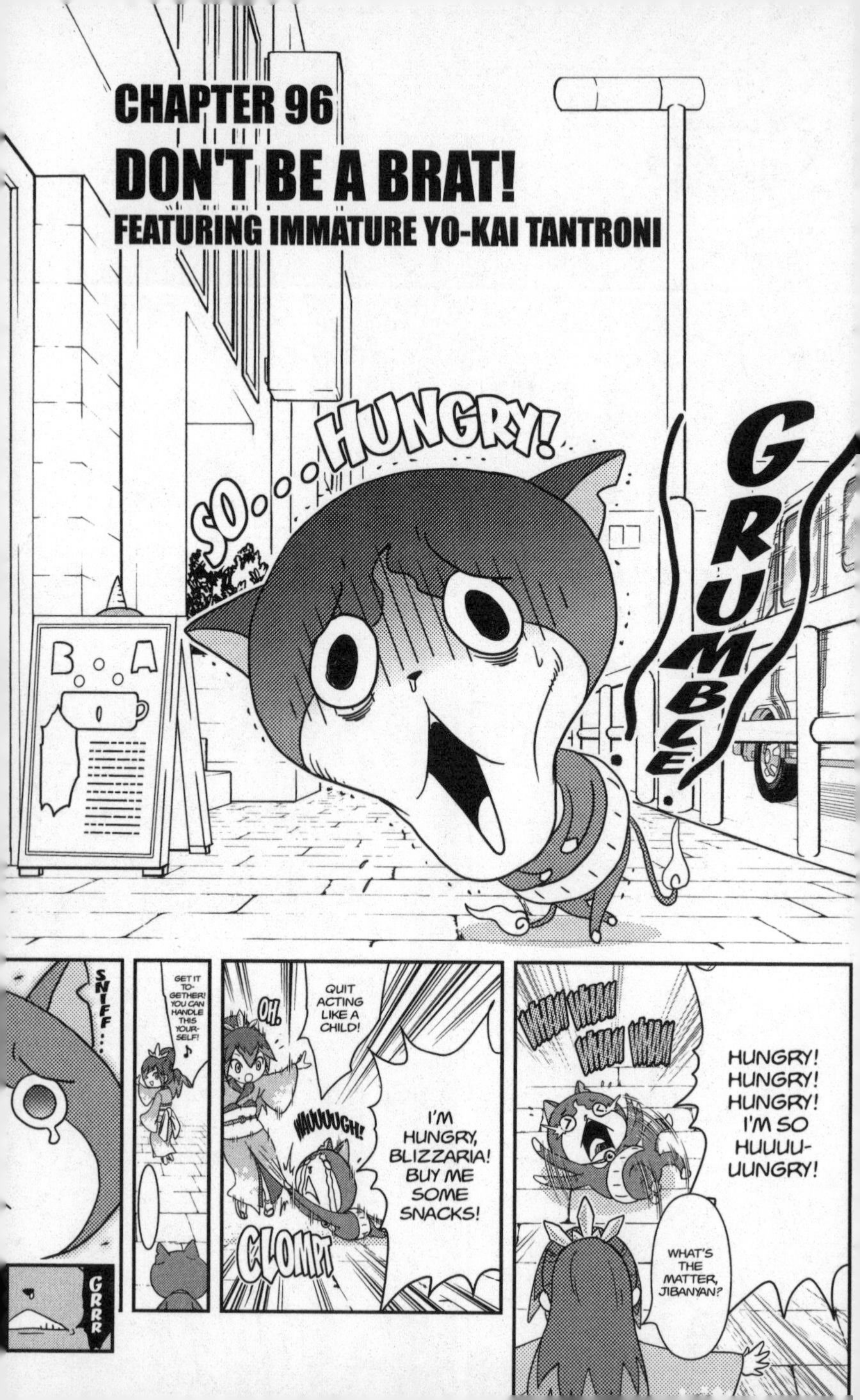
CHAPTER 96
DON'T BE A BRAT!
FEATURING IMMATURE YO-KAI TANTRONI
GRUMBLE!
SO...HUNGRY!
HUNGRY! HUNGRY! HUNGRY! I'M SO HUUUU-UUNGRY!
WHAT'S THE MATTER, JIBANYAN?
QUIT ACTING LIKE A CHILD!
OH.
I'M HUNGRY, BLIZZARIA! BUY ME SOME SNACKS!
WAUUUGH!
CLOMP!
GET IT TO-GETHER! YOU CAN HANDLE THIS YOUR-SELF! ♪
SNIFF...
GRRR

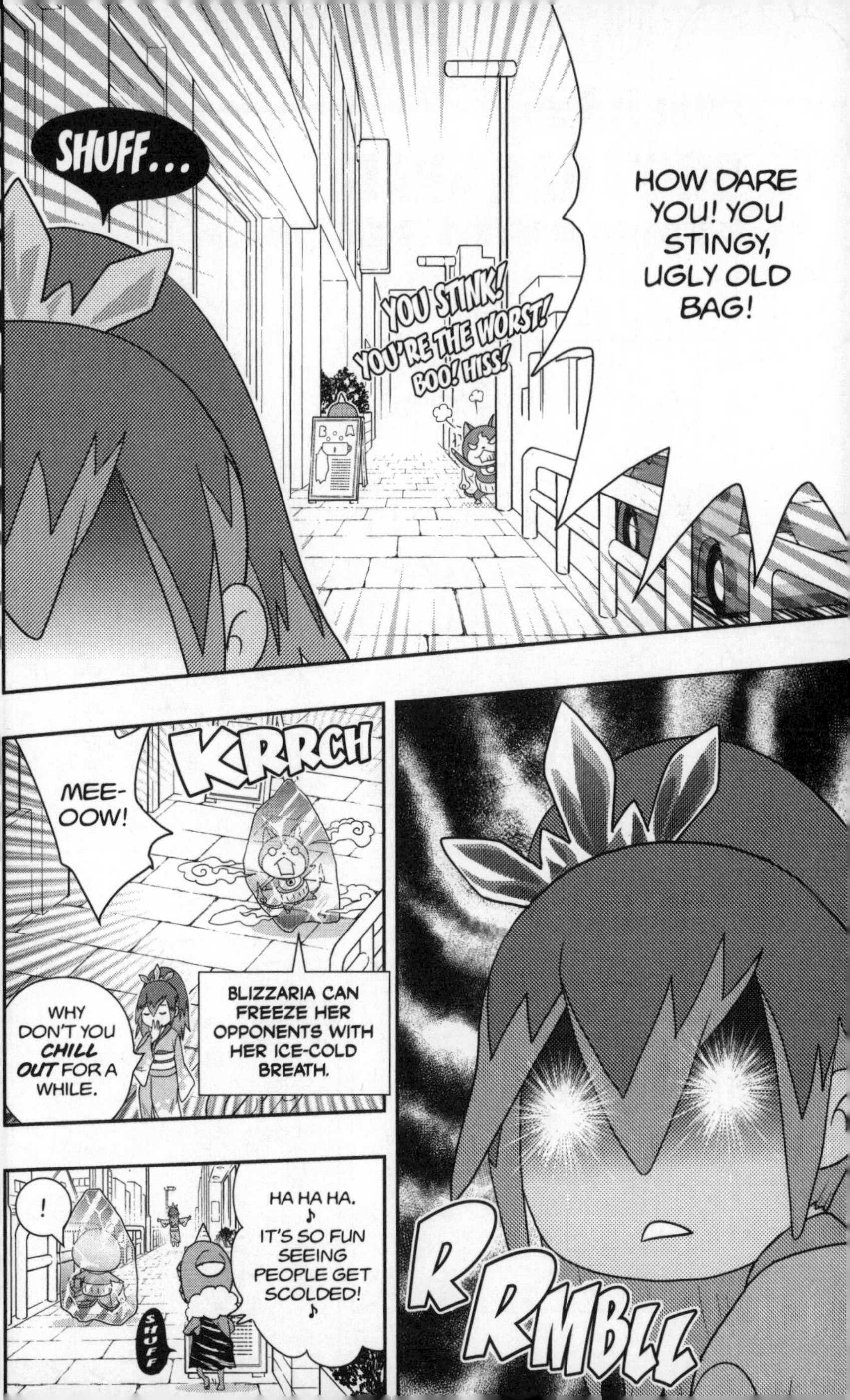
HOW DARE YOU! YOU STINGY, UGLY OLD BAG!
YOU STINK! YOU'RE THE WORST! BOO! HISS!
SHUFF...
RRMBLL
KRRCH
MEE-OOW!
BLIZZARIA CAN FREEZE HER OPPONENTS WITH HER ICE-COLD BREATH.
WHY DON'T YOU *CHILL OUT* FOR A WHILE.
HA HA HA. ♪ IT'S SO FUN SEEING PEOPLE GET SCOLDED! ♪
!
SHUFF

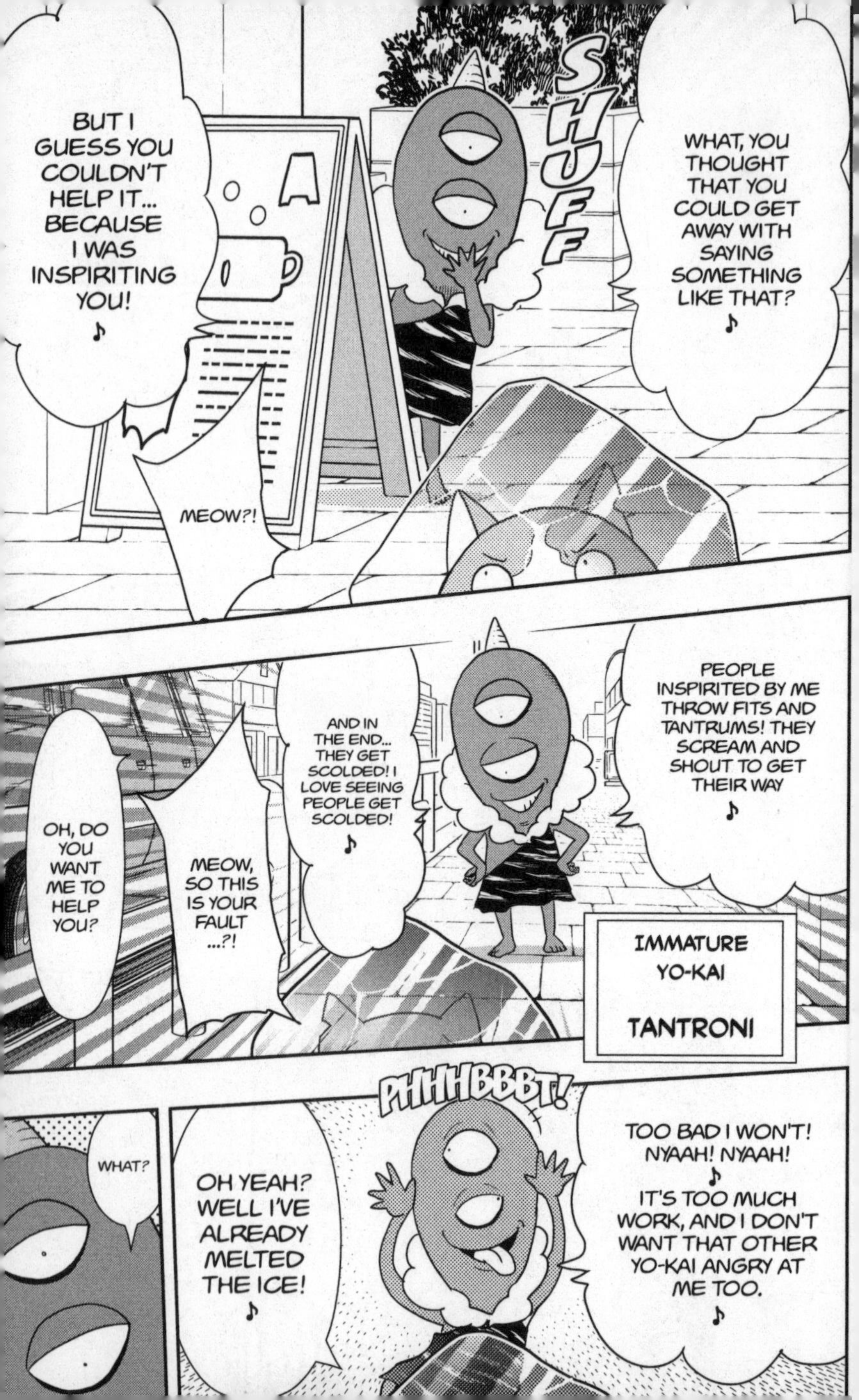
WHAT, YOU THOUGHT THAT YOU COULD GET AWAY WITH SAYING SOMETHING LIKE THAT? ♪
SHUFF
BUT I GUESS YOU COULDN'T HELP IT... BECAUSE I WAS INSPIRITING YOU! ♪
MEOW?!
PEOPLE INSPIRITED BY ME THROW FITS AND TANTRUMS! THEY SCREAM AND SHOUT TO GET THEIR WAY ♪
AND IN THE END... THEY GET SCOLDED! I LOVE SEEING PEOPLE GET SCOLDED! ♪
IMMATURE YO-KAI TANTRONI
MEOW, SO THIS IS YOUR FAULT ...?!
OH, DO YOU WANT ME TO HELP YOU?
PHHHBBBT!
TOO BAD I WON'T! NYAAH! NYAAH! ♪ IT'S TOO MUCH WORK, AND I DON'T WANT THAT OTHER YO-KAI ANGRY AT ME TOO. ♪
OH YEAH? WELL I'VE ALREADY MELTED THE ICE! ♪
WHAT?

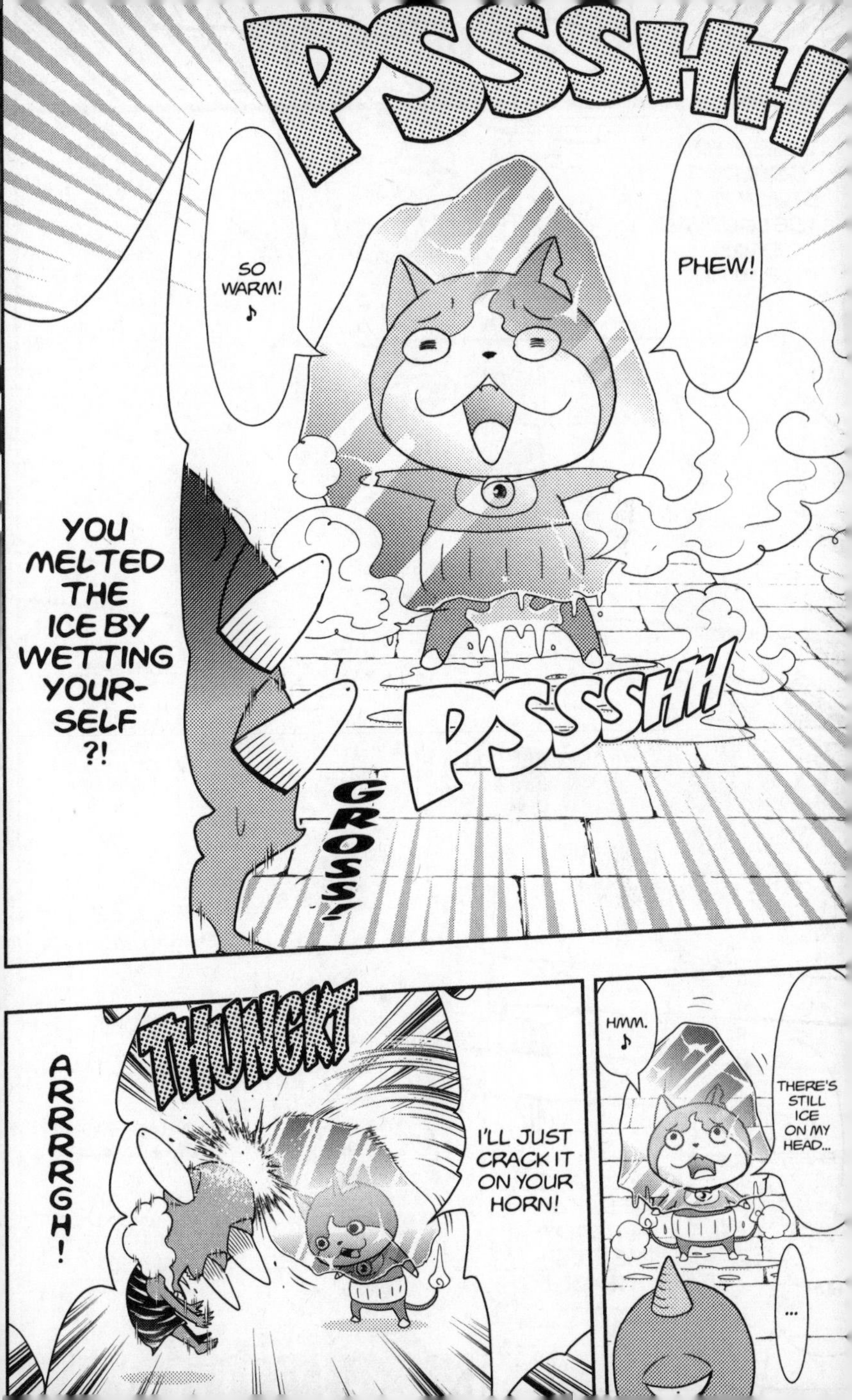
PSSSHH
PHEW!
SO WARM! ♪
YOU MELTED THE ICE BY WETTING YOUR-SELF ?!
PSSSHH
GROSS!
THERE'S STILL ICE ON MY HEAD...
HMM. ♪
...
I'LL JUST CRACK IT ON YOUR HORN!
THUNCKT
ARRRRGH!

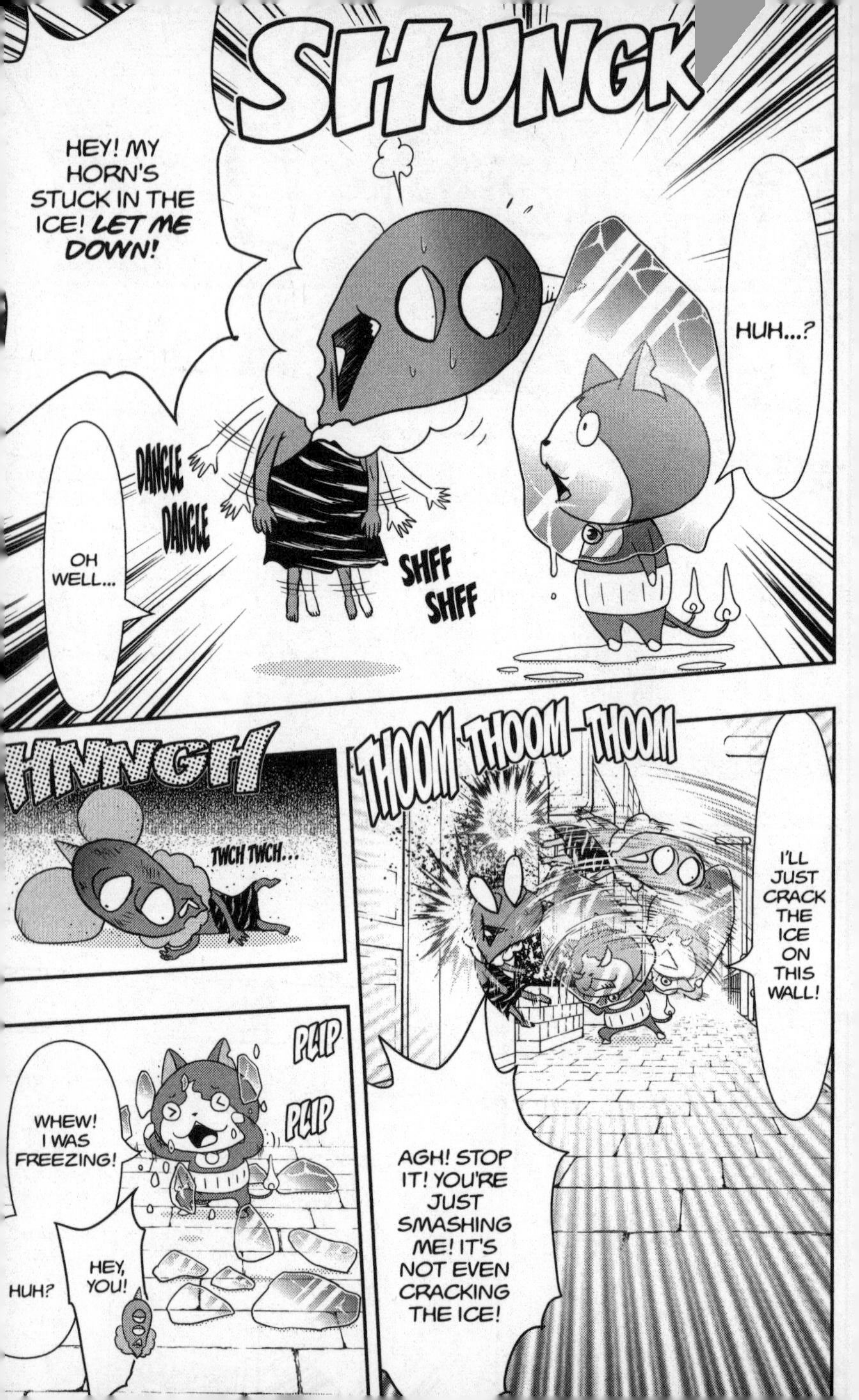
SHUNGK
HUH...?
HEY! MY HORN'S STUCK IN THE ICE! LET ME DOWN!
SHFF SHFF
DANGLE DANGLE
OH WELL...
I'LL JUST CRACK THE ICE ON THIS WALL!
THOOM THOOM THOOM
AGH! STOP IT! YOU'RE JUST SMASHING ME! IT'S NOT EVEN CRACKING THE ICE!
HNNGH
TWCH TWCH...
PLIP PLIP
WHEW! I WAS FREEZING!
HEY, YOU!
HUH?

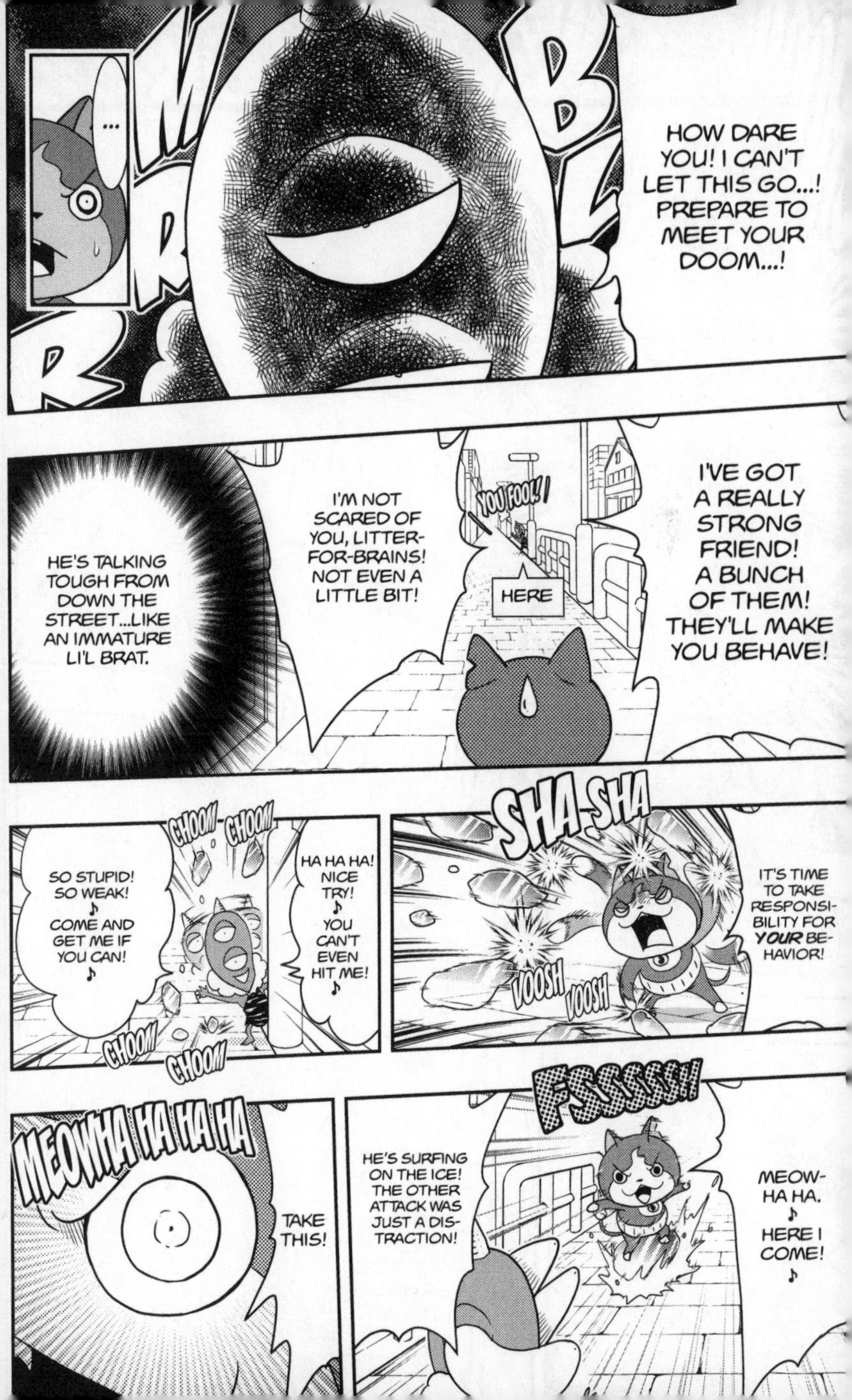
HOW DARE YOU! I CAN'T LET THIS GO...! PREPARE TO MEET YOUR DOOM...!
...
I'VE GOT A REALLY STRONG FRIEND! A BUNCH OF THEM! THEY'LL MAKE YOU BEHAVE!
HERE
YOU FOOL!
I'M NOT SCARED OF YOU, LITTER-FOR-BRAINS! NOT EVEN A LITTLE BIT!
HE'S TALKING TOUGH FROM DOWN THE STREET...LIKE AN IMMATURE LI'L BRAT.
SHA-SHA
IT'S TIME TO TAKE RESPONSIBILITY FOR **YOUR** BEHAVIOR!
VOOSH VOOSH
CHOOM CHOOM
HA HA HA! NICE TRY! ♪ YOU CAN'T EVEN HIT ME! ♪
SO STUPID! SO WEAK! ♪ COME AND GET ME IF YOU CAN! ♪
CHOOM CHOOM
FSSSSSH!
MEOW-HA HA. ♪ HERE I COME! ♪
HE'S SURFING ON THE ICE! THE OTHER ATTACK WAS JUST A DISTRACTION!
MEOWHA HA HA HA
TAKE THIS!

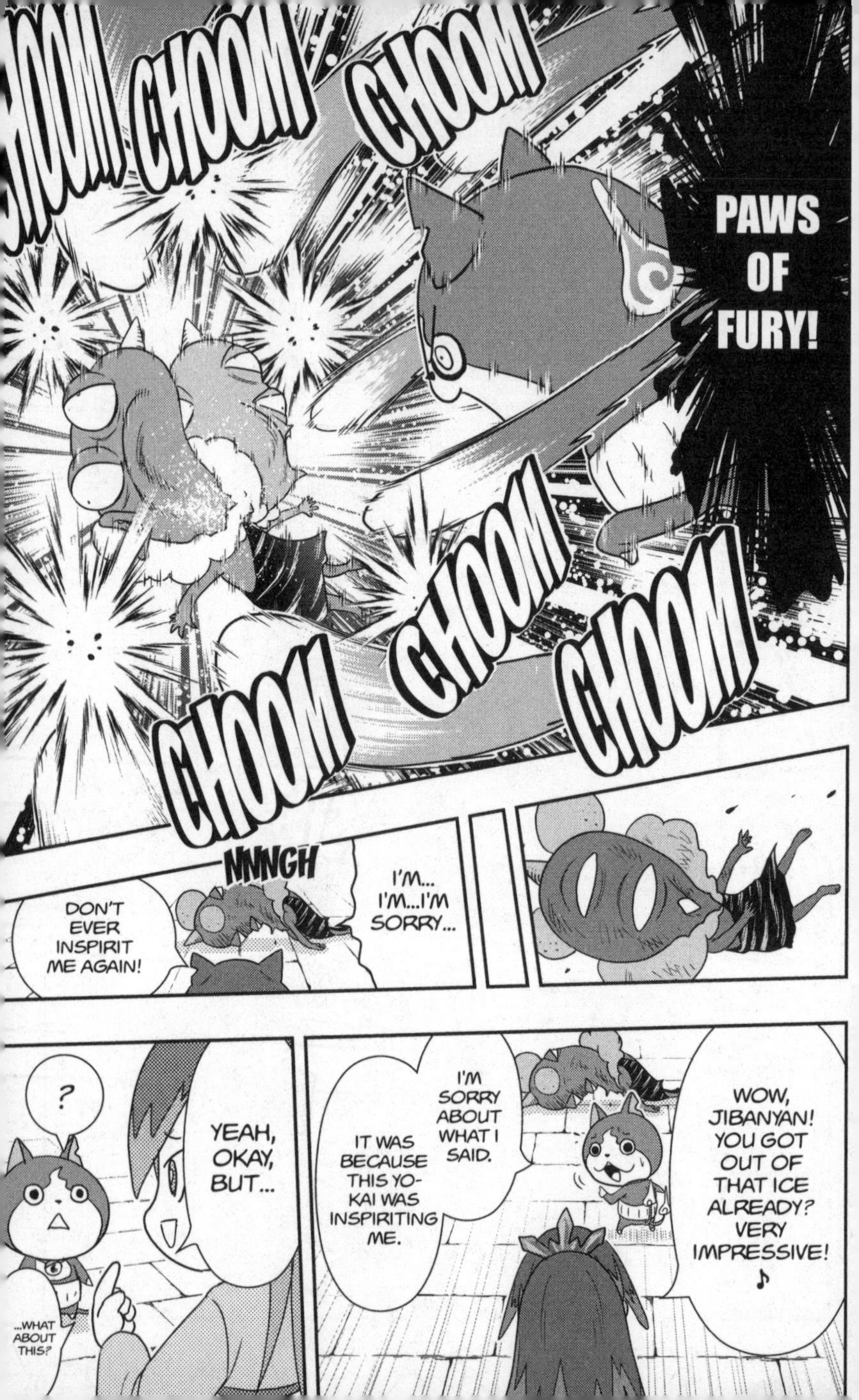
PAWS OF FURY!
CHOOM CHOOM CHOOM
CHOOM CHOOM CHOOM
NNNGH
I'M... I'M...I'M SORRY...
DON'T EVER INSPIRIT ME AGAIN!
WOW, JIBANYAN! YOU GOT OUT OF THAT ICE ALREADY? VERY IMPRESSIVE! ♪
I'M SORRY ABOUT WHAT I SAID.
IT WAS BECAUSE THIS YO-KAI WAS INSPIRITING ME.
YEAH, OKAY, BUT...
?
...WHAT ABOUT THIS?

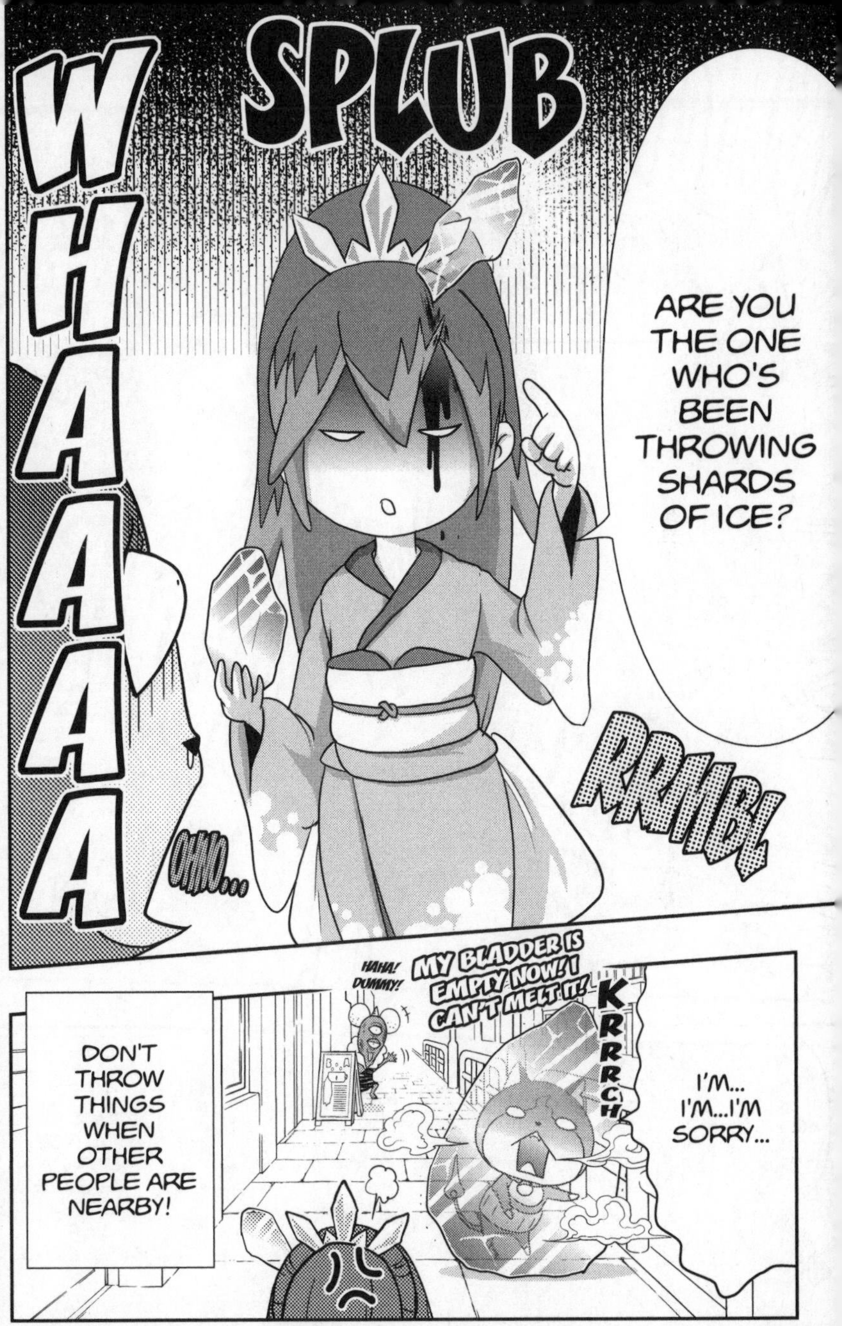
SPLUB
ARE YOU THE ONE WHO'S BEEN THROWING SHARDS OF ICE?
RRMBL
WHAAAAA
OHHO...
I'M... I'M...I'M SORRY...
KRRRCH
MY BLADDER IS EMPTY NOW! I CAN'T MELT IT!
HAHA! DUMMY!
DON'T THROW THINGS WHEN OTHER PEOPLE ARE NEARBY!

CHAPTER 97
ALWAYS FIGHT FAIR IN BATTLE!
FEATURING TRAINEE SAMURAI YO-KAI LIE-IN

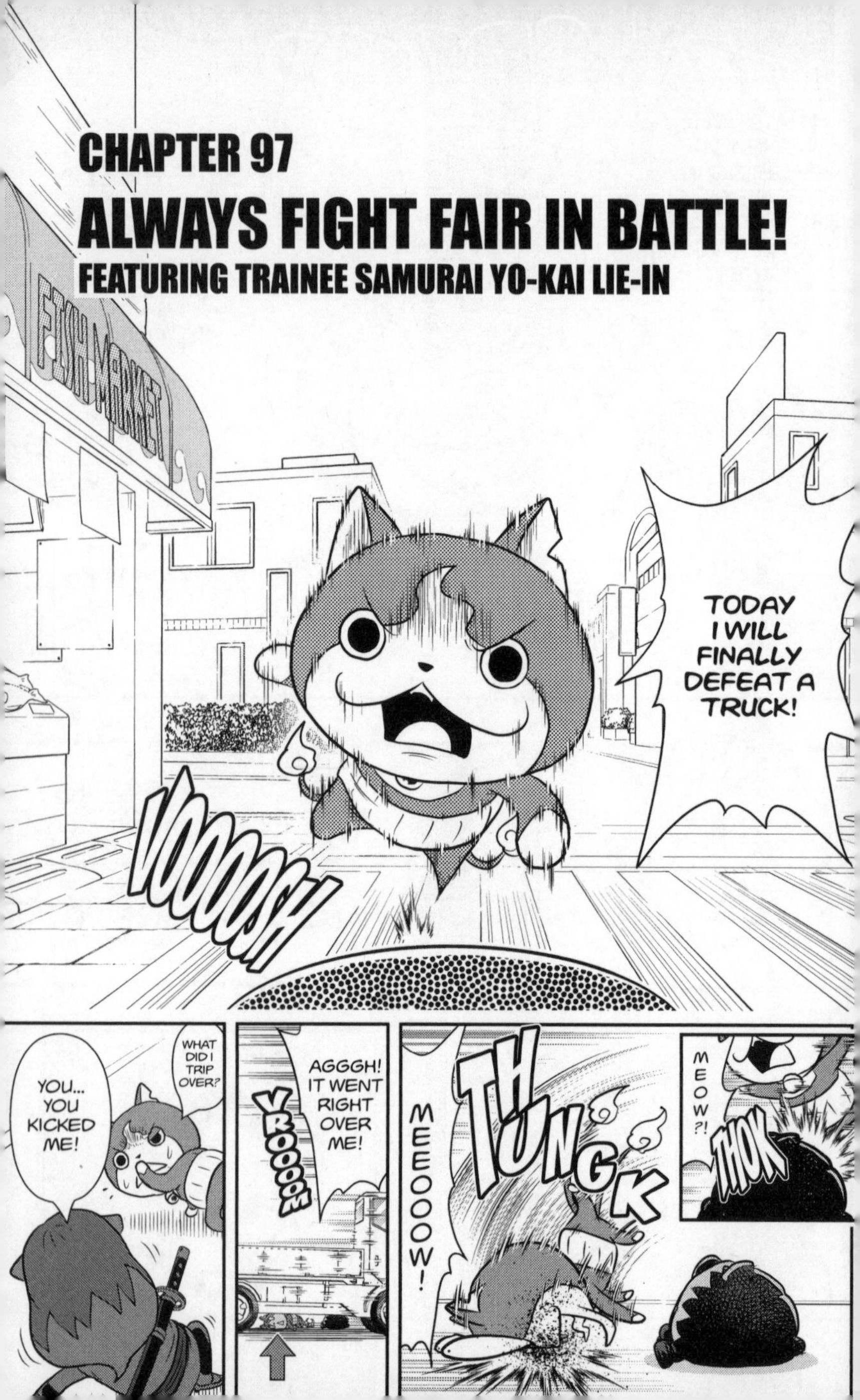
FISH MARKET
TODAY I WILL FINALLY DEFEAT A TRUCK!
VOOOOSH
MEOW?!
THOK
THUNGK
MEEOOOOW!
AGGGH! IT WENT RIGHT OVER ME!
VROOOOM
WHAT DID I TRIP OVER?
YOU... YOU KICKED ME!

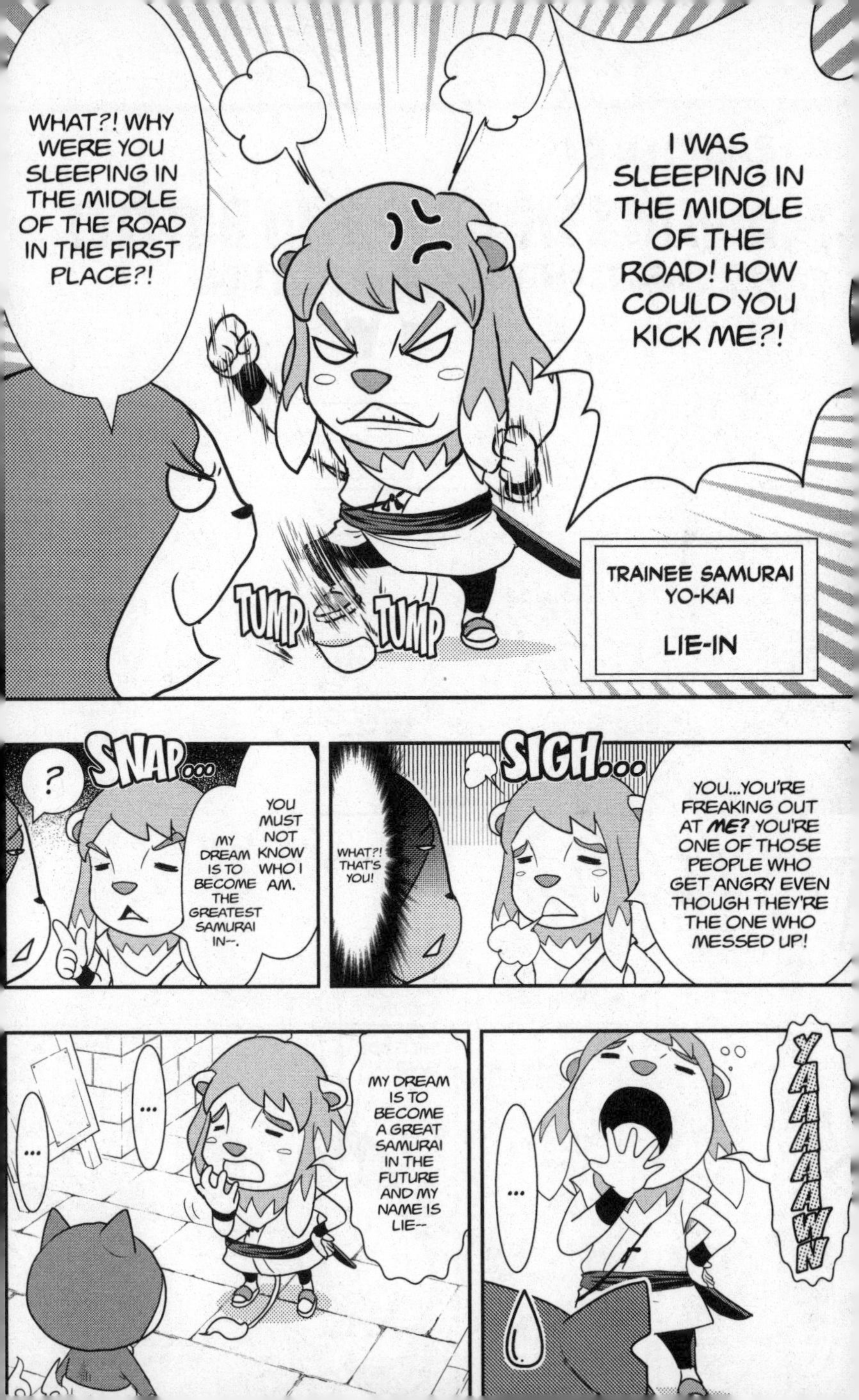
I WAS SLEEPING IN THE MIDDLE OF THE ROAD! HOW COULD YOU KICK ME?!
WHAT?! WHY WERE YOU SLEEPING IN THE MIDDLE OF THE ROAD IN THE FIRST PLACE?!
TRAINEE SAMURAI YO-KAI
LIE-IN
TUMP
TUMP
SIGH...
YOU...YOU'RE FREAKING OUT AT *ME?* YOU'RE ONE OF THOSE PEOPLE WHO GET ANGRY EVEN THOUGH THEY'RE THE ONE WHO MESSED UP!
WHAT?! THAT'S YOU!
SNAP...
?
YOU MUST NOT KNOW WHO I AM.
MY DREAM IS TO BECOME THE GREATEST SAMURAI IN--.
YAAAAAWN
...
MY DREAM IS TO BECOME A GREAT SAMURAI IN THE FUTURE AND MY NAME IS LIE--
...
...

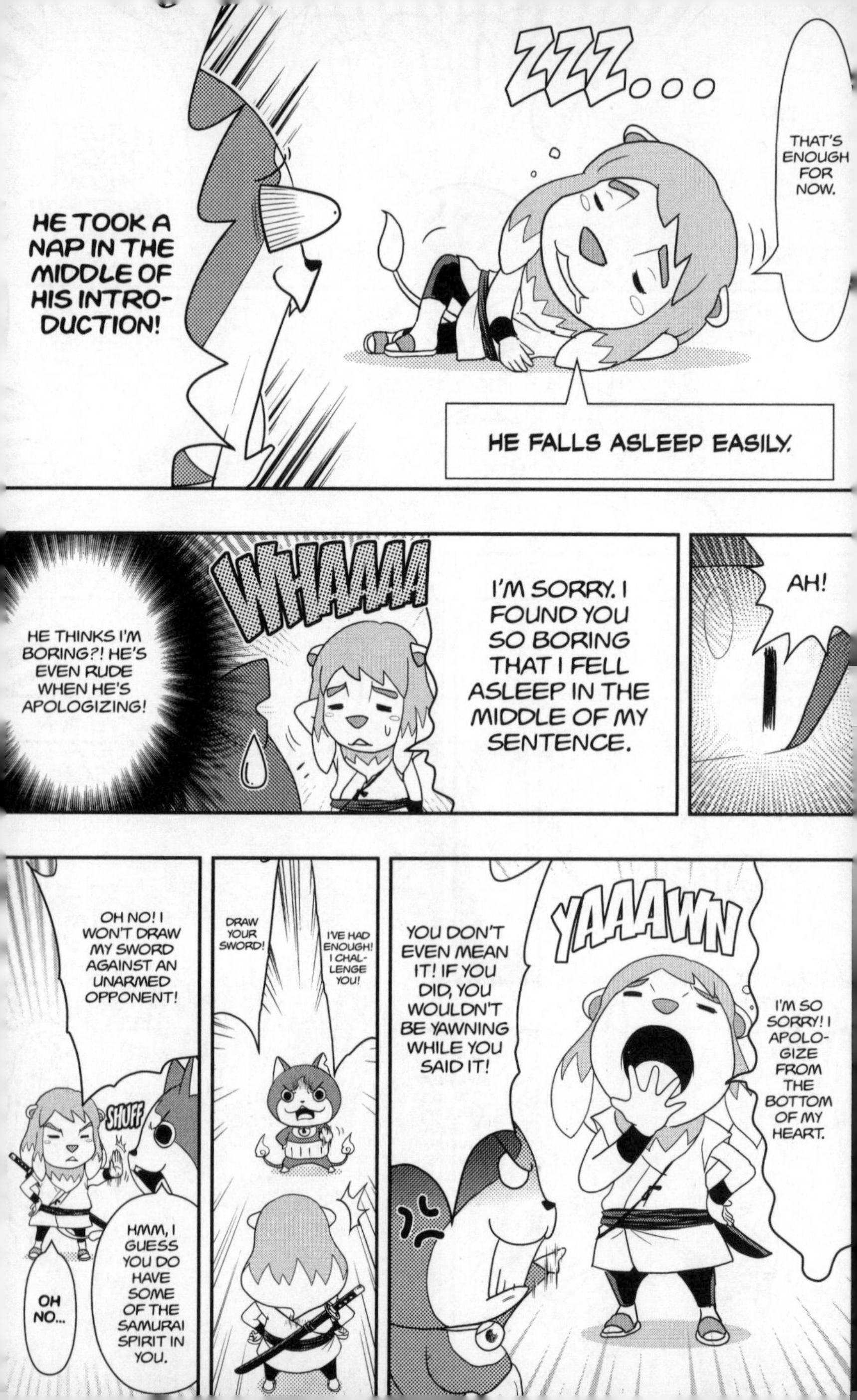
ZZZ...
THAT'S ENOUGH FOR NOW.
HE TOOK A NAP IN THE MIDDLE OF HIS INTRODUCTION!
HE FALLS ASLEEP EASILY.
AH!
I'M SORRY. I FOUND YOU SO BORING THAT I FELL ASLEEP IN THE MIDDLE OF MY SENTENCE.
WHAAAAA
HE THINKS I'M BORING?! HE'S EVEN RUDE WHEN HE'S APOLOGIZING!
YAAAWN
I'M SO SORRY! I APOLOGIZE FROM THE BOTTOM OF MY HEART.
YOU DON'T EVEN MEAN IT! IF YOU DID, YOU WOULDN'T BE YAWNING WHILE YOU SAID IT!
I'VE HAD ENOUGH! I CHALLENGE YOU!
DRAW YOUR SWORD!
OH NO! I WON'T DRAW MY SWORD AGAINST AN UNARMED OPPONENT!
SHUFF
HMM, I GUESS YOU DO HAVE SOME OF THE SAMURAI SPIRIT IN YOU.
OH NO...

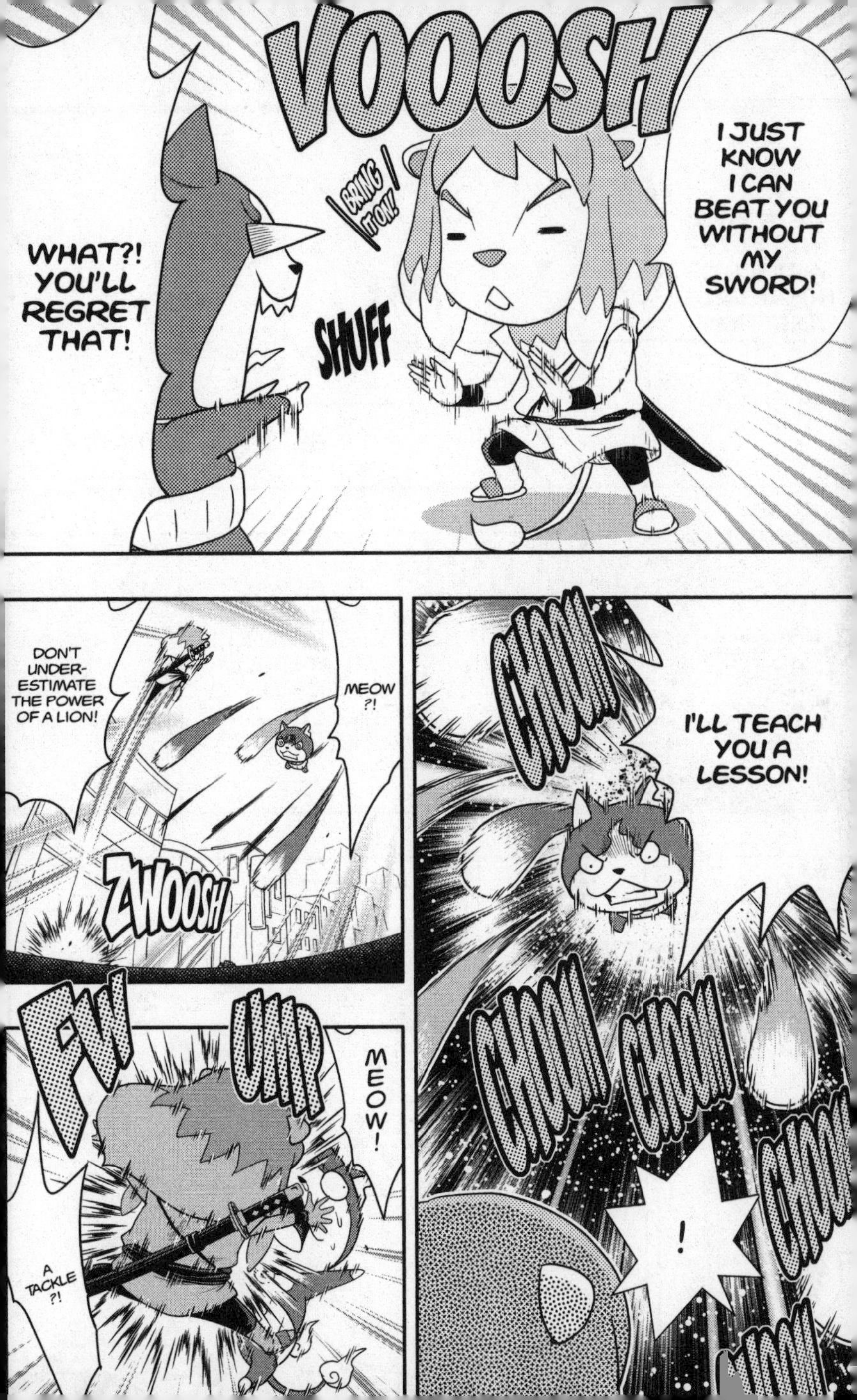
VOOOSH
I JUST KNOW I CAN BEAT YOU WITHOUT MY SWORD!
BRING IT ON!
WHAT?! YOU'LL REGRET THAT!
SHUFF
CHOMM
I'LL TEACH YOU A LESSON!
CHOMM
CHOMM
!
DON'T UNDER-ESTIMATE THE POWER OF A LION!
MEOW ?!
ZWOOSH
PW
UMP
MEOW!
A TACKLE ?!

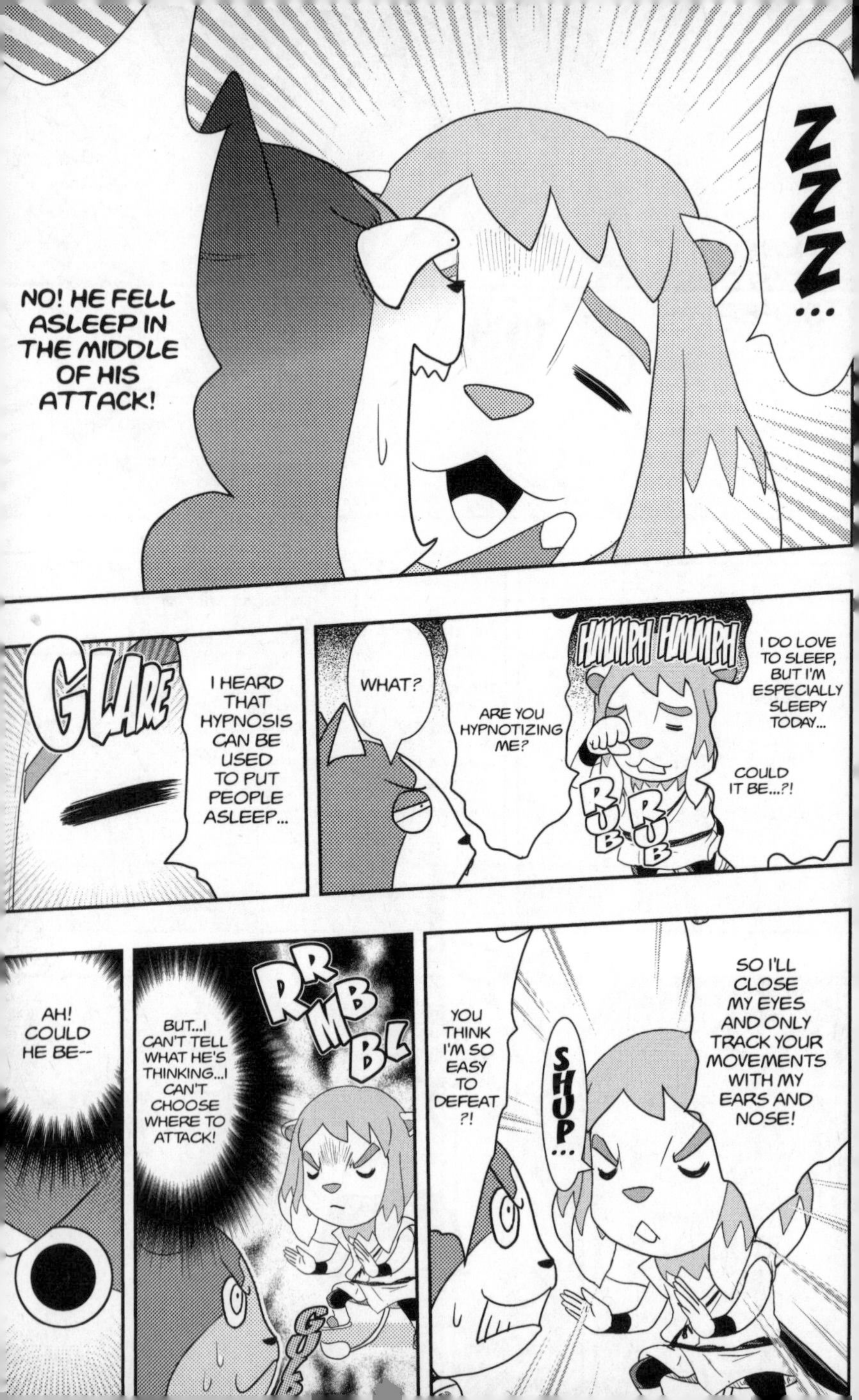
ZZZ...
NO! HE FELL ASLEEP IN THE MIDDLE OF HIS ATTACK!
HMMPH HMMPH
I DO LOVE TO SLEEP, BUT I'M ESPECIALLY SLEEPY TODAY...
RUB RUB
COULD IT BE...?!
ARE YOU HYPNOTIZING ME?
WHAT?
GLARE
I HEARD THAT HYPNOSIS CAN BE USED TO PUT PEOPLE ASLEEP...
YOU THINK I'M SO EASY TO DEFEAT?!
SO I'LL CLOSE MY EYES AND ONLY TRACK YOUR MOVEMENTS WITH MY EARS AND NOSE!
SHUP...
RRMBBL
BUT...I CAN'T TELL WHAT HE'S THINKING...I CAN'T CHOOSE WHERE TO ATTACK!
AH! COULD HE BE--

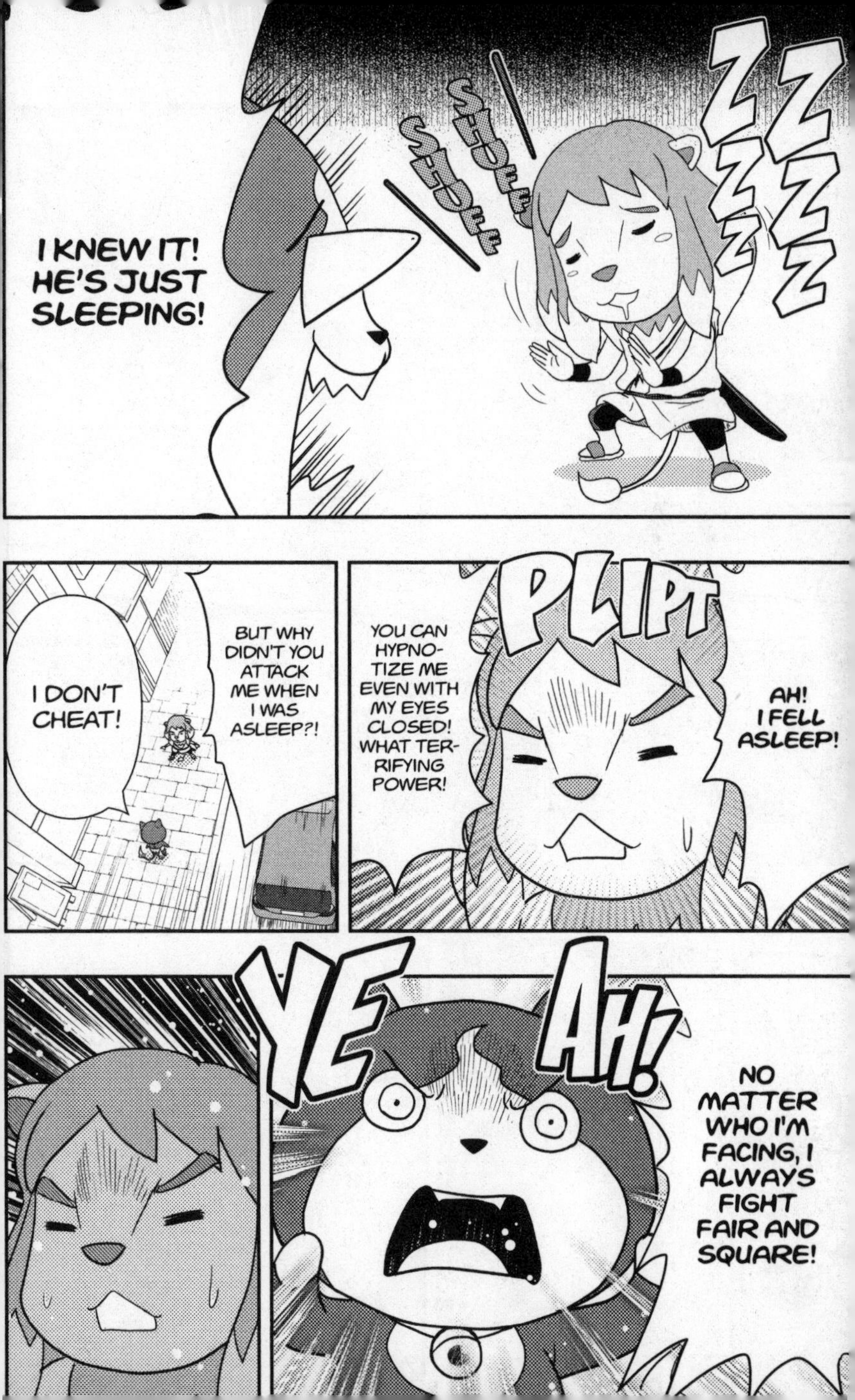
ZZZZ
ZZZZ
SHUFF
SHUFF
I KNEW IT! HE'S JUST SLEEPING!
PLIPT
AH! I FELL ASLEEP!
YOU CAN HYPNO-TIZE ME EVEN WITH MY EYES CLOSED! WHAT TER-RIFYING POWER!
BUT WHY DIDN'T YOU ATTACK ME WHEN I WAS ASLEEP?!
I DON'T CHEAT!
YEAH!
NO MATTER WHO I'M FACING, I ALWAYS FIGHT FAIR AND SQUARE!

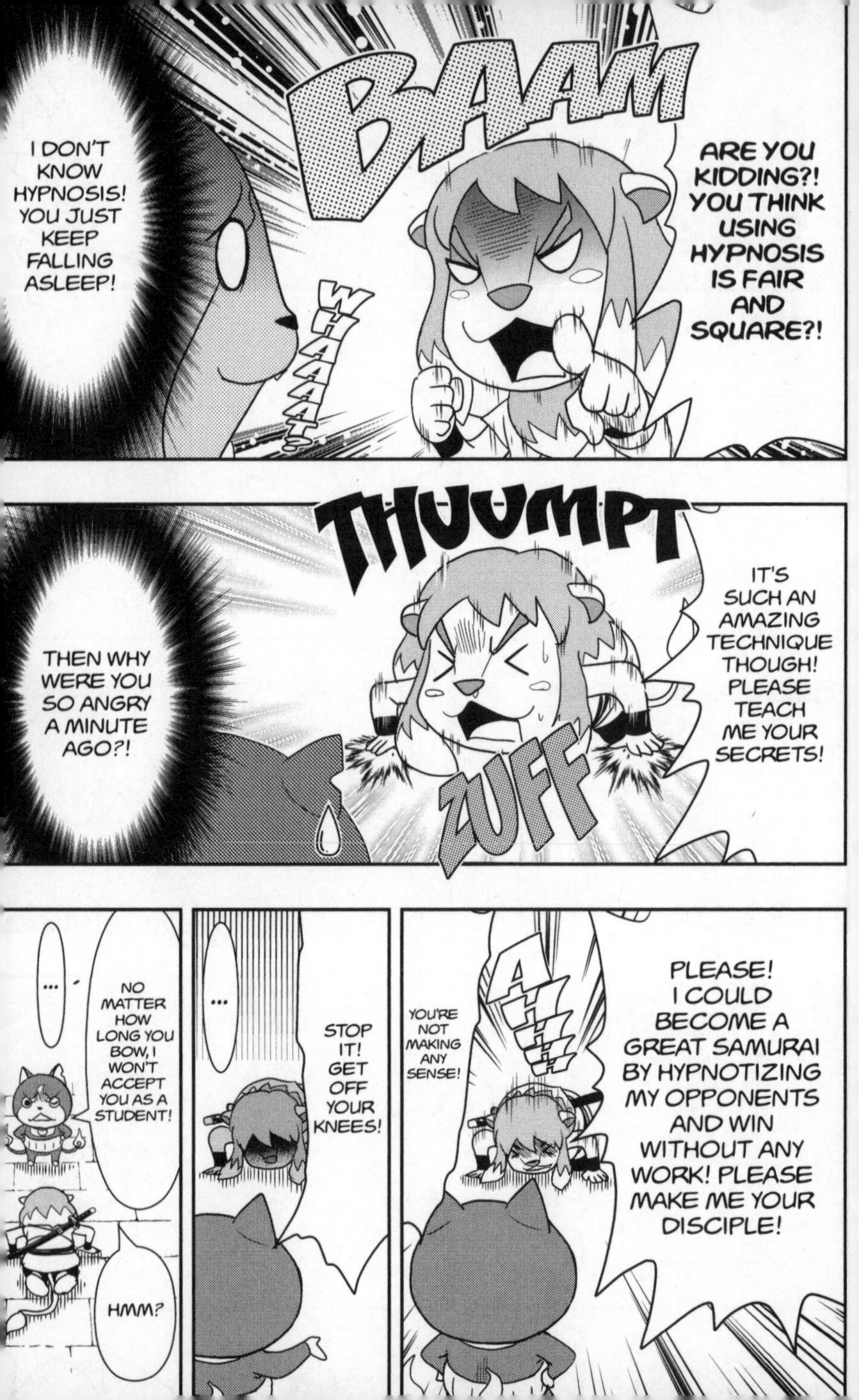
BAAM
ARE YOU KIDDING?! YOU THINK USING HYPNOSIS IS FAIR AND SQUARE?!
WHAAAAAT?!
I DON'T KNOW HYPNOSIS! YOU JUST KEEP FALLING ASLEEP!
THUUMPT
IT'S SUCH AN AMAZING TECHNIQUE THOUGH! PLEASE TEACH ME YOUR SECRETS!
ZUFF
THEN WHY WERE YOU SO ANGRY A MINUTE AGO?!
PLEASE! I COULD BECOME A GREAT SAMURAI BY HYPNOTIZING MY OPPONENTS AND WIN WITHOUT ANY WORK! PLEASE MAKE ME YOUR DISCIPLE!
YOU'RE NOT MAKING ANY SENSE!
STOP IT! GET OFF YOUR KNEES!
...
NO MATTER HOW LONG YOU BOW, I WON'T ACCEPT YOU AS A STUDENT!
...
HMM?

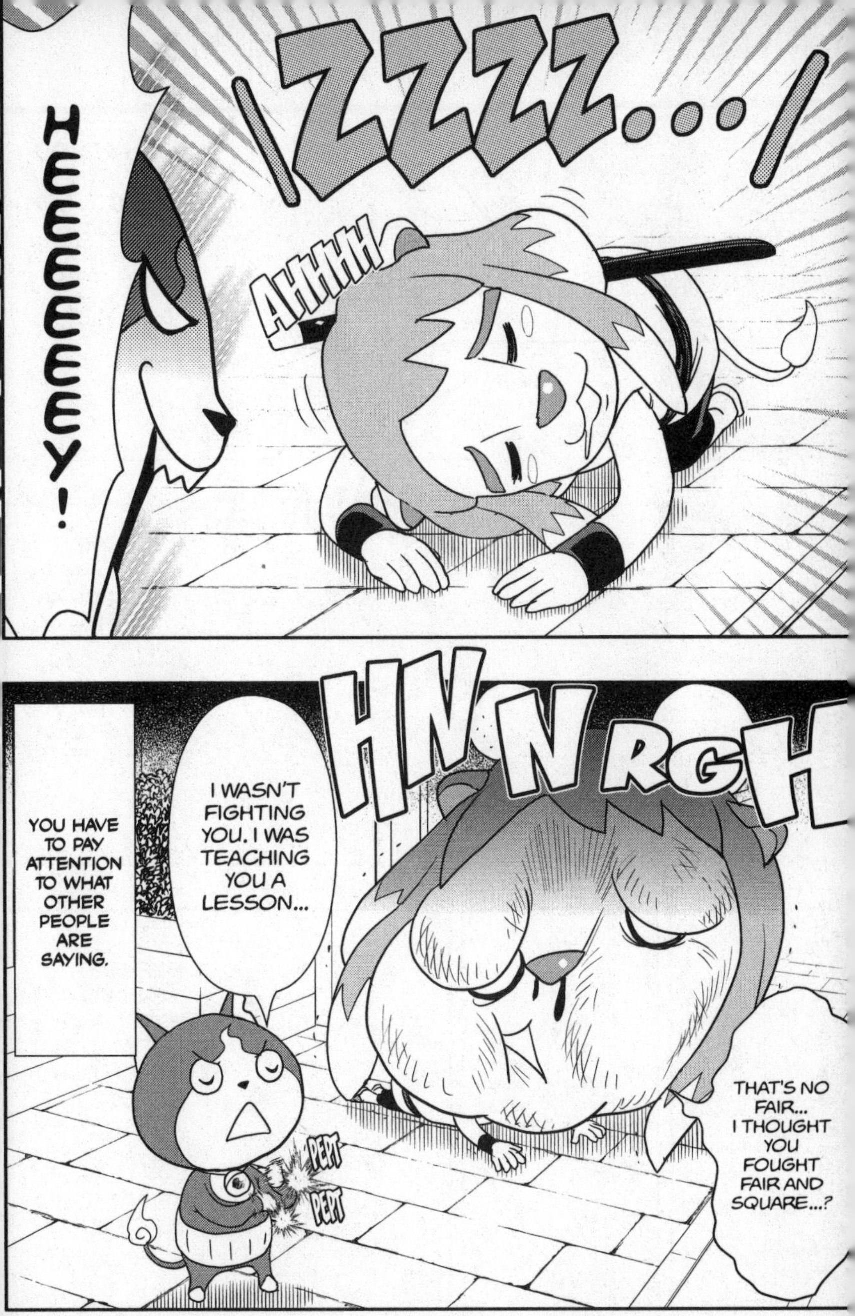

ZZZZ...
AHHHH
HEEEEEEEY!
HNNRGH
THAT'S NO FAIR... I THOUGHT YOU FOUGHT FAIR AND SQUARE...?
I WASN'T FIGHTING YOU. I WAS TEACHING YOU A LESSON...
YOU HAVE TO PAY ATTENTION TO WHAT OTHER PEOPLE ARE SAYING.
PEPT
PEPT

CHAPTER 98
I WANT TO BE HANDSOME!
FEATURING HANDSOME YO-KAI DANDOODLE

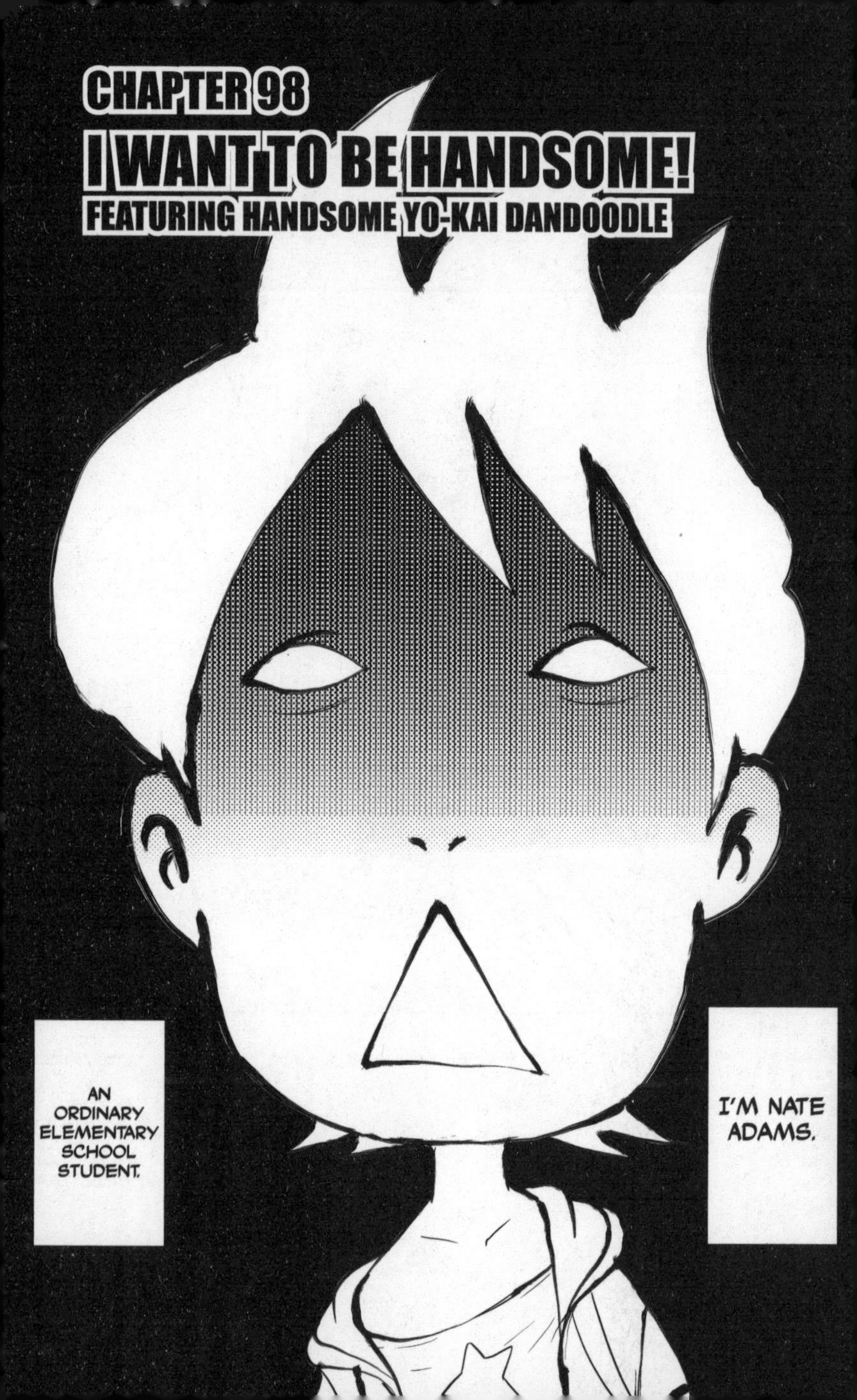

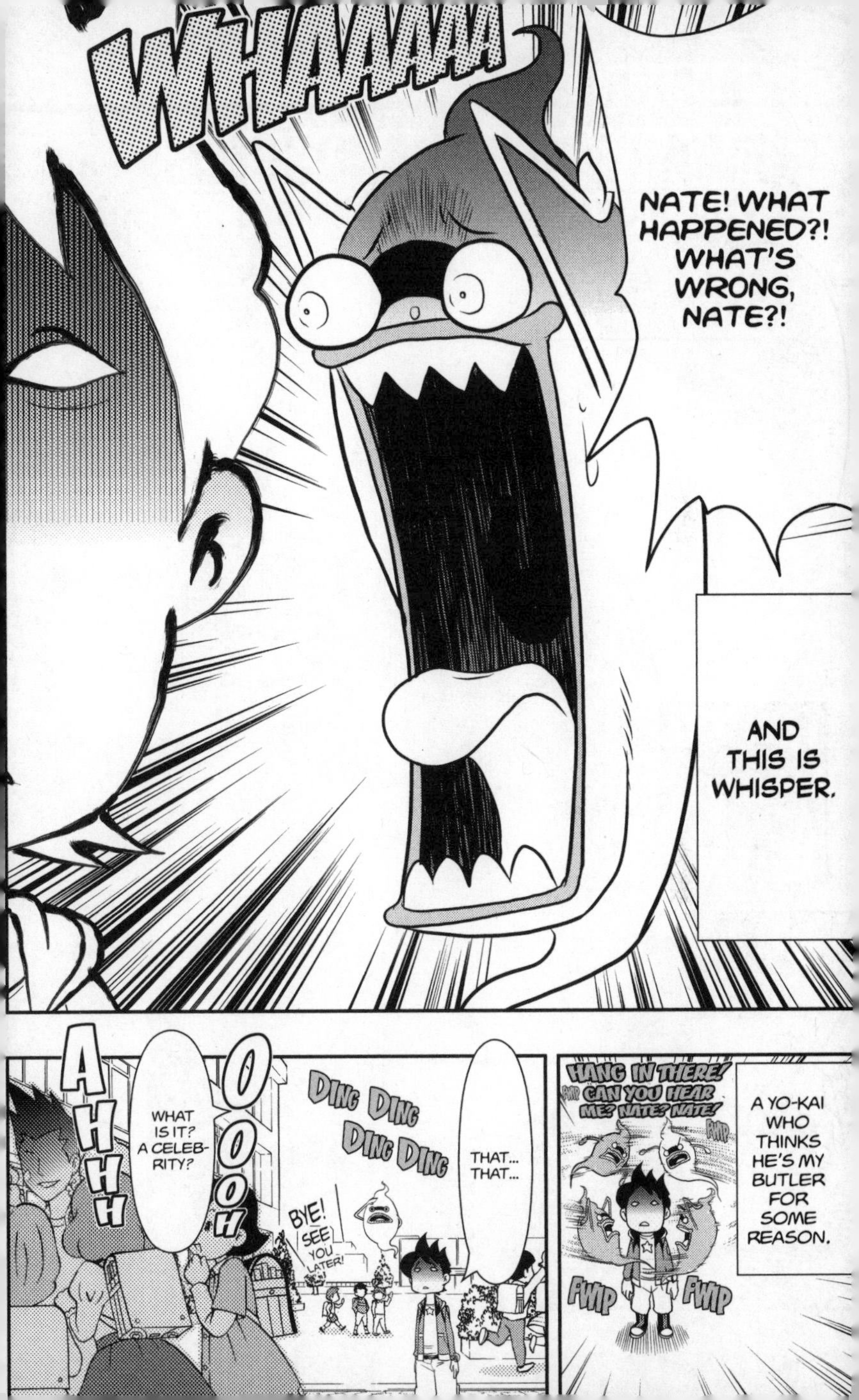
WHAAAAA
NATE! WHAT HAPPENED?! WHAT'S WRONG, NATE?!
AND THIS IS WHISPER.
A YO-KAI WHO THINKS HE'S MY BUTLER FOR SOME REASON.
HANG IN THERE! CAN YOU HEAR ME? NATE? NATE!
FWIP
FWIP
FWIP
FWIP
DING DING
DING DING
THAT... THAT...
BYE! SEE YOU LATER!
AHHHH
OOOOH
WHAT IS IT? A CELEB-RITY?

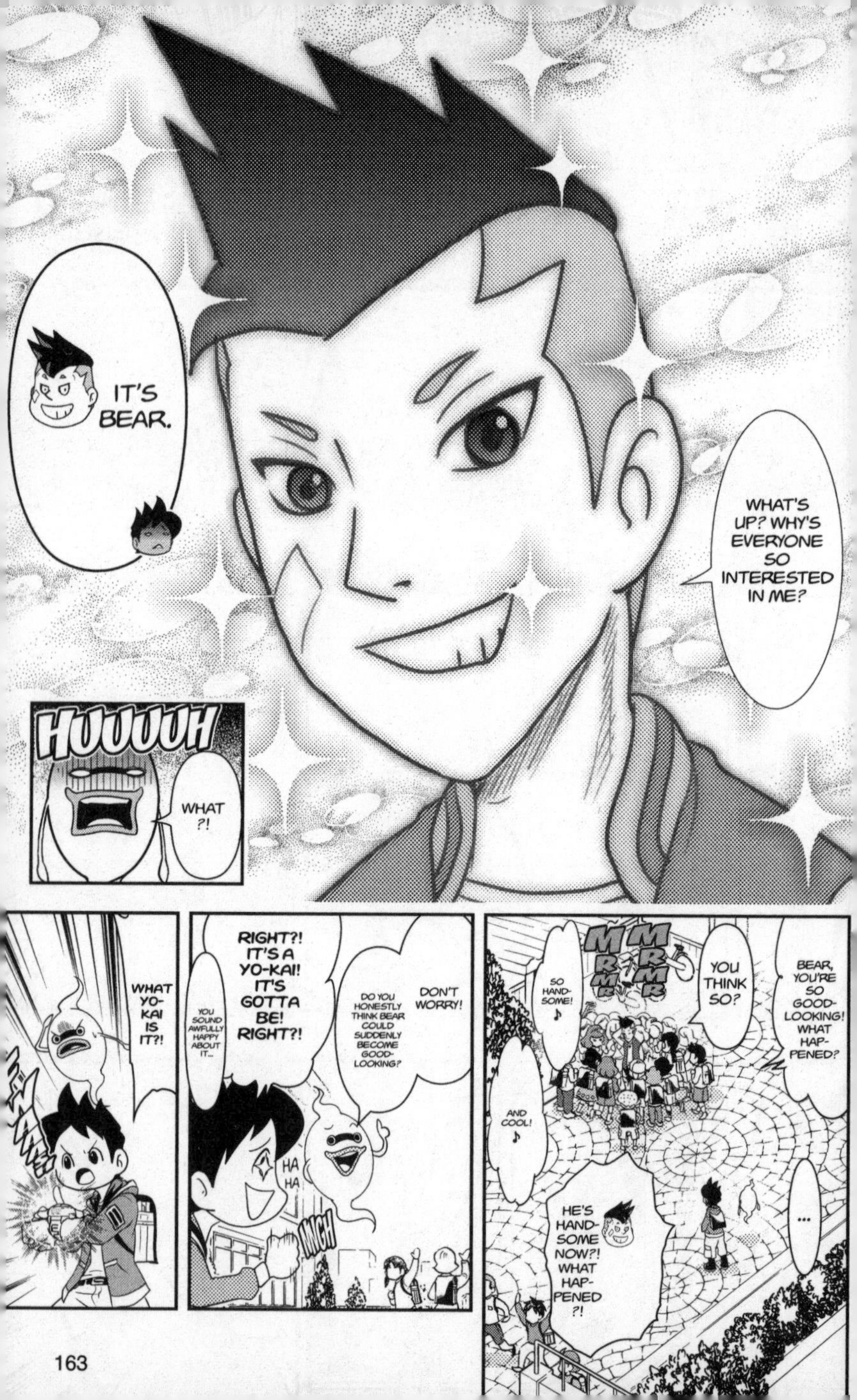
WHAT'S UP? WHY'S EVERYONE SO INTERESTED IN ME?
IT'S BEAR.
HUUUUH
WHAT?!
BEAR, YOU'RE SO GOOD-LOOKING! WHAT HAP-PENED?
YOU THINK SO?
MMRMRMR
SO HAND-SOME! ♪
AND COOL! ♪
...
HE'S HAND-SOME NOW?! WHAT HAP-PENED?!
DON'T WORRY!
DO YOU HONESTLY THINK BEAR COULD SUDDENLY BECOME GOOD-LOOKING?
RIGHT?! IT'S A YO-KAI! IT'S GOTTA BE! RIGHT?!
YOU SOUND AWFULLY HAPPY ABOUT IT...
HA HA
WHAT YO-KAI IS IT?!

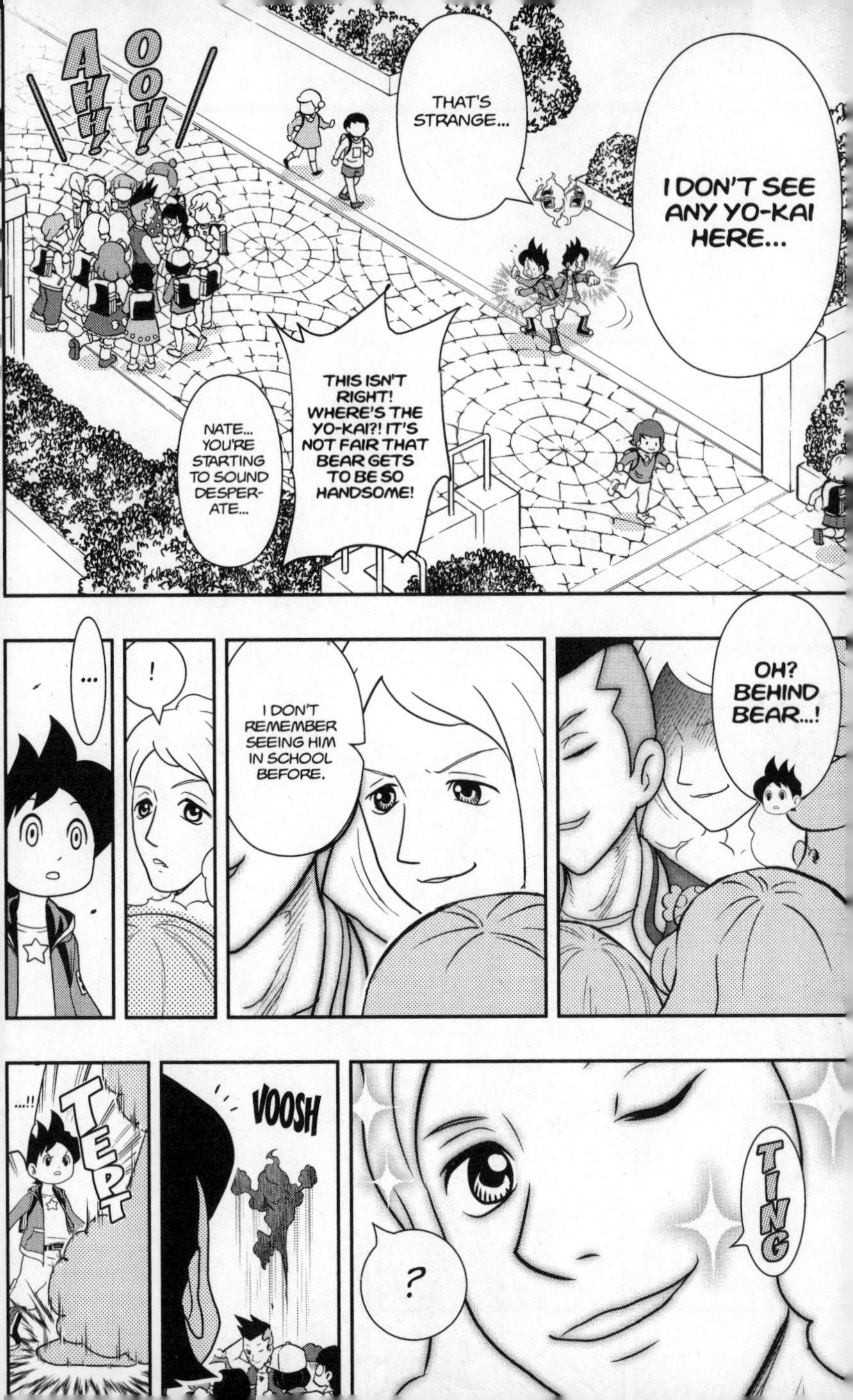

THAT'S STRANGE...
I DON'T SEE ANY YO-KAI HERE...
OOH!
AHH!
THIS ISN'T RIGHT! WHERE'S THE YO-KAI?! IT'S NOT FAIR THAT BEAR GETS TO BE SO HANDSOME!
NATE... YOU'RE STARTING TO SOUND DESPER-ATE...
OH? BEHIND BEAR...!
I DON'T REMEMBER SEEING HIM IN SCHOOL BEFORE.
!
...
TING
?
VOOSH
TEPT
...!!

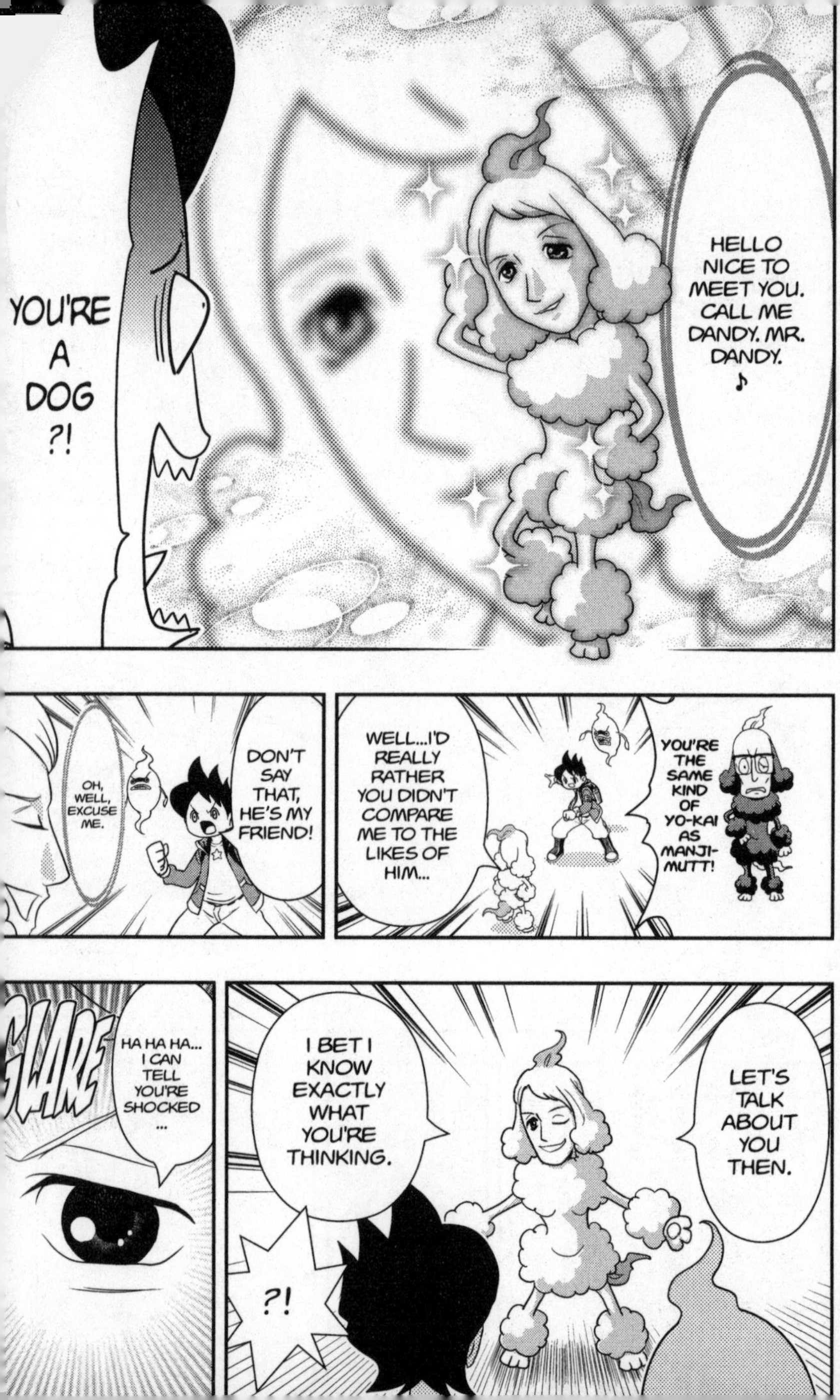
HELLO NICE TO MEET YOU. CALL ME DANDY. MR. DANDY. ♪
YOU'RE A DOG ?!
YOU'RE THE SAME KIND OF YO-KAI AS MANJI-MUTT!
WELL...I'D REALLY RATHER YOU DIDN'T COMPARE ME TO THE LIKES OF HIM...
DON'T SAY THAT, HE'S MY FRIEND!
OH, WELL, EXCUSE ME.
LET'S TALK ABOUT YOU THEN.
I BET I KNOW EXACTLY WHAT YOU'RE THINKING.
?!
HA HA HA... I CAN TELL YOU'RE SHOCKED ...
GLARE

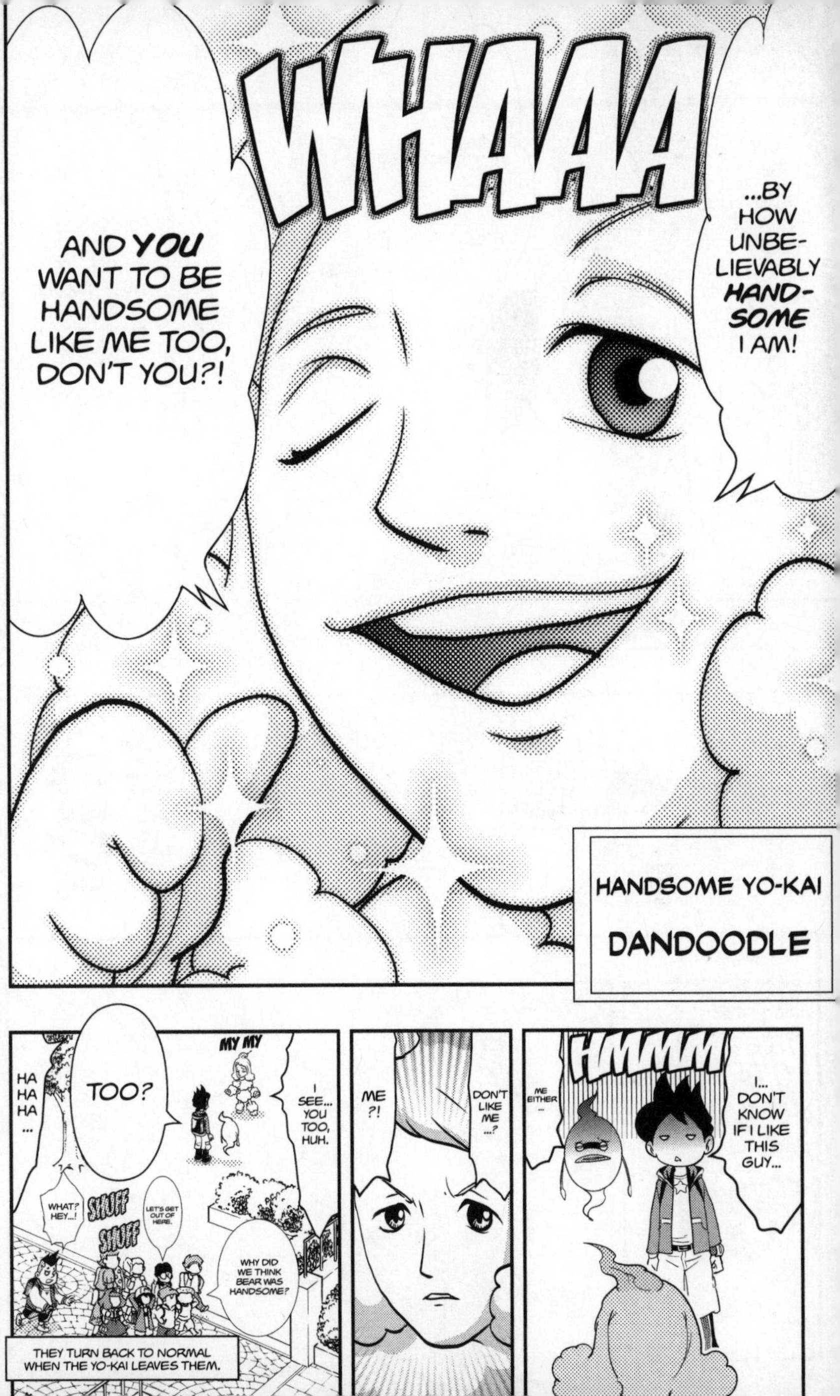
...BY HOW UNBE-LIEVABLY HAND-SOME I AM!
WHAAA
AND YOU WANT TO BE HANDSOME LIKE ME TOO, DON'T YOU?!
HANDSOME YO-KAI
DANDOODLE
HMMMM
I... DON'T KNOW IF I LIKE THIS GUY...
ME EITHER...
DON'T LIKE ME ...?
ME ?!
I SEE... YOU TOO, HUH.
MY MY
TOO?
HA HA HA ...
LET'S GET OUT OF HERE.
SHUFF
SHUFF
WHAT? HEY...!
WHY DID WE THINK BEAR WAS HANDSOME?
THEY TURN BACK TO NORMAL WHEN THE YO-KAI LEAVES THEM.

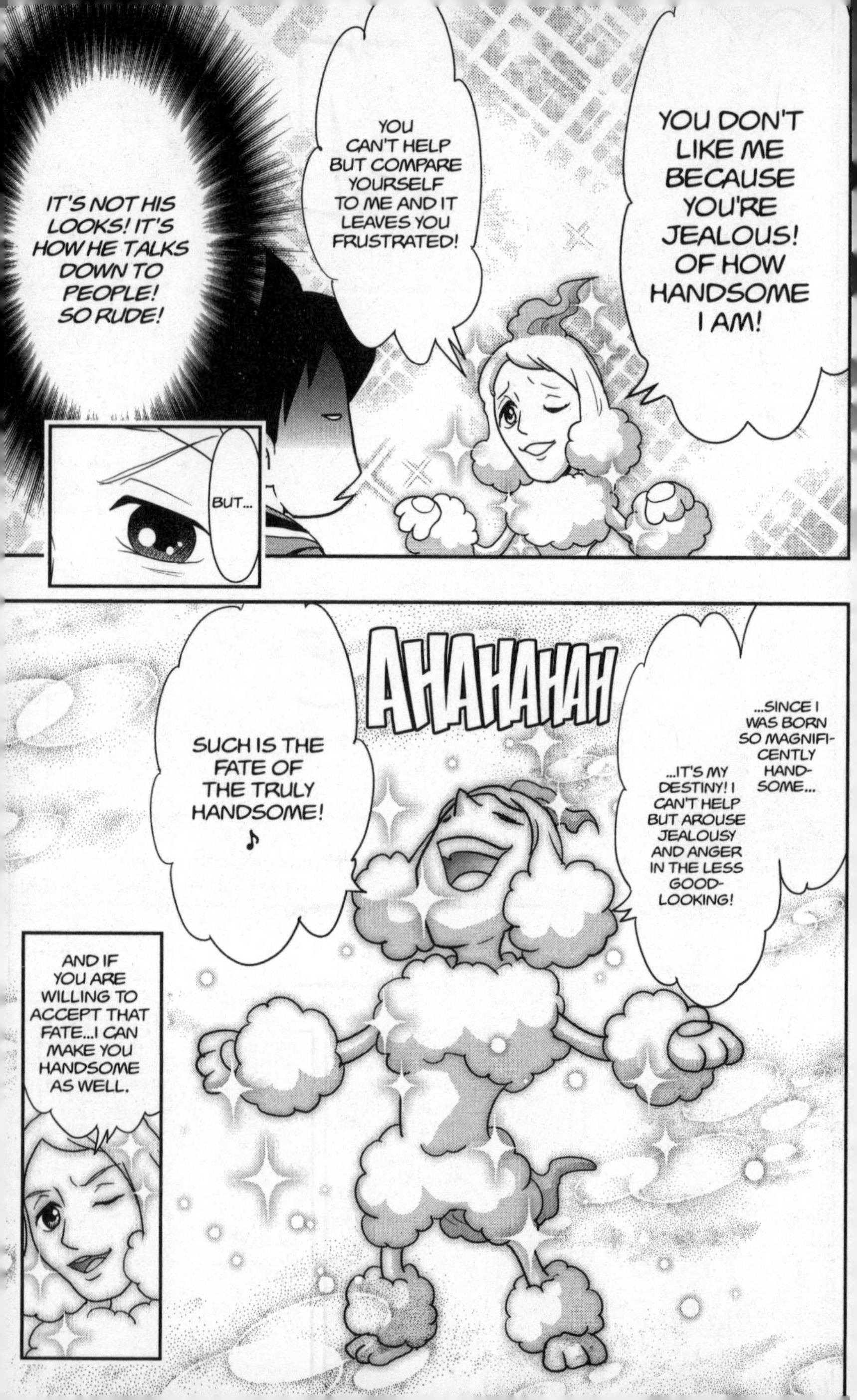
YOU DON'T LIKE ME BECAUSE YOU'RE JEALOUS! OF HOW HANDSOME I AM!
YOU CAN'T HELP BUT COMPARE YOURSELF TO ME AND IT LEAVES YOU FRUSTRATED!
IT'S NOT HIS LOOKS! IT'S HOW HE TALKS DOWN TO PEOPLE! SO RUDE!
BUT...
...SINCE I WAS BORN SO MAGNIFI-CENTLY HAND-SOME...
...IT'S MY DESTINY! I CAN'T HELP BUT AROUSE JEALOUSY AND ANGER IN THE LESS GOOD-LOOKING!
AHAHAHAH
SUCH IS THE FATE OF THE TRULY HANDSOME! ♪
AND IF YOU ARE WILLING TO ACCEPT THAT FATE...I CAN MAKE YOU HANDSOME AS WELL.

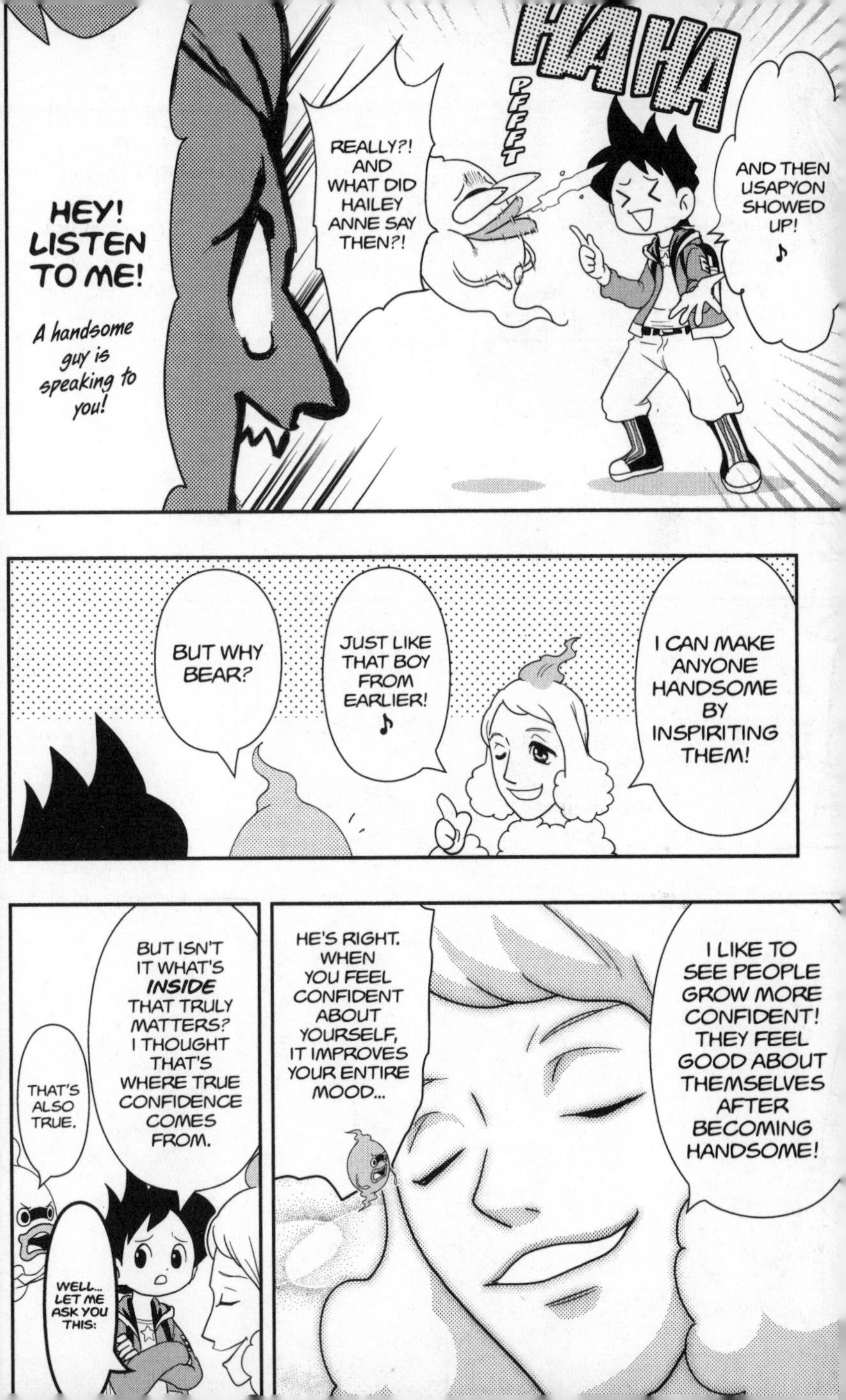
HAHA
AND THEN USAPYON SHOWED UP! ♪
PFFFT
REALLY?! AND WHAT DID HAILEY ANNE SAY THEN?!
HEY! LISTEN TO ME!
A handsome guy is speaking to you!
I CAN MAKE ANYONE HANDSOME BY INSPIRITING THEM!
JUST LIKE THAT BOY FROM EARLIER! ♪
BUT WHY BEAR?
I LIKE TO SEE PEOPLE GROW MORE CONFIDENT! THEY FEEL GOOD ABOUT THEMSELVES AFTER BECOMING HANDSOME!
HE'S RIGHT. WHEN YOU FEEL CONFIDENT ABOUT YOURSELF, IT IMPROVES YOUR ENTIRE MOOD...
BUT ISN'T IT WHAT'S INSIDE THAT TRULY MATTERS? I THOUGHT THAT'S WHERE TRUE CONFIDENCE COMES FROM.
THAT'S ALSO TRUE.
WELL... LET ME ASK YOU THIS:

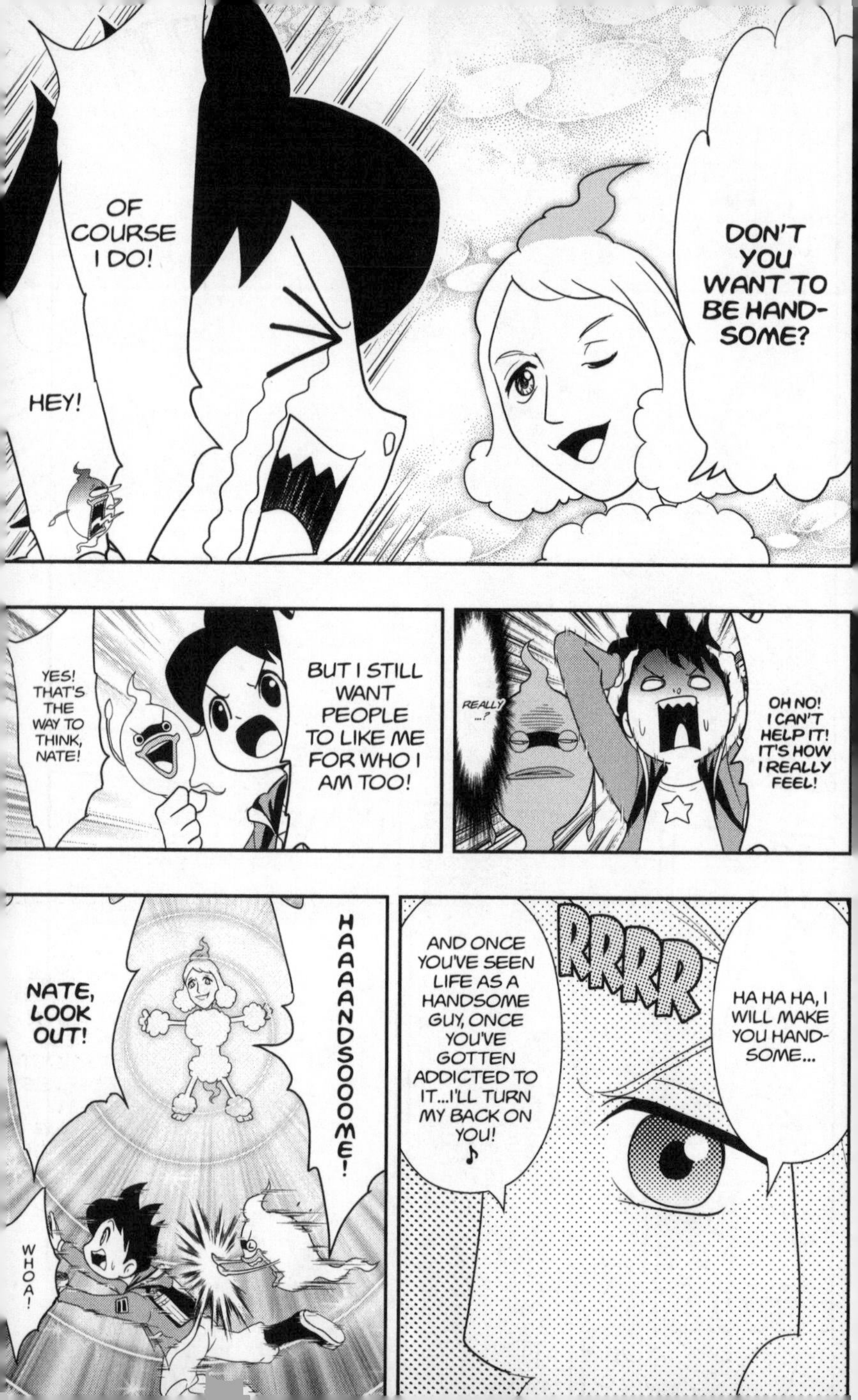
DON'T YOU WANT TO BE HAND-SOME?
OF COURSE I DO!
HEY!
OH NO! I CAN'T HELP IT! IT'S HOW I REALLY FEEL!
REALLY ...?
BUT I STILL WANT PEOPLE TO LIKE ME FOR WHO I AM TOO!
YES! THAT'S THE WAY TO THINK, NATE!
HA HA HA, I WILL MAKE YOU HAND-SOME...
RRRR
AND ONCE YOU'VE SEEN LIFE AS A HANDSOME GUY, ONCE YOU'VE GOTTEN ADDICTED TO IT...I'LL TURN MY BACK ON YOU! ♪
HAAAAANDSOOOOME!
NATE, LOOK OUT!
WHOA!

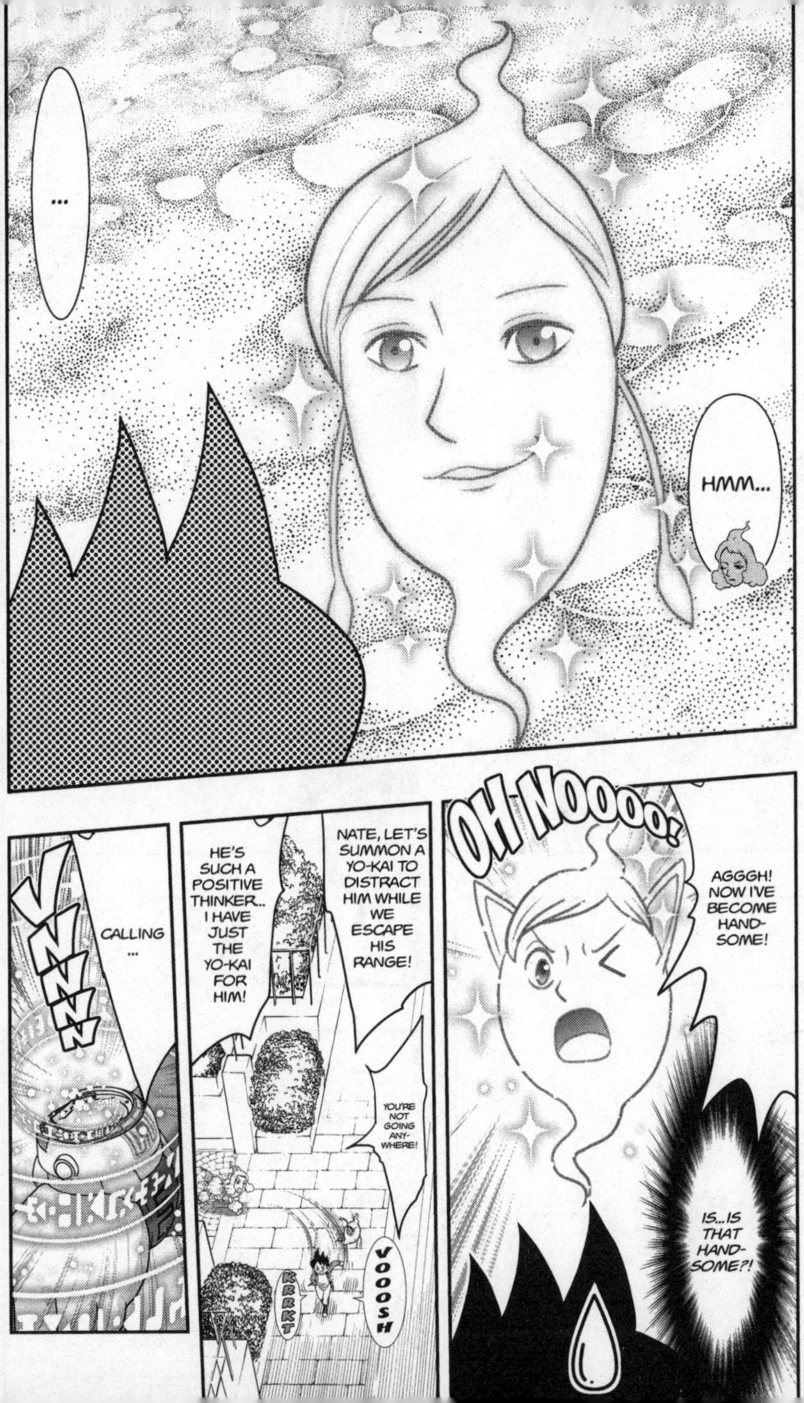
HMM...
...
OH NOOOO!
AGGGH! NOW I'VE BECOME HAND-SOME!
IS...IS THAT HAND-SOME?!
NATE, LET'S SUMMON A YO-KAI TO DISTRACT HIM WHILE WE ESCAPE HIS RANGE!
HE'S SUCH A POSITIVE THINKER.. I HAVE JUST THE YO-KAI FOR HIM!
YOU'RE NOT GOING ANY-WHERE!
VOOOSH
KRRKT
CALLING ...
VNNNN

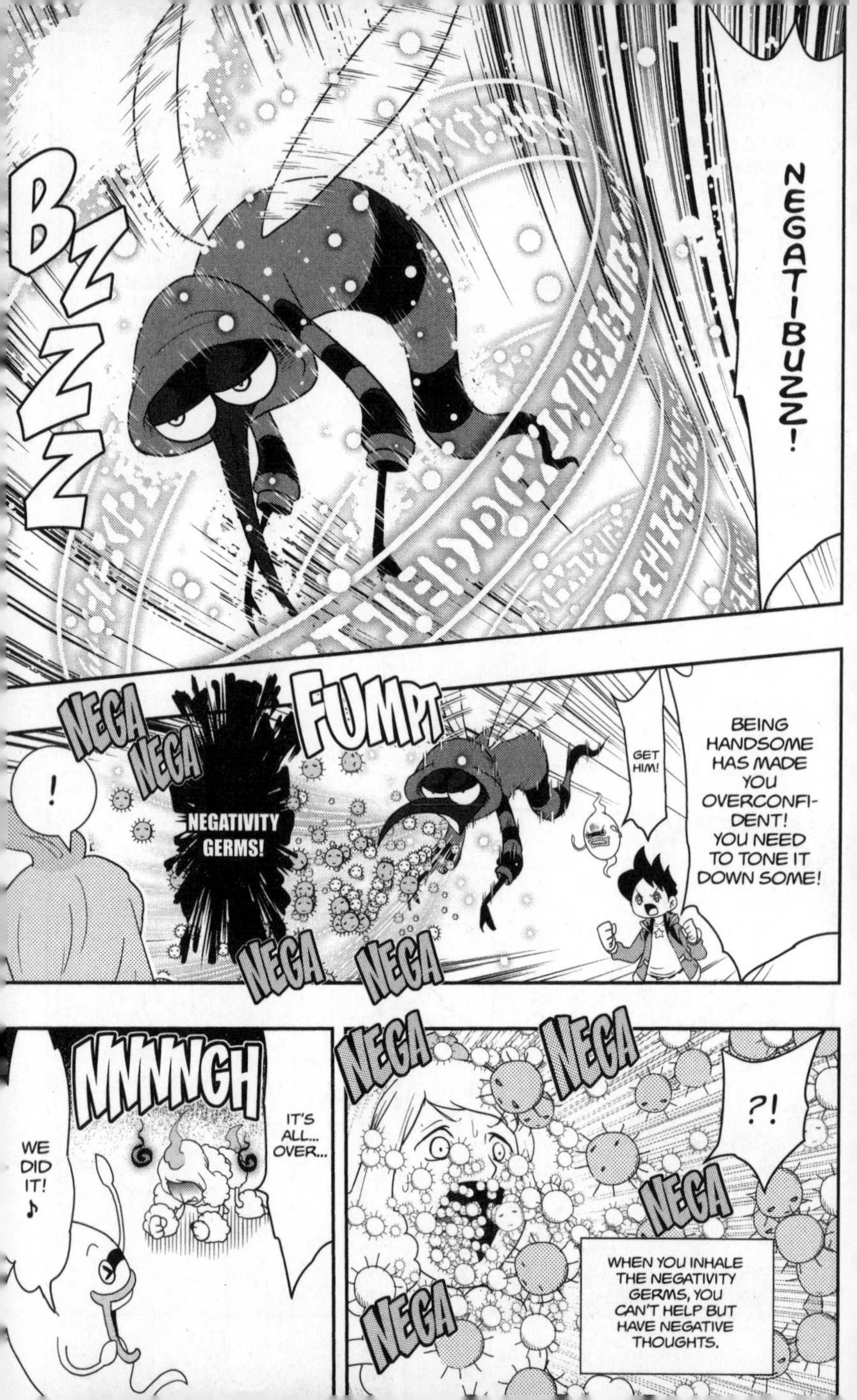
NEGATIBUZZ!
BZZZZ
BEING HANDSOME HAS MADE YOU OVERCONFIDENT! YOU NEED TO TONE IT DOWN SOME!
GET HIM!
FUMPT
NEGA NEGA
NEGATIVITY GERMS!
!
NEGA NEGA
?!
NEGA NEGA
NEGA
WHEN YOU INHALE THE NEGATIVITY GERMS, YOU CAN'T HELP BUT HAVE NEGATIVE THOUGHTS.
NEGA
NNNNNGH
IT'S ALL... OVER...
WE DID IT! ♪

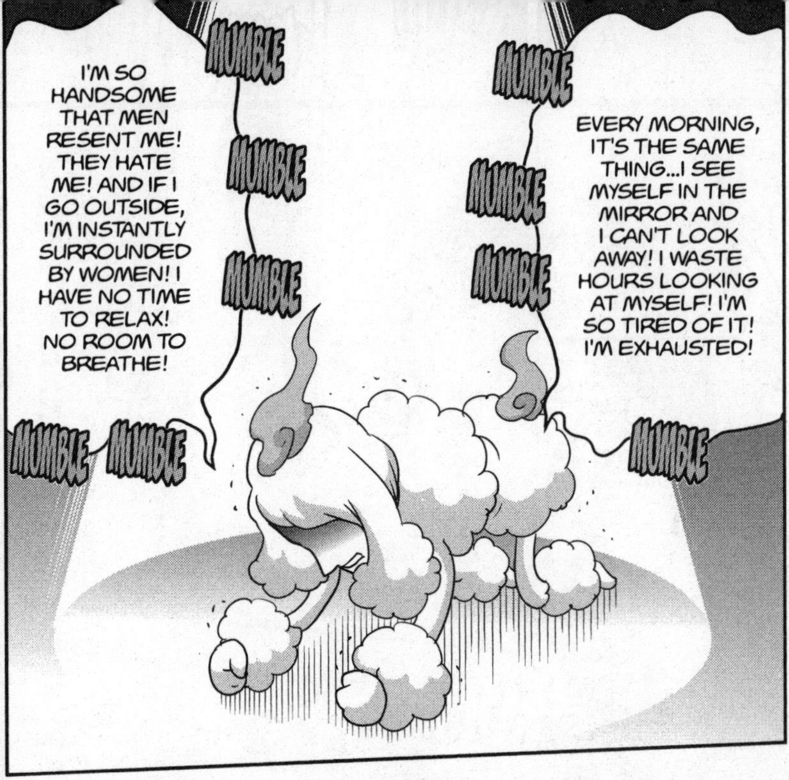
MUMBLE
MUMBLE
MUMBLE
EVERY MORNING, IT'S THE SAME THING...I SEE MYSELF IN THE MIRROR AND I CAN'T LOOK AWAY! I WASTE HOURS LOOKING AT MYSELF! I'M SO TIRED OF IT! I'M EXHAUSTED!
MUMBLE
MUMBLE
MUMBLE
MUMBLE
I'M SO HANDSOME THAT MEN RESENT ME! THEY HATE ME! AND IF I GO OUTSIDE, I'M INSTANTLY SURROUNDED BY WOMEN! I HAVE NO TIME TO RELAX! NO ROOM TO BREATHE!
MUMBLE
MUMBLE

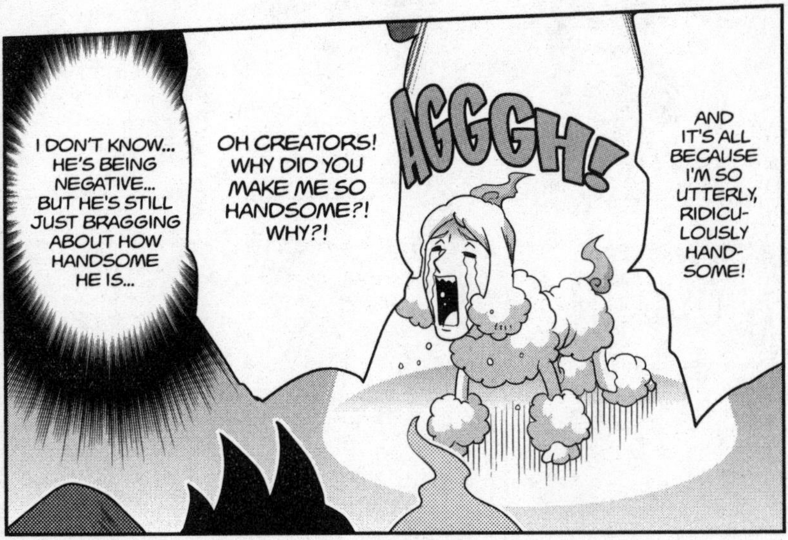
AND IT'S ALL BECAUSE I'M SO UTTERLY, RIDICU-LOUSLY HAND-SOME!
AGGGH!
OH CREATORS! WHY DID YOU MAKE ME SO HANDSOME?! WHY?!
I DON'T KNOW... HE'S BEING NEGATIVE... BUT HE'S STILL JUST BRAGGING ABOUT HOW HANDSOME HE IS...

VOOSH
I'M SURE JIBANYAN CAN TAKE CARE OF IT!
YO-KAI MEDAL, DO YOUR THING!
CALLING ...
VNNNNOOO
JIBANYAN!!

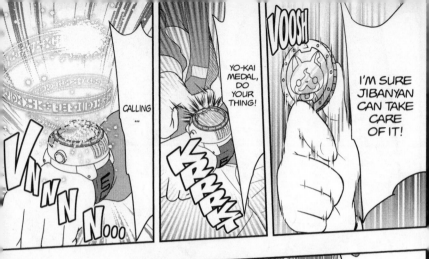

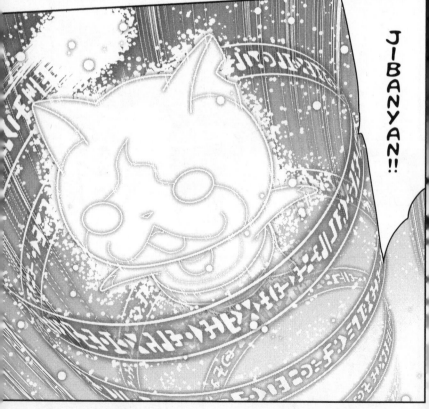

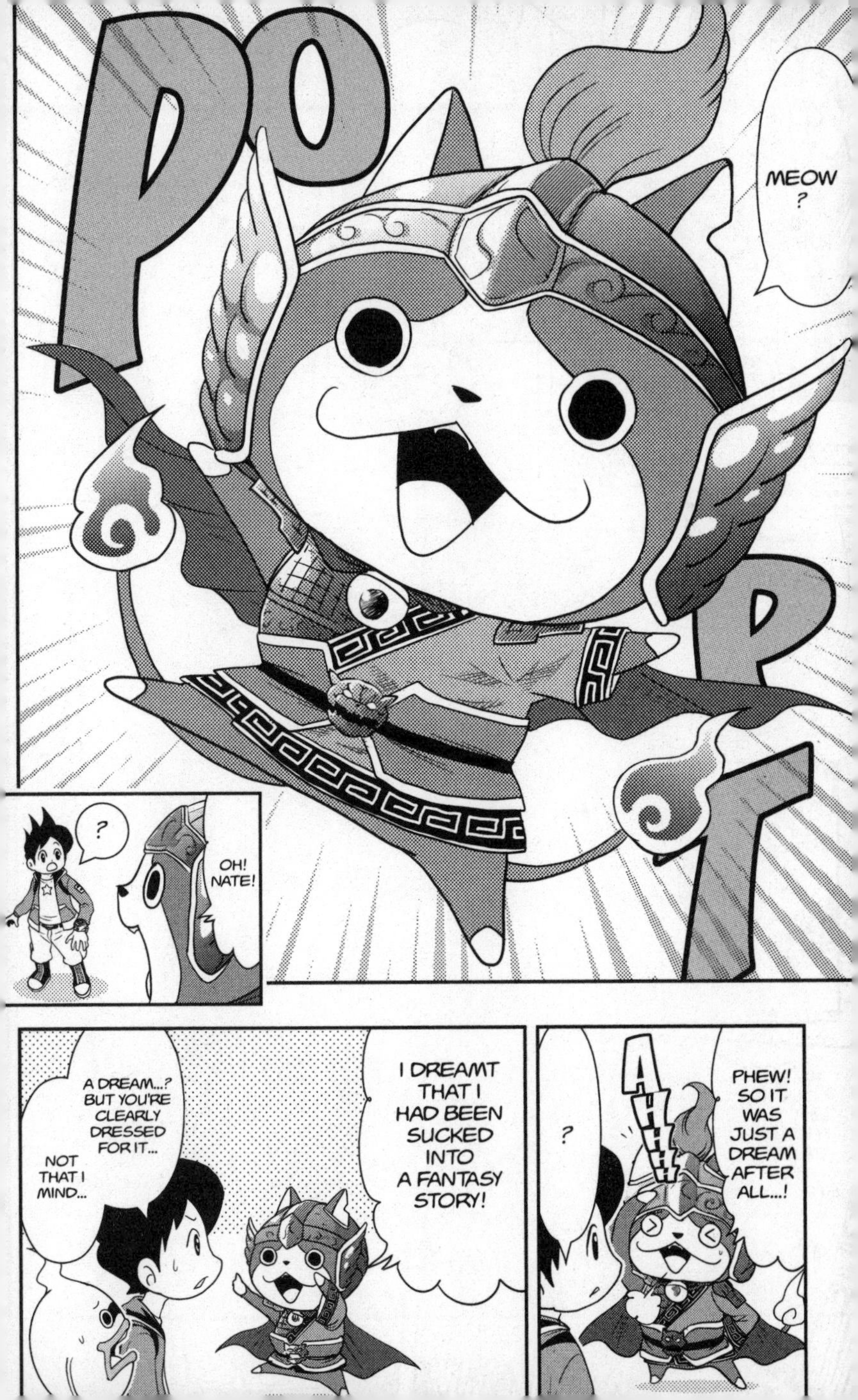
MEOW ?
?
OH! NATE!
PHEW! SO IT WAS JUST A DREAM AFTER ALL...!
?
I DREAMT THAT I HAD BEEN SUCKED INTO A FANTASY STORY!
A DREAM...? BUT YOU'RE CLEARLY DRESSED FOR IT...
NOT THAT I MIND...

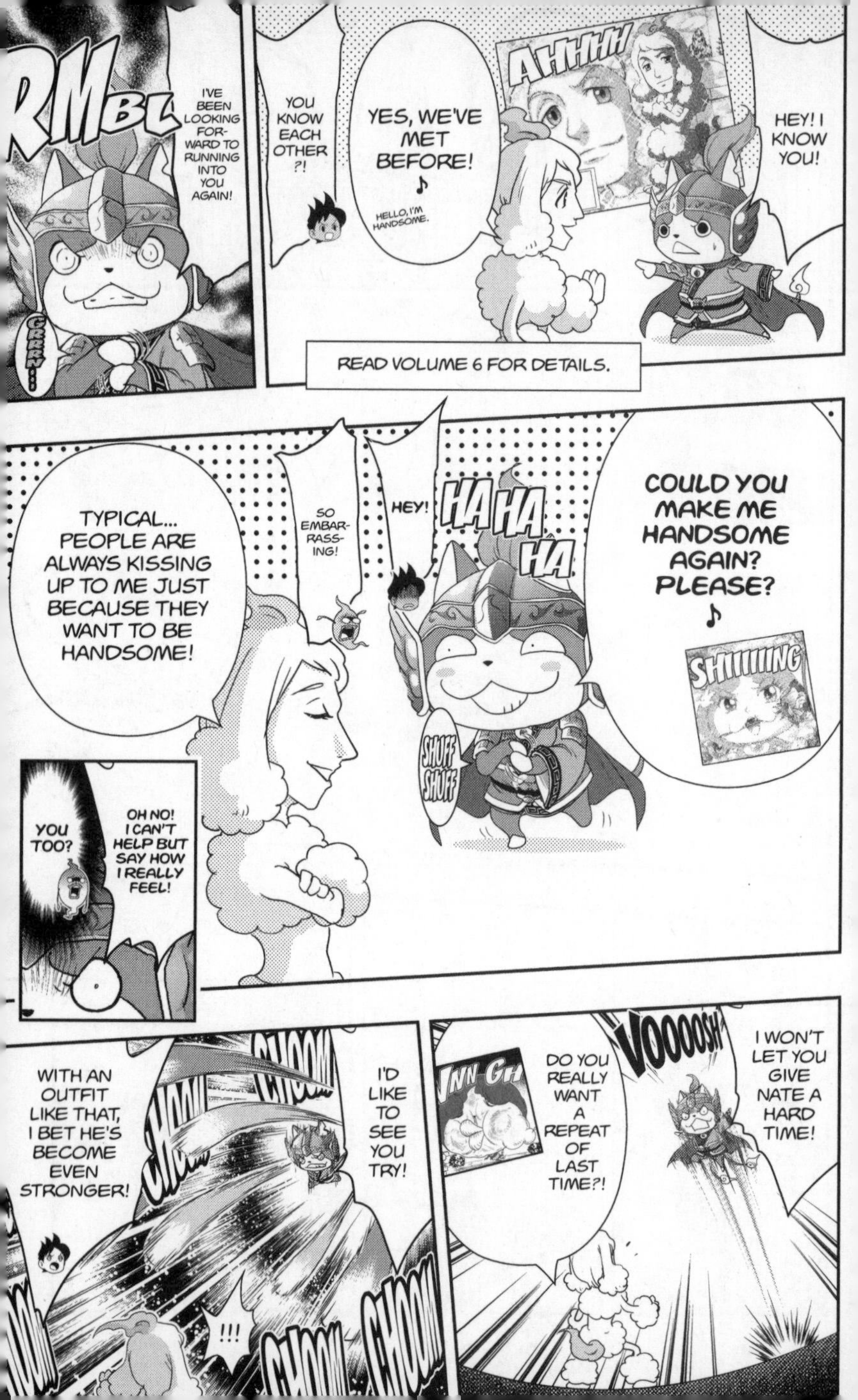
HEY! I KNOW YOU!
AHHHHH
YES, WE'VE MET BEFORE! ♪
HELLO, I'M HANDSOME.
YOU KNOW EACH OTHER ?!
READ VOLUME 6 FOR DETAILS.
RMBL
I'VE BEEN LOOKING FORWARD TO RUNNING INTO YOU AGAIN!
GRRRN...
COULD YOU MAKE ME HANDSOME AGAIN? PLEASE? ♪
SHIIIIING
HA HA HA
SHUFF SHUFF
HEY!
SO EMBARRASSING!
TYPICAL... PEOPLE ARE ALWAYS KISSING UP TO ME JUST BECAUSE THEY WANT TO BE HANDSOME!
OH NO! I CAN'T HELP BUT SAY HOW I REALLY FEEL!
YOU TOO?
VOOOOSH
I WON'T LET YOU GIVE NATE A HARD TIME!
DO YOU REALLY WANT A REPEAT OF LAST TIME?!
NNN GH
I'D LIKE TO SEE YOU TRY!
WITH AN OUTFIT LIKE THAT, I BET HE'S BECOME EVEN STRONGER!
CHOOM
!!!

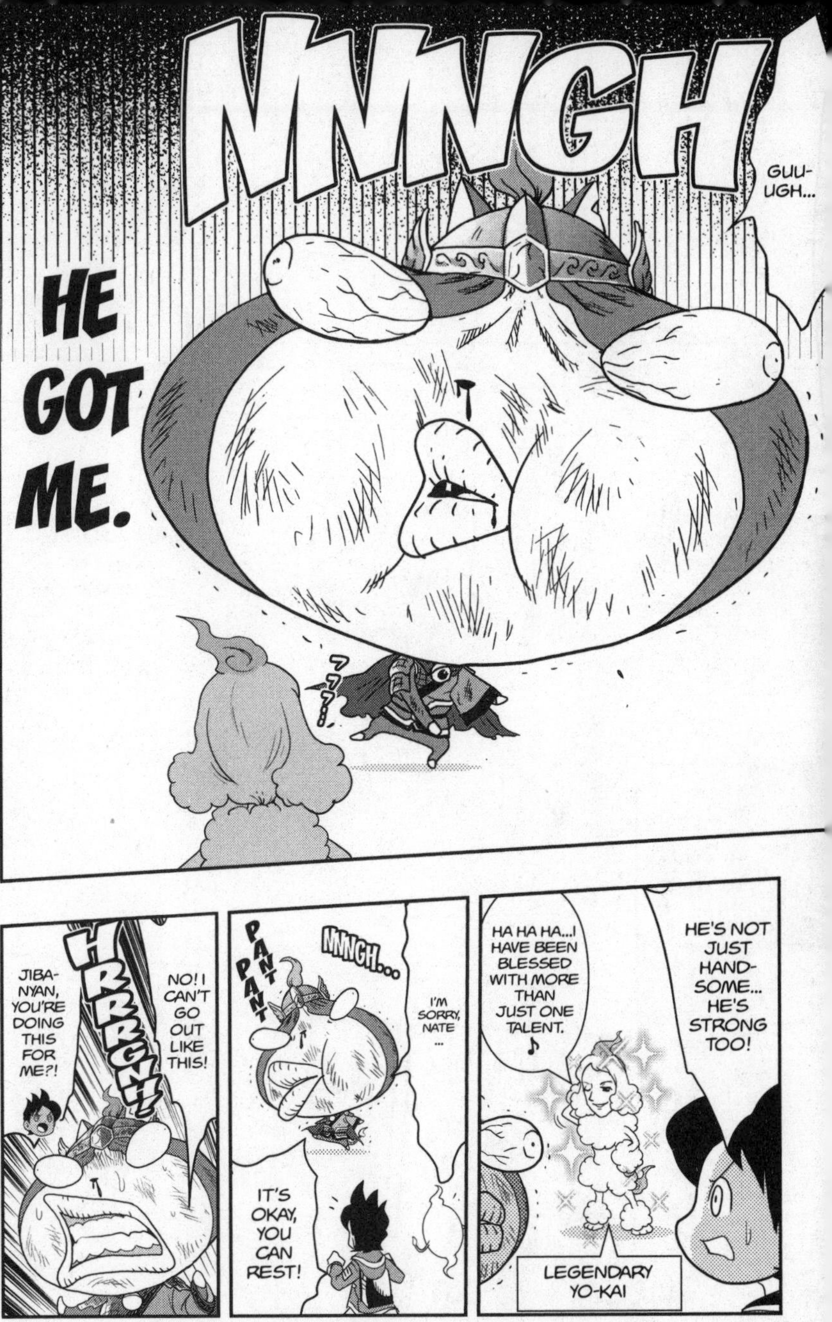
NNNGH
GUU-UGH...
HE GOT ME.
フフフ…
HE'S NOT JUST HAND-SOME... HE'S STRONG TOO!
HA HA HA...I HAVE BEEN BLESSED WITH MORE THAN JUST ONE TALENT. ♪
LEGENDARY YO-KAI
MNNGH...
I'M SORRY, NATE ...
PANT PANT
IT'S OKAY, YOU CAN REST!
NO! I CAN'T GO OUT LIKE THIS!
HRRRGN!!
JIBA-NYAN, YOU'RE DOING THIS FOR ME?!

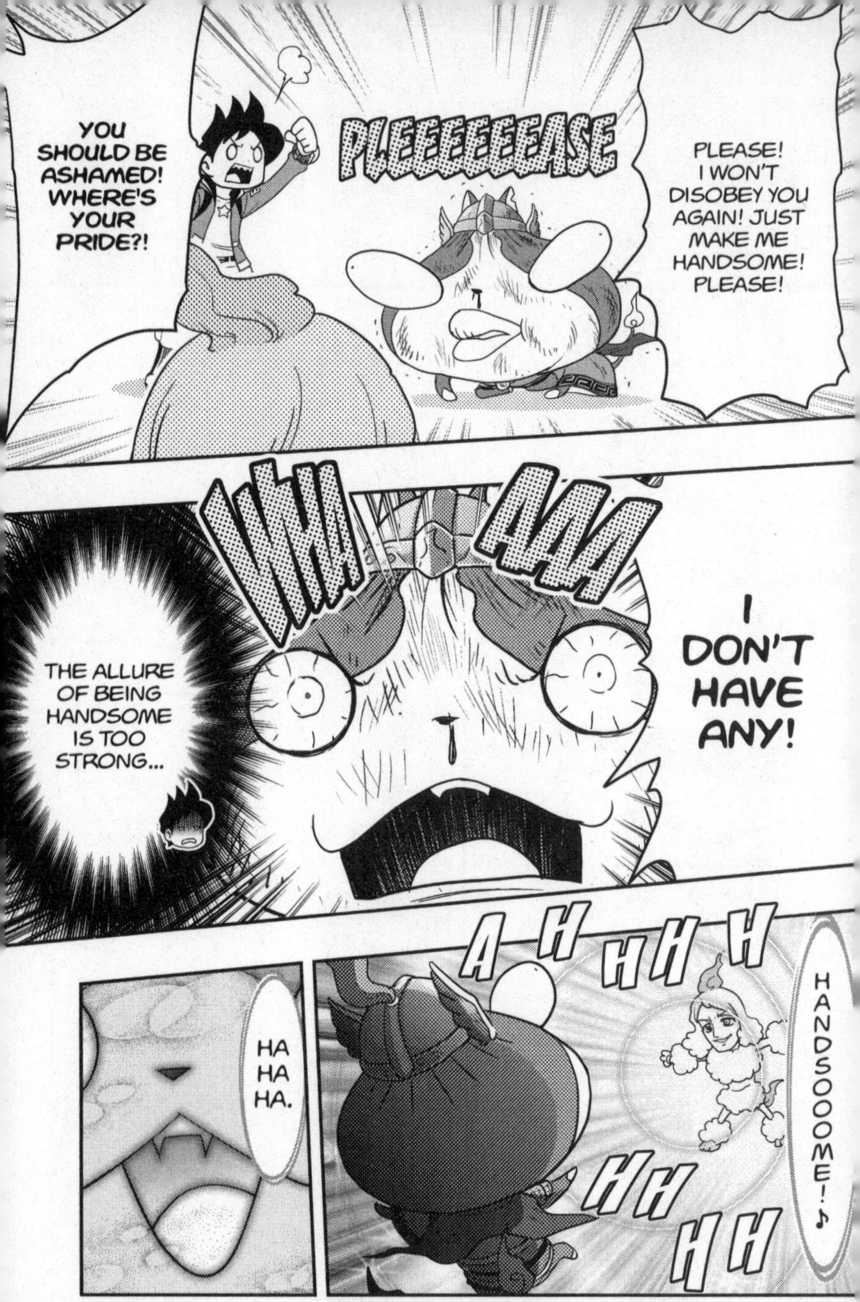
PLEASE! I WON'T DISOBEY YOU AGAIN! JUST MAKE ME HANDSOME! PLEASE!
PLEEEEEEEASE
YOU SHOULD BE ASHAMED! WHERE'S YOUR PRIDE?!
I DON'T HAVE ANY!
WHAAAA
THE ALLURE OF BEING HANDSOME IS TOO STRONG...
HANDSOOOOME!♪
AHHHHH
HHHH
HA HA HA.

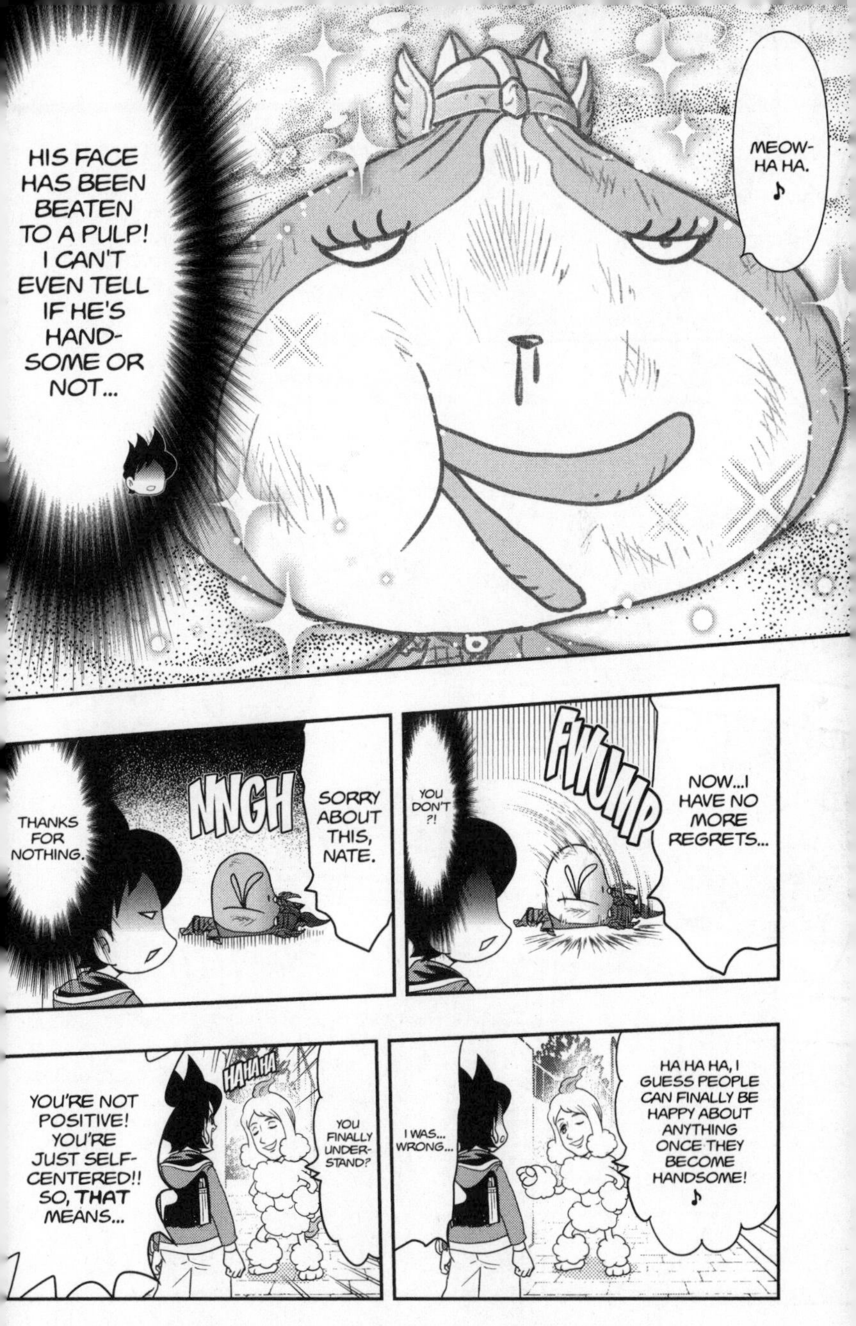
MEOW-HA HA. ♪
HIS FACE HAS BEEN BEATEN TO A PULP! I CAN'T EVEN TELL IF HE'S HANDSOME OR NOT...
NOW...I HAVE NO MORE REGRETS...
FWUMP
YOU DON'T?!
SORRY ABOUT THIS, NATE.
NNGH
THANKS FOR NOTHING.
HA HA HA, I GUESS PEOPLE CAN FINALLY BE HAPPY ABOUT ANYTHING ONCE THEY BECOME HANDSOME! ♪
I WAS... WRONG...
YOU FINALLY UNDERSTAND?
HAHAHA
YOU'RE NOT POSITIVE! YOU'RE JUST SELF-CENTERED!! SO, THAT MEANS...

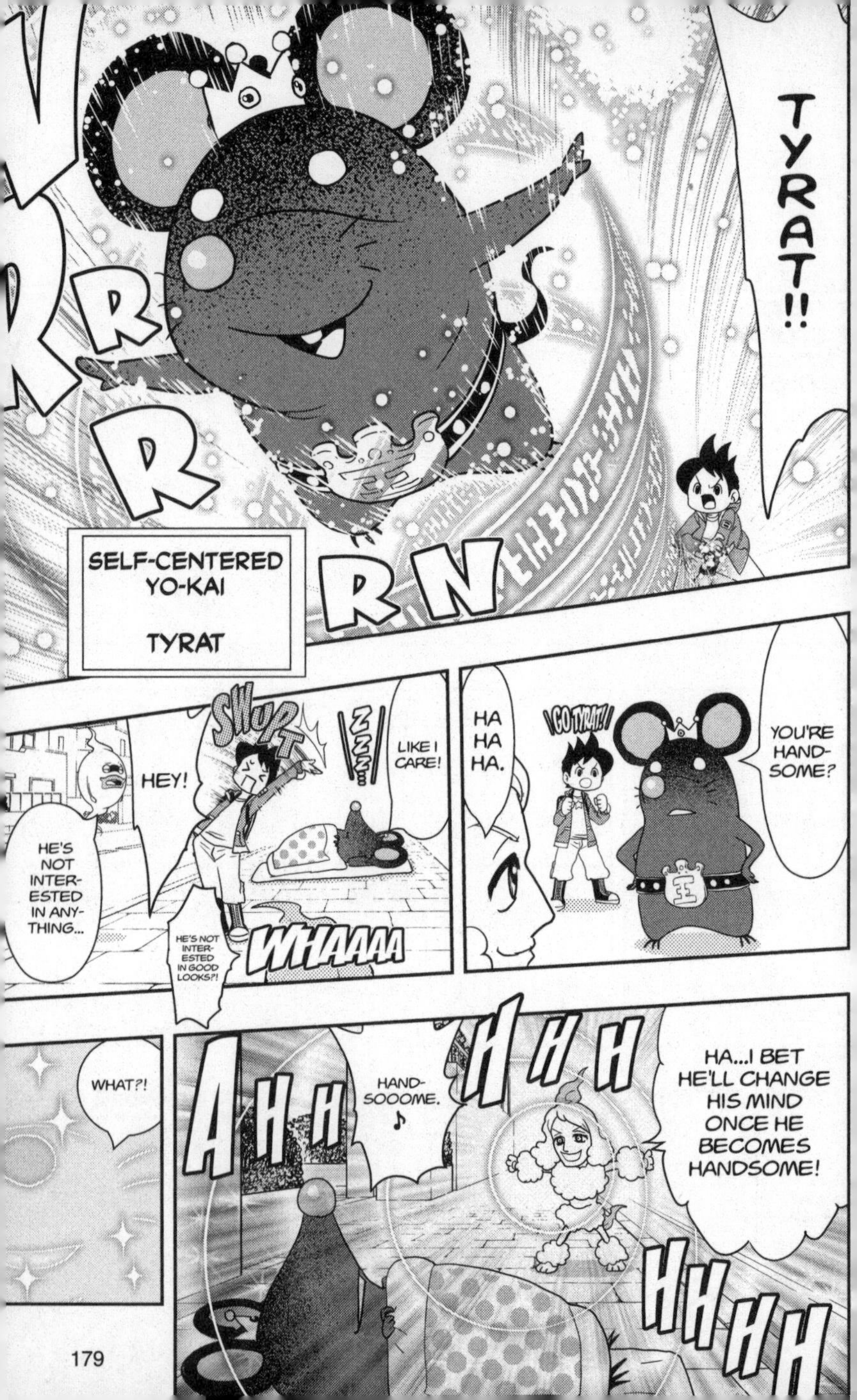
TYRAT!!
VRRRRRN
SELF-CENTERED YO-KAI
TYRAT
YOU'RE HANDSOME?
GO TYRAT!
HA HA HA.
LIKE I CARE!
ZZZ
SHUFT
HEY!
HE'S NOT INTERESTED IN ANYTHING...
WHAAAAA
HE'S NOT INTERESTED IN GOOD LOOKS?!
HA...I BET HE'LL CHANGE HIS MIND ONCE HE BECOMES HANDSOME!
HHHHHHHH
AHHHHH
HANDSOOOME. ♪
WHAT?!

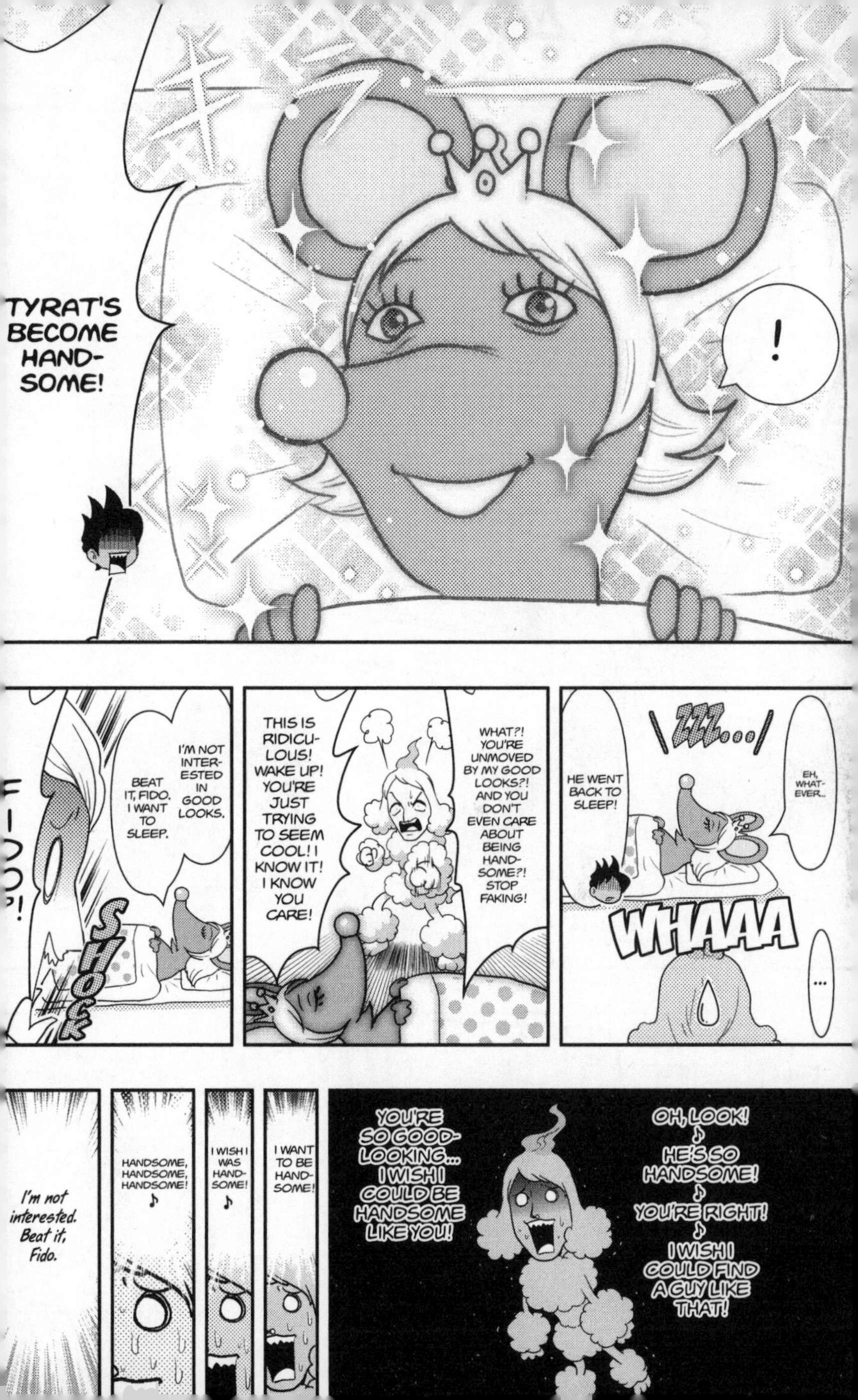
!
TYRAT'S BECOME HANDSOME!
EH, WHATEVER...
ZZZ...
HE WENT BACK TO SLEEP!
...
WHAAAA
WHAT?! YOU'RE UNMOVED BY MY GOOD LOOKS?! AND YOU DON'T EVEN CARE ABOUT BEING HANDSOME?! STOP FAKING!
THIS IS RIDICULOUS! WAKE UP! YOU'RE JUST TRYING TO SEEM COOL! I KNOW IT! I KNOW YOU CARE!
I'M NOT INTERESTED IN GOOD LOOKS.
BEAT IT, FIDO. I WANT TO SLEEP.
FIDO?!
SHOCK
OH, LOOK! ♪ HE'S SO HANDSOME! ♪ YOU'RE RIGHT! ♪ I WISH I COULD FIND A GUY LIKE THAT!
YOU'RE SO GOOD-LOOKING... I WISH I COULD BE HANDSOME LIKE YOU!
I WANT TO BE HANDSOME!
I WISH I WAS HANDSOME! ♪
HANDSOME, HANDSOME, HANDSOME! ♪
I'm not interested. Beat it, Fido.

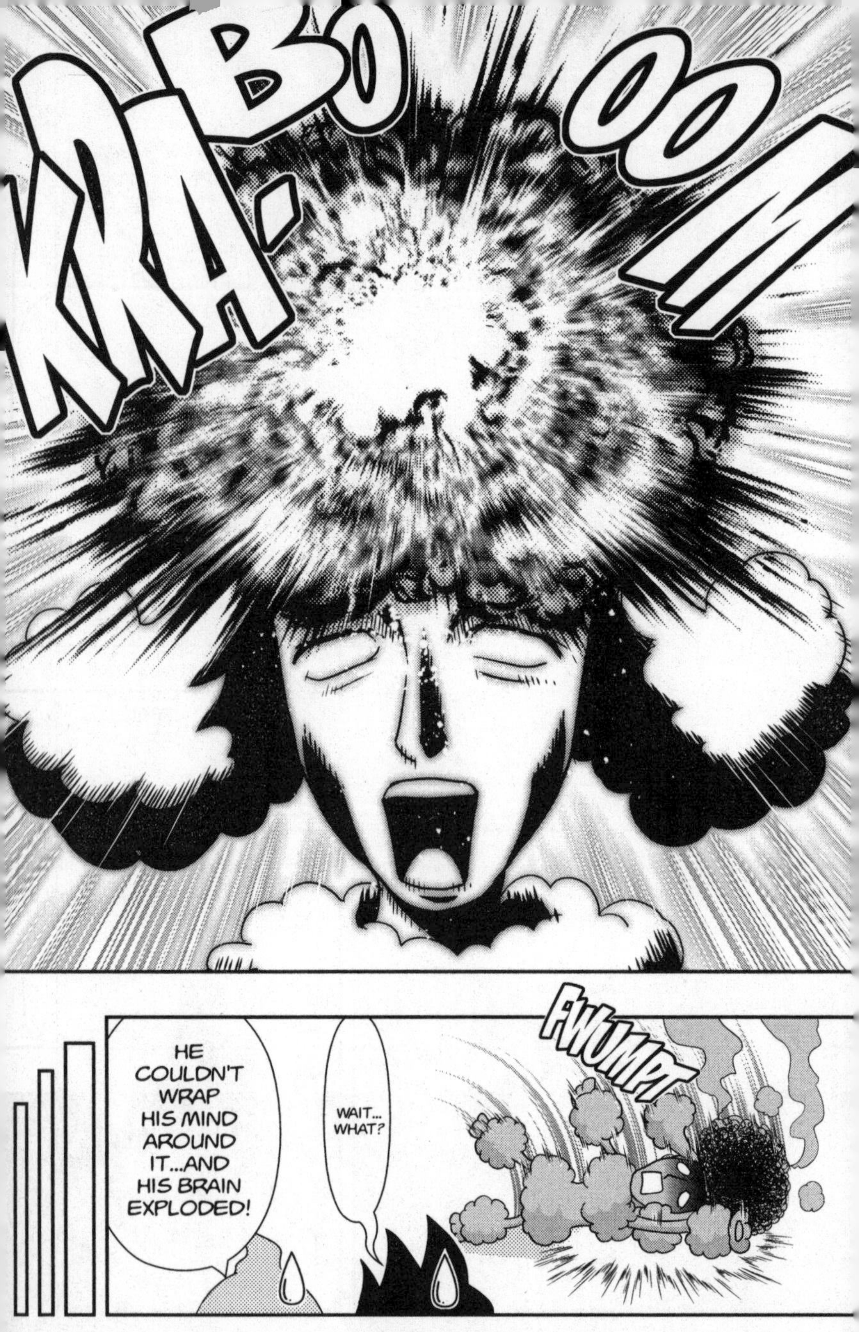
KRA-BOOOM!!
FWUMP!
WAIT... WHAT?
HE COULDN'T WRAP HIS MIND AROUND IT...AND HIS BRAIN EXPLODED!

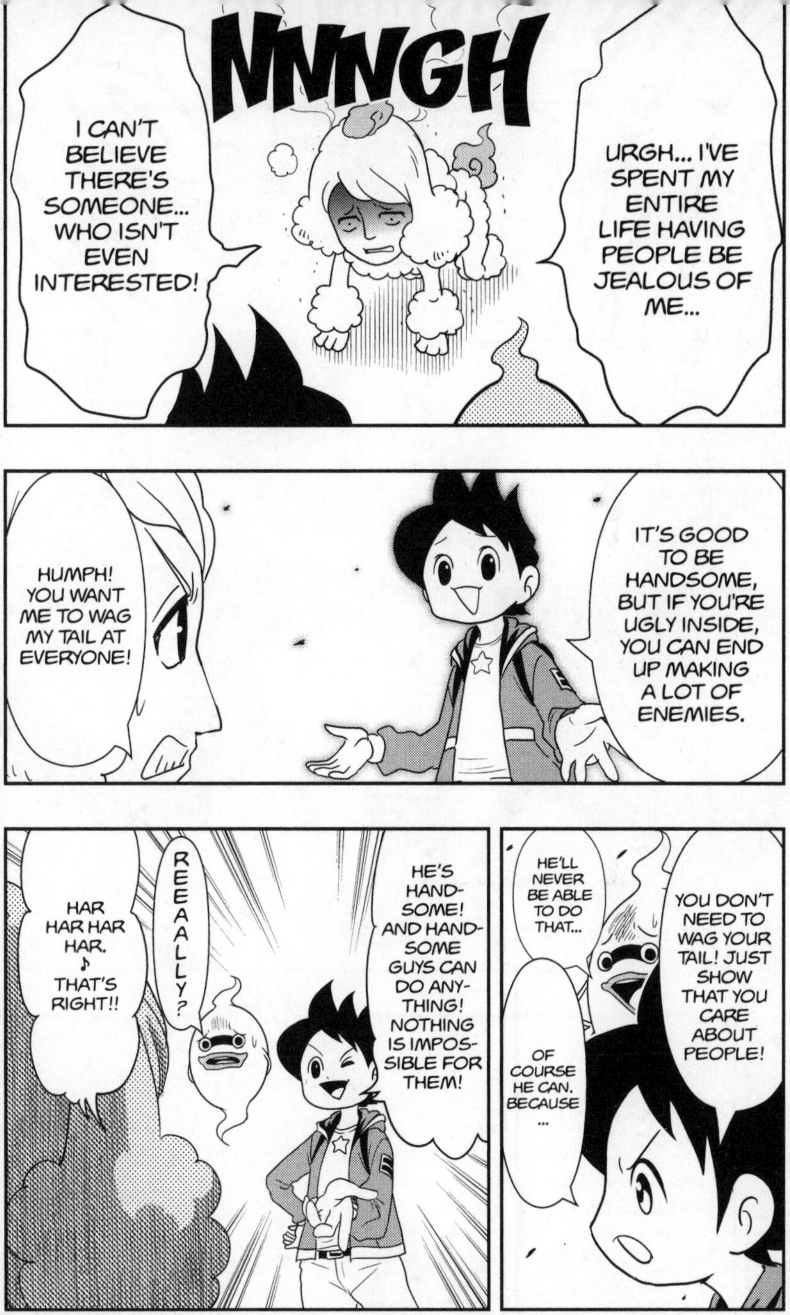
URGH... I'VE SPENT MY ENTIRE LIFE HAVING PEOPLE BE JEALOUS OF ME...
NNNGH
I CAN'T BELIEVE THERE'S SOMEONE... WHO ISN'T EVEN INTERESTED!
IT'S GOOD TO BE HANDSOME, BUT IF YOU'RE UGLY INSIDE, YOU CAN END UP MAKING A LOT OF ENEMIES.
HUMPH! YOU WANT ME TO WAG MY TAIL AT EVERYONE!
YOU DON'T NEED TO WAG YOUR TAIL! JUST SHOW THAT YOU CARE ABOUT PEOPLE!
HE'LL NEVER BE ABLE TO DO THAT...
OF COURSE HE CAN. BECAUSE ...
HE'S HAND-SOME! AND HAND-SOME GUYS CAN DO ANY-THING! NOTHING IS IMPOS-SIBLE FOR THEM!
REEEAALLY?
HAR HAR HAR HAR. ♪ THAT'S RIGHT!!

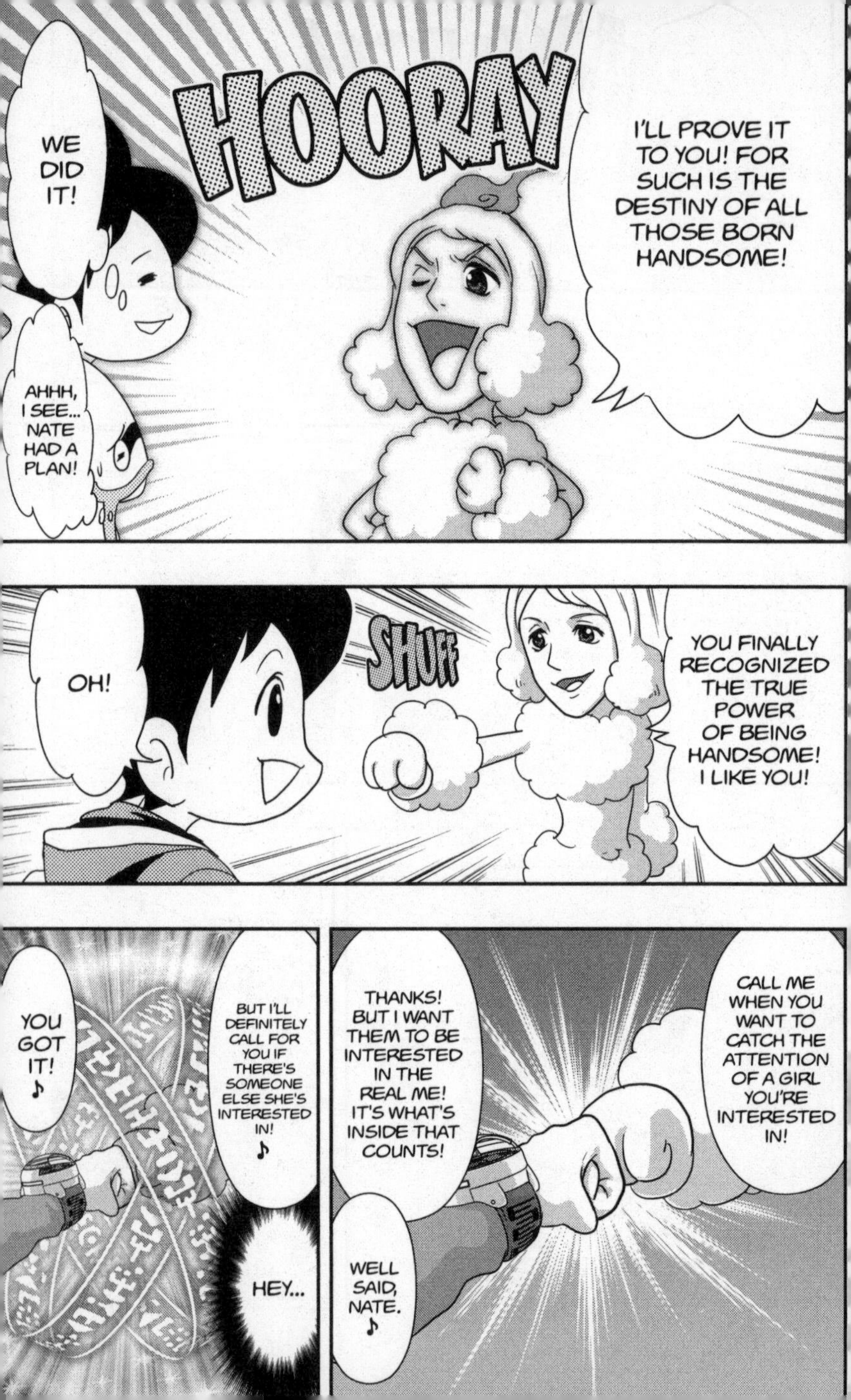
I'LL PROVE IT TO YOU! FOR SUCH IS THE DESTINY OF ALL THOSE BORN HANDSOME!
HOORAY
WE DID IT!
AHHH, I SEE... NATE HAD A PLAN!
YOU FINALLY RECOGNIZED THE TRUE POWER OF BEING HANDSOME! I LIKE YOU!
SHUFF
OH!
CALL ME WHEN YOU WANT TO CATCH THE ATTENTION OF A GIRL YOU'RE INTERESTED IN!
THANKS! BUT I WANT THEM TO BE INTERESTED IN THE REAL ME! IT'S WHAT'S INSIDE THAT COUNTS!
WELL SAID, NATE. ♪
BUT I'LL DEFINITELY CALL FOR YOU IF THERE'S SOMEONE ELSE SHE'S INTERESTED IN! ♪
YOU GOT IT! ♪
HEY...

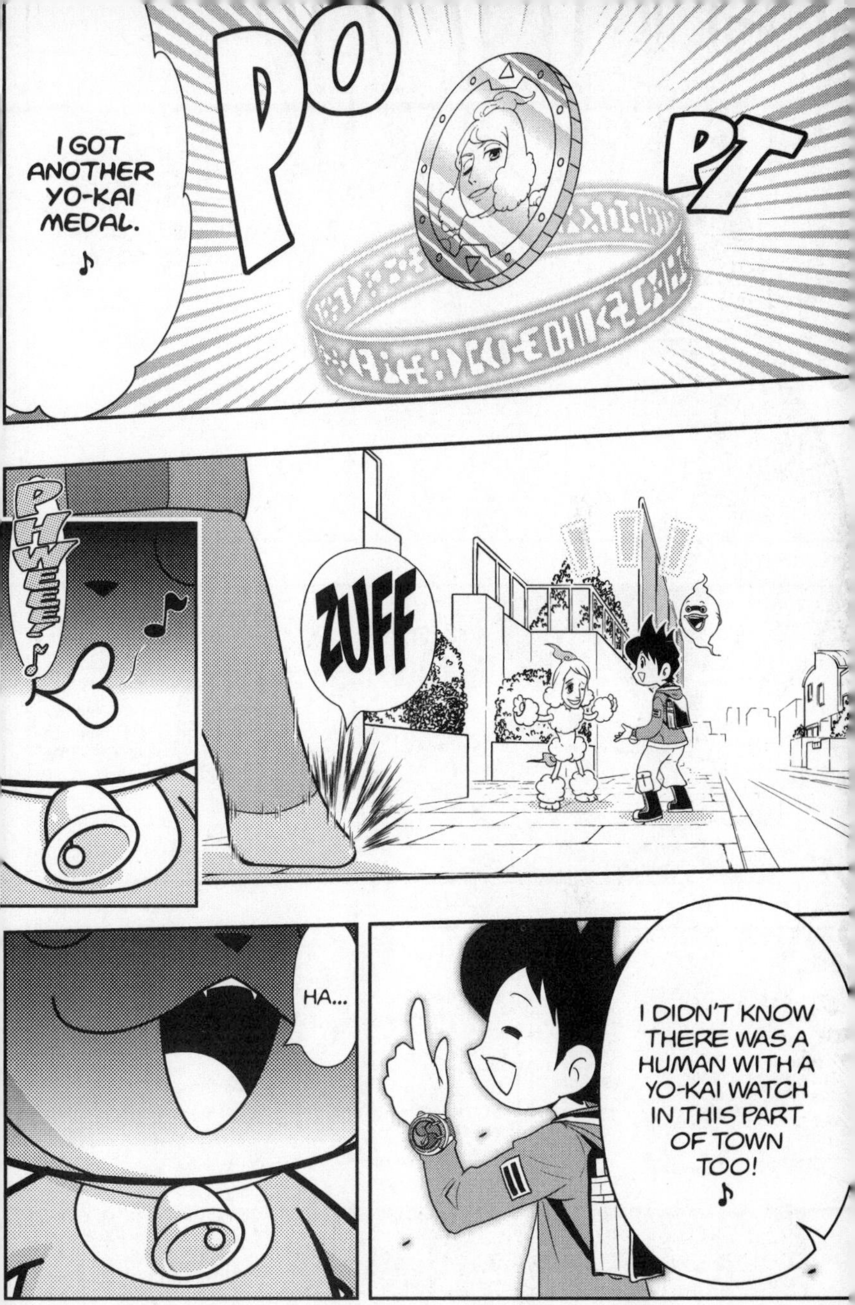
POOPT
I GOT ANOTHER YO-KAI MEDAL. ♪
ZUFF
!!!
PHWEEE♪
I DIDN'T KNOW THERE WAS A HUMAN WITH A YO-KAI WATCH IN THIS PART OF TOWN TOO! ♪
HA...

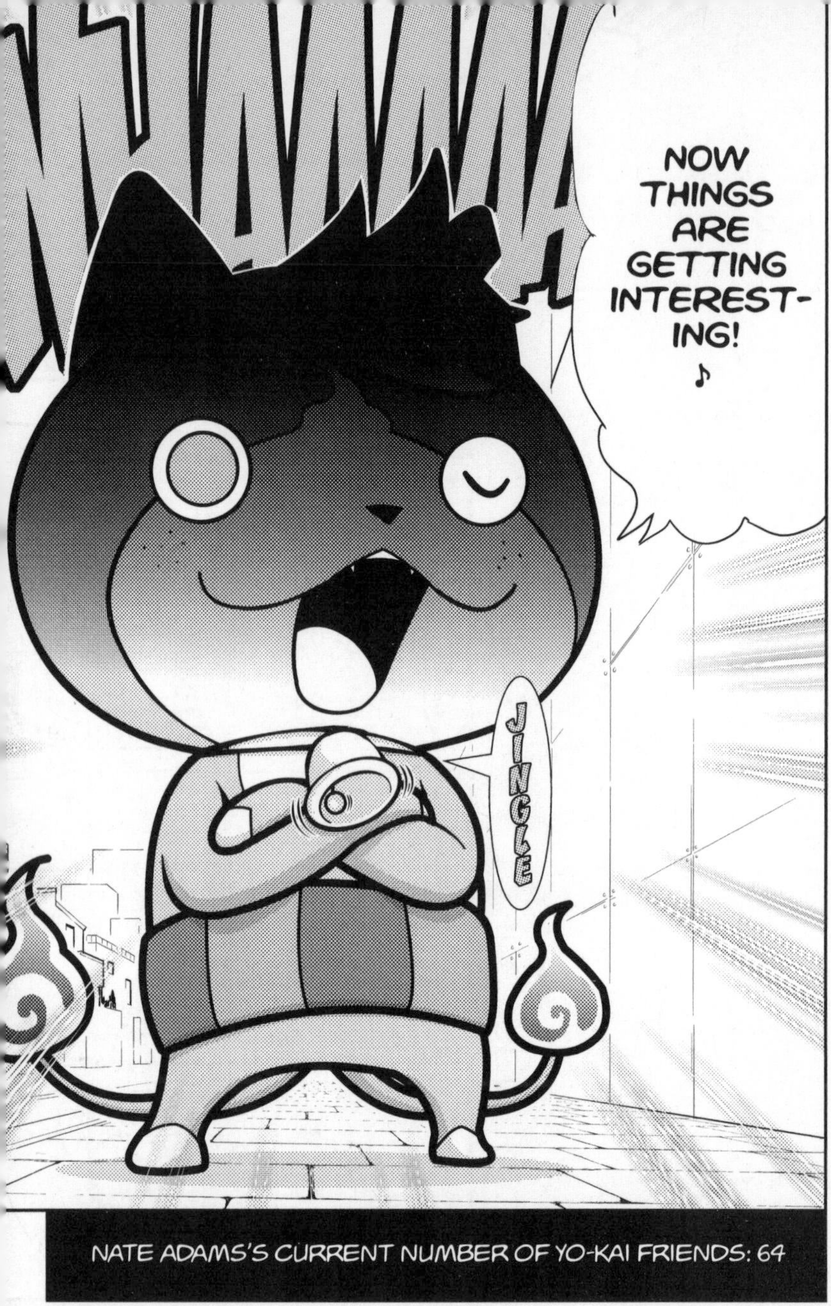
NOW THINGS ARE GETTING INTEREST-ING! ♪
JINGLE
NATE ADAMS'S CURRENT NUMBER OF YO-KAI FRIENDS: 64

MOVING HEART!

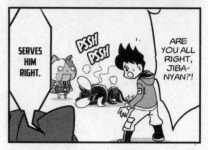

ARE YOU ALL RIGHT, JIBA-NYAN?!

SERVES HIM RIGHT.

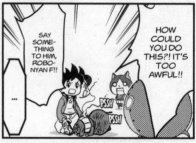

HOW COULD YOU DO THIS?! IT'S TOO AWFUL!!

SAY SOME-THING TO HIM, ROBO-NYAN F!!

...

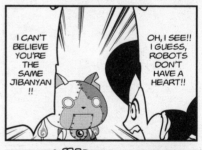

OH, I SEE!! I GUESS, ROBOTS DON'T HAVE A HEART!!

I CAN'T BELIEVE YOU'RE THE SAME JIBANYAN!!

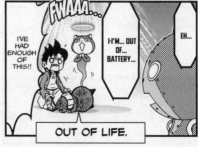

EH...

I-I'M... OUT OF... BATTERY...

I'VE HAD ENOUGH OF THIS!!

FWAAA...

OUT OF LIFE.

ENCOUNTERS WITH THE SPACE YO-KAI

BAAM
WHAT?! AN ALIEN?!
OOOH!
A SPACE YO-KAI TO BE EXACT. ☆
HURRAY!
I WAS GETTING BORED OF REGULAR YO-KAI. ♪
BORED ?!
...
HOW COULD YOU SAY YOU'RE BORED WHEN YOU'VE ONLY MET A HANDFUL OF YO-KAI?!
WHAT?! THERE'S MORE?!
TONS MORE.
...
YEE HAW!
I'M SORRY I GET BORED EASILY. LET'S GO LOOK FOR A NEW YO-KAI. ♪
SHF SHF
HE'S ALREADY BORED OF ME...

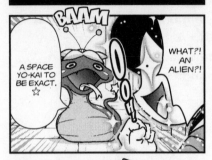

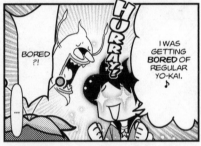

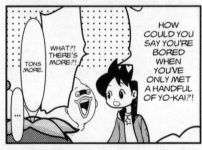

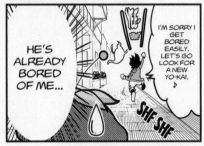

Welcome to the world of Little Battlers eXperience! In the near future, a boy named Van Yamano owns Achilles, a miniaturized robot that battles on command! But Achilles is no ordinary LBX. Hidden inside him is secret data that Van must keep out of the hands of evil at all costs!

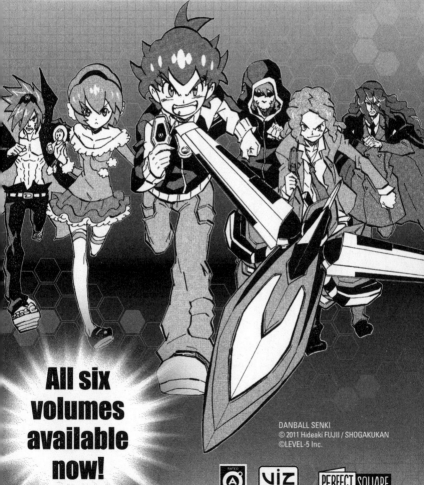

All six volumes available now!

DANBALL SENKI
© 2011 Hideaki FUJII / SHOGAKUKAN
©LEVEL-5 Inc.

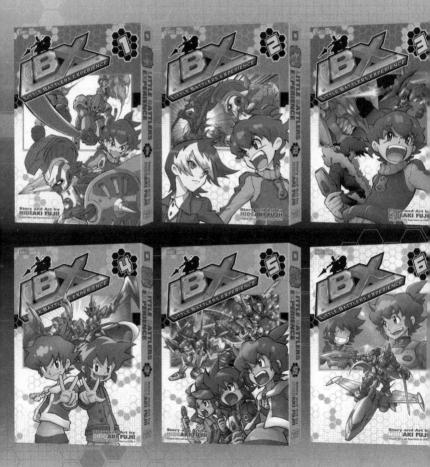

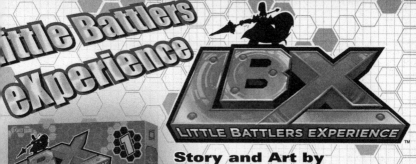
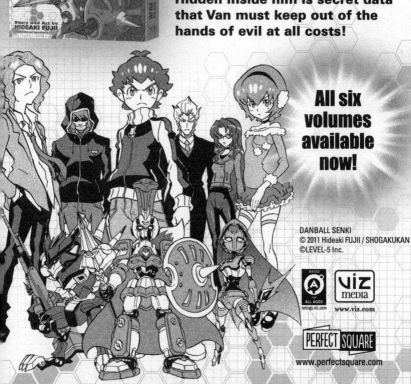

AUTHOR BIO

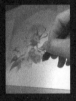

Thanks to your support, we've made
it to volume 10! Thank you so much!
And with that twist, we move ahead
to more of the brand-new story in
volume 11. ♪
—Noriyuki Konishi

Noriyuki Konishi hails from Shimabara City in Nagasaki
Prefecture, Japan. He debuted with the one-shot
E-CUFF in *Monthly Shonen Jump Original* in 1997. He is
known for writing manga adaptations of *AM Driver* and
Mushiking: King of the Beetles, along with *Saiyuki Hiro
Go-Kū Den!*, *Chōhenshin Gag Gaiden!! Card Warrior
Kamen Riders*, *Go-Go-Go Saiyuki: Shin Gokūden* and
more. Konishi was the recipient of the 38th Kodansha
manga award in 2014 and the 60th Shogakukan manga
award in 2015.